DEDICATION

To Jeremy.

My grandmother always told me, marry a man who loves you more.

And so I did.

Water's Threshold

Book 1
The Elementals Trilogy

Jillian Jacobs

Published by Green Moose Productions
Copyright 2014 by Jillian Jacobs

ISBN: 978-1-942313-00-7

Cover art and logo design: www.shelbybertsch.

ACKNOWLEDGMENTS

The first person I'd like to thank is my Mom. By her example, I read romance. Although, we agree to disagree on the Outlander series, without her, I never would have ventured into other worlds. Her love of reading is now my own.

Next on this list are Sabrina Jeffries and Christina Dodd who, on their websites, suggested starting a writing career by joining Romance Writers of America.

That decision led me to LaNora Mangano and Tia Catalina. LaNora guided me through my first year at Indiana Romance Writers of America. She patiently answered every question and concern. Thanks, LaNora. And to Tia, this book would not exist without her. As my critique partner, she took me step-by-step through the writing process and "rules". She steered me through each roadblock, and for that she'll forever have my gratitude.

My beta readers: Sherry Weir, Jennifer Hill, and my Mom. You're the best.

I would also like to acknowledge every member at Indiana Romance Writers of America. Without that chapter's positive reassurance and helpful comments, I would not have the confidence to continue.

My cover artist, Shelby Bertsch. Because of her, this cover tells my story in a single picture.

And finally, to Donya Lynne, the ultimate Juicebox.

PROLOGUE

Maya

I often wonder over the human fascination with vampires, werewolves, shape shifters, and other mystical creatures.

Vampires are especially intriguing as they are glorified for their sexual prowess, strength, and immortality. Why does only blood keep them alive? What is blood, really, but water when you break it down? Water flows through us and is part of what allowed our escape from the sea millions of years ago. Why isn't water part of the mystique? Water becomes steam, ice, and fog. It breaks down mountains, swirls in a rage, destroys entire cities, and is a much stronger life force than blood alone.

Water is the staple of our existence, especially so in my case. It is the only force that flows within me and gives me life. Unlike the vampire who must live by consuming the blood of another, I stand in the rain to renew.

Does that make me fascinating? Will I be celebrated? Will I claim a place in history, or just wash away? Deep inside, I feel the drip, drip, drip as my link to humanity etches away. I stay afloat, stuck in time—in order to serve those whose blood continues to flow, pulsing along, unaware that the real monsters exist right beside them.

CHAPTER 1

Terran Forrester turned up the radio and cracked open the driver's side window, hoping the cold mountain air flowing down from the Tetons would revive him. Driving home this late was not a brilliant decision. Where his headlights lit the empty road, he scanned for skittering wildlife.

Deer dash is not my game of choice at 2 am.

He would already be home if he hadn't left the National Park Service fundraiser halfway through the evening. As a department head at The Conservancy, his presence was required, although he'd have preferred to skip the affair all together. Black tie events were not his style. A lab coat was his suit of choice.

Talking with Dr. Melinda Givens had offered an escape from stale golf course discussions and details of who had joined who on the Grand Teton ski slopes this past season. He followed her back to her place for coffee, where she informed him "coffee" was code for kitchen sex. Message received, he stayed for round two in the bedroom. Melinda hadn't expected anything more and that suited him fine. She drifted to sleep with a satisfied smile. So, he threw on his T-shirt, dress pants, and shrugged on his dress shirt before heading out the door. At some point, he would connect with a woman who shared his passion for studying ways to conserve earth's natural resources, but for now, sex fulfilled a basic need, just like food or water.

As the gas needle tipped toward E, he realized his truck also had basic needs. Terran pulled into the only station still lit up on the outskirts of Morgan Junction. Dust stirred as he drove across the gravel lot. While paying for gas inside, he'd grab an apple. The natural sugars would generate a much-needed energy jolt.

After filling the gas tank, he stepped through the automatic doors. A nicely framed young lady, most likely in her mid-twenties, sat at a table by the window. Her long, jean-clad legs were propped against the table's edge as she tipped back in her chair. Her bare toes twitched and her hooded head bopped, no doubt due to the ear buds attached to the iPod in her hand.

Why is she out at this time of night? Why isn't she wearing shoes?

As Terran walked over to the coolers, he spotted a brown minivan pulling up for gas, which sounded a chime at the store's counter. He picked the least-bruised apple from the wicker basket placed inside the cooler and retraced his steps. Stopping next to Shoeless Girl's table, he lightly tapped her shoulder.

She removed one ear bud and raised a brow.

"Excuse me, I'm sorry to bother you. Do you need a ride back to town? Are you waiting for someone?"

She turned away and focused her attention out the window. "No," she answered, and met his gaze in the reflection of the glass. Her sweatshirt hood framed her delicate features and aqua blue eyes. A tendril of blonde hair escaped from under the hood and shone in bright contrast against the black fabric.

"Kind of late, handsome. Maybe you should hurry home." With a scrape of her chair, she pushed away from the table and exited through the back of the building.

That's what you get for being a nice guy, Forrester.

He shrugged then headed for the counter, juggling his apple from hand to hand.

"Hands up!"

Terran halted upon hearing those words shouted by a bearded man waving a pistol and standing between him and the counter.

"Stay back." Pointing the gun in Terran's direction, the gunman yelled, "Get down on your stomach. Face on the floor."

As Terran raised both hands in a show of compliance, he kept his gaze on the crazed man. "Stay calm. I'm going down." Not quite sure if his comments were meant for the robber or himself. He'd come in for an energy jolt, and by the way his heart was pounding, he'd succeeded. On his way down, he glanced out the window.

Shoeless Girl stood talking to a young lady in a red wool cap on the van's driver's side.

Is she crazy? The van lady is part of the robbery.

The robber ordered the night clerk to give him the money.

Bruised apple still in his hand, Terran considered using it as a weapon. *Better not chance it.* He braced his weight on his forearms. No way was he lying face down on this sticky, slushie-covered floor. He tilted his head to the side, keeping an eye on the action at the counter.

A thick fog seeped under the automatic doors, filled the front of the store, and made seeing even an inch in front of his face impossible.

Odd. Is this a new kind of security system?

The robber, the gun, the fog—the tableau playing out before him was so bizarre he refused to blink. Steady, slow breaths did nothing to calm his pounding heart. This thief was unstable enough, adding in this unknown element might push him to fire his gun. *Where are the exits?* Hadn't Shoeless Girl left out the back?

"Turn it off. Turn it off," the robber shouted at the clerk.

Terran waved a hand in front of his face, attempting to clear the hazy soup blocking his vision. His sense of hearing kicked into overdrive.

A desperate cry startled him and further accelerated his heartbeat.

Two shots were fired and glass shattered, tinkling onto the floor.

Reverberations from the gunshots made his ears ring. Sound was muffled, but he made out a clatter of metal against the tile floor.

A muted ding from the sliding of the automatic doors preceded a woman's horror-filled scream.

The fog grew thicker.

Fine beads of mist covered his arms and face. Only the sound of his quick, shallow breaths broke the eerie calm.

Terran rose and crouched on the balls of his feet. He unbuttoned his dress shirt and wiped the condensation from his glasses with the T-shirt underneath. Streaks of water still clung to his lenses as he glanced over his shoulder to determine the distance from his current location to the red blur indicating the rear exit sign. He stuck out a hand and heard the slight crackle of a bag of chips. That sound guided his way as he bent level with the aisle and slipped toward the red beacon of freedom. With quick steps, he moved toward the back, but stiffened when a heavy water drop trickled from his earlobe to his neck. He remained rooted in place as a wet glide rasped against his cheek, and a voice commanded, "Back door, now!"

What?

An unearthly shriek kicked his adrenaline in gear, and he raced down the aisle, away from the chaos shaking his usually rational mind.

Where's my apple? Do I still need to pay for gas?

Steps away from the back exit, he stopped and glanced over his shoulder to determine if anyone had noticed his flight to safety. The fog had lifted enough to reveal the incredulous scene by the counter.

The woman from the van now sat on the floor next to her cohort. Their faces were contorted, and their bodies thrashed. Fog wrapped around them and red blotches like steam blisters appeared on their skin.

How is that possible? Where is the clerk?

Their screams tore through the misty air. "It burns…make it stop…please stop…they're in the van…the van." Their cries halted when the entire store once more filled with fog.

As fear engulfed him, Terran strove to maintain his focus on reality and not succumb to the panic bounding down his spine. The vapor reached him, but did not burn his skin. He froze as the eerie mist swirled around his body. Aqua blue eyes flashed against a white cloud, and a wet hand caressed his face.

"In sleep forget," a soothing voice, murmured in his ear.

A vision of Shoeless Girl crossed his mind before he fell to his knees, weightless as if floating in a clear, blue pool. Drifting down, down until surrounded by sapphire darkness that faded into black.

# # #

After making too many changes over a short period of time, Maya Conway needed to recharge. A portion of the criminals' evil she'd absorbed tonight at the gas station still pulsed through her veins. Earlier in the evening, she'd gleaned the couple's intentions to abduct two little girls. Knowing they'd need fast cash, she mentally tracked their plans to rob the station on the outskirts of town. The showdown ended well and kept the children safe. After she dealt with

5

the criminals, she placed an anonymous call to the police with the woman's cell phone. When sirens blared across the morning quiet, Maya used her elemental connection with water to evaporate.

Now she needed to refuel.

Her well-hidden freshwater hot spring waited at the bottom of Signal Mountain. The warm water would wash off the filth that had crept down deep and would wipe the slate clean.

The film of pain and despair filtered away as she reformed from mist to body then drifted deeper and deeper toward the bottom of the spring. Revolting images from the criminal couple's minds vanished as she settled beneath the water's surface, eyes closed, with her body completely submerged in the naturally heated water.

Landing in a place between dreams and consciousness, she healed, fed on water—Adam's Ale—in order to renew. Sustenance flowed through her, and she breathed in water as if it were air. Though she preferred salt water, this fresh water spring served its purpose. Mother Nature had sent her to this mountainous region to conduct her Elemental duties—saving innocents and using her gifts for good.

Since arriving in Wyoming only a few months ago, Maya had experienced a strange energy pattern that interrupted her sense of peace. A consciousness never felt before, as if something attempted to anchor her in place—a pull unlike anything she had experienced since starting this new life nearly one hundred and fifteen years ago.

This internal strife was because of him—Terran Forrester. Mother had warned this would come. He was part of her purpose in being in this place at this time. Her orders were to guide him, because their destinies were entwined. Having Mother Nature set her up on a "fate date" left her feeling like a contestant on a game show. During her human life, Maya strove to control her own destiny, never handing over power. As an Elemental, she remained determined to give her all to their cause, but it chafed when Mother asked for more—to open her heart. Why now? Why was this burden of love thrust upon her with a mate she had not chosen?

Mate. What a ridiculous word.

Maya blew out a breath, causing a bevy of bubbles to dance their way to the surface. She couldn't have children so Mother using that specific word made the whole idea more ludicrous. Yet, Mother's wishes had come to fruition and that fact rankled. When spying on

Terran, Maya experienced emotions surfacing she'd thought buried in a deep well long ago.

Her duties included watching him as he went about his daily human life. She enjoyed observing his frequent visits to the banks of the Snake River where he filled little glass vials. A soft hum raced through her body each time she spied him doing ordinary things, like working up a sweat at the gym or grabbing a cup of coffee at the local café. Since her last sexual adventure occurred in the free-love laced 70's, she was more than overdue for male attention. Terran would, no doubt, approach sex with the same care he did his experiments—meticulously and thoroughly.

That trickle of lust thrummed especially strong tonight at the gas station, when he'd touched her shoulder, all concerned citizen, seeking to offer assistance to an unfamiliar woman. Her waterlogged heart had pumped like a steam engine traveling uphill.

There he'd stood—destiny's eternal match—a tall, handsome, dark-haired scientist, wearing spectacles that seemed to have no frames.

Tonight, he'd smelled of sex, earthy and appealing. Peering into those dark brown eyes, she'd been drawn in, entranced by the stabilizing force surrounding him.

Thinking of Terran's steady nature, perhaps she should verify he'd suffered no ill effects after tonight's traumatic events. He wouldn't remember anything after she'd disappeared out the back door. She had wiped his memories clean. *And gotten him very wet.*

A fountain of desire flowed through her as she remembered the way her body had molded to his, although only in fog. Kicking to the surface, Maya hauled herself out of the spring, sat nude along the edge, and dangled her feet in the water.

A clamping sensation tightened her chest and dryness wrinkled her skin.

How can this be?

Her lips puckered against her teeth as an intense wave of salt crossed over her tongue. Eyes burning, she blinked, attempting to remove the brackish substance drying her body. Seawater could renew her life force, but pure salt would desiccate her.

Someone had found her secluded spring—someone who meant her harm.

Only two people triggered this tempest within her body.

Apparently, her night of fighting scourges wasn't over. Maya transformed into a misty cloud and floated just above the spring's surface, where the steam re-hydrated her.

A great gust of wind struck, attempting to force her into the water. She fought the subtle nudge to take the easy escape.

Changing back to her human form, she let the breeze lower her, rolling with the wind's energy so she landed on the shore. A stark laugh across the morning quiet made Maya turn to face the intruder.

A woman watched her—Pillar, salt of the earth. Her white-blonde hair shone bright against the gray glow of pre-dawn. A sneer marred her beautiful face. A forceful gale beat against her, which billowed her hair and dress around her body.

"Oh come now, Nodin. I was just seasoning the water. It's so bland." Pillar's raspy laugh echoed in the air, and then her body transformed into a white whirlwind.

Salt particles beat against Maya's skin before a violent wind knocked Pillar off course. Maya stepped back as the salty funnel twisted with the wind, their forms dancing back and forth. The erotic tango ended when the shot of white salt separated and travelled alone into the lightening sky.

Maya stood by the spring's edge as the breeze died down and a man formed out of the air by her side—Nodin. He had the same symbiotic relationship with air as she did with the water. Together with Flint, who was fire, they represented the Elementals. Mother Nature had bestowed upon them "the gleaning," which was the ability to read and compel minds. They used their elemental abilities to protect the Earth and its people.

Nodin spent most days in the Plains States, like Nebraska and Kansas. Mother split them up and sent them where the need was strongest. Prior to coming here, Maya had lived in California. She hadn't seen Nodin in months. Six months had passed since she'd seen Flint.

"Are you all right?" Nodin wrapped his hands around her shoulders. His sky blue eyes assessed her, and an airy breeze floated through her consciousness.

An elemental connection linked their minds, although they allowed each other as much privacy as possible, no distance was too great for them to communicate. With a single distress call sent across Earth's frequencies, either Nodin or Flint would appear.

Comforting thought.

Maya gleaned conflicting emotions stirring within Nodin, battering his mind. A cool breeze floated across her face and reassured her. Nodin put others first, seeing to her comfort while he suffered an inner turmoil—a sadness brought on by Pillar and love lost.

He rested his forehead against hers.

Maya took his face in her hands and lightly kissed him. "It's good to see you." She left his embrace and pulled out a waterproof bag she kept hidden in a small gap between two rocks. Shaking out her shirt, she pulled it over her head. "Where have you been?"

"I go wherever the wind takes me."

"Still using the same joke, I see."

"It's a good joke." He shrugged.

"I would say it's more of a truth, Nodin."

As she buttoned her jeans, she scrutinized him. He looked as he had months ago—a perk of being peri-mortal. Jet-black hair fell straight past his square jaw. His deep-bronzed skin accentuated his whipcord-lean body. His clear blue eyes always stood in stark contrast to his Native American coloring.

Drifting a few steps away, he looked off into the distance. His gaze trailing the path the salty, white swirl had taken. "Pillar's been causing trouble again."

"That salty Schickster, I wish you wouldn't hold out hope. She tried to dehydrate me. Again." Maya sighed when he didn't reply. "You've been keeping track of her?"

"At times."

Maya sank down on a boulder and whipped her socks out of her bag. "I have one word Pillar would do well not to forget—deliquescence. Ms. Saltypants can only absorb so much water before dissolving herself." She stood and shoved her feet into her tennis shoes. "Perhaps Pillar should've taken a chemistry class at some point in her over-seasoned existence."

Nodin shared a past with Pillar. Maya had never asked for details, as he wasn't one to share his feelings. He tended more toward philosophical conversations. Flint, however, had filled her in on the more pertinent details. Pillar had lived for centuries as the personification of the salt of the Earth. Nodin received his gifts at a time long before the Europeans invaded America. Pillar found a partner in Nodin, and they fought side by side. Then something came between them, creating a distance, like the snap of a kite string on a windy day.

Pillar turned to the opposite of all light—Quintessence, the fifth element, or Aether, as he was known in ancient Greece and India. Maya only knew him as Quint.

Over eons, Quint had evolved from dark matter into the lecherous being he now used to exist as a living, breathing human. Together, Quint and Pillar haunted the Earth, intent on destroying all the Elementals held dear.

If both Pillar and Quint were here, perhaps that would explain Maya's strange sense of foreboding. Her last encounter with Quint had not ended well.

Pillar had launched her first attack tonight. Had Nodin not interfered, the battle between her and that salty square would still be raging. Maya did not harbor the same feelings of restraint as Nodin.

Stretching both arms above her head, Maya asked, "Do you plan to bunk with me tonight?"

"No, I made other arrangements." Nodin avoided eye contact.

Who is the lucky girl in his bed tonight?

Nodin took comfort where and when he could in an existence decades longer than her own. At times, Maya had done the same. Developing lasting relationships only meant watching them die. She lived a lonely life and when Flint or Nodin appeared, she tried not to hold on too tightly.

Rocking back on her heels, she shrugged. "Will you be around for a while?"

"I'm heading east tonight, but I'll be back in a day or two."

Maya nodded and wandered over to her faded green, three-speed bike leaning against a boulder. A strong breeze fingered through her hair then whipped into the sky—Nodin's form of farewell. The leaves of aspen and cottonwood trees rustled as he blew past.

Not surprising, Nodin had other sleeping arrangements. Never allowing close relationships—a remnant of his time with Pillar, perhaps.

Hopping on her bike, Maya took a worn path through the trees, headed toward town, and thought of the scientist. A question surfaced as the bright band of the dawn lit the horizon. Could

Terran, for a short time, be a beacon on the shore in her endless sea of life?

CHAPTER 2

Quint observed the fit and cut of Crowder's Brooks Brothers suit. While no Gieves & Hawkes, it would do for a time.

The research he'd ordered Pillar to gather on Carlyle Crowder proved correct. Crowder possessed a fit frame for his age, which must be somewhere south of sixty. He had earned his iron gray hair by handling the day-to-day business of ranching and oil reserves on his holdings in Wyoming and Texas.

Quint studied the books on the rancher's shelf. Crowder's endless drone and condescending manner needled against his nerves. Pulling an astronomy book from the shelf, he feigned interest as he flipped through the ridiculous book passing for science.

"I asked you here today because I understand, sir, that you are a 'Fixer.' We've tried to resolve this situation on our own, but it's reached a point where we need containment." Crowder fidgeted with his collar. "That Forrester kid found a half-burnt cow that wolves had dragged off the property. I've tried to assure everyone there's no cause for alarm, but the Conservancy is demanding access."

Crowder's ranch sat at the top of the Snake River by Morgan Junction. His land covered an area above Grand Teton National Park on the northeast side.

Crowder leaned back in his chair and snipped off the end of his cigar. "The disease is spreading. We're using an experimental vaccine from a start-up Seattle drug company, but it hasn't helped the animals already infected. I don't want every federal agency and fucking green-thumbed hippy crawling over my land, burning down everything I've built. We've separated the ones with the bacteria, and we'll burn them off as needed."

"This disease isn't caused by a bacteria." Quint folded both arms across his chest as he leaned against the bookcase. "It's a prion, a misfolded protein. In this form, it's known as Bovine Spongiform Encephalopathy or BSE for short. Don't want to scare anyone with Mad Cow, so let's stick with BSE, shall we? You do know it can't be cured?" Raising a perfectly sculpted brow, he continued, "You *will* most likely have to burn the majority of your stock."

"Don't worry, we haven't sent any cattle to the slaughterhouse. We have a contact at the drug company who, as I said, gave us access to their vaccine. This wonder drug is supposed to erase the protein in animals that have the potential to develop Mad Cow."

Quint's host explained that the Conservancy would expect him to take samples to a USDA-approved state veterinary diagnostic lab. Crowder expected "the Fixer" to contain the problem before it got to that stage.

With a swipe of his hand, Quint cut off Crowder and pinned him with a cold, black-eyed stare. "My name is Quint. I do not suggest using the moniker, 'The Fixer,' again, as it's starting to grate like fingernails across a chalkboard. Do you recall this sound? No? Then let me remind you."

Quint created a screeching echo that reverberated through the rancher's head.

Crowder cringed and clasped his hands over his ears.

"Irritating, isn't it?" Quint smirked. "How old are you?"

Crowder pulled his shaking hands from his ears. Blood spotted his palms. His face turned ashen as he observed the damage. "What have you done? I didn't bring you here so you could play these magician's games." His voice rose and he turned his head from side-to-side, looking for the source of the sound invading his mind. He came around his desk and jabbed a finger against Quint's chest. "I want to know what you plan to do to fix this problem. That's why you're here. I'm paying you a lot of money to handle this situation."

Quint stepped away from the sputtering fool, sat in a leather chair placed in front of the desk, and surveyed his manicure. "I find your threats quite entertaining. I'm surprised you didn't stomp your foot while you were at it."

Crowder stammered, "You, sir—"

"Quiet now." Quint silenced him, no longer amused.

Crowder clutched his throat, a slight cry squeaking from his wide-open mouth. His face turned beet red as he stepped toward Quint.

With a not-so-gentle mental nudge, Quint used his powers to compel his host's mind. "Sit down. It's time to explain your situation."

Crowder crumpled into the accompanying chair, hand at his throat, eyes wide as he stared at Quint.

"I will fix this problem for you, Crowder. Although not in the way you may wish. You see, I must take on many different personas to accomplish my goals. I could stay as I am for a few more months, but I tire of looking at the same face day after day and signs of strain are beginning to appear." He sniffed and straightened the cuff of his jacket. "Plus, I find your position, and of course, the fact you're worth millions, extremely appealing. Your status in life is conducive with my future plans." Quint sighed and reached into his jacket pocket for his vibrating phone.

Interruptions during playtime irritated.

He read the text then took his time responding.

Attention once more on Crowder, he inquired, "Do you know what dark matter is? No one really does. Does it repel or is it a gravitational force? Never seen, never detected. You see, Crowder, I cannot exist without coming here and grasping what I can of this world, of its people. I stay on this plane to be acknowledged. To live. You humans act as if you are the center of the universe, but you don't even make up five percent."

Quint laughed upon detecting a pitiful wave of resistant energy flowing from Crowder as he tried to escape the dark prison of mental and physical control.

Pinching the bridge of his nose, Quint continued, "And yet I have to debase myself with humans in order to breathe. I suffer to endure your skin. I find regular human hosts aren't enough, but I'm getting there. Very soon, I'll have the one who can sustain me forever. No longer will I have to feed off weak tits like you."

Crowder released a deep breath, his face a mottled red. He spit out, "What—what are you?" He shuffled to his feet and sidled toward his shotgun cabinet.

Quint scoffed and prodded against Crowder's mind, halting his forward motion toward his arsenal.

"Foolish human, you think something as simple as buckshot can end me after what I've just done to your body? Now, do you want my help or not?" Unwinding from the chair, Quint moved to stand between a stone-still Crowder and his vast assortment of rifles.

His host's gaze flickered toward the gun case.

Quint didn't allow movement, but since doing so amused, he'd grant Crowder a few final words. "Was there something you wished to say? Make it interesting as they're your final words."

Crowder ground out, "I think you should leave. I won't be recommending you to anyone else. I don't know your game, but—"

"That's all right, because I know it quite well." Grasping Crowder's arm, Quint pulled him closer. "This may hurt a little." While stretching his mouth wide over his host's lips, Quint transferred his essence.

Crowder's eyes turned inky black as dark matter coursed through his body. His horrific scream was unable to bypass the murky essence creeping into every corner of his being. A single tear fell from his eye as a veil crashed and extinguished his existence.

Quint stored all of Crowder's memories in order to maintain the identity. His former host body—the Fixer, a thirty-year-old private investigator from California—slowly deflated. The energy of his life force converted into a tiny orb of mass, which contracted, and then exploded into the air. The blast's force rocketed a chair across the room, shattered frames, and knocked books off shelves.

Running a hand along the custom-built Parnian desk, Quint shook his head at the ease with which he took over their lives. Just once, he wished for a challenge, a struggle before the shades were drawn and the lights went out.

Quint considered the available options as he sat on his new leather throne. The rancher's financial position would further his newly established drug company, Aether Pharmaceuticals. They were on the cusp of performing "miracles" with their newest vaccine. Once the prion spread, only Aether would have the drug to erase the effects.

Quite the profitable endeavor. Especially since his dark matter only masked the prion's presence, but did not erase it.

His reverie was interrupted when Pillar stepped into his office without first obtaining permission. She surveyed the damaged room and picked up a fallen tome then shook her head at Quint's new appearance. "Couldn't wait, I see."

"I wasn't aware I had to notify you of my timeline, Pillar." After shuffling through papers strewn across the desk, he met her gaze. "Is he here?"

Holding the book against her chest, Pillar nodded.

"Good. I'll make use of him soon. You found Maya's spring?"

"Yes. Nodin is in the area as well."

"Looking to add a little salt to his soufflé, are you?" Quint laughed as Pillar shoved the book back on the shelf. "Forget the wind whip for now. First, we'll handle the water wench."

CHAPTER 3

Terran tapped a finger against his steering wheel while driving to a Snake River outlet stream. The slithering river veered away from the main body only to wrap back around and rejoin its journey south. He checked his rearview mirror, very concerned that Crowder's ranch hands would come upon him investigating the area where he'd first discovered the cow carcass. And yet, the consequences of discovery were far less critical than determining how far the BSE contamination had spread from point zero—Crowder Ranch.

His plan involved catching a few channel catfish, taking brain tissue samples, and performing an initial rapid test for BSE. If the results were inconclusive, he'd send the samples to the National Veterinary Services Laboratories and the National Animal Disease Center. Since Terran had never known of a prion strain to present in an aquatic species before, he reveled in the opportunity to make a new discovery.

Terran walked a fine line after a key Conservancy donor had called a board member two days ago and suggested his team focus on other projects. This served as a not-so-subtle reminder that Carlyle Crowder had influential friends. Big money trumped all, even at the Conservancy, which subsisted primarily on grants and fundraisers. With any threat to their financial foundation, the board panicked and threw up roadblocks.

Since hard rock music better suited his mood, he punched the pre-set radio button and changed the station. Board members and businessmen would not undermine his focus. Crowder's practices were wrong—end of discussion.

After calling in sick this morning, Terran had loaded up the supplies necessary to gather proof in support of his theory. Three weeks prior, while taking water samples for another project, Terran had come upon wolves dragging a half-seared cow across this stream. A warning shot fired from his rifle scared off the scavengers. The stench exuding from the carcass overwhelmed him to the point that he retrieved a T-shirt from his truck and tied it around his nose and mouth. After almost retching, his anger further erupted at Crowder's blatant disregard of a creature that, in essence, lined his pockets with cash.

Shocked at the audacity of Crowder bypassing proper disposal laws, Terran took samples from the cow's slightly charred brain, knowing even before testing what he would find. Crowder's ranch was experiencing an outbreak of BSE. Why else would he take his cattle to a secluded area and have them burned?

He drove to the ranch to confront Crowder, but spoke to the veterinarian instead, who feigned ignorance. Upon returning to the carcass, Terran noted channel catfish were gnawing on the cow's flesh. The sun set while he dug a deep hole and buried the cow.

With a doctorate in Environmental and Organic Chemistry and a Masters in Biology, his upbringing and subsequent education made it impossible to stop investigating a potential health threat just because "big money" Crowder had thrown the hammer down.

After receiving Terran's initial test results, the Conservancy met with their lawyers. The next step was gaining legal access to Crowder's cattle so they could officially test for BSE.

Terran, however, refused to wait for all the legal posturing—immediate action was crucial. He parked on the side of the stream across from Crowder's property, hopped down, and pulled his tackle box off the truck's backseat.

Steps crunched against the rocky shore's gravel behind him. His heartbeat kicked-up as he glanced over his shoulder, but no one was there.

Standing still for a moment, he listened. Nothing but the usual sounds of the forest filled the air. He rested his pole against a nearby rock and worked at releasing the fishing hook from the ring on his pole, but the line was a tangled mess. He kneeled and dug through his tackle box for scissors. Finding them, he turned back to cut the line, but a pair of shapely calves blocked his vision. Long legs led all the way up to a blue-eyed blonde who stood in the cool water, which couldn't be more than fifty-five degrees. She peered down at him with her head slightly cocked to the side.

Where did she come from? Aren't her feet cold?

"Hello," he ventured, still crouched with scissors in hand.

She didn't speak, but looked at his tackle box and pole before returning her gaze to his. Water splashed around her calves as she stepped out of the stream and progressed in a circular path around him.

Not liking the disadvantage, Terran stood. "May I help you?"

Her eyes were clear as a lake, welcoming him to dive in and swim deep. Her hair flowed passed her shoulders, and the soft curls beckoned him to experience their waves.

"You're trespassing." Her voice cut across the quiet.

Her voice stirred a memory he couldn't quite place. He turned with her as she continued her trail around him in a wider circle—half-in, half-out of the water. "I'm sorry. Have we met?"

Her smile went stiff, and she stopped her slow turn. "We have not met. You need to leave." She pointed to his truck, pointed at him, and then made a shooing motion with her fingers.

"Why? I'm not trespassing." He reached around her to grab his fishing pole before it slid into the water.

"You are." She poked a finger against his chest.

"No. I hesitate to correct a lady, but I measured the distance to Crowder's land. It ends at that tree." Using the fishing rod's tip, he indicated a Lodge Pole pine directly across from where they stood.

Something was familiar about her. And that something caused a rumble through his body. A primal, raw need to capture and conquer her had him envisioning cavemen with clubs. *Too bad I only have this thin pole.*

"I'm sorry. You look very familiar." He shook his finger at her before tapping his forehead as if that would shake loose his memories. "Why are you here? Do you live nearby? Aren't your feet cold?"

"You ask a lot of questions."

"Do you work for Crowder?"

"And another question." She raised a brow and tossed her hair off her shoulder.

With that flick of hair, he recalled a golden tendril against a black sweatshirt. "I know." He snapped his fingers as he recollected the vision. "At the gas station the other night before the robbery, Shoeless Girl, that was you, right?"

"You remember this?" She moved closer, searched his eyes then glanced away. "What's in your kit? Why do you have all those vials? Do you plan to do experiments on the fish?"

"Looks like I'm not the only one with questions." He smiled. A charming smile, one that generally disarmed the female populace. "May I introduce myself?" He held out his hand. "Terran Forrester."

Her gaze stayed focused on his as she shook his hand. Her hand lingered in his, and she twisted his wrist. With her hand directly on top of his, she ran her fingertips down his palm then traced the etched lines with an index finger.

The sensual caress shot a lustful jolt down his body.

"Terran. It means 'of the earth.'" She ran a hand up his arm to his shoulder.

"Yes, my parents own Earth Wrap." His voice took on a husky tone in response to her bold touch. "It's a company that manufactures environmental packaging." His fingers twitched with the same need to explore her body. Her scent evoked images of yellow lily blossoms on a rainy spring day.

"And you, Terran Forrester, you study the earth for them?" She released her hold on his shoulder and bent to run her fingers through the stream.

"I don't work for them. I work at The Conservancy in Morgan Junction." No longer able to stand by while she waded through the cold water, he pointed out, "Your feet have got to be freezing. The body freezes at 32 degrees, excluding variations, of course. Please, let me get you a towel. I'm sure I've got one in my truck." He took her arm and helped her from the water.

Her pixie nose wrinkled as she stepped onto the bank. "You have a towel in your truck?"

"I always carry extra towels. When I was young, I fell into a Colorado stream. I got very sick after, so..." He dug around in the backseat. "Found it." He waved the towel above his head then turned to offer it to her. "I'm sorry I didn't catch your name?"

Empty space. No blonde.

What the hell?

Were Crowder's men here? Did she leave with them? No, there were no other vehicles around and no sounds. Nothing.

She couldn't have gotten far on foot. Perhaps she was a water sprite conjured from his over-caffeinated mind—no, that wasn't logical.

Where is she?

"I found the towel," he stated in a louder voice.

As he stepped over to where she'd stood only moments before, he felt a light mist brush the back of his neck. He spun and spotted her by his truck.

She held a rusted three-speed bicycle by the handlebars. "Terran, please leave. This is a hazardous place, unbalanced. Do not come back. You cannot change what has become." After making that strange statement, the Shoeless Girl hopped on her bike and rode off.

He threw the towel over his shoulder and walked back to the stream. The water bubbled and churned—a chorus in the quiet, summoning him to stand at the shore and explore its depths. He grabbed his pole and got back to business. If she was working with Crowder then he didn't have much time.

CHAPTER 4

Terran slapped his best friend, Clay Ellis, on the shoulder as they sat in a stretch limo's backseat. Clay's words were slurred from too many toasts to his bride-to-be. "Shtill can't believe it. I'm sho happy."

Bottles clanked against their feet as the entire crew stepped out of the car and followed the loud thump of music into Tattered Tetons. After hitting a few of the local pubs, the bachelor party crew decided this strip club was the proper way to end the evening. As best man and bachelor party planner, Terran checked off the last stop on his whisky-stained list.

An aromatic mix of cumin and onion permeated the air from a food truck labeled, "The Tangy Taco." The truck occupied the only handicapped parking spot on the lot. Ironic, as the food attracted customers hindered by various chemical intoxicants.

Tattered Tetons tinted glass door was covered in advertisements for weight loss and male enhancement drugs. When he stepped inside, Terran blinked as his eyes adjusted to the flashing lights. Vision cleared, he noted flesh bulging out of tight tops and ass-baring shorts as the waitresses carried drink-filled trays from table to table. A local group standing by the bar included Ethan Crowder. The only son of Carlyle Crowder, Ethan threw around his money to cover up the fact that ninety percent of the time he was a complete jackass.

Ethan glanced over as they headed to a large table set up in front of the stage. Two bottles gripped in one hand, a monster cigar in the other, Crowder maneuvered through the tables with his arms open wide. "What's up? What is zzzzuuup?"

He punched Clay on the shoulder with his cigar-filled hand and a hunk of ash drifted to the floor. "Hey, Ellis, hear you're taking the plunge next weekend. Why ya wanna go and get hitched for?" He wrapped an arm around Clay's shoulder. "Forrester," he slurred. "Surprised to see you here."

"Surprising how?"

"These girls aren't interested in your little science projects. Right, baby?" Ethan grabbed a waitress walking by and pinched her ass.

Terran refused to debate with someone who thought a cup of dirt qualified as a science project. Instead, he nudged Clay's arm. "I'll grab some beers and meet you at the table. Crowder, always a pleasure."

As Terran walked off, he smiled at a passing waitress. Quite a few girls here were a lot smarter than Crowder realized. He wasn't surprised to find Crowder and his crew in attendance on a Friday night. Word around town indicated Ethan had a tendency to play it rough in the bedroom. Unfortunately, Crowder's money might seem worth the pain to a desperate girl. Ethan took advantage of people, and everyone in town turned the other way while it happened.

After paying for an extremely overpriced bucket of Green Moose beer, Terran headed to where his friends were gathered.

"Ish amashers night," Clay struggled with his words as he reached into the bucket. He gestured toward the stage with his beer bottle. "Maybe that meansh they'll try harder. Shake it, don't break it, baaybee." He laughed and tipped sideways in his chair. Righting himself, he proceeded to down half his beer in one big swallow.

Great. The last time Clay got this drunk, he'd passed out on the back deck of their rental house. Terran decided to stop drinking, or he and Clay would be sharing porch space.

Strobe lights flashed across the stage and the bar lights dimmed when an announcer dressed in a red suit, with the requisite amount of gold chains, stepped onto the stage. "Welcome, everyone. We have a bevy of beauties lined up for you tonight, but first off are some amateurs to titillate you. Handpicked, these girls went through extensive tryouts before being allowed to entertain. Remember, these girls are worth every dollar, so drink up and hit the private rooms."

A popular dance song thumped through the room before a

pretty brunette appeared on stage. A little jerky and nervous at first, she eventually got through the song. The next girl lacked a bit in the chest department, but had some steamy moves. Crowder and his friends yelled for her to get off the stage. Terran slipped her a fifty.

The next number kicked off with a blonde in a cop outfit, wearing knee-high black leather boots and silver-mirrored sunglasses. Smoke machines billowed fog around her body.

A tingle of recognition struck—the fog, the hair, the legs.

What the hell?

It couldn't be her. *Why would she do this?*

A slow hypnotic beat pulsed through the club as Shoeless Girl twirled a police baton. The room fell silent as she danced. Her body was fluid and smooth, inviting him closer. When a light mist fell across his face, Terran checked the ceiling for the water source— must be a new 4D effects system.

He shifted in his seat as she worked her way over to where Crowder and his crew beckoned. No longer silent, they whistled and waved bills to get her attention. She danced in front of Ethan, removed her sunglasses, placed them on his nose, and then finished by running her hand down the side of his face.

Is she crazy? Why is she taunting that jackass?

She dropped to her knees, spread open her thighs, and ripped off her shirt.

Damn it. He'd figured she had a very fit body, but hadn't realized the package came that well-endowed, barely covered now by a pair of hot pink triangles.

She shouldn't be up there revealing her body. Her purity flowed in waves around her. Awareness of a connection had erupted that day at the stream, and he still felt it now. He struggled to remain seated while she continued her flagrant display. His fingers curled around the sticky table as he glanced at his friends—they, too, enjoyed her charms.

Her hips rocked back and forth as she centered her svelte body on the stage. With her back to the audience, she bent and ripped off her shorts. Every pulse of blood in his body went south. Permanently. Toned, yet curvy, she completed the picture of his fantasy woman.

She is mine.

Why that thought came as an absolute, he couldn't say, but he would not allow her to uncover anymore. He stood, tucked his index finger and thumb into his mouth, and whistled—loudly. Summoning her.

This produced the desired effect. She swayed over and crouched with her backside facing him. Everyone rushed to where he stood, tucking dollars under her black G-string. She subtly pushed away any exploring hands and stood, winking at him before dancing away.

A ruckus in Crowder's crew erupted just before Ethan jumped on stage. He grabbed the blonde by the back of her head and kissed her—hard. The bouncers were apparently tipped well, because no one moved to stop him.

A swell of rage erupted through Terran at the sight of his Shoeless Girl in another man's arms. He jumped onto the stage and wrenched Crowder away.

Unwilling to be thwarted, Ethan threw a wild haymaker.

Terran ducked then surged forward. He wrapped his arms behind Ethan's knees and used forward momentum to drive them onto the stage floor. Years of Brazilian Jiu-jitsu training kicked-in to control the fight, along with the primal need to defend his mate. Terran sat with his knees on each side of Ethan's torso and pinned his arms by holding his wrists. He growled out, "Keep your hands off her."

"What's it to you, forest fucker?" Crowder spit back.

Blood pumping hot and fast through his veins, Terran punched Ethan in the nose, which knocked his head against the stage floor and silenced him.

Sprinklers went off, blasting water onto the stage and throughout the bar. The power of the spray stung his skin. Terran stood and glanced around for the fire, but didn't see any flames. Must be a faulty system, or some new sort of security, because the power of the water's stream seemed excessive.

The crowd looked like a wet T-shirt contest gone wild as employees and patrons rushed for the exits. Their shouts overpowered the announcer's voice as he stepped on stage and tried to maintain calm.

Terran gripped the silver stage pole to steady his footing on the slick floor and surveyed the area for his blonde. *Gone.* Shoving aside the red-velvet curtain, he went backstage. Not finding her in the dressing rooms, he detoured out the back door.

"Terran," she spoke from behind him.

Startled, he spun to face her. "What?"

Now dressed in faded cut-off shorts and a light blue sweater, she stepped back as the door swung open and a very soaked girl exited the building.

Where are the fire trucks?

They needed to move away from the building if there was a fire. Terran eyed her feet.

No shoes. *Again.*

Rocking back on her heels, she joked, "So, you might say my dance routine was a little washed out."

"Not funny."

She chuckled and shook her head. "Ahhh... I don't know, I thought that joke was a good one. I sense you're not in the mood for my nonsense. Why not? Your gander party appeared in full swing. Celebrating the end of a friend's bachelorhood, right?"

"What the hell were you doing?"

Flinching slightly, she answered with a patronizing tone, "Stripping."

Jaw tight, he clipped out, "I understand that. What I cannot comprehend is why."

"Again, so many questions."

Terran tried wiping his glasses with his wet shirt, remaining completely baffled by this blonde beauty before him. Why did he feel this unearthly need to contain her? Why should any of this matter? Had his friends left? Why wasn't she wet?

Frowning, he considered the price he would pay for striking Ethan. He wouldn't be surprised if the local Sheriff was already waiting outside his home, ready to arrest him for assault.

"Crowder won't call a Copper," the blonde before him piped out. "He may bother your apartment, your car, or your office, but he won't involve the law. If he does, his father will find out he's been spending time in dives again."

"Excuse me?" *Copper? Who used that word? Why is she talking about the police?*

"You looked a little worried."

"Listen, I don't think you should encourage a guy like Crowder. He isn't known for his kindness to women."

"How kind of you to be concerned."

Rubbing his forehead with his fist, he tried to contain an impending headache. Too much alcohol and difficult women didn't mix. "Where the hell are your shoes? Why are you always roaming around without them? Come on. I'll take you home." He took her hand and led her toward the main parking lot.

She stopped and tugged her hand from his grip. "I can get home on my own. I still have work to do tonight. Work I would have finished sooner if you hadn't interrupted."

"And what 'work' is that?" He sneered.

"Are you implying I would prostitute myself?"

"Are you?"

She burst out laughing, holding her sides as her head rocked back. "Ah, Terran…" She began walking in a slow circle around him. *Again.* "Curious is what you are. I find I am a little curious about you, as well. What kind of man is hiding behind those spectacles and starched button-down shirts?" Grabbing both ends of his collar, she pulled him closer.

Placing his hands on her waist, he locked her hips against his body.

"Have you ever watched waves crash upon a rocky shore?" She whispered against his lips. "What happens when the earth yields? When it breaks and crashes into the sea. What then?"

He bent his head.

Her lips parted.

"Foressher," Clay's voice interrupted. "Whadaya doing, Foressher?"

His friends issued catcalls from the windows of the limo, which idled at the end of the alley.

She stepped away and issued another warning. "Stay away from Crowder, Terran."

His mind and body remained mired in lust. Her voice had washed over him, wrapping him in the scene, in the motion of the water rolling against the shore, her body into his. She wouldn't leave without some answers this time.

With a fast paced stride, he caught up with her, grabbed her arm, and wrapped her wrist against the hollow of her back. Towering over her, he spoke in a low steady voice. "Don't walk away. Not this time. Who are you? Tell me."

Her gaze flicked to her shoulder, where her arm was bent

around her back. She raised a brow and parried, "Commands instead of questions. Interesting."

"Terran, lesh go!" Clay yelled. The top half of his body stuck out of the limo's sunroof, and a bottle of whisky tipped in his hand.

Terran flashed the fingers of his free hand, asking for five more minutes. He released her arm.

She sighed and complied with his request. "My name is Maya Conway."

"Maya Conway," he repeated and offered his hand. "Nice to meet you. I believe for our first date, I'll take you to a shoe store and buy you some shoes, since you don't seem to understand the concept. They come in quite handy, especially—"

This time, when he took her hand, every molecule in his body clicked into place. Through that small connection, he glimpsed the answer to every question, every doubt, and every sensation he'd ever had. Another plane of mental awareness opened and stretched wide as long as they remained linked together. Waves crashed in her blue eyes, and traces of salt water and sea musk flared in the air.

She squeezed his hand before breaking contact.

Terran scratched his head. "What?...What was I saying? Your shoes. Right. In parking lots like this it is unclear what kinds of particulates and dried fluids are on the concrete. Walking barefoot isn't safe or healthy."

"Terran, you're sweet to worry about me. And I do appreciate your efforts to protect me against Ethan, but you need to go with your friends now. When I've time for you and your shoe talk, I'll find you."

He shoved his hands in his pockets and remained silent as she hopped on her bicycle and rode off to who knew where.

She stopped at the end of the alley, turned back, and offered a cheeky grin. "Sorry you got so wet. Although, I must say, if there had been a wet T-shirt contest, you'd get my vote." She winked and laughed again.

The girl really got too much of a kick out of her own jokes.

He headed to the limo and replayed the evening's events in his mind. How could everything come together when he touched her then just as easily crumble into confusion? He would make it a point to learn everything he could about Maya Conway.

CHAPTER 5

Monday morning, Terran wet the drying nib of his pen as he transferred test results from the Transmission Electron Microscope into a lab notebook. Each day, he used scientific methods to break down problems piece by piece. The non-routine of each day in the lab helped sustain his passion for the work.

Clay crashed into the lab at twenty minutes after eight—late, as usual. "Hey Forrester, you'll never believe what I heard at the coffee shop."

Placing his finger where he'd left off on the page, Terran sighed then marked the spot with a small check. Almost every morning, Clay stopped at his desk and spent fifteen minutes regurgitating town gossip. This frequent distraction trained Terran to devote his early hours to paperwork that didn't require intense concentration. Clay wasn't the only threat to his focus this morning. The printout's letters and graphs blurred together at the memory of holding Ms. Conway's hand, not to mention how she'd looked when she'd ripped off those shorts.

Not the time, not the place.

He'd found a groove and hadn't thought of Maya in the last half hour. At Clay's interruption, Terran strove to keep the focus on work. "You're in the lab today. We've got water samples from quadrant four. Grab your lab coat and safety glasses."

"I'm putting them on. Chill, boss-man. I heard some interesting info this morning." Clay grabbed his lab coat off the hook by the door and approached Terran's desk. An obnoxious slurp whistled through Clay's lips as he sipped from the hole in his coffee cup's plastic lid. "Waaahh, still too hot."

Terran tossed his glasses onto his desk and rubbed his eyes. With a heavy sigh, he tried to move Clay along. "I have no idea what you're going to say, and I'm not guessing. Just tell me. What exciting information did you learn this morning?"

Clay frowned at Terran's apparent lack of enthusiasm, but forged on. "Ethan Crowder walked straight into the police station this morning and turned himself in for roughing up a stripper on Thursday night. Can you believe that? And they said he was soaking wet, like he'd been water-boarded into talking. He went in, confessed to smacking the girl, and asked to be arrested. Like he'd lost his mind, he kept—"

"Wait a minute, what did you say?" Terran straightened in his chair as he zeroed in on a portion of Clay's statement.

"I said he kept—"

Terran slashed a hand through the air. "No before that, you said he was all wet?"

"Yeah. Waterboarding, man, like somebody tortured him. Sick."

"The more reasonable theory would follow that there is a new security business in town, using some sort of hydraulic system. Interesting concept as water can be a powerful deterrent." The gas station, the strip club, and a soaked Crowder were all effective testimonials for the security system's salesman.

Terran tapped his pen against the papers on his desk. "It's unfortunate someone didn't put a stop to Ethan's behavior before this occurred."

"I understand you laid Ethan out pretty good." Clay jabbed his shoulder. "I don't remember much about Friday night, but I do remember that tight blonde from the strip club. You were talking to her outside after the sprinklers went off. She may be the same blonde who came in with the stripper when she gave her statement against Crowder."

How was Maya mixed up in all this? Why was she always around when there were crimes being committed?

"The 'tight' blonde has a name, Clay. It's Maya Conway. Quite the mystery."

"Forrester, I have no doubt with that monstrous brain of yours, you'll figure her out." Clay raised his cup in a mock toast then left to run his samples.

Terran huffed out a laugh. Now was not the time to be distracted with thoughts of Ethan Crowder or blonde hydrologists. Test results from the channel catfish had come back inconclusive. The next step was acquiring live specimens in order to test their blood. Prion testing was difficult because regular methods didn't work. He had developed a prototype test, in the hopes it would separate normal proteins from rogue prions. Proving the prions existed in an aquatic species would be groundbreaking, because no one had discovered their existence in anything other than mammals.

As he fired up his laptop, he calculated the economic impact his discovery would have on the area. The panic over purchasing diseased fish would devastate the market value and the income of local fishermen. If the prions existed in the fish, then they could potentially transfer to everything that ate the fish. Not to mention the outbreak at Crowder's Ranch.

The Conservancy may not want him to move forward with tests from Crowder's land, but this extreme threat against the local environment gave him no choice. He opened the bottom drawer of his desk, retrieved his brown binder, and reviewed his test results once more. His duty was to the land and its inhabitants—the problem required solutions.

# # #

Quint leaned against the wooden counter at the Sheriff's office. The smell of burnt coffee assaulted the air and mixed with the hearty blend of sweat and fear. He breathed in each scent. Every flavor, every nuance added an appealing layer to being human.

These peons didn't exult in being alive, didn't embrace the possibilities. Although more than a few had tried—based on the hustle and bustle behind the counter and whining criminals shoved into chairs next to officers' desks.

Unfortunately, they now faced the consequences of stifling human law. *Lowly fools.* These ridiculous humans let rules laid down in an ancient book fight against their true natures. Nothing held him back. He was everywhere, everything. He encompassed all and as long as he remained on this plane, he took as he pleased, not bound by archaic beliefs or physical boundaries.

A tall man with bushy gray sideburns leading to an equally bushy beard approached.

Quint adopted the mask of an outraged father. Not that he cared, but for now the façade entertained.

The ill-groomed bushman smiled, removed his hat, and offered his hand. From Crowder's memories, Quint drew forth the hairy creature's name and ignored the proffered greeting. "Sheriff Cody, I find I am greatly inconvenienced at this interruption to my day. Why wasn't I informed earlier? We both know my son has a weakness for beautiful women. This little jade is only after his money. Somehow, he was coerced into giving his statement. I make donations to your campaign so I don't have to come down here and deal with this nonsense. I want my son out. Now." He pounded a fist onto the counter and stifled a smile when Cody jumped.

"I can't do it this time," Cody confessed, worrying his hat in his hands. "The girl came in and gave her statement. She had an emergency room report. The arrest is out of my hands."

Nervous energy swirled within the sheriff, and Quint saw the thin line of sweat forming on his brow. The man only cared about Crowder's contributions to his political campaigns. This poor excuse for a human stood there contemplating how he could follow the law and still placate Crowder enough to remain in his good graces. Contemptible. This discussion no longer amused.

"I want to speak to him."

"We're still processing your son. I'm sorry, you'll have to wait."

"Take me to him. Now." Quint prodded against Cody's mind. His dark will brushed across Cody's high-strung nerves. This minion would not deny him.

The sheriff scratched his beard, and then led him to the back room.

Good boy.

Ethan sat alone on a lumpy cot in a six by eight feet brick cell.

Quint peered through the steel bars turned to Cody and ordered, "Unlock it and leave us."

Cody complied and wandered back down the hall. A torrent of colorful language erupted from the cell occupant closest to the door as the Sheriff walked past.

Quint returned his attention to Crowder's son. The man-child rocked back and forth as if lost in madness. Quint detected the blue wave of consciousness flowing through Ethan's body—Maya's influence. Her gifts had grown quite strong since their last encounter.

Still nothing compared to his capabilities.

"What have you done, boy?" Quint scolded, maintaining the mask of a disappointed father. "You only gave the teasing wench what she asked for. You are guilty of nothing."

An unpleasant mix of piss and tears struck Quint's nostrils. The ragged child clutched a hand to his chest as if in pain. An azure swell warred with the black heart in his chest. Maya's grip held strong against the dark hand struggling to maintain control over the soul of this quivering human mess.

"I hurt her." The boy sniveled out. "I had to make it right."

"Right? As if you understand the meaning of that word." Quint whipped open the cell door, slamming it against the wall. "Look at you balled up like a baby on a piss-filled cot. What kind of man allows a woman to put him in such a state? If you had come to me, I would have made it right. We could have paid the bitch some money, and that would have been the end of it. Just like before, but now you've inconvenienced me. Get up. Let's go."

"No, I need to stay. I'm not going back out there." Fear flowed within the child and he remained anchored in a mire of guilt. Quint gleaned the strength of Maya's influence that forced Ethan to comprehend the error in what he'd done. The boy's glazed eyes looked into a mirror of pain, which reflected back and pierced his soul with the shame and culpability of all his illicit deeds.

Quint's lip curled and he turned away from this human's feeble mind. How dare he submit to some water fairy. "What's the matter with you, boy?" He entered the cell and stood before the whimpering simpleton. "Do you want to stay close to that crashing wave of awareness, seeing and experiencing every wrong you've done? Are you so weak you cannot embrace the pain long enough to fight through it? Don't let that water witch control you."

Ethan's red-rimmed eyes glared and a defiant black glimmer emerged from the wash of blue in his eyes. The boy's hunger to prove his manhood to his father, that fierce need lingering in every little boy's heart, beat hard within this child. "Help me. Please. Make it stop."

"Child," Quint scoffed. "I don't believe you are worthy of the gift I can give you."

"I-I-I am. I am w-worthy." Ethan held the cot's metal edge in a white-knuckled grip.

"Listen to you sniffle and stutter. You disgust me. Stand up!"

"What?"

"Stand. Up." Quint's patience thinned at this foul creature's inability to follow a simple command.

Ethan shuffled to his feet and mumbled, "What's wrong with you?"

Quint gripped Ethan's chin. "What's wrong is I have a worthless waste of energy for a son." With his back to the cell door, he braced a hand at the back of the shocked stripling's neck then locked his lips over Ethan's mouth and released a burst of dark matter down his throat.

Ethan jerked away and wiped a hand across his mouth. Eyes wide, he stared at his father. "What are you doing? What did you kiss me for?"

Quint slapped him across the face. "What's this? What's that? Be grateful all I did was kiss you." He lodged his forearm against Ethan's throat and pressed him against the cell wall. "Are you a survivor? Or will my essence be too much? Embrace the gift, child, or die. It matters not to me."

CHAPTER 6

"So, you're stripping now?"

Maya glanced at Nodin over the rim of her teacup. "No, I explained what happened. I was helping that girl by going undercover on amateur night."

"Sorry I missed the show. Flint would have loved it."

"That Crowder kid is a menace to every woman in this town. I had to stop him."

A week had passed since she'd spoken to Terran at the strip club. Maya rubbed her fingers against her breastbone. Worry for him erupted in an area of her heart she believed dried up long ago.

After spending the past few days at the outlet stream removing catfish that had contracted the same disease as the charred cow, Maya understood a larger problem existed. Her link with nature allowed her to sense the negative energy patterns coursing through earth's creatures. After a bit of research at the library, she determined the name of the disease and its causes—Mad Cow or BSE. At sixes and sevens, she called on Nodin for guidance.

Nodin met her at a table outside the local coffee shop. Perfect timing, since Quint had struck again last night. A late night visit to rejuvenate in her hot spring resulted in finding nothing but an empty, dried-up hole.

They needed a plan. Why was Quint back? Why the continued attacks against her, specifically?

Nodin lounged with his head tilted back, basking in the sun's morning rays. Wisps of white vapor rose from an untouched cup of black coffee, sitting on the café table before him.

Maya sipped her green tea then clanged the mug against the glass tabletop, which jolted Nodin from his sun worship.

"Our next move should be a visit to Crowder's farm. We'll start at the stream and spread our efforts from there. We need Flint to burn the diseased animals. I've done what I can in the water, but I noticed a few wolves that fed on Crowder's charred cow are now shaky and disoriented. We'll have a good old-fashioned round-up. Where is Flint anyway?"

Nodin heaved a heavy sigh. His calm, philosophical mind always clashed against her emotional, dramatic need to act now and worry about the consequences later. "I am unaware of Mother's placement of Flint."

Maya tapped her empty teacup against the table.

Nodin reached over and stilled her hand.

"That's another thing…what is Mother thinking? I don't want an Elemental life for Terran. He deserves all the normal events a human life can offer." She ran both hands through her hair. Conflicting thoughts coursed through her mind. While she longed to journey through life with Terran, she realized this was a selfish hope and foolish dream since his path remained unclear. "I don't believe he'll ever accept becoming peri-mortal. I can just imagine the conversation, 'Hey, guess what Terran? You have to take daily mud baths or you will die. *Again.* You can't eat, can't sleep, and your life now entails fighting freaks of nature and every major criminal whose dirty deeds pop into your mind. What? What is that you say? Nope, sorry no choice in the matter, too bad for you, case closed. Destiny rules.'"

Nodin shook his head and ran a finger along the rim of his coffee cup. "Maya, you're over-exaggerating the facts."

"Am I? He should be allowed time to consider the consequences before having this life foisted upon him."

"The philosopher Kierkegaard says, 'Life can only be understood backward, but it must be lived forward.' Mother will do as she pleases. She always has. I understand your concerns, but once Terran sees the possibilities, I believe he will embrace his path."

The waitress came out to check on them for the third time that morning. The poor girl twitched and jittered either from too much coffee or the potency of Nodin's charm. After an innuendo-filled conversation, the girl left with a promise to return with a fresh cup of coffee.

"I guess my tea needs failed to register."

"She's pretty, but she's blonde."

"Poor thing isn't aware of your aversion to fair-haired females."

"I'm not averse to you."

"No, but you're not interested in me, either. Don't you ever wish for more? How long will we remain like this, Nodin?" She cast him a sideways glance before sighing heavily, and then resting her elbow on the table and cupping her forehead in her hand. "Does anyone know why we are what we are? What would be the reason for Terran joining us? It doesn't make sense. He's lived a good life. He isn't like us."

"We're all the same in the end. I think he'll surprise you."

"He's a scientist, Nodin." Rubbing at a sudden ache in her temple, she sighed then met his gaze. "I doubt he'll accept his Elemental gifts without question. He'll be stuck in his lab conducting experiments on himself."

"Really, Maya, sometimes I wonder at the things you come up with."

"How can you remain so calm when we are about to experience a major change in our Elemental crew?" She shoved his shoulder. "This poor man's life could undergo a radical shift. Are you so far removed from when you were human that you cannot sympathize?"

"Maya, Quint is at the forefront of my thoughts right now. As for Terran, he will complete our circle. The fact that he is an educated rational thinker only strengthens our cause. Aldous Huxley said, 'Scientists simplify, they abstract, they eliminate all that, for their purposes, is irrelevant and ignore whatever they choose to regard as inessential; they impose a style, they compel the facts to verify a favorite hypothesis, they consign to the waste paper basket all that, to their mind, falls short of perfection.'"

"Oh good God, you've moved to science quotes now?" Maya covered her face with both hands and shook her head. After running both hands up and down her face, she folded them together on the table and sent up a silent prayer for forbearance. "What happened? Did your book of great philosophical quotes get lost in the wind?"

Nodin laughed and adjusted the chair next to him so he could prop up his legs. He leaned back and closed his eyes. "I hope your

Earthman joins us soon, because I want to discuss the possibility of containing and potentially converting Quint by using a high-energy magnetic field. We need access to instrumentation that can produce this field and a person who can find the right resonant frequency. In theory, this would convert Quint from dark matter into a photon. I am not sure of the particulars or how we would even get him into our trap, but…" He opened his eyes, straightened, and tapped a finger against the table. "This is where Terran will prove invaluable."

Maya gleaned Nodin's brain patterns as they searched through his memory-banks for the appropriate quote. "Do not rattle off another quote that will take me ten minutes to decipher."

"Hmm, how about this quote? 'The desire that guides me in all I do is the desire to harness the forces of nature to the service of mankind.'"

"Nikola Tesla." Terran's deep baritone sounded directly behind her. "Great quote."

"Lordy lou, you snuck up on me." Maya pressed a hand over her heart.

"Good morning, Ms. Conway." Terran rested his hands on her shoulders.

Arching her neck, she flashed an upside-down grin.

He tapped her nose with a finger. "It's nice to see you again."

Nodin pushed back in his chair and offered his hand in introduction. "Forgive our girl, Terran. She's a bit water logged this morning. I'm Nodin." He gestured to the empty seat at their wrought-iron table. "So, Maya tells me you're a scientist?"

#

As Terran shook the man's hand, an image of an Indian riding bareback across a golden prairie flashed through his mind. Nodin could have stepped straight out of a history book. His square jaw, red-brown skin, and ebony hair—neatly braided and tied with what looked like twine, were all throwbacks to the quintessential Native American.

Introductions finished, Nodin sat and stretched his long legs under the faded wrought-iron table. His demeanor seemed friendly, not territorial. "Please, join us."

Maya stood and brushed her fingers against his arm. "May I get you something?"

"No, please sit. I ran out of coffee at home, so I came by here before going to work. You live in town?" Terran swept his hand before him to include them both in his question.

Maya reached for Nodin's coffee, swallowed visibly before scrunching her nose, and sticking out her tongue. "Coffee's cold."

Nodin rolled his eyes. "I prefer a more natural environment, so I live on the outskirts. Maya lives in a small apartment above the gym."

"To be clear, you don't live together?" Green fragments of jealousy rumbled across his mind. This man would pose quite a rival for Maya's affections.

How involved are they?

Nodin shook his head, and his lips lifted in a crooked grin.

Mindy, the waitress and long time local stepped outside and placed a steaming cup of coffee on the table. "Hey Terran, haven't seen you in awhile." She bumped his shoulder with her hip.

"I ran out of coffee, Mindy. Do you think you could set me up with a very black, very large to-go cup?"

"Absolutely. I'll be right back. I'll just take this cold coffee off the table. I can assure you this new cup *is* hot *and* sweet." Mindy winked at Nodin then walked back inside.

Nodin watched Mindy walk away before returning to the prior question. "Maya and I have known each other for a long, long time, but she is not for me."

Maya sipped Nodin's coffee then slammed down the cup, jostling liquid over the edge. "*She* has to get to work, so *she* will see you boys later."

Terran and Nodin rose when she stepped away from the patio table and flounced down the sidewalk.

Terran caught white sneakers peeking out from under her faded jeans. Today, she'd been sensible enough to wear shoes. He nodded in her direction. "Where does she work?"

"Today, I believe, she'll be at the library. She works there part-time."

"Today? Does she work other places?" Terran considered asking about the strip club but refrained.

"Yes."

"I haven't seen either of you around before. Are you new to the area?"

"Yes and no."

"You certainly answer questions in the same manner."

"Yes." Nodin tapped his finger against the side of the mug before dumping the contents into the shrubbery. He pinched his bottom lip before he spoke, "You are interested in her, but then you are interested in many things. She is unsure of the path she should take with you, but has been led to this crossroads by a hand that sees with an all-encompassing view. Maya's path will cross with yours, and as you join her journey, it may not be anything you seek. Choices are not given. Links will forge closed. She wishes to stop fate, but after meeting you, I see she will lose. I wonder with your science and your logic how long you will take to accept that life sometimes defies explanation."

"Our paths will cross? Links forging?" This conversation was too peculiar to quantify before caffeine fortification. "I'm sorry. I don't follow."

"You will. Soon." Nodin pushed away from the table, stood, and followed the same path as Maya.

They were both on the far side of odd. No wonder they were friends. No one else stood a chance in comprehending them.

CHAPTER 7

Maya pushed her library cart between shelves lined with children's books. The squeaky wheel joined the whispers of mothers reminding their children to use their inside voices, while allowing their own cell phones to blare with the popular ring tone du jour.

She hid her exasperation with smiles at the children as they chose their picture books and early readers.

The dusty smell of overused books calmed her, which was why she volunteered twice each week. People who visited the library generally thought about the books and videos they planned to rent, so any devious intent was readily apparent, but few mental images raised red flags.

Her abilities allowed her to glean negative energies. At times, the sheer amount of just one human's inner darkness could wear her down. In the beginning of her Elemental life, dark thoughts threatened to overtake her mind, and she had fought to differentiate her own thoughts from others. Under control now, she focused her energies on where true harm sprung and let the rest fade away. Years passed before she'd completely grasped whether or not a person was actually capable of their intent. Even now, there were times she followed someone who in the end became incapable of committing his or her planned crime. Or she'd encounter others whose minds were in a repetitive cycle of causing chaos and pain. Her powers cleansed their minds and pushed them to follow a better path. This mental gift, along with others, came packaged with her new existence. *No directions or shut off switch included.*

Her waterlogged heart pounded a little harder when she spotted her sexy scientist weaving past tiny tables and chairs in the children's area. Brown eyes caught blue as he walked down the aisle toward her cart.

"Mr. Forrester, I would have thought your reading level was a bit higher?" She teased as she placed another thin book upon the shelf.

"Hello, Maya."

One of Terran's hands was wrapped around a hardbound book, and the other was tucked away in the front pocket of his Dockers. Dockers he filled out very well. "May I help you find something?" She flashed a bubbly smile.

"Sure, I thought I might look for a book in the self-help department."

"Oh?"

"Yes, one on relationships, dating, that general topic."

"I do believe you know quite a bit on that subject already. If you were interested in a woman, I'm sure you would only have to crook your finger, and she would be more than willing."

"Really, and why is that?" He tapped his book against her cart.

"Well, it's obvious you take care of your body. You have a very attractive face and most importantly—you're smart, which allows for a successful career, which equals financial stability. You offer quite an appealing package." She bit her bottom lip as she considered just how attractive.

His gaze locked on her lips and his breath hitched. He cleared his throat before asking, "Am I appealing enough for you to join me for dinner?"

What? Good Lord, after a hundred years, Maya shouldn't be flustered when a man asked her on a date. It did happen on occasion, so why did his request have her blushing like a schoolgirl? *Not that my cheeks can turn pink. Maybe they turn blue. That's attractive.*

She flipped through the books on her cart. After picking one, she placed it where it belonged in order to avoid answering the question.

"It's actually more of a get-together with my friends. Since you're new to the area, I thought you might like to meet some people. We'll grill up burgers. Have a few beers. Would like you to come?"

"I have a restrictive diet." *A very restricted diet.* "I'm sorry, Terran. I don't attend many backyard barbeques."

"We can work with your diet. A lot of people don't eat meat or whatever your food allergies happen to be."

At that comment, she refrained from laughing out loud. There was no way for him to "work" with her food issues. "I won't come for the food, but I imagine your friends stay after sometimes and um… hang-out, right?"

"Yes. Some people stick around after."

Should I do this? Enter his world and befriend him. Her lonely heart and empty arms clashed with her Elemental duties. Destiny teased with an opportunity to explore their connection without spying from afar. Of course, she would follow her heart. Hadn't she always leapt without thinking?

His head was tilted a little to the side. His unease obvious by his incessant finger tapping on the book in his hand. *How sweet.* Time to relieve his mind. "I will come for that part, the not-eating part. Very kind of you to ask. Thank you."

He smiled, lighting up the room. Every drop of water in her body glistened from the warmth found in that simple expression.

"All right, I can give you my number. Call when you're ready and I'll pick you up."

"Terran, I'll get there on my own."

He nodded. "Good."

Her special skills weren't needed to glean the kicked-up beat of his blood. A wave of sexual energy bubbled through her as a red-hot vision broadcasted from his mind. Her legs were wrapped around his body, and her shoulders jostled the shelves as he kissed her. Appreciating the direction of his vision, she dusted off her flirting skills.

After watching him place the book he'd been holding on a shelf, she said, "Are you sure that's where that book belongs? If not, poor workers like me get in trouble." She reached over the cart and ran a hand down his arm.

He raised a brow, aware enough to interpret the not-so-subtle acceptance of him as a potential mate. Her body went from slow simmer to roiling boil, as his mental picture switched to him bending her over the library cart.

Terran kept his gaze locked on hers. "I'm not sure where this book belongs. Perhaps you should come closer and make sure I put it in the right slot."

Well, well, double-entendre much? She'd enjoy putting his thoughts into action, but not in the middle of Curious George and Clifford the Big Red Dog. "The right slot? Sorry, my cart seems to be in the way. What is the title of that book you so carelessly placed on the shelf?"

Terran tapped a finger against the binding. "*The Call the Cthulhu* by HP Lovecraft. It was in the Sci-Fi section."

Ironic. "I'm familiar with the story. An octopus like being with tentacles and tiny wings awaiting its awakening at the bottom of the sea. Interesting reading material. You should watch out for sea-creatures. You never know which ones will bite."

"Very true." He smiled and shook his head. "Where did you take off to the other night?"

What? He couldn't possibly remember seeing her the night of the gas station robbery. She'd wiped his memory clean. "What night?"

"The other night at the gas station when it was robbed. You were outside talking to this lady in the van. Stupid move by the way, since she was with the crazy guy waving around the gun. Where did you go? I didn't see you once the police came. Do you know what happened?"

"We already discussed this." She crouched and pulled some books from the cart's lower shelf, gathering her calm.

"No, not in depth." He filched one of her books and flipped through the pages.

She sighed. Obviously, he wouldn't drop the subject until she answered him. "I heard a child cry in the van, so I asked the lady if everything was all right. Then I went home. You're saying the place got robbed? Wow. I'm glad I left." She hated lying, but she had to tread carefully. Admitting she transformed into a menacing fog would send him searching for her straightjacket.

"Yes, it was robbed. One minute I was buying an apple, and then I woke up on the floor soaking wet."

Coughing to cover a laugh, Maya asked, "You don't remember anything other than that?"

"We spoke, don't you remember? You weren't very friendly."

"It was late and some strange man approached me. I'm not apologizing if that's what you're after."

Terran moved around her cart, placed his hands against the shelves, and pinned her between his arms. "No, that's not what I'm after."

Hazy heat shot through her body. "Not shy at all, are you?" If only he knew how easily she could push him away.

"I'm very clear about what I want." His dominant position was much too commanding, but at the same time, Maya found his boldness intriguing.

His lips hovered above hers and the scent of cinnamon enticed her senses. Their elemental connection vibrated throughout her body—strong, sensual, primal. Why him? Why had she never felt this attraction to Nodin or Flint? Was it because water flowed toward the shore? Was he the grounding force beneath her feet?

If she stretched, her lips would meet his. The flames from their kiss would burn down the building.

Fahrenheit 451 had nothing on them.

However, book burning in the children's section would most likely get her dismissed as a volunteer. Tonight was soon enough to find out just how good cinnamon-flavored Terran tasted.

"I'll drop by later." She pushed a book against his chest and waited until he took it before stepping from under his cage. "You should read that book. It's very informative."

His brows drew together as he read the title aloud, "*The Little Mermaid?*"

CHAPTER 8

A low beat of classic rock came from the backyard as Maya stood on Terran's front porch. Always one to forge her own trail, she fought the notion that this pull toward him was predestined. Hadn't she, so many years ago, left behind her birthplace to begin a new life? At eighteen, she had traveled across America by train to California. Forever frozen at age twenty-one, she fought the notion this relationship was chosen for her. Fate did not have her at Terran's doorstep—hope did.

At the door's threshold, indecision raced through her mind. Should she cross into his life and get release for this pent-up need, or should she walk away? If she left, could she keep him safe and ignore the pull attempting to anchor her in place? Could she stand still, neither in, nor out?

Nodin and Flint could keep an eye on Terran if she chose to leave. *No*, she refused to step back. She would take this one night, this one moment as her own. Only Terran could deliver the escape into pleasure she craved. Why not surrender to a night of bliss? The chance might never come again once Terran discovered her identity as an Elemental water-girl.

Indecision time was over.

Choice made, she knocked on the front door, but no one answered. She took a deep breath, turned the knob, and stepped over the threshold. Eyes closed, she searched for his mental signature— *upstairs and irritated.*

Her direction clear, she opened her eyes and observed Terran's home. A woven Navajo rug lay at her feet, offering a colorful protection for the wood floors that led from the front door to the kitchen. On her right, brown leather couches squared around a big screen TV. A half wall divided the living room from the kitchen area. A few guests stood by the fridge chatting, drinking, and living the normal life of those in their second decade. She gleaned their thoughts, which came across as a gentle wave of worry over a salsa blotch on a shirt, a low cell phone battery, and sex—of course.

The staircase to the left led to Terran. The intricately carved wooden banister slid smoothly against her hand as she snuck upstairs. He was alone, which worked out well for her plans. In her human life, she'd been called a soiled dove by co-workers. Tonight, they were right. Poor fella, she planned to keep him locked in his room, drunk as a boiled owl on the firewater burning between them.

Along the upstairs corridor were three bedrooms, a bathroom, and a closet. The closet door stood open, so she peeked inside. A laundry basket's contents overflowed onto the floor. Brown towels, bulk shampoo, and body wash bottles lined the shelves. Condensation beaded on a half-empty beer bottle that sat on top of a white tote with a pullout drawer.

Maya tapped her foot against the wood floor. Impatient. Jittery—as if she'd just downed four shots of double espresso.

Terran stepped out of the bathroom. His arms were loaded with cleaning supplies and a roll of paper towels.

"Good evening, Terran."

"Holy crap, you startled me. I was just—" A bleach wipes tub toppled to the floor. "Damn it." He cleared his throat. "Sorry. We… ah… hadn't cleaned up here, and so I thought…um…I thought I should get it done." He shoved the products onto the closet shelf, shut the doors, and then opened them again to grab his beer.

Still wearing plastic gloves.

"Nice gloves, Terran."

"Give me a minute, please."

Cute. His cheeks turned a slight pink. Handsome and cleans the bathroom—what more could a woman want? Water sloshed around in the sink and a great amount of mumbling came from behind the bathroom door.

Watching him step back out, she blinked and tilted her head. "Terran? Is that you? I didn't realize you were up here. What are you doing?"

A huge grin appeared along with a teasing twinkle in his brown eyes. "Maya, I haven't seen you in so long." He wrapped her in an embrace that lifted her off her feet. He swung her back and forth before he set her down, keeping his hands on her hips.

His faded jeans rested low on his hips, and a T-shirt adorned with Beaker from the Muppets was tucked behind a thick brown belt. No spectacles tonight. *Not bad for a Boffin.*

"I'm glad you could make it." Terran tucked a stray hair behind her ear. "Glad to see you're wearing shoes tonight, although I'd like a replay of those tall black boots someday."

She placed a finger over his lips. "No shoe talk tonight. Let's check out your room." Maya gestured toward the closed door behind them then pulled away and twisted open the knob. *Another threshold crossed.*

Terran trailed behind, his fingers threading through his thick, brown hair. "It's a black hole in here. Once you step in, you might not make it out."

"Who says I want out?"

His sharp intake of breath clarified she'd made her point.

She took a slow turn about the room. Socks and pants were strewn across the floor of his simple, square bedroom. The unmade king-size bed took up the majority of space. Papers and spiral binders teetered on an end table. His laptop sat perched on a small desk nestled between two windows. The curtains billowed as a cool evening breeze entered and stirred through the room.

Voices streamed up from the backyard through the half open windows. In his closet, a blue gym bag sat on the floor, topped with a pair of scuffed running shoes.

Her hand trembled as she brushed the change on his dresser. *Don't be nervous. You can do this.* "Does your door lock?"

"Yes. Why?"

Maya slipped out of her shoes and padded over to the bedroom door. A loud click reverberated through the room as she popped the lock in place. She leaned against the door and ran a finger down her neck then trailed between her breasts before advancing.

Terran stood with legs spread. He shoved his hands into his pockets. A single brow rose over heated brown eyes.

Moving slowly, she cupped his face in her hands and rose on

her toes to fit her mouth to his. With her tongue, she licked a wet wave across the seam of his lips.

He inhaled sharply, and then took over, slanting his mouth over hers. His hands were rough and urgent over her body. He wrapped a hand around her waist, drew her closer, and then traced a line from her collarbone to her neck before his thumb locked in place under her chin.

Heat flowed between them like a torrential downpour on a humid summer day. She moaned against his mouth as he led them in the exact direction she'd planned.

Their elemental connection flared in blues and greens behind her closed lids as each kiss welded shut a link in the chain between them. His wild need made him the perfect choice to end her sexual drought. Her waters burned hot, brewing within her, steaming with the need to pour over every inch of his body.

Momentarily breaking their bond, she lifted his shirt over his head. She ran her hands ran over his muscular chest and across his broad shoulders.

He clutched her arms and held her at a distance. His brow furrowed and he shook his head. A quick gleaning of his mind indicated his confusion over his extreme lack of control. Indecision fogged over his need and warned him to tread at a slower pace.

No!

She touched his inflamed lips with hers and tried to wrap her hand around his neck.

He stopped her by clasping her head in his hands. "Maya, what are we doing?"

"I believe you know and I imagine you do it quite well." She bit his thumb.

After drawing a sharp breath, he brushed a thumb over her bottom lip then stepped back and paced along the side of his bed. "I can't believe I'm saying this, but let's think about this for a minute. I don't understand." He pulled at his hair, which created two tufts making his appearance a bit like the comic book character, Wolverine.

"What is there to understand? It's sex." She waved a hand through the air.

"You don't even know me."

"I don't believe you're always best of friends with the girls you've slept with in the past. Why does it matter? This is basic, Terran. It's feeding our natural instincts." She placed his hand against her cheek then kissed his palm. "I want you on this level. Tonight. That's all I'm asking, all I expect. Do you deny you want this as much as I do?" She ran her hand over the bulge in his jeans and shuddered as she envisioned all that molded clay moving inside her.

Terran grabbed her wrist. "I'm sorry. I can't do this. Not right now."

"Why, because it's now instead of later? Based on how you feel against my hand, I would say you are well equipped and ready. You can't deny you planned on getting us here at some point. Well, here I am, ready for you, eager even." She trailed a finger across his chin then down to his throbbing pulse. "Stop worrying about the way things are supposed to be, or what you have been led to believe is the natural order of a sexual relationship. This isn't anything you need to analyze. It's just you and I, together, enjoying one another."

Why did he have to dissect this? They were two pieces of nature's puzzle and, eventually, they would lock into place. Why not tonight? His rejection stung and made her feel like a tart offering her body, only to be dismissed.

He leaned closer and kissed her forehead and the tip of her nose before wrapping her in his arms. Intimacy from a human seemed so foreign. The tenderness Terran shared through this gentle embrace brought tears to her eyes.

Terran tightened his hold and was silent for a moment before admitting, "I'll not deny I want you, but not like this. Not like two animals feasting on each other, mindless and out of control. At least, not the first time." He pulled back and winked.

She rested her forehead on his chest, so he wouldn't see the tears evoked by his soft touch. After re-absorbing the tears on her cheeks, she stated, "You're overthinking it."

"Maya—"

Stepping away, she peered out the window. "Are you pushing me away because *you* didn't make this decision? What does it matter if you know me? I am the same now as I'll be in three weeks, three months, thirty years. Why can't we have this one night? We'll forget the rules and shut out the world. Be with me."

Why couldn't he cooperate? She wanted to bathe in pleasure, release this dam of need. Her body felt like a steam engine and he'd sealed the lid shut.

"You say I have questions. This is true, but you never have answers. Who are you? Where did you come from? Why are you here?" His voice softened, and she turned and caught his whispered final question. "Why do I feel a link to you I've never felt with anyone else?" He leaned with his elbows against his dresser, facing away.

Maya wrapped her arms around him. "Let's resolve the question you most want answered. How it feels to sink inside my body, to feel me move beneath you, the crash of that final wave as it breaks over us. Then we'll do it all over again." She ran her hand over his heavy flesh covered by jeans and rocked her hips against his. A wicked thought flashed through her mind—*compel him*. A little prod against his will and she could have him.

No, I won't force him. Desire makes me crazy.

Terran twisted and grabbed her wrists before she slid them under his waistband. "I want more from you. Everything. Not just one night. I want you by my side tomorrow and the next day. Together, we can connect all the missing factors until I know every part of you." He softened his refusal with a sweet kiss. A gentle melding that calmed her.

"Has anybody seen Terran?" A voice carried on the wind through the window.

A female voice.

The man in question paused and tilted his head toward the sound. "Come on, let's head downstairs. They'll send up a search party soon."

"Is that your girlfriend?"

"No." A flush spread across his cheeks, and he avoided eye contact as he searched the floor for his shirt.

"Hmm...is she aware of this? I can see myself out. It's never good to have three kissing fish in the same tank."

Or a piranha with two sweet Kissing Gourami's.

"No, you came as my guest and you will stay. If you think I'm letting you leave after all this..." he waved his hand in a circle, "whatever *this* was, you're wrong."

"And how do you plan on making me stay?" She raised a brow. "Gonna tie me to the bed?" She cuffed her wrists together and lowered them before him. "Feel free."

He grabbed her wrists, wrenched her close, and placed his hands on both sides of her face before kissing her hard. His desire made clear as he branded her lips from deep pink to enflamed red. Their kiss took a hot turn as he teased her with his tongue, driving in and out of her mouth, imitating what he refused to do to her body.

Teasing wasn't what she craved. Her gifts allowed her power over others, and yet, she was powerless with this man.

She hopped up and wrapped her legs around his waist. In flagrant abandon, she kissed him as she ran her fingers through his hair.

He braced his legs against her assault and ran his hands under the back of her shirt.

A sound reached her clouded mind—a persistent pounding. A hard knock upon the door broke their rhythmic kiss. They eased apart, their gazes meeting as their labored breathing rushed out in short puffs against their lips, drying the glistening evidence of their passion.

"Terran?" A girl's muffled voice sounded from outside his bedroom door. "Are you in there?"

Quiet ensued for a moment.

Maya stifled nervous laughter against his neck.

The doorknob rattled.

"Why is this door locked?" The intruder asked whomever was listening—another persistent double tap against the door.

Go away, Chippy!

"Give me a minute." Terran hollered at the door as if the inanimate wood were the one speaking.

Intending to ignore the interruption, Maya bit his earlobe and kissed his face and neck.

He drew a ragged breath. "Maya, you have no idea what you're doing to me."

"Show me then."

He caught her mouth and gave her a hard buss. "Not tonight." He eased away and narrowed his eyes—a silent warning to stop her torment.

Young totties banging on doors would not deter her. She kissed him again.

To halt her renewed efforts, Terran nipped her bottom lip. He soothed the bite with the rasp of his tongue. A struggle ensued as he set her on her feet. "Maya, stop," he whispered. "I told you they'd send a search party."

She picked up his shirt and threw it at his head. "I don't play games, Terran." After she found her shoes, she shoved them on.

"I think you do and we are playing this one to the end. You've made your first move tonight. Mine will come, but only once I know you, Maya Conway. Why would you come here and offer yourself? Why are you so averse to footwear? Why do I dream of you swimming in the ocean as I sit in warm sand?"

An intense longing swept through her at his questions. A foolish wish for him to play out that exact scene trickled through her heart. "Terran, please understand, I'm not like that girl on the other side of the door. I just want this. Whether we're together weeks or months from now, I want you to remember I'm not the one who asked for more. I only wanted this moment. It's easy and it's primal. As you're the scientist, you must comprehend my meaning."

"That side of my nature almost swamps me completely when I'm with you. It's barely leashed right now. Anticipation will make our time together that much sweeter. Besides, I'm hungry—for food. By the aromas coming through the window, I imagine the burgers are ready." He drew her close and placed another kiss on the tip of her nose. "We'll get back to this soon enough."

Maya rocked back on her heels and chuckled. "Soon, right. I guess it's not like I don't have plenty of time."

A quick succession on the door—tap, tap, tap—louder, more forceful, this time.

Young tottie is tiffed.

"Terran? Who are you talking too?" A girl's voice summoned, the tone tinged with a hint of desperation.

"Katie, I'll be out in a minute."

"But why is your door locked?" Katie questioned.

Terran cast a sidelong glance at the door. "Go on down, Katie. I'll join you in a few minutes."

Maya basked in the feeling of Terran's arms around her. Affection was something so foreign and yet so wonderful. The gentle touch of another was an infrequent experience in her second life. Her sense of right and wrong pricked, but she peeked into his mind anyway. A very romantic view of their future relationship prevailed. Unnerving, because she had given up softer emotions and long-term relationships many years ago. Yet, wasn't this what fate had decreed? Was she strong enough to walk away if he chose a separate path? Their lives were meshed together now, like mixed paint on a canvas and nothing could separate the vibrant swirls of brown and blue without destroying the beauty they created together.

Terran swayed back and forth and whispered in a husky voice, "Now I know, I had dreamed of you in my arms. I'll have you here again, but when it's right, not before. You draw me in, but I won't allow myself to sink any further until I figure you out."

"Terran, do not build me into something I may never be. I am not one of your samples to process. I may be nothing but a passing wave, drifting by, unable to stop at any shore."

He bent and brushed her lips lightly with his own, "We'll see. I have an awfully large shore." The sound of his chuckle joined the sound of the lock popping as he opened the door.

CHAPTER 9

Terran had to escape before he changed his mind, threw Maya on his bed, and lost himself in the silky caress of her body. Why hadn't he taken what she'd been willing to give? Because her actions didn't add up, it was like an equation waiting to be solved on a chalkboard, but too many factors were missing.

One interesting puzzle piece was her names had water connotations: Maya meant "water" or "spring" and Conway meant "Holy River." Perhaps that was the reason he dreamed of her as water in various forms. His parents had named him for the earth. This peculiar connection almost had him believing in pre-destined relationships.

Maya tugged on his sleeve as he stepped into the hallway. Her sweet pink tongue trailed across her plump bottom lip. "Sure I can't change your mind?"

Sweet mother, have mercy.

Desire and an accelerated heartbeat had him pausing in his doorway.

Why am I leaving my bedroom again?

He shook his head, took her hand, and drew her into the hall. Primal urges screamed do not exit, but Terran ignored them and shut the bedroom door.

Maya chuckled and squeezed his hand. "I'll give you a minute," she said, before ducking into the bathroom.

Katie waited down the hall at the top of the stairs, whispering with her friend, Melissa.

As he approached, he was met with very different expressions on their faces. Melissa's gaze attempted to shoot daggers through his chest, while Katie appeared close to tears. *Damn.* She had made clear her interest—an interest he didn't return. Their outlook on life didn't run along parallel lines.

However, if his calculations were correct, the blonde in his bathroom embodied everything he wanted in a woman and more. How would they fit if he set her on the sink and—

"Terran, what…what's going on?" Katie gripped his upper arm.

Melissa narrowed her eyes at the bathroom door.

"Melissa." He nodded. "Katie, glad you could make it."

Katie gathered him close for an awkward one-armed hug and kissed his cheek.

He eased away and stuffed his hands in his front pockets. "Are you having a nice time?"

"Yes, Scotty greeted us downstairs," Katie answered. "What are you doing up here? Why were you in your—" she trailed off and stared over his shoulder.

A slight mist dampened the back of his neck, causing the hairs to stand on end. A single bead coalesced and trickled down his back, caressing his skin on the journey south before a fold in his T-shirt caught the drop. Maya slid up beside him. *What did she spray on me?*

"Oh, hello." Katie looked back and forth between him and Maya, before blurting, "Who are you?"

Although he had never led Katie to believe there could be an intimate relationship between them, he considered her a friend and didn't want her upset. She wasn't like Dr. Melinda Givens who wanted a one-night stand or like Maya who wanted whatever the hell it was she wanted. Katie made obvious her aspirations of love and marriage, but he wouldn't be the one taste-testing wedding cakes.

He stepped aside to make introductions. "Katie, this is Maya, my guest this evening. Maya, this is Katie and her friend, Melissa."

Maya bobbed her head and a soft "Hello" came from her lips. *What is this timid attitude?*

"Thanks for the advice, Terran. I'll keep what you said in mind." Maya nodded then exited down the steps.

She had given him an out by portraying innocence in their time together. Maya obviously read the tension in the air. He appreciated her consideration of Katie's feelings. One more thing in Maya's favor, she had a kind heart.

"And what were you helping her with, Terran?" Melissa charged.

"Who is she?" Katie said, a quiver to her voice.

"Maya is new in town, and I invited her tonight so she could meet everyone." *Escape. Escape.* Once more departure was necessary, although this time he welcomed the exit. Withdrawal was crucial before Katie asked all those questions likely circulating in her mind. Questions he did not want to answer. "I should head down and help Scotty. I'll catch you later."

A wet glimmer appeared in Katie's eyes, and he accepted the sneer from Melissa as he retreated down the stairs.

# # #

"I brought you a beer. We don't have any limes, though." Terran handed Maya the bottle and wrapped two fingers around his own as he juggled his full plate. "Were you able to find something you can eat?"

"Sorry, I'm a bit of a teetotaler. Would you happen to have water?" Maya relieved him of the bottle's burden and held it like a prop. "Scotty was explaining you're roommates. He said your other roommate, Clay, moved out after getting married."

Scotty dug around in a cooler set by his feet and pulled out a water bottle. "I told her since she's new to the area, if there was anywhere she'd like to go rafting, I'd take her in my four-man." He replaced Maya's beer with water.

Terran nodded and wiped the ketchup and grease from his fingers.

There will be only one-man for Maya. Me.

"Rafting sounds fun. I enjoy being out on the water." A mischievous smile played on Maya's lips before she covered it by taking a sip from her water.

Burger in hand, Terran took a bite, chewed, and then pointed out. "We'll have to get a group together and go sometime. We can use one of your larger rafts."

Scotty threw a chip at Terran's head, and it landed in his hair. "Oh, it's like that, is it? Moving in on my date."

"It's like that. Sorry, man, I saw her first."

"All right, all right, I can see Forrester isn't in a sharing mood. Maya, when you're ready for a real man, I'll be around." Scotty raised his beer in toast then weaved through the crowd toward the house.

Terran threw baby carrots and a cherry tomato at Scotty's head.

Maya brushed a hand through his hair. She smiled and showed him the chip. "Did you get things worked out with your Katie-girl?"

"Cute. Real cute." He crumpled his napkins, put them on his plate, and placed the entire mess on a picnic table.

"You're right. It isn't funny, is it? The poor daisy is dead-nuts over you. Her mind is very full of future visions, and you feature in every frame. You stand beside her on top of a pure white wedding cake." Maya licked her thumb then wiped at a spot on his cheek.

"I'm not interested in daisies or wedding cakes."

"Neither am I, but I am aware when I'm a thorn in someone's side. Ms. Katie and her friends are plotting my demise. Any minute now, she'll approach, claws bared, prepared to spit and hiss. So that's my cue to leave, as I don't deal with confrontations in the same kitty-cat manner. I'm much more direct, as you can attest." She handed over her water bottle. "Thanks for inviting me. I don't... I rarely get a chance to be involved in anything so conventional. Another time, Forrester." She inclined her head and headed toward the front of the house.

He took a long draw from her water then followed. Sidling alongside her, he spun her to face him. "I'll walk you home."

"That isn't necessary."

"It's just as necessary as this." He bent and kissed her. A soft kiss. With this gentle meeting of lips, he intended to send a message to her and the entire crew present—she was his. Again, he lightly brushed her lips, once, twice before drawing back.

She raised a single brow and locked her aqua-blue gaze with his. "Perhaps next time you'd like to lift a leg, always a much clearer form of marking your territory."

"I think I would have to mark my territory with you. Mark it and anchor you down so you won't drift off."

"Bondage. How romantic."

He chuckled, this cheeky Shoeless Girl got to him. "Come on, let's get you home."

Standing beside her, he recalled the time they crossed paths at the stream. The water bubbled and churned, creating a melody found only in nature. A harmony created in her presence, one that echoed in his mind even now. What would happen if he closed his eyes and allowed her to lead him further down the stream? Were there rapids ahead or a still pond?

With every intention of discovering the answers to those questions, he clasped her hand. Her smooth skin was like a clay piece on a potter's wheel waiting to be shaped by his touch. Together, they would create a rare piece of art. Fingers spread, he linked her fingers in his, setting an unbreakable mold.

CHAPTER 10

Maya kicked a rock down the sidewalk as Terran spoke about his friends at the party. Heat from their joined hands offered warmth on the cool night.

In a lifetime of fighting as an Elemental, Maya would take this moment as her reward. Highlighted by a gold star, she would lock away this memory and bring it out to treasure during moments of loneliness or despair.

During her stay here, she had rented an apartment in an historic building a couple blocks away from Terran's house. The second floor apartment served as a fitting place to store her steamer trunk that overflowed with paraphernalia from the last hundred years. The building's red brick façade had weathered many different signs hung from its scrolled metal post. A gym was the current ground floor occupant. Tourist shops and restaurants filled the town square only a few blocks away.

Lost in her own thoughts, she stumbled when a malicious chill of greed and impatience bit into her mind. A veil of darkness fell on the sidewalk and a stifling thickness filled the air. A sticky sheen cloyed in her nostrils, but left no trace. Maya stretched her elemental senses, searching for the crafty fox in his shaded burrow, awaiting an innocent rabbit to scurry by.

The sounds of the night vanished—no birds sang, no crickets chirped, no cars purred.

The streetlights flickered then sizzled and popped.

Extinguished.

Terran stopped and pulled her close.

As if he could protect her.

"That's odd. I wonder if a transformer blew." His body became a stiff wall of tension beside her.

It figured his scientific mind would attempt to explain these events rationally. Awareness of the menacing vibe thrumming through the air was palpable, even to a human. Unfortunately, in her world, only the irrational prevailed, the personification of her worst nightmare awaited.

Quint.

Her dream date turned into her worst nightmare. She could not defeat Quint alone.

Maya turned her back on the smug leech waiting farther down the sidewalk. A storm gathered in her body and an icy sheen prickled her skin. She refused to shiver and give away her alarm. Although, Quint had no doubt already gleaned her terror at facing him alone.

After steadying her thoughts, Maya rested a hand on Terran's shoulder. "I'll head back on my own from here. It's just a bit farther and you should get back to your party. Thanks for inviting me. I had—"

"Isn't this sweet?" Quint's vile voice erupted out of the darkness. "Two lovers walking under the moonlight on a mid-summer's eve. What a romantic picture you make."

Maya spun and shifted Terran behind her. Searching for the inky beast cloaked in black. An obsidian form separated itself from the curtain of night. Quint's monstrous silhouette crept across the sidewalk. All wrong, his shadow didn't seam with this earthly plane.

The surrounding darkness receded. Maya recognized Quint's current human form as the rancher, Carlyle Crowder.

Quint wagged a finger. "Maya, aren't you a little old for young Forrester here? Never figured you for a...what do they call it these days...a cougar?"

Terran took her arm and pulled her to his side. "Mr. Crowder? I'm sorry, but I don't understand what you're doing out here? Is there something I can help you with?"

"No," Quint smirked. "Not yet anyway, but I do need to speak to Ms. Conway. I'll see she makes it back to her watering hole." He tapped his index finger against his bottom lip. "Oh wait, hmm, that's all dried up now, isn't it?"

Anger replaced the fear storming through her body. She stepped away from Terran, but she felt his grip tighten. "Terran, as I said, my apartment's just ahead. Please, let go of my arm. I have some things I need to discuss with Crowder. Just go." She yanked her arm out of his grip, focused on his mind, reached deep, and compelled him to leave.

An icy chill shot down her spine as she heard a twig snap behind her.

Run. Mist. Escape with Terran now.

Quint's voice grated across her nerves. "On second thought, I'm more than happy to have Terran stay. He's quite a specimen. I do believe with the right person operating beneath the surface, he'd go far."

Terran stepped toward Quint, his fists clenched at his sides. "What is going on here? How do you two know each other? I don't like people talking in circles around me."

Maya wrapped a hand around Terran's fist and tried calming him, prodding at his mind.

Terran fought her waves of influence, shaking his head.

Quint posed an unpredictable danger. The connotations behind his words were never completely comprehendible. Anything was fair game in the twisted black miasma of his mind, because he had no moral scruples. His not-so-subtle hints at taking over Terran's body with his coal black core would not become reality during her existence. She would sacrifice herself before letting that vile deed occur.

Using the earth's energy frequencies, she sent out a mental distress signal for Nodin. Her fear and anxiety broadcasted across the waves. Urgency rippled with her need for elemental aid. Quint would pick up on her waving red flag, but she had no choice. He already knew her deep-seated fear of him. Years ago she'd spent six months recuperating from their battle, so her unease was well founded.

Her thoughts shifted to Flint. *Please come.*

What was Quint planning? His idea of fun ranged from fast cars to slow torture. He seemed fascinated by the unbearable pain a human could endure.

Maya had to keep his focus on her. "Quint, whatever it is you're doing, you have to know we won't allow you to succeed. Why don't you disperse back into whatever black hole you were derived from."

Her goading continued, "You want to be human, but you're playing a part. Being human requires having a heart, one thing you will never have. Change your path, dark man. This insane fantasy you have to be human is all played out."

Terran turned and faced her, blocking her view of Quint. Searching her eyes, he asked, "Maya? What is going on here? Why are you calling Mr. Crowder, Quint? How do you know him?"

"Yes, Maya, how do you know me?" Quint jeered, in a voice incongruent with the distinguished face of Carlyle Crowder. "Everything I seek is within my reach. Terran's elemental nature is dormant inside his body, longing to be set free. You do know who he is to become?"

Damn it! How does Quint know so much about Terran?

She grasped Terran's hand and pulled him to her side. Ready at any moment to flee.

Quint smiled like a serial killer before he guts you with a knife. "I plan on absorbing myself in every aspect of Mr. Forrester's life after he undergoes a few alterations." A feral light flashed in Quint's eyes, eagerness broadcasted its signal straight into her mind. His intentions now clear.

A heavy swell surged through her body, ready to pour forth and defend her mate. "I won't allow it."

Quint gave a hard laugh and rocked back on his high-dollar heels. "As if you have any say in the matter. He and I will mesh well together, don't you think? He is so young, intelligent with the added bonus of being attractive to the female sex. Or male. I like to try new things. With my boy here, the possibilities are endless."

Terran's frustration was palpable. Maya gleaned the bafflement in his mind, but he wouldn't back down from the incongruously menacing behavior coming from a man he had known his whole life.

Terran paced in front of her. "Mr. Crowder, we will not be working together on any projects now or in the future." He stilled, and then pointed a finger at Quint. "I'm aware of your unlawful deeds with your cattle and that is not how I conduct myself. I do not let others, human or animal, contract diseases then cover up the evidence by sprinkling the ashes with money. I don't know how you know Maya, and I don't care at this point. What I do know is, you should leave. Now."

Quint raised a brow and sneered, "Is that what you know? How unfortunate, as we were just getting to the good part. Are you sure you wouldn't like to know more about Maya? I can smell the unspent lust seeping out of your every pore. She's a tricky siren, son. She'll tempt you then leave you dry. Isn't that right, water witch?"

Quint's essence drifted, like fingers, across her face. A shady brush painted a black stain down her neck and trailed between her breasts.

Maya clenched her jaw against the pain. Could Terran see Quint's dark mark on her body? She trembled and covered her neck with her hands.

A flaming bolt flashed across the sky, striking down in the backyard of the house behind them.

Finally. Flint.

Quint shook his head and rolled his eyes. "Always such a dramatic entrance. He's a flaming fool. I've no desire to remain and listen to his ridiculous threats. Terran is mine, Maya. You will not stop me." Quint focused on Terran, a conciliatory smile on his face. "If you would like answers to your questions, pay me a visit at the ranch. I have the answers you are pursuing in your BSE research, as well. We will work well together." His gaze skimmed over Terran's body. "I'm looking forward to it."

Maya sensed Quint's dark energy scouring through Terran's mind, compelling him to come. To blindly follow where he led. She used everything she had to block his attempt. If Terran were destined to be her man, then she would be the only one messing with his mind—a woman's prerogative.

Quint turned his raven gaze on her. A deep roar echoed across her mind when his connection did not hold up against hers in their struggle for supremacy in Terran's mind. "Maya, you know how I handle those who interfere."

He stepped closer, cupped his palms, and blew a handful of black particles in her face. They struck, like tiny pin pricks against her cheeks and eyes, and began to melt into her skin. Her field of vision began to narrow. The murky lead drew a trail through her body—an eraser of her existence. Deep ebony mixed with the clear blue lifeblood in her veins. Her fingertips turned black and panic screamed through her mind. She struggled to maintain her grasp on reality, knowing she would heal, but she couldn't leave Terran.

"Flint," she shouted. "I need to go"

What is taking him so long? And where is Quint?

She collapsed, but strong arms caught her fall—Terran's arms.

A faint rustle sounded on the pavement beside her then an intense heat wave blasted through her ice-cold system. Flint's fire boiled through her body and helped release a portion of Quint's black matter as dark gray vapor.

Terran's voice reverberated like a foghorn through a dense haze, "What the hell are you doing? Move. I need to get her to a hospital. He blew some kind of contaminant into her face. You need to leave. It may still be in the air."

"No, Earthman," Flint answered. "I'll take it from here."

Maya shivered as Quint's darkness continued to slither through her body. This pain was not as strong as what she experienced during their last encounter. This was more of an irritant, like trying to shake water out of her ears after a long day at the beach.

She mentally reached out to Flint, *"I can't stay. Get Terran to leave."* Maya sensed the energy wave Flint fired through Terran. Her vision remained distorted, but she blinked away the black specs. *"Flint, Where is Quint?"*

"He's gone, Maya. Focus on Terran."

"Terran, look at me," Flint commanded. "Everything is fine. Maya is not injured. You met up with me while walking her home. I took her the rest of the way. You will remember nothing about meeting Crowder. Turn around and go home."

Maya blinked through the black matter filming in her eyes. The folly of this moment evoked a burst of nervous laughter. Flint's hands were placed upon Terran's shoulders as he gazed deep into his eyes. Terran's expression was pure shock over Flint's naked, warrior body. They posed in the street like two lovers who'd quarreled at the start of a tryst. Flint's intense amber eyes stared into eyes of deep brown, attempting to reach that portion of Terran's mind which would persuade him to move on and forget all he'd seen tonight.

"I ca... can't... this does... doesn't..." Terran stuttered.

Maya bit her lower lip, stifling a moan. Digging her nails into her arms, she struggled to focus. "He's fighting it, Flint. And I can't stay."

"Terran, go now." She joined with Flint's fiery energy wave, and together they compelled Terran to leave and forget.

Terran held strong. His world existed in absolutes. Much was needed to shake his mind that understood the world only through scientific facts. Terran grabbed his head and pulled at his hair as if that would release the compulsive bombardment striving to re-direct his reality. His intense concern for her safety fought to break through their gleaning grip.

Maya misted and whispered a plea into his mind, laying a dewy drizzle across his consciousness. *"Terran, please let go. Stop fighting."* Wrapping him in fog, she strove to calm him by urging him to forget the latter portion of the evening and directed him home.

Finally, he retreated, not once looking back.

If she had tears to waste, she'd have shed them. She hated altering his beautiful mind. She shifted back to human form and held out her arms to Flint. "Quint still gone?"

"Yes, he's close, but I don't believe he'll come back tonight."

"Can you look after Terran, please?"

"What's in it for me, Baby?" Flint chucked her chin.

"If my head didn't hurt so much, I'd roll my eyes right now. Take me to water, please. And then come back and watch Terran."

"Always the damsel in distress." Flint lifted her in his arms and transformed—a flash of gold fire across the night sky.

After traveling for a few minutes, Maya felt a warm breeze drift across her face then Flint abruptly released her. Without his heat, her free-fall through the cool evening air almost turned her into an icicle. She hit the water's surface with a splash.

Not fighting to re-surface, she scrunched into a fetal position and called on the water to heal her. Waves of hydration immersed every pore and she arched in pain. The darkness receded as healing liquid irrigated her body. A soundless energy boom rippled through the water as she freed herself from the clawing grasp of Quint's nefarious pepper.

When the pain receded, she released all consciousness, like dead weight, she drifted along the bottom. She woke hours later. Her only companions were water-smoothed rocks with green tufts of algae sticking out like mad scientist hair. Lake trout swam past, not registering her existence. Fully healed, she surfaced. Upon getting her bearings, she realized she was floating in the middle of Jackson Lake.

Trust Flint to go big.

CHAPTER 11

Three women huddled together on the corner. The orange-red glow from their cigarette tips stood out next to pale fingers. Streetlights emitted a hazy glow against the dark. Moths bumped against the glass crowns, seeking the light and heat.

Quint sought heat, as well. Just standing near Terran tonight had done unimaginable things to his body, creating a raw human need. Desire's greedy claw and the yearning to possess had him wound tight. Tonight verified how close he was to attaining one perfect form to house him forever.

A punishing ache coursed through his body, and he rubbed a palm against his erection, solid since connecting with Terran's mind. That water whore, Maya, had blocked him. He could have compelled Terran to do many things. So many games they could have played tonight, if she hadn't interfered.

These thin substitutes standing on the street corner were quite repulsive, but he needed to feed this gluttonous desire surging through his body. These women would take the edge off.

He pulled alongside them in Crowder's silver Mercedes and rolled down his window. Two brunettes strutted around the car's front, came alongside the driver's door, and peered inside. The smell of unfiltered cigarettes, cheap perfume, and sex surrounded them. The third girl, who had remained at the curb, exuded disease and a drug-induced mental bliss.

"Get in." Quint jerked a thumb toward the backseat.

The girls climbed in the back, but the third girl ignored his command.

He rolled down the passenger window. "Get in."

She glared from glazed eyes and shook her head.

A defiant one, how promising.

"Get. In." He struck his dark will against her mind, forcing her acquiescence.

She flicked her cigarette on the concrete and crushed it with her shoe's red tip before sliding into the passenger seat.

"Do not speak," he ordered. His bold passenger turned on the radio, and he endured the latest drivel while driving to Crowder's house. He pulled into the garage and informed them they would shower.

"What are we doing here?" Ms. Defiant hooked her purse over her shoulder.

Quint turned and took in her ratty jeans and red button-down sweater. "I believe I said not to speak. I will, however, allow you to answer one question. What type of mind-altering chemical are you harboring in your bag? Come now, don't be shy. Didn't your mother teach you to share?"

She pulled her bag tighter against her chest.

He smiled at the other two. "I just love the rebellious ones." After wrenching the bag from her grip, he rifled through and found a plastic bag full of needles and ivory nuggets. "Euphoria in a needle. Let's go."

He led them into the massive open shower in the master bedroom. He watched as they cleaned themselves under the spray, even encouraged them to play, as they seemed to enjoy one another.

This might do, after all.

Once they were clean, he dove right in, impatient to satisfy his voracious need. He took them each again, and again, wrapped in their flesh, aching to relieve his unrelenting desire in the most human way.

Unable to fulfill his fantasy with Terran, he gorged on the willing women before him. Over and over, he sought to appease his insatiable excitement over his final link to becoming peri-mortal.

Still on edge, he tried a different tack. He bent each brunette over the office desk and entered her from behind. He imagined Terran in their place, and his human body took him to a place of sexual bliss he had never been before.

Yes, this is the answer.

The drugged defiant was the last to take a turn. She shook her head and held up a hand. "I don't do that."

His body dripped with sweat. The smell of spent lust filled the air. He grabbed her arm, pulled her closer, and brought down his mouth on hers. He drove his tongue deep and let loose his essence in her body.

Her eyes went wide, and she struggled against him.

He easily contained her feeble attempts to break free. His tongue moved in and out of her mouth until her body shook and turned black. He dropped her on the floor and spit her taste from his mouth.

The other girls gaped with wide eyes and slack mouths as Ms. Defiant disappeared into nothing, and a burst of energy blasted through the room. They screamed, cowered, and held each other close as they kneeled on the floor at his feet.

He silenced them with a slash of his will against their weak minds.

His cell rang. Pillar's number appeared on the caller ID.

"Get me a drink." He flicked his hand at the brunette and sat in a chair before Crowder's desk. "Yes?" he questioned Pillar.

"Aether is willing to meet in Prague, next Tuesday."

Quint had pegged Neb Aether, a renowned virologist, as Crowder's replacement. Aether's respected expertise provided the perfect public face for his drug company. After Quint switched into the scientist's body, he could go public with his enterprise—Aether Pharmaceuticals. Crowder's vast worth had served its purpose in preparing the company for new leadership.

"Set it up." He disconnected.

The brunette stood before him, holding his drink with a shaky hand. The golden liquid threatened to slosh out of the glass.

"I wouldn't suggest spilling a single drop." His mood darkened once more as he considered Pillar. Her wayward behavior had become more frequent of late. Upon her return, he would take special care in reminding her of her loyalties.

For now, he'd punish the whore who stood at his side. He removed the glass from her shaking hand and yanked her arm. "Kneel."

The smooth burn of forty-year-old Glenfiddich seeped down

his throat and heated his belly. He grabbed the brunette by the back of her neck and shoved her face in his lap. With a sharp wave, he beckoned the other girl to join them.

Ethan appeared in the doorway. "What's with all the noise in here?" He blinked against the glare of bright light in the room.

A shell of his former self, Ethan's cheeks were hollow, his skin pale, and his eyes bulged out of their sockets. His sweatpants hung off his emaciated body.

Quint raised his glass in greeting and smirked as the boy stared in shock at his naked father.

Ethan met Quint's gaze and shivered visibly.

The stench of death exuded off Ethan's body. Poor child had squandered his life in vice and yet, when given the ability to truly transgress he couldn't contain it.

Quint placed a hand on the top of the brunette's head and waved Ethan over. "Care to join us?"

CHAPTER 12

Maya plucked apart a pinecone and kicked another down the sidewalk. On the way to her night job, she no longer detected the energy patterns of either Flint or Nodin.

She was alone—again.

She stomped the pinecone under her heel.

Very aware her behavior was like a toddler in a snit, she couldn't overcome her frustration. It grew tiresome, constantly waiting for her Elemental partners to return. Didn't they know they had work to do?

Recon at Crowder's Ranch to determine Quint's schemes should be their top priority, along with figuring out why Crowder's body was Quint's host du jour. Was Quint behind the spread of BSE in the area? Not a far stretch to assume he was the creator of this brand of chaos.

Heated from the afternoon sun, the silver handle on the heavy metal back door of Mo-swa's bar warmed her palm. She paused a moment, and deeply inhaled the fresh, pine-scented air, before entering the smoky saloon.

After working at the library earlier, she'd taken a scenic bike ride. Soaking up the sun and nature, she'd found a modicum of peace as summer breezes rippled across her face. The noble faces of the Tetons peered down their noses at her insignificant meanderings.

Three days had passed while Maya healed in Jackson Lake. Last night, she misted through Terran's open window and hovered over his bed as he slept. Agreeably creepy and a scene straight out of a horror movie, but she was now assured of his well-being.

He had fallen asleep with his glasses still perched on his nose. A report with some scientific gibberish laid in disorder across his chest. A light mat of brown hair sprinkled over his well-toned body and narrowed to a V that led to a bedspread-covered area calling on her strong sense of curiosity. She refrained. Better to allow him the honor of unveiling.

As she pushed open Mo-swa's door, she paused at the threshold as her eyes adjusted to the poorly lit bar that was in intense contrast to the bright sunshine outside. Familiar smells of popcorn and cigarettes filled the air. Her shoe soles ground against empty peanut shells with each step across the sticky tile floor—time to prepare for the night shift. Her boss was never one for mundane chores like mopping the floor. She shook her head at the thought of what the bathrooms would look like. Even water-girls felt dirty after a foray into the latrine following a busy night.

She and the owner, Moose, had an agreement. She agreed to work weekends and various days of the week. He agreed to let her. Her earnings came through tips. Cash was the best arrangement for her off-the-grid lifestyle. Occasionally, he played the trickster by slipping her extra funds with the ridiculous story people had left him tips intended for her.

His nickname—Moose was well suited. At six foot six, he was rangy, with a solitary, taciturn disposition, and he constantly chewed on toothpicks, gum, or the bar's tiny plastic swords. Glass bottles lined the bar shelves behind him, and the requisite glass mirror offered a glimpse of his black silver-streaked hair, which was twisted in a long braid.

He nodded in greeting as she swiped two empty glasses off a table on her way to the u-shaped oak bar. The wooden relic was layered in shellac, whiskey, and secrets revealed across the grain. The perfect frame for Moose's Indian ancestry, which was evident in his square jaw, sun-touched skin, and eyes so dark they appeared black.

Maya lifted the damp wood pass-thru and stepped behind the bar. She tied on her apron and grabbed her tray.

"Is all well?" Moose said, working a toothpick in his mouth.

She shrugged then grabbed a glass from a rack above the bar, filled it with water, and added a twist of lemon. Grabbing a straw, she stirred the mixture and took a long drink. "Sorry about missing the past couple nights." She offered a half smile.

Moose shook his head. "I've told you not to apologize."

After giving him a quick hug, she got to work. The tables required a serious wipe down. The floor needed a proper hosing by the local fire department, but she made do with steaming hot water and bleach.

Where are my plastic gloves?

Her sunny yellow mitts were crucial pieces of equipment for bathroom decontamination. These menial tasks occupied her time and mind. Regulars would soon drift in, and others would stop by for happy hour with co-workers. Tourists crossed the threshold attracted by the flashing neon beer lights and the chance to experience another western adventure in a city surrounded by the woodlands of Grand Teton National Park.

"Gonna be a busy one tonight, I'd imagine." Moose's rough baritone broke into her reverie.

"How so?" Maya leaned against the mop handle, raising a brow when he walked across her newly scrubbed floor.

He looked down, flashed a sheepish grin, and sat on a nearby stool while she continued her monotonous swiping.

Back and forth. Back and forth.

Moose followed her movements, and then announced, "Ethan Crowder died."

As she turned to face him, she jumped when her mop clattered to the floor. "What? When?"

"About two days ago. I imagine after the funeral people will be milling about the place, gossiping about how it happened."

"How did it happen?"

And how did I miss this?

"Real strange. Ethan got sick and sort of folded in on himself. A nurse I know said they could hear him screaming at night about the darkness. Said he was twitching and jerking around in his bed. Maybe a bad batch of drugs." He shrugged and fiddled with the beer-stained table tent. "His funeral is tonight, up the road at Basin's."

Darkness, screaming, twitching all added up to one thing—Quint. Even though Ethan lived his life as a bad egg, he hadn't deserved Quint's push off the wall. Her efforts to save him after his dealings with the girl at the strip club had failed.

Ethan's death added one more life that foul-black stain, Quint could mark on his ever-increasing list of lives taken. Quint's escalating actions gave viability to the necessity of Terran's transformation into Earthman. Everything hinged on using his knowledge to discover a way of transferring Quint's essence into another form. Quint's blight on humanity had gone on far too long. Their Elemental team needed more firepower. If Terran were forced to join them, would he accept that the needs of the many outweighed the needs of few?

Why am I quoting Star Trek? Desperate times have flooded my brain.

#

Maya's shirt and shoes were damp from various spilt whiskies, wines, and beers. In her constant trek from thirsty tables to the waitress station, she'd worked up quite a sweat. She placed an order with Moose then took a long draw from her tepid water.

Glancing into the mirror behind the bar, she grinned as a tabby party walked in that included "the Sticker" Katie. Poor girl hadn't given up on her infatuation. Her mind still flashed with visions of Terran, which were nice to glean because he was finely dressed.

Katie and her friends joined the already overflowing patrons at Mo-swa's. Citizens of Morgan Junction had gathered to remember Ethan Crowder's spirit in a way that would have made him proud.

Her breath caught as an invigorating rush of bubbles fizzled up her spine. Terran was near. Her mind reached out and the troubled storm that had thundered all night through her consciousness stilled.

Is this the gift he will give me?

This feeling of stability and peace as he guided her along like a compass in her drifting sea of life. She did not turn and acknowledge him. Instead, she monitored his trek into the bar from the spyglass mirror, searched his mind, and waited for the moment he became aware of her presence.

Can he detect me through our elemental connection? Will destiny nudge him in my direction?

It wasn't fair to cheat, to pick through the energy patterns in his mind. Her impatience wrapped her tight.

As waves surged, rising high before crashing through her body, she gasped. Lust swelled as a coursing magnetic attraction connected them at their very cores. She closed her eyes and released a calming breath as his desire overwhelmed her senses. Her answer was crystal clear. *Yes, his effect is the same.*

Terran twisted through the crowd and approached the bar. Worry erupted that her need might present as steam pouring off her body.

Strong hands landed on her hips, and she smiled when their gaze met in the mirror. Aware she looked like a sap, but she couldn't cork the excited bubbles that threatened to pop due to his presence.

He brushed her hair from her nape and kissed beneath her ear. With a gentle nudge at her waist, he shifted her around. Worried brown eyes peered downward. "Where have you been?"

"Just waiting for you, Terran. What shall I do now that you're here?"

"You work here." A statement not a question, as he tugged at the apron string wrapped and tied around her waist.

After giving his fingers a quick squeeze, she replied, "Yes, I work here, which means I've got to deliver these drinks. Have a seat. I'll be over in a minute." She lightened her brush-off with a quick kiss on his cheek.

Circling the tables, she noted Terran had joined his friends, who were surrounded by the tabby party.

Katie bumped Melissa off a barstool to make room for him.

Maya waited until he surveyed the room and caught her eye. She winked, letting him know she had watched his progress.

Terran winked back then turned to Katie, who attempted to tug off his sleeve in order to gain his attention. "The sticker" perched next to him, hands animated as she related some exciting tale then listened, entranced by his response.

What a moon-calf.

Maya delivered drinks and engaged in light flirtations with regulars before stopping at Terran's table.

Katie's mental shock hit like a mighty squall, followed by jealousy and a not so nice opinion of Maya's person. Her heavily lashed eyes narrowed as she considered ways to make Maya's evening hell.

Oh, my little daisy, don't go swimming in the big pool.

Maya bared her teeth in a grin, looked directly at Terran, and bit her lower lip. Keeping her gaze on his, she blew a bubble with her gum, and then used the tip of her tongue to draw it back into her mouth. "What can I get you, handsome?"

Terran shifted forward in his chair, a slight flush on his cheeks.

"If Green Moose is on draft, would you mind bringing three pitchers and seven glasses?" *Trust him to be precise.*

"Anything you need, honey." She capped off the flirtation with another teasing wink. After gathering more orders, she returned to the bar. A glance in the bar mirror gave Maya a moment's pause as she repeated her orders to Moose.

A very perturbed Katie approached.

Maya turned to allow Katie her say.

With pinched lips and fisted hands, Katie blurted, "I don't know what's going on, but I want you to leave Terran alone." She paused and folded both arms across her chest. "I'm not sure what kind of girl you are, but we're trying to develop our relationship."

"That's a nice thing to say—'develop our relationship.' I bet you're a college girl, ain't ya?" Maya picked at her front teeth with a plastic cocktail sword.

Katie's brow furrowed, and she tapped her foot against the sticky floor. "I'm not sure what you mean."

Maya smiled at Moose as he finished her first order. "Katie-girl, I'm sorry, I truly am, but I don't believe you'll 'develop a relationship' with Terran. Your heart may hurt now, but there are a lot of men who would be interested in what you have to offer. Terran is not a good match." She lightly squeezed Katie's hand. "I apologize for my bluntness, but your life is short. Don't waste time chasing after a man you cannot have."

Maya walked away while Katie sputtered and tried to pick her jaw off the floor. When Maya delivered the pitchers to Terran's table, she gleaned an extremely hostile vibe coming from the tabbies all huddled together. They glared as she placed their glasses on the table.

Why were they angry about truthful words? Was allowing Katie to believe she had a chance with Terran, a kindness? Humans had such short lives. Why permit them to waste time hoping for something that would never happen?

Maya had used harsh words to clarify the facts. Heartbreak was something she'd experienced during her human life, so she had sympathy for the girl. Katie was too young to realize this moment was only a quick flash. A fleeting instant of temporary heartbreak in a life filled with more sorrows and joys. Katie would find happiness when she found the right person to share her life.

As Maya walked away from the table, she heard someone ask—

Who is that girl?

Very good question and after almost one hundred thirty years, she still didn't have an answer.

CHAPTER 13

Terran tipped back his bottle and drained the last swallow. His gaze followed Maya as she flowed from one table to the next, her laugh a balm to his soul each time the husky echo hit. Still a mystery, but at the same time, he understood they fit together. Behind their physical attraction was an indefinable chemistry, bubbling like the potent mix of an acid and base.

The bar stool by Maya's station opened. He crammed his empty bottleneck into the ice-filled bucket on the table and hustled through the crowd to fill the empty seat.

He nodded and smiled at a blonde lady with a very low cut V-neck shirt as he sat beside her. The deep crease of her breasts, created by the visible straps of her purple Wonder Bra, was adorned by a variety of gold necklaces. Terran motioned for Moose, ordered a shot of Zaya rum for himself and his jeweled companion, and waited for Maya's return.

Throughout the rest of the evening, he chatted with Maya when she came to pass along her drink orders. They discussed people in attendance, the town, and Ethan's funeral. Moose and his barstool buddy, Margie, piped in at times.

Terran rolled his empty shot glass on the bar. When Maya placed her tray full of empty glasses beside him, he said, "When do you get to clock out?"

The crowd had died down. Funeral attendees, regulars, and tourists all headed to their homes or wherever they had found comfort for the evening.

"Why?"

"I thought we could take a drive." He placed his hands on the sides of her waist and pulled her between his legs.

She reached past him to grab her drink. "Sounds perfect." After taking a sip, she placed the empty glass back on the bar.

"What were you drinking?" He lifted the glass and sniffed.

"Adam's Ale."

"Never heard of it." He sniffed again, but didn't detect any lingering beer aromas.

"Adam's Ale is water, Terran." She ran a finger along his bottom lip. "Just water." Wrapping her arms around his neck, she swayed back and forth to the rhythm of an old country song playing on the jukebox.

He remained on the stool and drew her closer. Their bodies perfectly aligned. Even after a night delivering all flavors of alcohol, she still smelled like a freshwater spring. He rested his head against the soft blonde waves of her hair. Eyes closed, he flowed with her dance.

She stepped back after the song ended and motioned for Moose. "Rafferty's on a toot again. You'll have to call his wife. I'm heading out with Forrester here, all right?"

Moose pulled his phone from his pocket and nodded as he eyed Rafferty tottering by the pool tables.

Maya shot her apron into a basket sitting by the sink.

Terran stood and jiggled the keys in his pocket, while he watched his blonde retrieve her bag from behind the bar.

She took his hand. "Are you ready?"

He nodded, but caught a flash of uncertainty as it crossed Maya's features before she turned away. She squeezed his hand and drew him toward the door.

Are you ready? Had she meant more by that question? If not, then why the uncertainty? Had a greater question gone unasked?

This woman tied his mind in knots. Dizziness threatened each time he stared into her eyes' blue depths. The only thing he was sure of right now was, yes, he was ready.

CHAPTER 14

A crisp chill remained in the air, but the skies were clear. The stars radiance had shuttered out long ago, yet their light still traveled across the night sky. The only other illumination came from a lamppost erected in the center of the parking lot. The lamp's beam cast a glow in a wide circle around the solitary pole. Terran unbuttoned his long-sleeved navy shirt and slipped it around Maya's shoulders.

Pine trees formed a line that blocked the bar's parking area from neighboring businesses. His truck sat alone, parked along the back aisle.

Following Maya to the passenger side, he hit unlock on the key fob. After glancing at her feet, he commented, "Glad to see you're wearing shoes tonight." He took her hand before she could hop into the seat.

She raised a single brow as he traced his finger down the edge of her cheek.

"So fair, like a pale moon beckoning until your curiosity about what lies on the dark side has you willing to risk any journey to unearth its mysteries." He kissed her, tilting his head to deepen the plunge.

Their linked hands were held at his side, restraining any exploration of those mysteries here in the parking lot.

She met him with intense eagerness, dueling for mastery over the kiss.

On the verge of losing control, he pulled back. "Get in the

truck."

Maya shoved his chest. "I was trying to get in the truck. You're the one who stopped me."

He chuckled. "You're right. I'm sorry." After helping her up, he circled around to the driver's side. Clicking his seatbelt, he left the parking lot and drove to the south end of Emma Matilda Lake. He talked about Ethan's death, and the town's shock that his father, Carlyle Crowder, hadn't attended the funeral.

His truck bumped along a forgotten dirt road. Deep pits filled with remnants of the summer rains jostled them in the cab and water splashed against the sides of his truck. He followed two narrow strips lit by his headlights before stopping along an outlet stream's grassy bank. Pine forest densely populated with spruce and fir surrounded the lake. The white-tipped Teton peaks were illuminated by moonlight.

"This is a popular area for serious climbers during the day. Most novice hikers don't make it this far from the main road. We should be alone out here tonight. Hold on a minute." Terran twisted and reached behind the seat for his backpack. He dragged it over the top and onto the seat between them, pulling out a thermal camping blanket. "Would you like to sit outside?"

Maya nodded. "Let's sit in the truck bed. I've been inside most of the day. I'd like to enjoy the night."

He went around to open her door, but he found she'd already jumped down. "I've been inside all day as well. Everything seems fresher at night, like the world is renewing in the darkness. I hike out here sometimes and sit along the bank. I enjoy the earthy smell of wet grass."

A frog croaking and the rustle of night creatures created a musical chorus only a forest lake could provide. Sounds of hoo's and whoop's from a female great gray owl echoed across the night, which added a comical element to the mix.

Terran pulled down the tailgate and helped Maya into the truck bed. He settled the extra wide blanket and sat with his back against the truck. "Sit with me." He pulled her down between his legs. "Are you cold?" He wrapped his arms around her.

"No. I don't really get cold." Yet, she snuggled between his thighs.

Odd, women were always cold, or maybe he wanted an excuse

to warm her. He played with her hands, running his fingers between hers, and then massaging her palms. Her skin was smooth against his rough hands. "How long have you worked at Mo-swa's?"

"Is that really what you want to talk about?"

"Sure, why not? Let's do small talk." He kissed the back of her hand, returned it to her lap, and continued toying with her fingers.

Maya sighed and relaxed against him. "The bar isn't a full-time job. I go in on the weekends and sometimes Thursday nights. Moose doesn't mind the help, and I make good tips. I've only been here a few months. I don't know how much longer I'll get to stay." She ran a hand down his thigh and squeezed his knee.

The pressure trembled up his leg straight to his groin.

"Mother has me moving all the time. I think the longest I've stayed in one place was…um… a long time ago. I lived in Hawaii for a couple years. I liked being on an island surrounded on all sides by water." Her hair tickled his chin when she laughed and shook her head.

"Where is your Mother now?"

"She's around."

"Are you tired? I got tired just watching you work." He rubbed her shoulders.

She bent forward so he had better access to her entire back. "I'm not tired, but don't stop. That feels wonderful."

A soft moan erupted from her throat, shooting a jolt of lust straight through his body. The wild side of his nature threatened to stand up and howl.

He maintained his calm when she asked about his family, childhood, and school years. Her interest sparked when he commented on his Conservancy projects. Shifting to face him, she fired off question after question on water's ecosystems and whether or not prions could affect other animals besides cows and sheep. She had a ready grasp of everything and appeared to absorb all he said like a sponge. "Have you been to college, Maya?"

"No, attending college wasn't possible. I left home when I was young. I wish I was smart, like you." She slumped a bit and rested her head against his shoulder then pointed to a grouping of stars. "Do you know the constellations?"

"That is Cepheus-the King and there is Cassiopeia-the Queen." He pulled her against his chest, and then used his hand to guide her finger. Together, they traced the star patterns in the sky.

"Stars are amazing, aren't they?" Maya sighed. "And the moon, he and I, we're friends of a sort. He guides me. I drift with the tides at his direction. Would you like to be a star, Terran? Your light remaining, spanning lifetimes, and appearing to never die out?"

He brushed a kiss against her temple. "Stars are spheres of gas, technically plasma, held together by their own gravity."

"That's a very practical answer. Apparently, for you, stars aren't glowing beacons to wish upon." She sat quietly for a moment before questioning in a soft voice, "Do you think there is something more? A place where we go when we die?"

"No." He softened his short response by kissing the top of her head. Religion was not a discussion to delve into at the moment.

"Would you wish to live longer? To walk the earth, never dying. If someone offered you a perpetuating life, would you accept it?"

He combed his fingers through her hair, pulling the strands away from her neck. Dropping a kiss against her pulse point, he answered, "That's not possible."

She twisted in his arms and clutched his bicep. "Consider it for a moment, please." A slight quiver shook her voice, and her eyes sparkled from the moon's light. "You are free from disease, hunger, and death. Your scientific knowledge would grow and you could develop ways to protect the environment. If you became peri-mortal the earth would benefit. I would—"

"Hey, what's wrong?" He winced as her nails dug half-moon-shaped grooves on his arm. "Why are you so upset? It's not something I can consider, because immortal life is not possible." He brushed her hair away from her face.

She peered into his eyes, and her grip on his arm loosened. A single tear shimmered and fell down her cheek. "But what if a long life was possible? Why can't you have a hypothetical conversation?" Rising, she tilted her head toward the sky and wrapped both arms around her body.

His arms empty and chilled without her close, he watched her shoulders rise and fall as she took a deep breath. This was why he didn't discuss religion. The conversation never ended well. His mind didn't process life in "what ifs"?

Hands fisted at her sides, she turned and said, "What if you received special abilities? Perhaps you could read minds or compel others to do your will. Would you choose forever then?"

These questions meant something to her, but why? "All right, Maya, I'll consider your questions. I didn't bring you here to upset you. So, would I choose an immortal life? This is what you wish to know?"

"Yes. Not really immortal per se, but continuous or long lasting." She sat on the edge of the truck bed, and her knee bounced up and down.

"No," He shrugged. "This is my one shot. I have a passion for life, now. If I could live forever that would be erased. I would get up and think, why not just do it tomorrow?" He reached over and stilled her knee. "The thought of what science will discover ten, twenty years from now does appeal, but I'm happy with this life. I don't need more."

With her elbows resting on her knees, she bent and scrubbed her fingers through her hair. After nodding a few times, she sighed, and then lifted her head.

The mood turned gray.

His heart lodged in his throat. *What did I say?* Why did a wave of sadness and loss seem to flow from her? Like a dead tree branch breaking away and floating down the river away from his reach.

"I. Don't. Need. More. Do you mean that?"

"Yes." He hadn't wanted to upset her, but he wouldn't lie. He did need more. Only *she* was the more he craved.

"You're very sure in your answers."

"I know what I want."

"A passion for life now, you say, and yet, all you've done tonight is talk. Since you're not planning on becoming a peri-mortal, let's not waste another minute." She dropped to her knees before him.

He rose to meet her and gripped her head in his hands. "I have more than just passion for you. I cannot guess at tomorrow, but if you want absolutes then I'll be clear. I want more moments like this. I want to know you. I want to lay you down and make love to you. I want to erase the sadness in your eyes. What is it *you* want?"

In answer, she gripped his hips, drew him closer, and locked her mouth over his, leading them in a flagrant kiss.

Spreading his fingers through her hair, he angled her so he could plunge deeper into her mouth's warm depths. He spread his knees and leaned back, supporting her as she wrapped her legs around his waist. Not close enough. He craved the balmy heat of her skin, the cascade of her hair against his body. Withdrawing from the kiss, he leaned back and removed his T-shirt.

She reached out to touch his bare chest, but he stayed her hands. She still wore his flannel so he tugged it down her arms and off. She lifted her dampened T-shirt over her head.

He worked loose the bra hooks at her back, and then he fingered the straps over her shoulders. He arched her over his forearm, and ran a hand over her silky skin. Her bounty filled his hands and he teased her straining peaks.

"You might not choose forever, but choose this, choose me. Here. Now." Maya locked her lips to his. Their mouths molded together in perfect union. Her fingers trickled up his chest and over his shoulders. She rocked against him, brushing her body against his, as their kiss grew more heated.

Her motions were fluid, like water in a warm spring flowing through his fingers. He jerked as her hand worked across his stomach and under his waistband. She ran a thumb over the tip of his straining flesh. His body shuddered, and his control crashed into dust when her pleased moans filled his mouth. *Now.* This was happening now. Her single finger's caress had him lost in a sea of need.

He twisted and laid her against the blanket.

Desperation poured heavy and strong to complete their connection. The force of his desire was like water crashing against a rocky shore. Relentless and strong, they would break against each other again and again.

"Yes, yes." She answered and pulled him down for a kiss so steamy, it heated his tongue.

Their fingers tangled in the fight to free his erection until together they shoved down his jeans. He gazed into her eyes, now swimming with lust.

She smiled a siren's smile. "Terran, I've waited so long for you. You may not believe in eternity, but I do, and I'll remember this moment forever."

"Are you sure you're ready for me?" He sank back on his knees.

She wiggled her jeans down her hips.

Impatient to touch her, he pulled back the cotton wrapping covering the gift of her body. He ran his fingers over her slick folds, and sank a single finger deep. His thumb and finger worked in tandem, stoking the fire between them even higher.

She lifted her hips and gasped, the sound like a beacon calling to his now-seeping cock.

"So wet, you flow right over my fingers." He centered himself at her core. More than ready to calm the stormy seas raging between them. Her fingers dug deep into his shoulders, ready for his initial thrust into her welcoming, wet cave.

A bug bite burned the back of his neck. His shoulder twitched. Another flaming sting bit his shoulder and another struck his upper thigh. "Ouch." He flinched. *Must be one hell of a mosquito.*

"What? What's wrong?" Maya's eyes were wide, and then she stiffened, covering her chest with her arms.

"Something bit me." He rubbed his shoulder and a singed hair smell filled the air. A cool wind battered against him. Terran eyed the sky. Perhaps an early morning storm was brewing.

Maya released a string of curses that lit his eardrums, and she reached for her T-shirt.

"Maya, wait…What are you—"

"How old are you two again?" She sighed loudly.

Terran figured she was flustered because she put on his shirt instead of her own. What had she asked him? How old was he? What was she talking about?

Footsteps crunched against the dried grass. The hairs on the back of his neck prickled.

They were not alone.

Still on his knees above Maya, he twisted to assess the threat.

Two men stood at the end of his tailgate.

Two naked men. *What the hell?*

Terran rose and rubbed at the bite on his back. The racing of his mind matched the racing of his blood. Unfortunately, the majority of his blood was still pooled south. What kind of scenario was this?

"Maya, finish getting dressed and stay behind me." Upon recognizing Nodin from the coffee shop, Terran tried grasping rational thought while still clouded in sensations of Maya's scent on his skin. "What are you doing here?" He threw the blanket toward the tailgate. "Will you please cover yourself?"

CHAPTER 15

Of course. Flintus Interuptus and Nodin No-fun.

Of course, they'd show up seconds before her decades old dry spell ended and quite gloriously at that. She'd been so close to the downpour. So close to reveling in the pounding storm. A torrent of pleasure would've spilled through her body, and she'd planned on experiencing that thundering bliss over and over until Terran couldn't move. But no, these two jokesters had ruined it all. Ruined. It. All.

Hadn't they gleaned the waves of hunger writhing off her mind and body? How dare they interfere. Would she never have anything of her own?

"I believe I'm old enough not to need a chaperone, *boys*. So feel free to move along. Go about your business elsewhere." She made a shooing motion with her hand. Not that they would heed it.

Flint chuckled. "Oh? I'm sorry. Were you in the middle of something?"

Maya blasted him with a torrent of water.

Flint laughed and shook the water from his body like a wet dog. "Thanks, I was feeling a bit dry. Too bad, that's the only geyser erupting tonight."

"Excuse me?" Terran stepped toward the edge of the truck bed.

Upon hearing Terran's voice and gleaning his confusion and dissatisfaction, her anger shot past the boiling point.

Again, she doused Flint.

"Enough, you got me wet that time." Nodin interrupted her play. "Maya, you need to come."

"I had planned to do just that, but then you two showed up." She wiggled into her jeans then shoved her bra in her pocket. "Real covert, by the way, you handle all your operations like this?"

Flint smirked, "Maya, are you feeling a little tense? We can wait here while you finish. I'd be happy to offer Terran advice."

Maya narrowed her eyes. Poor Terran was so confused. They were talking in circles around him again, and all he wanted was to protect her from the two naked freaks standing at the back of his truck. This moonlight drive had been a mistake, especially now that she understood his thoughts on living a peri-mortal life. If he were given a choice, he would not walk beside her along destiny's path.

Fates intertwined. *Ha!* Mother had played her for a fool. Hope remained a dangerous emotion for a lonely water-girl.

Terran buttoned his jeans then moved her behind him. "She isn't going anywhere. She's staying with me." He kept one hand behind him, pressed against her thigh.

Flint stepped forward and pounded his fist against the tailgate. "What is it you think to do, Earthman?"

Terran maintained his stance. "Have we met?"

Flint laughed. "What? You don't remember?"

This male chest beating was heading in a dangerous direction. Terran was disturbed, tense, and unfulfilled. Ready to fight Flint. Maya preferred to do that herself.

One thing she did not prefer doing was changing Terran's memories. An unrealistic wish, since her doubts about his willingness to join their team had been vocalized clearly and without question. Nodin wouldn't allow Terran to retain his memories of the latter part of the evening.

She wrapped her arms around him from behind and rested her forehead against his back. Anger and helplessness overwhelmed at the thought of altering his mind. His thoughts were such complex, wondrous things, but she'd have to erase them. Mask them with a brush of sapphire blue across fertile greens and browns—artistic melancholy across the canvas of Terran's mind.

Maya took a deep breath, released her hold, and began the lie. "Is Mother ill? Is that why you and Flint felt it necessary to come all the way out here?"

Nodin gleaned her distress and the direction of her thoughts. "Yes, we need your help with a problem she's discovered."

"Hold on a minute." Terran pointed a finger at Nodin. "First of all, how did you get here? I see no vehicles. Second, you all have the same mother? Third, why in the hell are you naked? How did you even know we were out here? This is a thoroughly incomprehensible situation you realize that, right?" He sat on the edge of the truck bed, shoved on his shoes then pointed a finger at Nodin. "Let me be clear. Again. Maya is staying with me. I will take her home, and I agree it would be best if you both just went on your way."

Maya took Terran's hand in hers and appealed to Nodin, "Couldn't you have waited until I got back to town."

"No." Nodin wrapped himself in the blanket Terran had thrown on the tailgate.

"What am I supposed to do now? I'm not dealing with this. I won't be the one to change him. You do it." Her heart ached at the thought of their special night being erased from Terran's memory. She released Terran's hand and leapt to the ground.

The scoreboard of her life had Team Normal blown out by the cheating Team Elemental. Elemental's field of play went on and on into the abyss of plasma-filled stars. Team Normal would never win.

Nodin's will drifted around and through Terran's mind. "Terran, step out of the truck."

Terran shot her a sideways glance before he jumped down.

After that, she blocked his conversation with Nodin from her mind. She waited by the stream's edge for Nodin and Flint. A simmer of heat along her back alerted her to Terran's presence.

"Nodin says he'll take you to your mother. I have to go. Next time, we'll finish what we started here."

She struggled to keep the surprise off her face. What had Nodin said? "Yes, go. I'll see you soon." She wrapped her arms around Terran and held tight. The thread running between them was like a wick on dynamite, but the resultant explosion would have to wait.

She lifted her face for a kiss and scanned through his mind. Nodin hadn't erased Terran's memories of the earlier portion of their evening. Terran no longer questioned the reasons for Nodin and Flint's presence, nor would he remember they were naked. Nodin was very skilled at how much of a memory swipe or alteration was necessary. A gush of gratitude toward her airy friend filled her.

Terran's kiss softened and fed fanciful fantasies she'd long since forgotten. When he released her, he said, "I'll see you soon. If you need me, you know where to find me."

Will I see him soon? Should I?

She blinked away tears as the back wheels of his truck stirred dust and he drove home alone. In enough physical discomfort from an interrupted sex-capade, she didn't appreciate this added rush of emotional distress.

Nodin wrapped her in his arms. Her cloud of sadness stirred then drifted away as a cool breeze swept her worries from her mind. She hated and yet wanted the brotherly comfort found in his arms. He and Flint were her only friends, the only two creatures on earth who understood this lonely existence. She forgave Nodin for the interruption, but maintained her anger toward Flint. Someone had to be on the receiving end of her frustrations.

Flaming fire-breathing ass.

She lifted her middle finger at Flint behind Nodin's back.

Flint laughed. "I know you secretly love me, my little sea serpent."

"Maya," Nodin scolded, and then patted her back.

Peering into Nodin's wise blue eyes, she said, "I don't like altering Terran's mind. It isn't right."

"We do it all the time." Nodin tweaked a strand of her hair. "And as you saw, it was only a slight nudge to ease his worry over leaving you with us."

"It's just not right shifting the mind our own teammate, or whatever he's supposed to be." She brushed her hair away from her face, wishing she had a hairclip. Her hair was driving her crazy, Flint was driving her crazy, and her stomach ached, which wasn't possible, but was the only explanation for this disturbance churning her gut. "Why did you bring Flint, anyway?"

Flint yawned and stretched. His semi-flaccid matchstick twitched in her direction.

She rolled her eyes, and huffed out a laugh. "Flint, please. That smoked jerky bit is not even close to what I held in *both* my hands moments ago. Speaking of that..." with her index finger, she drew a circle in the air around his crotchal-region. "Next time, do not interrupt. It's been a hell of a lot longer for me, and now that I have someone I am interested in—do not interfere. I'm a woman on the edge of a sexual feast, and if I don't get to slake my hunger from the banquet soon, someone will get stabbed with a fork. A very sharp silver serving fork, although for you, Flint, I'm sure I'd get by with a tiny crab fork."

CHAPTER 16

"I'm not doing it." Flint crossed both arms against his chest, like a defiant two-year old.

Maya knocked her fists against her forehead, shook them at Flint, and pleaded, "Can you please do as he asks? We're running short on night. I don't particularly want to do it either but … just cooperate. Please."

Nodin had suggested they join hands and pool their abilities to detect the nearby diseased animals. Their combined power to glean "off" mental patterns would be more efficient and effective.

Flint shook his head and slashed his hands through the air. "This is ridiculous. Let's just do an aerial search. This standing around chanting camp songs won't get us anywhere."

Maya ground out a sigh, took Flint's hand, and pulled him closer to Nodin.

Nodin took Maya's hand. "Hazrat Inayat Kahan says, 'A soul who is not close to nature is far away from what is called spirituality. In order to be spiritual one must communicate, and especially one must communicate with nature; one must feel nature.' We must communicate with nature together, Flint. Our combined spirits will convene and show us the way forward."

Flint jerked away his hand and jabbed a finger against Nodin's chest. "We don't all live in that philosophical world you do, Nodin. You let that mask who you really are. You hide behind platitudes to explain your existence. We just are. Someday, you'll have to accept there are no answers. You'll never find reason in this unreasonable existence."

"Flint, leave him be," Maya scolded.

Flint's fiery will and impatience often had him leaving scorch marks with his flaming tongue. His words burned a little too close to home for her, as well. She didn't want echoes of her own discontent mixed with her ability to locate the sick animals.

Nodin shot back, "I don't need lectures from you who flickers around the world never stopping, never taking the time to appreciate your surroundings. *You* are the one always moving on, so you never have to show anyone even a glimmer of who you really are. I may not have lived as long as you, but unlike you, I'll never give up questioning the whys of this existence. Enough though, we need to focus. We must destroy this unbalanced vein running through the forest. We'll debate our natures another time. For now, take my hand, brother."

Maya slumped to the ground and waited.

Flint took Nodin's hand and yanked him down.

Such children.

Nodin turned to Flint. "Close your eyes and concentrate. The sooner we do this, the sooner you can torch things."

Sitting Indian-style in the dew-covered grass, they joined hands. The elemental force of their linked minds rippled in waves of energy and flowed over the forest floor. Together, they traveled, across sage-covered hills, and mule deer pulling at grass, farther and farther as rustic greens and browns of the pine forest meshed and blurred. A river trickled and bubbled as they sailed over it in a swell of consciousness. The earthy smell of moss-covered trees and the grassy shore reminded her of Terran. A dead spruce whose bark had been rubbed raw by moose antlers revealed a smooth tan trunk similar to the hue of Terran's skin. She squirmed as a memory blazed through her mind of her hand as it glided across the tight planes of his body. The rasp of his tongue as it dueled with hers.

"Maya," Nodin snapped. He shook free from her hand.

"Come now, Nodin," Flint smirked. "Let her finish. The play-by-play was getting good."

"Shut. Up." She squeezed her hand then once again reached for Nodin's. Jaw clenched, mind blank, she pushed ahead to where they had left off in the forest.

Yellow eyes glowed against the dark. Snarls and growls rose

from deep in the wolves' throats. Their fang-baring mouths dripped saliva from their black lips. These visions re-focused her mind on their mission.

A group of four wolves stood removed from their pack. Their bodies convulsively twitching and their wobbly legs made standing and walking difficult. They growled at each other and scratched their sharp-clawed paws against their heads. Their pack mates avoided them with their natural ability to sense sickness.

After returning from their mind travels, Maya said, "Did you sense the cattle, as well when we first connected? They are closer and will be easier to obtain. Nodin, I suggest you start there. I only picked up around five sick in Crowder's pasture. Let's get this bonfire started."

"I agree. I'll bring them back." Nodin spun into a funnel. He would use that spiral force to lift and transport the diseased cattle to this remote location.

Maya turned to Flint. "See, you shouldn't have given him such a hard time. Joining together worked well."

Flint shrugged. "He lost his mind about fifty years ago."

"Really? As if you've ever found yours."

Mooing beasts interrupted their verbal sparring as cows dropped one by one. A strong wind had Maya and Flint backing away.

Flint stood with his arms crossed as Nodin reappeared in his human form. "I hope you're not expecting us to do a cow dance now."

"Actually, we do have a dance. It goes like this—" Nodin punched Flint in the jaw, knocking him off balance, but not down.

"Thanks for the spark, brother." Flint laughed then turned into fire. He burned the cattle and the smell of charred meat filled the air.

Ash drifted—specs of black and white dancing against dawn's early morning gray.

Nodin tensed.

Maya looked through the smoke rising above the charred grass to determine what affected him.

Pillar stood in a sagebrush field, high on a hill. Her white-blonde hair whipped wildly in a breeze affecting only her. *Nodin's touch.* Pillar observed them a moment longer then disappeared in a white whirl.

Nodin turned back, brows drawn. Regret flowed from his mind.

Flint slapped Nodin on the back. "Let's move. No time to

worry about white foxes when wolves are in need of peaceful rest."

Nodin lifted Maya into the air, and they traveled to stand before the diseased wolves.

Gray hairs at the beast's necks bristled and they snarled and snapped.

Maya stepped into the middle of the scared, sick creatures. Sadness and pity flowed at seeing the ancestral throwbacks of every domesticated dog brought so low. Their gray coats were ragged and bare in spots. Growls curled up from deep in their throats. They guarded each other even with the stain of madness in their minds. Pain was evident in their tarnished golden eyes and crippled attack efforts.

Their pack mates weaved through the forest in a wide circle. The natural urge to protect was a product of their bound nature. The alpha couple howled and raced through the forest, calling on their sick brothers to move—to fight against these human invaders.

A strong breeze flowed through the trees and pressed back the wolf pack's healthy members.

Maya offered a hand to a sick female who shook with fear and the ravages of the disease. The wolf's instincts kicked in, and she lunged and sank her fangs deep into Maya's hand.

Water seeped from her wound as Maya brushed the soft fur on the female's head. Another set of fangs ripped into her leg.

Flint batted away the beast. "Maya, what are you doing?"

"I can give them a few moments peace before they die. I'll heal. They will not."

Maya stroked the female's back. Sadness echoed deep as she felt their fight to live, to remain sane, even as the disease blanketed their minds. She released a wash of soothing, cleansing water through the female wolf, giving a temporary respite before the animal's yellow eyes drifted closed for the last time.

Flint lifted the wolf into his arms and added her to the pyre.

Another wolf approached and the process began again until Maya arched in pain and collapsed. A blood-curling scream erupted as the disease streamed through her body. The heat of Flint's bonfire scorched her skin, and the foul stench of charred flesh struck her nostrils.

Awash in the sooty flakes of death, she envisioned snapping teeth and ripping flesh as darkness took over, blackening her mind.

Paralyzed in place with no control over her movements, black vultures picked at her cracked brain. Her vision clouded into a red-and-black mush. Lifted into the air by black wings, she fought off the sharp beak holding her and struggled to regain sanity.

The smell of salt water replaced burnt hair and flesh. A gull screeched before she was plunged into cool life-giving water. Clumps of her hair floated past her face. Her skin was puckered and pale. Maya opened her mouth wide and drank deep to eradicate the disease now rampant in her body. *Not enough.* She dispersed and became one with the sea. Each molecule healing on its own before coalescing once more and forming her human body.

"You are strong. A survivor. You are woman." Mother's voice whispered *across the sea. "Call on Goddess Isis, Mother of the Universe, Mistress of the Elements, to heal with life-giving water. Ask for purification. Allow her to cleanse you with her golden light. Glorious Isis, come to my daughter, Maya. Free her and restore her fount of elemental gifts."*

CHAPTER 17

Quint's attention was diverted from the papers in his hand when Pillar walked by the glass walls encasing his office. Veimhet Schwarz, his top research scientist, brushed against her in the doorway, even though the double doors offered ample space. The little German mouse had a ridiculous obsession with the pale blonde. However, Pillar's preference for alpha males did not bode well for this scrawny creature. Schwarz's prominent forehead receded into a hairline circling the back of his head. His ears stuck out in a cupped fashion, and his beady eyes were set close together. The little mouse preened like a lion in her presence.

Schwarz remained rooted in place, staring at Pillar. Images of her, disturbing even to Quint's depraved mind, broadcasted from his mad scientist. No doubt Schwarz's nights were filled with dreams of using her to further his inhumane experimentation addiction.

Quint cared not who used Pillar's body. She had amused him for a time, but as with all things, the thrill waned, so he'd moved on to more daring prey. The current fascination humans had with bondage and dominance suited his nature quite well.

Safe words, however, did not.

He and Schwarz had finished a conference call with Jing Pingfang, a Japanese scientist, who offered advice on their studies. Pingfang was the foremost historical expert on Unit 731, a chemical and biological warfare research unit of the Imperial Japanese Army during the Second World War.

Pillar's visit actually pleased Quint, because now he wouldn't be forced to endure Schwarz's drivel about his experiments, or his tedious recitation of Pingfang's information. The mouse chased after his mission in life as if it were a rare piece of cheese. His fondest desire was to create a soldier impervious to any and all forms of injury or chemical agents. And like him, Schwarz allowed no human laws to impede his goals. There was always at least one human immune to a specific disease, and they were tracking down those cases and conducting experiments. The lure of quick money made bringing in new test subjects easy. Death typically took them out.

Pillar sat before his desk. "You wished to see me?"

Quint sat forward in his chair and steepled his forefingers against his lips. "So, tell me, how are things back at the ranch?"

Pillar sniffed and glanced around his office. "They had quite the bonfire last night, gathering and burning the diseased cattle and wolves. Maya will be out of the picture for a while."

Quint's gaze sharpened. "And our boy? Is he still the same?"

Pillar squirmed after noticing his intense regard.

That's right. Don't disregard me.

"Yes, Terran's still human."

"I'll give him a few more weeks before I intervene. I have some time to spare. Plus, running this lab with Schwarz has been entertaining, to say the least. I need you to follow-up on a rumor."

Pillar flicked her hair over her shoulder and raised a brow in question.

"I need you to retrieve a girl in Switzerland, Violet Levina. From what I understand from Schwarz, her family dabbles in witchcraft, and the girl's been hexed by a spell of extraordinary magnitude. It's imperative she's brought into the fold before falling into the hands of the Elementals. Not that I'd want to intrude on any of your plans, dear."

Pillar shot a glance his way and inquired, "Where in Switzerland?"

"I believe you'll find her near Meyrin, at the Franco-Swiss border. She's currently employed at CERN. An expert in the field of Quantum Mechanics."

"And why is she of interest?"

Ms. Inquisitive apparently needed a reminder of her place in his domain. Quint rose from his chair and walked around his desk to sit at the table in front of Pillar.

She leaned back.

Smart girl.

"Pillar, you seem to be laboring under a certain misconception. We are not partners. You chose this bargain and in doing so placed your life in my service." He ran his hands over her knees and locked down on her upper thighs. "It isn't important you know who she is or my plans for her. I asked you to retrieve her, and that is the end of the matter. No questions. No discussion."

Pillar gripped his wrists. "Get your hands off of me."

"Now dear, you used to like my hands on you. All over you." He gripped her hips and yanked her onto his lap. Wrapping a handful of her hair in his fist, he used his grip to snap back her neck. "You are mine, my well-seasoned wench. Mine to do with as I please. I suggest you don't forget who is in charge of our arrangement. You wanted your revenge and you'll have it. I can just as easily take it all away." He bit and pulled her earlobe.

A wash of salt crossed his tongue, so he thrust her onto the floor at his feet. "I tire of your constant pout, Pillar. I suggest using your time acquiring my prize in Switzerland to reflect on your future path. If not, we'll end this right now."

"I am not yours to bid. I do as I wish when I wish." Pillar glared as she rubbed her hip.

Quint wrapped his hand around her neck, and then he lifted her until her gaze was even with his. "Careful with that tone, my dear. I believe you forget with whom you're speaking." He threw her across the room and laughed as she coughed and sputtered. "Don't come back without Violet."

CHAPTER 18

Lying on top of the sleeping bag on her apartment floor, Maya rustled around, contemplating the current state of affairs in her ever-changing Elemental world. They had contained the infected wolves and incinerated the sick cattle, but that didn't mean the disease wouldn't continue to present. Verification the tainted feed was no longer in use at Crowder's ranch was the next step.

What larger scheme was Quint planning? Perhaps during her absence, Nodin and Flint had investigated Quint and the ranch. On her way back from the ocean, she gleaned only a faint hum of their energy signatures. They weren't far, but they weren't in the immediate vicinity either. She rarely worried about their whereabouts, but they were supposed keep an eye on their reluctant future partner. She'd called Terran this morning using the phone in the gym below her apartment, but he hadn't answered.

Frustrated by inactivity, she dressed and padded down the apartment's back stairs. Perhaps shuffling amongst library shelves would provide clarity, and she could zero in on Terran's location. Later, she'd waitress at Mo-swa and plunge into the patrons' brew-filled minds to determine potential trouble. Wound tight after a three-day Pacific Ocean immersion, Maya was primed for the physical outlet of thwarting criminals.

Most nights, the voices in her head filtered out and only remained in her mental strainer if a half-baked noodle was present. The sheer volume of voices sometimes overwhelmed—but not tonight. Tonight, she'd chew those al dente noodles and spit them out.

With one foot raised to take the last step, Maya faltered, almost tripping as a wave of dizziness blurred her mind. She clutched the handrail to keep from collapsing, earning a wooden sliver in her palm. As she scraped at the splinter, an odd vibration trickled down her spine and a great roar erupted in her head. Maya clasped both hands over her ears and looked around at the people heading into the brick building's first-floor gym. No one else seemed affected by the sound.

Her body wobbled and a fissure in the earth spread open at her feet. A searing pain jolted her head to the side, as if she'd been physically struck.

The crack grew wider and deeper.

Dizziness threatened and she fought not to teeter into the abyss. Taking deep shallow breaths, she tried regaining control as her inner waters boiled and steamed.

Earth beckoned, urging her to follow the path split open at her feet. Eyes closed, Maya let earth's energy surge around her. Visions punched through her mind. *A stream. Dust rising from boots. Clenched fists. Crazed male laughter.*

Bright red blood dripped from a man's nose and mouth— Terran.

As pain shot through her body, Maya gasped. *No!*

His elemental tie to the earth had reached across the miles alerting her to his extreme danger.

Taking her apartment steps two at a time, she thrust open the door, stepped inside, and misted. She shot back out and arrived at the stream in minutes. Terran's beaten body rested half in, half out of the water.

Rage and fear converged inside her body and matched the red blotches marring his face and arms. His lips were swollen and his right eye was a half-closed, bloody mess. Internal injuries caused blood to dribble out his nose. Rocks stabbed her knees as she knelt beside him and laid her head upon his chest. His heartbeat was a faint thump against her ear.

Dust stirred from his perpetrators' vehicle as they sped off. Tears fell from Terran's eyes. His mind sought escape from the pain and welcomed the Reaper standing on the horizon. He tried to speak, but she quieted him with gentle murmurs.

Maya brushed tears from his cheeks and licked the salty substance from her thumb. "I believe I warned you about staying away from this stream. Now look at you beaten to edge of death."

Terran's hair lay on his forehead, matted with blood.

The water streamed red from wounds on the back of his head.

She compelled his mind to calm and release the pain.

Each Elemental received one additional gift. Hers was the ability to heal. She rarely used this gift, not believing in interfering with death's plans. Today, she believed. Strongly. Dreams of a life with Terran remained buried deep in her heart, and she refused to watch him die.

The stream bubbled around her, seeking guidance upon sensing her need for additional strength. Maya drew Terran deeper into the water and wrapped her arms around his chest. As she spilled cool water down his throat, her healing elixir flowed into his body.

He drank like a man lost in a desert for weeks. With each swallow, her essence drifted into his body and repaired the injured internal organs.

Through their connection, she caught glimpses of men's faces and portions of the fight he'd endured. Terran was strong, but no human could withstand the savagery of four men. She, however, was far from human and vowed they would pay.

Terran moaned and thrashed in the water.

The sound affected her heart's deepest recesses. "No, my brave, Boffin. Be at peace. You are safe." Tears rolled down her cheeks. Calm words were whispered into his ear, guiding his mind away from the trauma and pain of his beating.

More and more, Maya absorbed each tear, split, and scrape. Her body twitched and a scream dared to escape her lips as she cleared each blow.

Time to pull away and regain strength before continuing the healing process. She tugged Terran toward the bank.

Why did he return? How did the ranch hands know he was here?

Weakened by her healing efforts, she returned to the stream. Positioned just below the surface, her body rejuvenated. She kept her eyes above the water line and watched the steady rise and fall of his chest. *Up and down. Up and down.* The movement offered assurance they'd passed the critical point. As she swallowed water and floated in the stream, she trembled as battle dregs ejected from her body in a continuous flow.

Terran remained still and rested on his back, breathing steady and calm.

Her feelings for the brave man ran deeper than just desire or destiny. His will to do the right thing, and his bravery in the face of uncertainty, made him stand out from every human she'd ever known. Their connection proved real today. How else could earth's call stretch across the miles? Terran would be an extraordinary Elemental. The troubling question remained, would he accept his role?

Worry for another time.

After rising from the water, she kneeled at his side, covered his mouth, and delivered a dose of healing liquid. Once his bones began to re-set and she healed the worst of his internal injuries, she gauged the distance to his truck.

Not far, because he'd parked along the bank. She prepared for his transfer by opening the truck's back door then returning to his side. "All right, Terran, I'm going to carry you to the backseat now."

After getting him settled, she used his ever-handy towel as a head cushion. His cheeks, no longer the pale white of impending death, blossomed with a mix of red and purple bruises across his jaw. A line of dried blood remained on his upper lip and across his left cheek from a nasal fracture. His breathing steadied, but his body shivered from the clinging wet clothes.

He opened his eyes and stuttered out. "My...Maya ... you...you came."

His rasped-out words were alarming. *What did this mean?* Was their link so strong, she would continue to receive his distress calls? Nodin and Flint had never used their elemental link with fire or air to contact her. Their mode of communication entailed mental messages. Terran's use of the earth to reach her was an interesting discovery and, based on this experience, the call was wired to her alone.

Now was not the time for stewing over the implications of Terran using the earth like a cell signal. He stirred, so she seeped through his mind's distress. *"Sleep now, Terran. Release your pain. You'll not die today."*

Optimistic her gentle mental croon would hold him on their journey to the hospital, she kissed his forehead and the tip of his nose. She jumped into the driver's seat and downed water from a bottle in the cup holder.

Flooring the truck's gas pedal, she drove like the lead in a Nascar truck series dirt race. Pits in the road jostled her precious cargo, so she swerved to avoid the larger ruts.

On the highway, she kept the pedal flat against the floor mat during the final lap into town. The red-and-white emergency room sign loomed ahead. The truck tires squealed as she turned into the drive and slammed on the brakes. She hopped from the truck, rushed inside, and misted past the waiting room and check-in counter, heading directly through the double doors in search of a nurse. A shorthaired brunette with streaks of gray leaned against a counter, chatting with another nurse. Maya engaged her mind and convinced her to come out with a gurney.

After reforming, she and the nurse transferred Terran to the wheeled cot. Maya searched his memories by holding his head between her hands. She flipped through his mind for a complete picture of the four faces involved in beating him and leaving him to die.

"Show me, Terran," she whispered. She stopped the gurney and rested her forehead against his. Visions of Crowder's vet and three ranch hands broadcasted from his mind to hers. They had argued with Terran and accused him of trespassing. Terran turned his back to gather his things when a blow to the back of his head dropped him to his knees. *Cowards.* They attacked and beat him with a frenzy of blows and kicks. How had he survived the gang's aggressive onslaught?

His breathing came in short rasps as he fought to resurface into consciousness. She kissed him, gushing her own blend of Maya Kool-Aid down his throat—a thick coating to brush over the pain. Breaking contact, she staggered back and did her best to focus on those around them.

"Are you all right, Miss?" With a perplexed frown, the nurse waited alongside the gurney. "What happened to him? Why are you naked?"

Maya looked into the nurse's kind hazel eyes, held her hand, and nudged deep into her mind. "He was dropped off here in his truck. You will not remember me."

Unblinking, the nurse nodded.

Maya headed for the exit, and yet, the pull between her and

Terran was like an elastic band she could stretch, but not escape. She hit the pavement and headed for a copse of trees. Once past, she swirled into mist, and traveled closer and closer to water. That final kiss to ease his discomfort had taken her reserves.

She prayed Quint remained unaware of Terran's weakened state. A long soak was crucial in order to accomplish her task tonight. Tiny droplets of her misty form rained down on Emma Matilda Lake. Under the surface, she coalesced into her human form.

Adrift at the bottom, she renewed her body and strength until darkness fell. Tonight, she had to look her best.

She had a date with four men.

CHAPTER 19

At a dive on the outskirts of Morgan Junction, Crowder's ranch hands cozied up to a heartbroken brunette. Two made their play, while the other two, which included Crowder's vet, played pool in the backroom.

Maya slouched in a back booth, wearing deep-indigo skinny jeans and a hooded black sweatshirt. Biding time until one of the hands made a move outside—then recess would begin. Her knee bounced under the table as anticipation thrummed in rhythm with the hard rock blaring from her ear buds.

Misery eddied through the brown-haired girl's mind. Tonight's barroom visit was a sad attempt at revenge over a cheating husband. Her mind radiated pain over the betrayal and a solid wish for retaliation. Over all, she was a good woman, one who hadn't deserved such cavalier treatment. The ranch hands' interest fed her bruised ego. If only she understood their intent was the stuff that gave women nightmares.

Lucky for her, Maya had followed the bastards. Mrs. Brunette Brokenheart's night would not end in an inescapable haze of terror.

Maya watched as the younger blond fella dropped a light colored powder into the brunette's drink. Liquid X—used on the street to increase sociability and promote libido by lowering inhibitions. The drug mixed with the amber liquid—undetected.

Raccoon eyed Betty-bartender, with orange hair and wrinkled lips, witnessed the drop, but refused to comment. She lit another cigarette and walked to the other end of the bar. Worry over massive gambling debts swamped her, so she no longer cared about her patrons. To Betty's mind, the brunette deserved what she got for coming in here all high and mighty, with her fancy outfit and massive rock twinkling on her finger.

Disgust shot through Maya as Betty-bartender considered making a deal with the ranch hands in order to pawn the ring. Maya chewed through ten pieces of Dubble Bubble as the tableau played out at the bar.

Loud laughter and slurred words, followed by allowing various tongues down her throat, indicated the brunette was severely intoxicated. The effects of the drug and alcohol mixture had worked wonders on Mrs. Brokenheart's libido.

The party of three moved to the back door. The men openly groped her, laughing and smiling at each other with their foul faces. Mrs. Brokenheart stumbled. Her purse hit the floor and spilled its contents. The two fools helped keep her upright and led her out the door.

Maya noted the red-and-white sign above the door as she exited. Only the X remained lit, a sure omen for anyone who believed in signs. At the threshold of the back door, she watched as the drunken brunette and half-spiffed ranch hands made their way over to a truck. Parking lot sex seemed to appeal at the moment.

Voyeurism, however, wasn't her style. Maya threw back her sweatshirt hood and unzipped enough to reveal the top of her lacy black bra. She stepped over the threshold and moved closer to the party, then hollered over the sounds of their love play. "Hey boys, what cha' doin'?"

The older blond, who was hopeful the night would turn into a threesome due to his secret crush on the younger fella, turned to give her a very blatant once-over. "Well, aren't you a pretty thing. Come here, baby. Let, Uncle Walt show you a real good time."

Upon spotting fresh prey, the younger blond removed his tongue from the brunette's mouth. "We're heading back to my place. How's 'bout you join us? I got plenty for you, too, doll."

"Oh, you have no idea how much I want to give you everything you deserve." Maya beckoned with her index finger.

Interested, the young blond tried propping Mrs. Brokenheart against the side of his truck. She bent over, vomited, and then fell face first into the gravel. Drugs and alcohol did not mix, and her stomach was apparently revolting against the addition to her beverage.

"It's unfortunate your friend has passed out. I think she and I would've liked each other." Maya turned as the back door banged open behind her, and the final party members stepped out. "Hey, boys. Glad you could join us."

Anticipation pasted a wide grin across her face, as she stood her ground in-between the two groups of men. The two pool players, a chubby brown-haired guy with a chicken wing sauce stain on his shirt and the bald veterinarian, joined the motley parking lot crew.

They had all planned to take advantage of this one woman. Standing around watching each other rape an unconscious lady was not something they would ever take part in again.

Maya raised her hands to her sides in welcome. "I am ready, boys. How about you start with me?"

The cocky young blond walked up and grabbed her hair. He yanked back her locks and kissed her hard.

She poured water into his mouth, gagging him.

He fell to the ground, coughing and spitting up water.

The young blond's smitten friend, Uncle Walt, approached. Golf ball-sized hail rained down on the men in a torrential downpour. Uncle Walt screamed and cowered next to his friend, who had recovered from his drenching. They attempted escape, but Maya stopped them with a wave that slammed them both into the back of their truck.

Chicken-wing stain pulled a knife from his pocket.

With a water blast, Maya knocked the weapon from his hand then she spun into a hurricane and brought all four men together at the parking lot's center. Evil steamed off their skin as her water washed over them.

She captured their minds. *You meant to cause harm, and you've done this foul deed before. You also beat a man and left him for dead. Why should I let you live when destroying you would be a gift to mankind? What have you ever done but ruin everyone and everything you touch? While I would love for you to die by my hand, I'm not allowed. I will, however, leave this bitter pill within you. You shall have my cleansing water to wash away your filth. If you do not change your path, then you will die. I am your last chance at redemption. Pay for your crimes. Admit your guilt and change your ways.*

She mixed her crystal clear elixir with their murky gray hearts.

Humans this far gone typically wilted and died, rather than change. Their shady souls were incapable of accepting awareness of the torment they inflicted.

One man had caused more damage to Terran than the others— Uncle Walt. His confusion over his sexuality and self-hatred warped his mind. Unable to satisfy his appetites with his young friend, he unleashed his frustrations by exerting pain and bullying others. Terran's body beaten and bloody at his feet had provided a sexual high.

Maya stood before Uncle Walt and took both his hands in hers. She squeezed until she'd crushed the bones in each of his fingers. He crumbled to his knees, screaming, and begging for release. A long time would pass before he hurt another with those hands.

She released him then grabbed the vet by his protruding ears. Water poured out of his nostrils and mouth, as he gasped for breath. The coughs and pleading screams were a cacophony of distraction.

"Quiet," Maya ordered, and with a swipe of her hand, compelled them to silence. Focused on the vet, she again placed her hands on each side of his head and peered into his eyes. Clues to Quint's plans were buried within this man's mind, so she delved deep—*animals at Quint's ranch, tainted feed, a vaccine vial, a syringe.*

Deeper still, she searched for the vaccine's origin. "Show me the source." *Invoices. Letterhead. An address—Phinney Ave. N., Seattle, Washington.*

"Thanks." She released the vet's head with a shove and surveyed the disgusting excuse for humans at her feet. "Understand this, the pain you attempt to inflict on others will now be your own times two. You will choke and feel the sensation of drowning every time you harm another." She circled the pile of cowering men. "I am a rain cloud that will thunder down should you stray from the right path. Only misery and death will follow if you stay in the shadows. Emerge. Free yourself from this foul existence."

Maya walked over to Mrs. Heartbreak, who would be worshiping the porcelain goddess tomorrow, and lifted her off the ground.

A raspy cough had Maya turning back to the four men kneeling in a circle. "Lights out, boys."

They slumped to the ground.

Date over.

CHAPTER 20

After a cleansing dip in the lake, Maya returned to her apartment and quickly dressed. Too early for hospital visiting hours, but that was a human rule—incapable of keeping her from Terran.

She hopped on her bike and rode through the morning fog. A rack near the employee entrance provided the perfect place to park her two wheels. A few employees glanced over as she walked toward the front of the building. She removed her impression from their minds.

Anxious to see Terran, she rushed through the doors. She hadn't wanted to leave him. His poor face was so bruised and bloodied. Though she'd alleviated the majority of his pain, he would still experience some discomfort. The sooner she arrived at his side, the sooner she could ease any lingering aches.

Where were Nodin and Flint anyway? She could use their help. Just like a man to disappear after the heavy lifting and barbequing were done and expect a woman to clean up the mess.

Once inside, Maya zeroed in on the volunteer desk as her destination. She spotted the Welcome Center next to the gift shop. No one sat there this early, so she made herself at home. Too much pain and distress from hospital patients echoed in her mind, making honing in on Terran's location difficult, so she'd have to find him using technology—not her preferred method.

Maya shook the mouse. "Wake up, computer." Not overly familiar with these machines, she pecked out each letter, searching for Terran's room number. Writing letters was more her style, but she had practiced with computers over the years after closing time at various libraries.

She punched in his name. Room #333

After taking the stairwell to the third floor, she peeked around the door and stepped into the hallway. The wall had numbers and arrows directing her to his room.

Wait.

Stop.

Danger.

A briny-tang drifted across her tongue.

Pillar.

Maya crept around the corner as Pillar stepped out of Terran's room.

Oh, hell no.

Maya rushed her, pressed her against the wall, and buried her forearm against Pillar's neck. "Leave him alone. He. Is. Mine." Maya could feel Pillar's salty push, burning her nostrils and drying her arm where it levered against the blonde's neck. *Not this time.* Maya jerked away.

"I was just visiting *our* patient." Pillar smirked. "I wouldn't get too attached if I were you. Men are known for their ability to change allegiances."

"Says you. Really? Of all people." Maya got right in Pillar's face. "Who owns you?"

Pillar narrowed her eyes and shook her head, refusing to engage in the argument.

"I assume your cryptic statement has something to do with Nodin. I'll never believe it. You've misjudged him."

Salt stung Maya's eyes. Blinking, she stepped back and tripped over a wheelchair left sitting against the wall. In retaliation, Maya released a rocket of water against Pillar's chest, which knocked her flat and sent her floating down the hallway toward the elevators.

"You're on the wrong side, Pillar. Whatever happened to bring you to this state, let it go."

Pillar released a sharp bark of laughter. "Everything's so easy for you, isn't it? I have walked this earth far longer than you. I've seen water-girls, like you, come and go. Why don't you ask Mother what happened to the last one?"

"I'm aware of the history of my kind and past choices. There is an end for everything, even a peri-mortal. I know this. The question is, do you?"

"Mother doesn't care about you." Pillar gave a quick, disgusted snort. "All she cares about is using you to get the job done. And for what? I've watched as humans have devoured this land and done unspeakable things to each other. I see no reason not to join them on their selfish path toward self-destruction. I live for myself. No one else. I suggest you do the same, because you cannot win against Quint. He wants Terran and nothing you three 'Elementals' do, will stop him. Prepare yourself, Maya. Harden your heart."

Maya fisted a hand over her heart. "Your heart isn't hard, Pillar. You couldn't possess this much hate if you weren't capable of deep love at some point in your existence. Find that girl again. Let her out of the cage. Nodin has suffered enough. And so, I believe, have you."

Pillar rubbed a hand against her chest where her heart no longer beat with softer emotions. A wave of grief and indecision coursed through Maya's mind before Pillar blocked her.

"Quint will come for Terran after his transformation. If the change isn't soon, he'll force Mother to expedite matters." Pillar twisted water from her shirt and punched the elevator button. "Don't hold out hope Mother will switch Terran, if she knows Quint's plan. In her mind, if Terran were to die, she could easily select another Earthman."

Mother would never view another creature's life as expendable. Worry about Mother's intentions and Quint's plans would wait. Terran was her focus now. "What did you do to him?"

"I did nothing but verify he's alive. I was about to board my plane when I was called back to check on Quint's baby boy. He was not pleased when he learned those ranch hands had left Terran to die. There will come a day when you'll wish you'd let that happen." Pillar's words were punctuated by the elevator's ding. She stepped into the elevator and propped a hand against the door. Her coarse voice whispered through Maya's mind. *"Love is a golden pear shining at the top of the tree. The sunlight glints against it, the beauty of the shining skin so ripe and alluring. It remains elusive. You cannot reach it. You jump, you climb, but you never quite grasp it. The next day, you return to find the pear on the ground, bruised and tarnished. You reach for the ripe fruit and take a bite, but inside is a rotted core. Never say I didn't warn you, fellow daughter of Isis."*

Maya closed her eyes against the vivid picture painted in her mind and rejected the entire notion. Love may be elusive, but with Terran, she had reached the top. When she finally sank her teeth into love's golden surface, she'd taste an exquisite explosion of flavors. Pillar was mistaken. In her grief, she'd lost her way. Maya allowed herself a moment's sympathy, but that was all she could offer.

One good thing had come from their little tête-à-tête. Pillar clarified why Quint wanted Terran. So, how would Maya keep that from happening?

Maya reabsorbed the water covering the floor and stepped into Terran's room. His eyelids twitched as he slept, perhaps in a disturbed dream. Such a handsome man, his square jaw housed the bristle of his morning beard. The whiskers outlined perfectly formed lips, which were alive, whole and pink once more.

She closed her eyes to lock this vision in her mind. His steady breathing was the only sound breaking the calm quiet of his room. The smell of antiseptics and the twang of sickness permeated the corridors and helped seal the moment in her memory.

Her healing blue energy mixed with the pure red blood in his veins. His scent was a fragrant blend of them both. He smelled of earth on a humid day after a heavy downpour, the ground sizzling as it absorbed the quick drenching. A muggy heat surrounded his body as it strove to heal.

Already, his Elemental gifts were evident. His human body should not have healed this quickly, even with the majority of his injuries being treated by her special medicine. This proof of his extraordinary recovery offered a sliver of hope.

She pulled a chair close to the bed and plopped down against the seat's worn padding. Worry remained that Pillar's prediction would come to fruition. Would fate be so cruel to offer a chance at love only to have their relationship destroyed before they had time together?

Maya tried calming her thoughts, rotating her neck around and around. A human technique, but the motion relaxed her. Worry for a future she could not envision raced through her mind. Would Terran agree to an Elemental life? Should she warn him of his fate? Give him time to prepare? Hadn't Mother conveyed that was her duty?

No, this life could not be prepared for or explained. All it encompassed was too much to comprehend. This life must be lived and learned from everyday. Questions still plagued her about being an Elemental, which meant she wouldn't have all the answers to the many questions Terran would inevitably ask.

Unlike Pillar, she hadn't given up hope on the human race. She made herself search for good when her mind was weary from constant battle. The world was full of darkness, but there were always stray moments of light—a child's laughter over a balloon tied to their wrist. A father who built castles in the sand with his little girl. An elderly couple with wrinkled, arthritic hands clasped together, sealing their continued devotion as they walked through the park.

She opened her eyes and wiped tears on her sleeve. Pictures like that would never be showcased in her life's photo album. Longing for a simpler human life gave her short moments of despair.

An awareness of being watched prickled. A pair of deep brown eyes regarded her intently.

"You are so beautiful." Terran's voice was gruff when he spoke. "Whatever you were thinking just then made your face so serene. I don't know any other way to explain it. What were you thinking? Why did it make you sad?"

Maya grabbed a tissue from a box on the side table and dabbed her nose. "He awakes and begins his perpetual round of questions." Though the fact he could actually ask questions brought a surge of relief. Their link had saved him.

"Questions that remain unanswered, Shoeless Girl." He settled against the pillow and groaned while stretching his arms over his head.

That sexy sound shot straight through Maya. She wanted to lie with her head upon his chest and feel that sound vibrate through his body every time he woke. After which she would mount him, lock his arms above his head, and torture him with her mouth and tongue. She squirmed in her seat and shook that carnal image from her mind. "How are you feeling this morning? Can you remember what happened?"

After visibly running his tongue over the roof of his mouth, he wet his dry lips. "I suppose I'm not dead since I'm talking to you, but I have no idea how I arrived at the hospital. My mouth is so dry. Could I have some water, please?"

Maya hid a smile while pouring a cup of water from the pitcher on the moveable tray.

He drank like he was experiencing some kind of sexual peak.

"Mmm…may I have some more?"

Using the pitcher as a blind, she let her healing waters flow from her hand into the cup.

In one greedy gulp, Terran drained it all, smacked his lips, and stretched with that groan again. He handed her his empty cup, smiling lazily.

Drunk off the effects of Eau de Maya.

"I had a strange dream. I was alone in the ocean, drowning, gasping for air, and then a calm came over me. I didn't panic. I just floated along with the waves as they broke against me time and again. They struck my body as if they were washing straight through me. You were there, holding my hand and whispering in my ear. I felt you in every part of my body. How is that, Maya? How can you enter my dreams? Make me feel like every inch of me is tied to every inch of you with a force stronger than anything I understand?" He ran a hand through his blood-matted hair, wincing when he pulled and tried to break up a clump.

Maya was unclear if he required a response. "Don't pull at your hair, Fancy Man. You can wash it soon. They smashed your blinkers. Can you see without them? Your glasses?"

"I can see a blurry you. That's all that matters." He stretched a hand toward her over the bed slats.

How could such a simple thing almost liquefy her? It would be better if she were to reject his invitation. Find Nodin and Flint and watch him from afar.

She took his hand, tracing the veins running under his wrist. The crisscrossed mix of blues and purples, pumped blood from his heart to his hands, warmed them, and proved he was alive. Human.

He would not die or become Quint's puppet as long as she was alive. She held tight, vowing not to allow that potent flow to end completely.

She gleaned his thought patterns as they rumbled through his mind. People to contact, arrests to be made, experiments to conduct, legal action against Crowder, and, of course, he worried about calling his mother. In his vision, his father was leaning over his mother's shoulder and listening in on the call. *How sweet.* Terran shook his head at the distress that conversation would cause his mother. She'd want to come straight to town.

Maya's watery heart bubbled, because Terran planned to ask her assistance with his recuperation, although his visions of her in a nurse's outfit were naughty. Nurses didn't dress like that anymore, but maybe a costume store—

"I figured it out," Terran announced.

She jerked, startled by his abrupt verbal declaration when she'd been flowing through his thoughts. *Privacy, Maya!*

He recited the history of finding a charred cow at the stream and confronting Crowder's men. How they lied and he'd gone back to take a sample from the cow and run off wolves feeding on its flesh. His tests were inconclusive for BSE so he sent his findings to government agencies. He returned to take more samples and Crowder's men caught him. After the men learned Terran was aware of their unlawful practices, they circled him like vultures, picking and jabbing until he'd fallen into oblivion.

She straightened in her chair, grasping the cool metal armrests. "So, that's why they tried to kill you? You told them what you knew." She slowly shook her head. "That is the one thing you never do, Terran. Never give them your ace."

"They didn't care about the repercussions of their actions. I regret instigating their physical response, but only because I almost died. I thought of you. I lay next to the water, pain searing through my body, and cool water lapping against me. I know now I won't ever take anything for granted again. I won't let them win, Maya. We have to make everyone aware of the danger." He leaned forward and threw the blankets off his body.

"What do you think you're doing? Lie down," she ordered and gave thought to compelling him to rest.

He fisted his hands in the white sheets. "I'm not going to sit here while that disease spreads. We have to contain it. Now."

CHAPTER 21

Terran's empty stomach churned and dizziness cloaked his vision. *Or is that due to lack of glasses? Nope.* Not when black patches danced before his eyes. He waited for the room to stop spinning then attempted to move his legs to the side of the bed. *Not happening.* He slowly angled back down on his pillow.

A caffeine-deprivation headache, along with having his face used as a punching bag, was not conducive to rising quickly.

Maya squeezed his hand and gently pushed against his chest. "Terran, please lie back."

He closed his eyes, and took slow even breaths until the nausea subsided. "I need coffee."

"That sort of defeats the whole rest scenario."

He shot her a sideways glance. "My head is pounding. Coffee is the only medicine I need right now. Can you rustle up some?" Maybe he could talk her into massaging his temples.

"It's before visiting hours. I'm not even supposed to be here."

"Maya, my life depends on it." He offered a pleading smile. "Please, I'll buy you all the shoes you need."

She rolled her eyes. "I can think of other things I need more."

"Get me coffee, my little lily, and I'll see what I can do."

"In your condition, I doubt you could do much of anything."

He chuckled. "You're probably right. I'm covered in dried blood, ache all over, and I need coffee." He kicked the blankets off his feet. The air seemed a bit muggy.

"Your poor face. How's your head feeling?" She stood and massaged his temples.

The girl must have read my mind. "That's heaven, but I still need

117

caffeine."

A wide smile lit her face before she kissed his forehead and walked out.

Hopefully on a coffee-finding mission.

Maya's absence since their moonlight drive had troubled him. He had stopped at the library and Mo-swa's, but she hadn't been around. The night at the lake remained on his mind. The way she fit next to him, her beautiful fluid body, was something he was anxious to experience again. He hadn't wanted to leave her with Nodin, but their mother was ill. Maya's relationship with Nodin continued to puzzle him. When she returned, he'd inquire after her mother's health, along with finding out her plan for the next couple days.

When he'd first opened his eyes, he thought her presence was a dream. Her head was tilted back, her eyes closed, and tears streamed down her cheeks. His heart wrenched at her sorrow. He hoped she was not crying over him.

The woman drove him mad, but she was here now, and they would be discussing the fact that he didn't want her disappearing again. An inner sense of purpose and peace came from being in her presence. He craved that feeling, almost needed it to survive. Rationally, a relationship took time, but his mind refused to follow his normal thought patterns when it came to Miss Maya Conway. How she managed to make him feel so much in such a short time baffled, but the forward motion of his life would roll along much smoother with her alongside.

Maya would come to understand no more questions would be left unanswered, and no more taking off to who knew where. He would build a dam around her and lock her down.

He glanced around the room for a mirror and a bathroom. He sighed as he realized it was too far to go without help. Running a hand over his unshaven cheeks, he rotated his jaw back and forth. His body ached all over, but thankfully, he had no broken bones. The fight had started when he'd been struck from behind. He'd rallied, but lost ground when they all attacked at once. How had he escaped any internal bleeding? However it happened, he had no time to lose. A new mission formed in his mind. He needed a pen and a notepad to write everything out, or his laptop.

He groaned and rubbed his temples. Even thinking hurt. He really did drink too much coffee. Funny how he could be beat by four men, yet his caffeine addiction was what would kill him.

#

After three life-altering cups of coffee and a round of helpful nurses, Terran drifted into a peaceful mid-morning nap.

He awoke to a blurry Maya quietly sitting in a chair by his bed. *New glasses—priority one.* The TV was on and she seemed mesmerized by a talk show with four fuzzy women sitting together at a table. She must have sensed he was awake because she turned and smiled. "Nice nap?"

"It'd be better if you were in here with me."

"Hmmm…men always have a one-track mind." She rolled her eyes, and then pointed to the TV. "Look at this woman. She's addicted to plastic surgery. Just imagine when a thousand years from now, someone digs up her body and wonders what she did to herself. I mean look at her …ah… enhanced chest. Do you find that attractive?"

"Maya, I can't even see the screen. I prefer a more natural body. Yours comes to mind." Terran took her hand and lined their palms together then linked their fingers. How could he make her understand he wanted her to stay? "Would you mind—"

"Good afternoon." A cheery nurse came in to poke and prod, which prevented him from asking Maya her plans.

A few moments after the nurse left, he straightened as Sheriff Cody entered the room. "Mr. Forrester. I understand there was a spot of trouble."

How would this interrogation work since Cody was in Crowder's pocket? Terran didn't trust him to follow through.

"Sheriff Cody, may I get you something to drink?" Maya released Terran's hand and padded toward the door.

Cody nodded and placed his hat on the food tray next to the water pitcher. "Sure. Coffee. Black. Thank you, miss."

"Me too." Terran piped.

Maya shook her head. "Terran, Terran, what shall we do about your fluid intake? Drink the water I left on the tray. I'll be back with your coffee."

He downed the water as she disappeared into the hallway.

Sheriff Cody took her chair.

Terran gave an account of the attack, as well as the names of the men involved. He told the Sheriff to expect contact from the CDC and National Animal Disease Center. They would explain the proper protocol to initiate quarantine now that his suspicions about Mad Cow were verified. The ranch hands had taunted him with their secrets, never expecting him to survive.

Cody stood and tapped his hat against the table. "We'll look into your allegations. Have a word with Crowder and his men."

Clay dropped by during his lunch hour and brought Terran's lab glasses.

After the barrage of visitors, Terran could barely keep his eyes open.

His mind, however, refused to rest. How he had arrived at the hospital? The last thing he remembered was unbearable pain and lying by the stream. Thoughts of Maya had flashed through his mind as his body drifted in and out of consciousness.

A headache threatened to return as he turned these questions over in his mind. His lids drew heavier and sleep eased the bewilderment plaguing his mind.

A whispered argument woke him.

Nodin and Maya stood at the foot of his bed. Nodin swiped his hand in the air, cutting her off.

She stepped back, glanced over, and noticed him watching her.

"What are you two fighting about?"

"Nodin wants me to go home, but I want to stay. He's always forcing me to do things before I'm ready. It's good you're awake. I believe you'll be checking out soon." She walked over to the side of the bed and placed her cool hand across his forehead. "How are you feeling?"

He kissed her palm and placed her hand on his chest. "Much better, thanks." Surprisingly, his body felt rejuvenated. A slight twinge remained along his right jaw and rib cage, but that last nap must have done the trick.

Nodin grabbed the rail at the end of the bed. "Those boys sure did a number on you, brother. Glad you're recuperating. I'll let the nurse know you're awake so you can go home."

The TV glared bright in the dark room, causing Terran to blink against the flashing pictures on the screen. The title of the person standing behind a podium and the news ticker below were blurred due to his near-sightedness.

"Maya, do you know where my glasses went?"

"I removed them while you slept." She still seemed perturbed. The food tray squeaked as the plastic caster wheels attempted to go sideways before she yanked the table toward her and grabbed his glasses off the faux-wood top.

Ah, the clarity of vision.

"Can you unmute the TV, please?" He adjusted the frames on his nose, and the man behind the podium came into focus.

The man standing to the side of the speaker looked like Carlyle Crowder, and beside him stood the renowned Virologist, Neb Aether. "Is that Carlyle Crowder?"

"Terran, no need to get your blood pressure up." Maya ran her hand up and down his arm. "You aren't completely healed."

He cast her a glance and thought about mentioning his blood pressure had been fine until she touched him.

Nodin returned and glared at the screen.

Maya pushed the button on the side of the bed, raising the volume. "Do you want to sit up?"

Terran nodded.

She pushed another button, which elevated his back.

The man behind the podium was Dr. Veimhet Schwarz. He announced Aether Pharmaceuticals had created a vaccine to cure BSE, the prion causing Mad Cow disease. Three eminent scientists debated this astonishing announcement, which must have been recorded earlier today. Their heads appeared in square boxes on the screen. The newsman focused on Dr. Dennis Houser, the head research scientist at The National Prion Clinic.

"All right, Mr. Forrester, let's get you checked out." The nurse's voice overlapped comments made by Houser. She placed a folder on the table and pointed to the places requiring his signature.

Impatient to leave, he read through the papers quickly and signed off.

The nurse shuffled the signed sheets together, returned her copies to a folder, and handed him a large manila envelope. "I'll be back with a wheelchair to see you out."

Terran's focus returned to the news channel as Houser explained his doubts and expressed his wish to visit Aether Pharmaceuticals to review the results of this supposed cure. "What is Crowder doing there? Does he own that company?" He questioned

Maya who had moved to the other side of the bed when the nurse entered.

Nodin responded, "Yes, Crowder owns Aether. He hopes to gain prestige and money with this move. I don't trust this information. He lies."

A breeze disturbed the room, rustling the napkins left on Terran's tray.

Odd, no windows are open.

"Nodin," Maya said. Her tone was even, but with a hint of something Terran couldn't distinguish.

Nodin turned his steely blue gaze on her. "Are you ready *now?*"

The nurse returned with Terran's wheelchair. "Mr. Forrester, let's get you over to the bathroom so you can get dressed and on your way home."

Terran swung his legs to the side of the bed, no longer impeded by dizziness. Maya stood in front of Nodin. They made an odd picture as she stared into his eyes before he threw up his hands and left the room.

She followed.

"Maya?" Terran didn't want her to leave. Not yet. They were way over-due for a long, informative, and very private conversation.

At the doorway, she sank her fingers in her hair and wrapped the golden strands into some sort of bun on the top of her head. "I'll be right back. Don't worry."

After getting dressed and using a damp paper towel to wipe off his face, he stepped out of the bathroom.

Maya waited behind the wheelchair. "Let's get you home."

"How are you planning on doing that?" Winking as he eased into the seat, he said, "Gonna put me on your handlebars?"

She gently tugged his earlobe. "I just might."

After wheeling down the hall, they rode the elevator to the lobby.

Once outside, he hopped out of the wheelchair, wrapped Maya in his arms, and twirled. Blue skies, crisp summer air, he breathed everything in, grateful for the sensations of the sun's warmth against his skin, the warbling of a Mountain Bluebird, and the tickling brush of Maya's hair against his chin.

"Come on, happy feet." She wrapped an arm around his waist and led him to his truck.

He stopped in the middle of the parking lot. "Maya, how did my truck get here?"

"I drove it."

"When? From where?"

"The stream."

"But how did you know it was at the stream?" *Did I tell her I was at the stream?* The past day and a half was jumbled in his mind.

"The day you were injured."

"Maya, please start making sense. I'm not having another unexplainable and exhausting conversation with you. How did my truck get here? Answer the question, please." He leaned against his truck and tipped her chin with his forefinger.

"I was out looking for you. Moose said you'd been by to see me, so I went on a search." She removed his hand from under her chin and brushed her fingers over his bruised knuckles. "I found you bloody and beaten by the stream, so I hauled you into your truck and drove you here."

"Thank you. I can't imagine how hard it was to get me into the truck. Do you have super strength or something?"

"Yes, actually I do." Maya ruffled his hair. "Would you like to see?"

He responded to her flirtations in kind. "Yes, I would like to see. Do you have plans now? I mean for after you drop me off?"

"No, but I have to leave with Nodin in the morning." She avoided eye contact, glancing around the parking lot and fiddling with the bun on her head.

"Where are you going?"

"He has an interview so I'm going along as moral support."

"How is your mother?" One question, he knew, she would answer when others were racing through his mind. Was she really related to Nodin? Where was her father? So much he didn't know, and yet, she drew him like a siren, keeping him under her spell.

"Nodin and I...I mean, what did you ask? About my mother? Uh...yeah, she's much better. She was sick, but the fever burned out." She was silent a moment, kicking the truck tire. "I'm sorry about that night." With a one-shouldered shrug, she smiled and took the manila envelope he had tucked under his arm and shook out the keys. "I'll drive."

CHAPTER 22

Silence reigned on the drive home, both very aware of what would happen once they crossed the threshold. The sexual tension ratcheted up a notch as thoughts of their "almost moment" by the stream rumbled through Terran's mind. His head bumped against the headrest as Maya suddenly accelerated down the road.

The truck lurched to a halt in front of his house.

While no longer in any discomfort, he needed a long, hot shower, preferably with Maya in attendance. After guiding Maya down the sidewalk, he stepped inside the front door and shouted, "Scotty, you home?"

No response.

"Come upstairs with me?" He offered Maya his hand. Taking this next step in their relationship would be her choice.

She stood at the threshold. Her hands stuffed in her back pockets, but then she smiled and took his hand.

Choice made, they walked upstairs.

Memories of the last time she was here rolled through his mind. This time, no voice outside the door would stop them, nor would the bruises on his body.

At the top of the stairs, Maya took a deep breath. "I imagine you're glad to be home."

Wrapping his arms around her, Terran held tight. He buried his face in the richness of her hair. The clean smell, like citrus scented raindrops, reminded him he did not exude the same freshness. He ran both hands up and down her back. "Are you ready for this?"

"Yes."

"All of it?"

She pulled away and brushed her fingers across his cheek. "I'm willing to give you all I can for as long as you wish."

He nodded. That sealed her fate as far as he was concerned. "I wish for it all. Here. Now." He dropped a quick kiss against her lips. "Let's shower."

After grabbing two brown towels off the hall closet shelf, he guided her into the bathroom. He reached into the shower and turned the knob a little hotter than his usual temperature.

"Are you sure you're up for this?" Maya leaned against the counter. "You did just get out of the hospital after knocking at death's door."

"We'll take this first time slow and easy. I want the moment to last. No interruptions. You said you're all in. I'm not backing off now." He reached for his toothbrush, and then raised a brow when she continued studying him.

"I thought you had questions."

"I do, but we'll find the answers together."

"Terran, perhaps we should...maybe first I should..." She blew out a breath and rubbed her temple.

"What is it?"

"Nothing. You're right, we'll find the answers together so this has to be now." She tugged her shirt up and off then unzipped her jeans, revealing a hint of black lace.

"Stop. Give me a minute here." He rinsed out his mouth and studied the man in the mirror. A colorful mix of purple and yellow bruises painted his right cheek, and his eye was puffy pink. "Crowder's men did quite a number on me. I'm alive because of you." He turned and faced her. "Would you like me to show you how grateful I am?"

"I'm hoping you'll show me a lot more than gratitude."

Appreciation was too small a word for the vision standing before him now. The hourglass shape of her body would mold perfectly to his hands. Black lace cups overflowed with the fullness of her pale breasts. Matching black panties covered valleys and a peak he longed to scale.

"When I watched you up on that stage, I knew your body was mine. Not meant to be seen or shared by anyone. Only me. To think,

I almost died without getting to feel every inch of your skin." He shook his head at the thought.

"You're alive, I'm alive. Touch me…please, Terran. You have no idea how long I've waited for you."

Terran reached for her hands and steered them under his T-shirt and over his chest. Together, they lifted off his shirt. Then, he guided her hand down to unsnap his jeans.

Under his boxer briefs, her hand teased and stroked his thick flesh and caressed his swollen sacs.

"Enough," he growled and attempted to pull away her hand.

She resisted and ran a finger over his seeping, rigid tip then circled in a spiral from the center slit to the outer edge of his crown. Her fingertip glistened with the silky result of her touch. Her chest rose and fell with each panted breath as her fingers stroked up and down his length.

He'd lose control if she kept up that torturous glide. He spun her around and unsnapped her bra. Lifting her fallen tendrils to the side, he feasted on her neck. Her full, firm breasts molded perfectly as he kneaded them with his hands. He brushed his thumb against her taut nipple.

She pressed more fully against his hand, straining for more. She wrapped her arm around his neck, and she rolled her hips back against him.

He traced his thumb along the edge of her lace-topped panties, and he pushed them down over her hips along with her jeans. Steam filled the bathroom and he could barely make out her clothes now puddled at her feet. From his position behind her, he walked her forward and stopped before the shower door. He stepped out of his jeans and briefs then nudged her under the hot spray. A faint russet red tinted the water as it swirled into the drain. The smell of hospital washed away as Maya gently bathed him.

"Mmmm, never underestimate the rejuvenating effects of a shower."

"Water can be quite a refresher. I agree." A secret smile lit Maya's face. "Look at your poor body, all bruised." She kissed his chest. "Poor man, let's make sure you're clean everywhere." The washcloth made its way south and she did a very thorough job.

Relieved to be scrubbed clean, he took the washcloth from Maya's hand, placed it aside, and reached for the soap.

She stayed his hand and lifted on her toes to slide her tongue over his bottom lip. "Kiss me."

As he wrapped his hand around the back of her neck, he tangled his fingers in her hair. Once again, the passion between them flared hot. Explosion was imminent. He claimed her lips, slanting his head to glide his tongue in a heated duel with hers.

The depths of her mouth drowned him, and he never wanted to surface. Water poured out of the showerhead, hard and strong. Steam engulfed them, rising and swirling in a dance around their bodies. He roamed his hands freely over her sleek skin. A sharp gasp escaped her lips as he rolled the tips of her breasts between his thumb and forefinger. The water served as liquid fire as he feverishly explored every inch of her body. Refusing to gain release without her, he drew her teasing hand from his rigid shaft.

"The water pressure seems really strong today." He adjusted the nozzle on the showerhead, but the pressure abated on its own. "Come here. It's your turn to get clean."

"Why? I like being dirty." She licked his nipple.

He jerked against her, more than ready to see how muddy they could make the waters. "I'm sure I'll enjoy 'dirty Maya' very soon. Right now, I want you as steamy as this shower."

She shoved him against the wall. "I'm past steam all the way to boiling. Can't you tell?" Placing her hands on his shoulders, she boosted up and wrapped her legs around his hips.

He dug his fingers into her bottom's firm globes and locked her in place.

She worked her hand over his enflamed erection as she flagrantly kissed him.

He bit her bottom lip and again stayed her hand. "Stop. I don't want to come without you."

A bit of a struggle ensued when she refused to release him.

He slid her down his body, smiling over her glare. He relieved her pout by gliding his soapy fingers against her core, creating a fluff of foamy bubbles in the wet curls at the apex of her thighs. She tried to kiss him, but he held her back. The sexiest sound he'd ever heard escaped her mouth. Running his hand along her inner thigh, he teased her as she had him.

She clamped her hand around his wrist when he slid his fingers over her sensitive folds.

Brushing a single finger against her wet cleft, he slid a finger inside.

Her entire body arched against his hand.

Amazed at the glory raining down upon his solitary finger, he clenched his teeth against the thunder of need tearing through his body. A continual glide, she moved her hips in time with each gentle stroke, he took their torment to a new level as he whispered his intentions in her ear, "You took care of me when I was lost in a dark cloud of agony. I plan to storm every inch of you until you're in the same state. But this time we'll die that little death together."

She ran her fingers through his hair, gripping tight, and pulling him close. Her bright blue eyes opened, gazing directly into his before she tugged on his lower lip with her teeth.

He took her lips in a kiss way past the point of primal into a new reality that could only be attained with her. His heart pounded and his body ached with the need to expel his seed deep within her—marking her, claiming her as his.

Her body began to tighten around his surging caress.

He pulled back and dropped to his knees. "Open for me." Kissing his way up her thigh to the tiny triangle covering her wet cavern, he licked her swollen folds and gently sucked her bud of pleasure.

Her knees buckled and she clenched his hair with each rasp of his tongue. "Terran, I'm going to fall."

"I've got you." He dug his fingers into her hips as he held her in place for the thrust of his tongue. Diving into her well, over and over, he held her still for his ministrations.

He nuzzled against her pale curls, learning her, assaulting her senses, as she pleaded with him not to stop until she broke with a shout. Her death grip on his head kept him in place as her body shuddered with release. Steam filled the shower so completely, he could barely make out her form through the dense mist. Water seemed to pour off her skin as she strained to catch her breath. Incoherent words came from her lips as tiny tremors continued to rack her body.

He rose and thrust his straining manhood between her wet thighs. Not entering only thrusting in that slick hollow, he whispered in her ear. "I'm not finished with you yet. Do you know what happens to your body when you come?" He placed a hard kiss on her mouth and continued his explanation while dropping heated kisses against the side of her neck. "Your clitoral glans moves inward under the clitoral hood, and your labia minora becomes darker." He pitched his voice lower. "As orgasm develops, the outer third of your vagina tightens and narrows, while overall the vagina lengthens, dilates and becomes congested from engorged soft tissue. Your uterus then experiences a series of muscular contractions then release as your uterus, vagina, anus, and pelvic muscles undergo a series of rhythmic contractions." These last words were growled from his throat.

Maya strained up on the balls of her feet and moaned against this mouth. "How can you make science sound so hot?"

"Are you hot? Let's check." He ran his fingers down and over her sensitive outer lips then slipped past her entrance, probing deep as he kissed her. His little science lesson had fanned his fire just as high.

He turned off the water, stepped out, and quickly patted dry. Wrapped in a towel, with his hair still plastered against his head, he led her across the hall to his bedroom. He briefly rubbed the towel over his body and hers before he pushed her back on the bed with a gentle nudge.

A strong ache coursed from his cock. His balls had to be Artic blue.

His gaze roved over the blonde bounty on his bed. "Quite a vision. Beyond beautiful. All that gorgeous golden hair against my pillow. Lips red. Chest heaving. Your eyes sleepy with satisfaction. Knees bent and open." He joined her, fitting himself between her thighs.

Maya quirked a brow. "I figured you for a by-the-book kind of lover, who knew you could be such a tease. I'm on a very thin ledge right now, Terran. If you don't get down to business soon, I'm flipping you over and riding you like a ship in a stormy sea."

"It's a ride you're after? I'm more than happy to give it to you. Ready?"

In answer, she reached down and settled him at her center.

His body shook at the connection. "Wait, we need protection."

"No, I'm covered. Don't stop now. It's safe. I promise."

Why he trusted her he couldn't say? Perhaps his mind was fogged with lust, but he didn't stop. If he was going to finish quickly, then so would she. He bent and drew one nipple deep, rubbing the hard peak against the roof of his mouth. His attentions continued to the next.

She sank her nails into his shoulders. The sharp claw of her arousal, raked against his intent to bathe in every nuisance of this moment.

Maya let out a few choice curses. Her body bowed, seeking that primal connection.

He rubbed his cock between her thighs, gliding back and forth, teasing her.

"Terran...please."

He dove deep, so deep and began that slow, repetitive glide.

She rose to meet each demanding stroke.

A light film of sweat covered his body as he held back from the final surrender.

The string winding them together went taut. His whole body contained in the pleasure of her yielding heat. The vision of her under him, her lips plumped and parted as she took short breaths, tied him to her. Her creamy skin flushed a soft pink across her chest.

She opened her eyes and a flash of dark blue sparked as she held tight to his upper arms. Her siren's smile beckoned him to join her as his waving rhythm finally broke against her shore.

Her hips erupted off the bed, taking him with her as fulfillment flowed through her body. He held her hips in place beneath him, answering her heated call, which led him to that final moment of release. Like the tip of a match, it stroked along the surface, then lit and burst into a bright yellow-gold flame. Burning with bliss again and again, he attempted to snuff out the erupting fire, but it only burned brighter and a white blue flare flashed before his eyes, taking him to a level of completion that seared this moment across his heart forever.

Their tremors slowly faded, and an instant addiction forged that would drive him to dive into her spring again and again.

This level of connection and physical fulfillment had never been attained with another woman. Her body aligned perfectly to his, and his climax had scorched like a white-hot magnesium burn—intense like the surface of the sun.

Once his breathing slowed, he dragged his head from its resting place between her breasts. He rose above her on his forearms and kissed her softly. An appreciative kiss, one that lingered and played a game of touch and retreat as he softened inside her. "What was that? Have you ever felt anything that hot? Do you think there are scorch marks on the sheets?" Brown eyes sought answers in her dreamy deep blue depths.

"Even now, you have questions." Maya chuckled and shook her head.

He joined her, caught up in the pleasure of the moment. He placed tons of smacking kisses all over her face. "Maya, I don't know how you feel, but I don't want this to be a one-time thing. I want to pursue this. I'm complete when I'm with you and after this, well… I…I know I'll never stop wanting you. I don't play games. My mind doesn't function like that. I'll need answers from you."

"My body did answer yours." She reached up and touched his face, avoiding his bruised skin. "We will have a chance at forever, Terran. The path of our relationship is for you to determine. I've never had any choice. Not even in this. I've accepted fates plan, knowing I belong here, with you. I've been alone for so long. I don't want to be sad or scared anymore. With you, I'll be stronger than I was before. You'll see."

"No, you're not alone. We'll always fit together one way or another." He demonstrated by nudging her with a semi-hard twitch.

"Looks like someone came primed."

"He did, indeed."

Throughout the night and early morning hours, Terran reached for her again and again. Exhaustion finally led into a sated dream-filled slumber.

A long trail leads to an isolated mountain lake. His feet sank into the mud as he ran down a narrow path, hedged in by evergreens. Maya waits at the end. Pine needles crunch under his feet. Bright green leaves. A cloudless blue sky. All is perfect. With each step he takes, he sees her moving farther away. The lake churns in angry waves behind her. A tree falls and blocks the road before him. A raging storm strikes downward and a huge funnel cloud envelopes his body, lifting him away from the earth. As he spins through the sky, he sees her at the end of the path—silent, still, waiting. Tears pour down her cheeks. He fights against the raging storm. She raises one arm and runs toward him. Their fingers touch, bending as they try to link. She grasps his hand tight and pulls him to stand beside her. All is quiet as she gazes into his eyes. Not a sound from the forest. Suddenly a deep crevasse forms in the earth and swallows him whole. He sees her bent at the edge, reaching for him, and screaming as he continues to fall.

Terran started as a moan deep in his throat tried to erupt into a scream. He wiped a hand over his sweat-covered chest. Still caught up in the dream, he swiveled his head back and forth, trying to determine his bearings.

A shiver racked his body, cold now from his damp skin. He reached for Maya, but found only empty space and rumpled brown sheets.

"Maya?" He rose on an elbow and glanced around the room, listening for sounds of movement in the house. He ran a hand over the bristle on his chin. That's right, she had an appointment with Nodin today.

What time is it anyway? And what was that strange dream about?

As he lay back, he turned his head and spotted a single bright yellow water lily in full bloom upon her pillow.

Proof that some dreams became reality.

CHAPTER 23

Their shadows meshed as they silently slipped around the redbrick building housing Quint's drug company. Light from the moon failed to filter through the dark sky covered in puffy gray clouds. A light rain left tiny water droplets on her skin.

Maya ran a hand over her wet arm, remembering the feel of Terran's hands on her body. The brush of his skin against hers, the wet-glide as—

"Maya!" Nodin scolded.

"Ouch. No need to shout. Sorry."

Now. Focus on now and emptying her mind in case Quint was listening. One never knew what he was capable of doing. Perhaps their sneak approach had already sounded alarm bells in his sludge-filled brain.

Nodin gestured to a window above them, and then he dispersed into the air. His energy pattern was apparent to her elemental senses, but she saw nothing.

This far north and close to the ocean the evening air still held a chill. She shivered as she waited for "invisible" Nodin to return from his floating spy perch.

Moments passed, when suddenly, he reappeared and wrapped his arms around her. "Mist," he whispered.

They spun in a funnel, crossed the street, and traveled down the sidewalk trail alongside Lake Union.

"So, were you able to get anything through your windy wiles?"

"Veimhet Schwarz is the name of Quint's top scientist. I was able to glean his thoughts. Pillar featured in his mind. She's in Switzerland. I had to weave around all his sexually deviant thoughts to catch something about a girl and radio waves or microwaves. I'm unclear on that. Schwarz wants Pillar and he thinks he could have her if Quint was out of the way. But she hadn't—" Nodin clammed up.

A burning sense of failure washed through her mind, which was an emotional echo from Nodin. A strong breeze rustled through the trees along the shore. The chill wind beat against her and created goose bumps on her droplet-covered skin.

She caressed his arm. "It's okay. Don't blame yourself for Pillar's choices. What else were you able to discern?"

Nodin peered out over the water, calming his thoughts. "Schwarz phoned someone about picking up a shipment of experimental vaccines for three ranches in Washington and Wyoming. Some humans don't mind using their cattle for experiments as long as they get paid. Houser, the head of that Prion Institute, is troubling him. They can't sway his opinion nor stop him from gaining access to their research. Schwarz wants him eliminated."

"Was Quint in the building?"

"Not that I could glean." Nodin scuffed his foot along a grass tuft sticking out of a crack in the sidewalk. "There's more."

Maya could see the images in Nodin's mind. The inhumane experiments Schwarz had done. A repulsive memory shivered down her spine.

"You remember the last time." Nodin wiped a hand across his mouth.

"Yes, I remember."

WWII had been a busy time for the Elementals.

"Schwarz is part of the problem now. These experiments he's involved in must be dealt with. I need to speak with Mother and gather Flint."

"I'll wait for you in Wyoming."

Nodin nodded, and then a wide smile appeared. A rare sight, but it transformed his already handsome face into a vision she couldn't describe.

"I'm happy for you, Maya. Terran will make a worthy addition to our team. We've been too long without our grounding force."

Maya raked her hair back from her face. How would Nodin take

Terran's refusal to submit to this new life? And after their glorious night together, how would she? "He may not choose this path."

"Then hold on while you can. Let love be your anchor, but remember that a strong storm can blow you off course." Sadness stirred in his sky-blue eyes.

"And love for you?" The words carried from her mind to his.

"A wasted breath."

A rush of regret filled his mind, before he disappeared and blocked her from his gray thoughts. He softened his abrupt exit by ruffling a light breeze through her hair.

Job done, she could return to Terran. Relief and anticipation rushed through her along with a strong dose of happiness. She ran along the trail, exulting in the misty drizzle fanning across her face. She breathed it in, enjoying every particle soaking her skin. Two-dinosaur topiary seemed to laugh at her frolics, the glow from their ornamental eyes sparkling as she ran past.

Ahead was a break in the trees, and she ran for it, ready to plunge into the lake. A short trail led down to the retaining wall, and she leapt off.

A vice squeezed around her throat and wrenched her out of the air. The force propelled her against the water's edge lined with blackberry bushes that scratched and tore as she tumbled. Her body remained out of her control when, once again, she was lifted right before she rolled into the water. An unforgiving energy slammed her onto the boulders hidden just beneath the lake's surface along the shore. The bones in her back crushed on impact. Darkness threatened, pain seared down her spine, and then *he* stood above her.

Quint.

With every ounce of power left, she screamed for Nodin to return. *Save me.*

Now that she'd found her true mate, she refused to die. She blinked against the vacuum of emptiness threatening to overtake her.

Water. Her ravaged body half-rested in the liquid perpetuator of her life force. But was it enough to save her?

What would Quint do now that she was at his mercy?

CHAPTER 24

"Look at you. Legs dangling in water, your supposed 'elemental' gift and yet, you're slowly circling the drain."

A slight moan came from the awkwardly arranged body at his feet.

Quint nudged Maya's head with his shoe. "Ah, ahh, no distress calls allowed."

A wild scream ripped from Maya's throat.

"That's right, my little water whore, scream. Let me hear you. The melody is music to my ears."

Maya's back was broken. Paralyzed. He'd let the water heal her for a time before he began her torture all over again. "Did you really think you and that air puff could spy and I wouldn't know? My dear, have you learned nothing after all this time?"

He gleaned her attempts to mist and escape into the water, but the poor creature was too weak. His hopes for more of a fight from Ms. Conway were dashed—literally. *Pity.*

"All you had to do was ask. I would have told you everything. What is it you want to know? The vaccine? It's not real. It just hides the prion. My dark matter masks it. Those scientists bumble around, but they'll never see the truth, nor detect it. So weak is the human mind, unable to fathom all that I am. Quite unfortunate, as there is so much I could show them. My company will make millions once the scare begins then I'll simply disappear."

A mumbling came from the body lying prone before him.

"I'm sorry. I didn't catch that. Did you say something?

Interesting, what's this?"

Her mind projected a strong vision of Terran above her, staring into her eyes. His face flushed. Apparently, they'd just fucked. Now this vision intrigued as it flashed from her mind through his. *Such a beautiful man.* Terran's body, once peri-mortal, would fit his needs perfectly, and soon. Very soon.

Gravel crunched under his feet as he paced beside her. "Good, was he? I knew Terran had potential, especially with that substantial package hanging between his thighs. Liked that, did you? Perhaps, I'll keep you alive so I can fill you with it again and again. Wouldn't that be a crowning glory?"

The water whore didn't respond. Too broken, the bottom half of her body lying half-immersed in the lake. Her eyes were closed, so he kicked her hip, jolting her to attention.

"Have you ever watched a house cat play with a mouse? I find it entertaining. The cat stalks, then pounces, hovering over the mouse's body. The mouse fights against the claws sunk deep into its flesh. The fun begins once the cat tosses the half-dead mouse in the air and bats it about with its paws. And then the cat bites off the poor creatures head. I thought perhaps we could play cat and mouse today, but your very X-rated picture show has changed my mind."

Choices, choices.

If he used Maya as a host, he might have a bit of fun with her body before receiving his true prize. He could use Maya's womanly wiles to seduce Terran. Once he discovered Mother Nature had transformed Terran into the peri-mortal Earthman, he would escape his watered-down shell.

The idea had interesting possibilities.

Torn from his contemplations due to bubbles boiling up around Maya, he grabbed her arm and hauled her out of the water onto the rocky shore.

Mounting her, he locked his mouth over hers and drove his tongue down her throat.

She gagged and coughed water into his mouth. Waves of lake water rose and splashed against him. Her body had become half mist, half human.

Quint wiped the water from his face. "Your water games have done nothing but irritate me, Maya. I really liked this suit."

Mouth to mouth, he again sealed against her, transferring his essence into her body. The force of her power shot a fissure of pleasure through his body—unlike anything he'd ever felt. Never had he gone this deep with an Elemental. Water began seeping from his hands braced on the sides of her head. *Incredible.*

Mays's eyes turned black, and her body began to wrinkle and concave. He released her. Too much, too soon, wasn't as fun. And his mind whirled with the shocking discovery that a portion of her gift had transferred to him.

How long will this ability last? Will the affect be the same with the other Elementals?

He squeezed his hand, but upon reopening his fist, only a small water-bead formed in his palm. A complete connection must be necessary to retain her full gift. This Elemental thing had interesting perks. Fortunately for them, he'd never realized this potential before, he'd only considered the peri-mortal factor.

A strong gust of wind struck his side, knocking him off balance. A faint twinge of sea salt struck his nostrils.

No!

Quint scrambled toward Maya, but a bright purple light burst between him and his prey. The flash burned his eyes, and he tumbled into the water, blinded. He shook his head against the white spots now dancing before his eyes.

What kind of power was this?

CHAPTER 25

"Thanks for the interview, Mr. Forrester." The blonde reporter crooked a charming half-smile and shook his hand, maintaining the grip longer than necessary.

Invitation was apparent by the glimmer in her eyes and the continual brush of her knee against his during the interview conducted in the Conservancy's conference room.

Blondes, at this point, are not more fun.

Terran had answered her questions about the Conservancy's discovery of BSE at Crowder's ranch. His beating was also discussed. News vans and reporters were all over town, so escaping his ignominious defeat was no longer possible. Getting his ass kicked was not anything he cared to dwell on or have the reading public privy to. The only thing keeping his chin up was the fact four men were needed to bring him down.

Unfortunately, the tale had not ended with him and had become especially sordid after all four of his fight club foes were found dead in a vacant barn on Crowder's land. Reports claimed their bodies looked like hollow emaciated shells, as if their blood, tissue, and organs were drained somehow. Some of the crazier stories had vampires running rampant in Teton National Park.

Sheriff Cody held him as a person of interest for all of a minute before his alibi checked out. Not to mention the fact that Carlyle Crowder had gone missing. No one had seen or heard from him since the Seattle news conference.

Dr. Dennis Houser had visited the Conservancy yesterday.

Terran welcomed the distraction from his unease over Maya's whereabouts. Houser came to town to determine the ramifications of this prion strain. As charismatic as he was smart, Houser fascinated him. Together, they hoped to educate people on the dangers inherent in a Mad Cow outbreak and calm fears. Terran expressed his doubts about the vaccine Aether Pharmaceuticals had developed—a belief Houser shared. The doctor related his unease at Aether's initial lack of cooperation with the Prion Institute. Once Houser's team was allowed in Aether's building, his top scientists found nothing. A complete absence of proof was, in essence, proof. Something wasn't quite right in those laboratory halls.

Terran drew back from his musings when the reporter stood after gathering all her items in her purse, which was the size of a small suitcase.

Women and their bags and shoes. Shoes. Where is Maya?

He paged Clay and asked him to give the reporter a facility tour, and then see her out. Leaving her in capable hands, Terran headed back to his desk. He thumbed through his notes, read e-mails, and checked his calendar for dates to schedule a visit to the Prion Institute in Ohio.

Rubbing his fingers against his temples, he sighed then downed the dregs of his now-cold coffee. A constant dull ache had set up shop and no amount of massage or medicine erased the unending throb. Eyes closed, he pictured the same vision, over and over. A cold, damp cave. Water lapping against the rocks. A deep pool. He peeked over the edge and saw nothing but filmy water. These thoughts were tied to Maya somehow. His subconscious was shouting danger by inflicting an unending, drilling pain that threatened to bore through his brain. An overwhelming sense of foreboding remained throughout every moment of the day. He couldn't shake the feeling that Maya was injured and needed him somehow.

A week had passed since he'd seen her. Sleep eluded and he could barely choke down even coffee. Each day, he visited both her job sites. No one knew where she was or how to contact her.

Why didn't I get her cell number?

Perhaps, her mother was ill again, or she and Nodin had lied about their relationship. No, he wouldn't believe she'd abandoned him for another. Their night together had been too raw, too real on every level. Her heart and body had opened. Why else would she leave a bloomed flower on his pillow? The bright yellow blossom was a sunny token left in her place. Something bad had happened. Nothing else could explain her disappearance and these visions of water, of danger pitching through his mind. The same nightmare woke him each night, his chest pounding out in fear as he peered over the dream pool's edge and glimpsed—what? *What can't I see?*

As if conjured by his thoughts, Terran caught a glimpse of Nodin out of the corner of his eye.

Terran shot out of his chair, which rolled back and slammed against the table behind him. "Where is she? What have you done? I know your 'interview' didn't last a week. Is she hurt?"

"She said you were full of questions." Nodin stood at the lab entrance, dressed only in black gym pants.

"Fuck you." Terran shoved a finger against Nodin's chest. "I want to know where the hell you've been for the past week. Where. Is. Maya?"

"No need to persist in these questions when I am willing to show you the answer. Come." Nodin ordered and stepped out of the lab offices.

Terran gripped the back of a chair sitting by the door, on the verge of whipping it across the room. This entire situation—Maya missing, all the unanswered questions, a man who walked around wearing only pants, their constant lack of footwear—was all an illogical farce. Still, only one path led to answers, so Terran followed behind the bronzed male as he padded, shoeless, out of the building.

Stripping off his lab coat, Terran draped it across a chair in the front lobby. "April, I'm heading out for the rest of the day. I'm not sure if I'll be in tomorrow. I'll call in the morning." He left his smiling receptionist and hoofed after Nodin who was halfway across the parking lot, heading towards his truck.

Nodin stopped at the passenger door and waited, watching his approach before stating, "We need to drive to a more secluded area."

Terran jammed a hand in his pocket, pulled out his keys, and clicked open the locks, but remained standing at the back of his truck. "I'm finding it difficult to accommodate you, but I'll agree if you take me to Maya."

Nodin kicked the stainless steel running board. "Drive to the top of Signal Mountain, and I'll take you to her."

Terran's head pounded with an overwhelming intensity. He rubbed his temples and swallowed hard as nausea threatened. "How sick is she?"

Nodin snapped to attention at his question. "How do you know she's unwell?"

"I just do."

"Then accommodating me should be easy. You understand we have no time to waste."

Terran huffed out an aggravated sigh, but jumped in the driver's seat.

Nodin guided them along an overgrown track that climbed vertically toward the mountaintop. Terran struggled to believe Maya awaited them there. Nothing about this computed in his rational mind. And yet the relief of finally getting answers solidified his intent. Where would this path truly lead? And why was Nodin, instead of Maya, leading him to the answers needed to relieve this sour tremor in his gut.

They reached the top without another word between them, until Nodin said, "This will do."

Terran pressed on the brake and slid the truck into Park.

"Follow me." Nodin stepped out.

Sparing him a sideways glance, Terran followed as Nodin trudged through the forest for about two miles, and then stopped along the side of a snowy peak. Silence reigned. The only proof of life was their footprint trail in the snow behind them.

Nodin stood barefoot in snow up to his ankles, apparently immune to the cold.

Perhaps Terran had been led here by Nodin as food for those marauding vampires, recently loosed in the mountains. At this point, that seemed a plausible explanation.

Nodin lifted his arms and face to the sky—like an ancient Indian in the throes of sun worship.

He laughed. "Sun worship? Really? You study the earth and everything it's composed of, yet there is much you do not comprehend. Maya needs you. She may reach an end without you. Are you willing to go to her?"

"Why did you mention sun worship? Wait...end? What end?" Terran grabbed Nodin's arm. "When will you start making sense?"

Nodin just shrugged.

"Of course, I want to go to her." He released his hold on Nodin and kicked the snow at his feet. "What are we doing up here? She's not here and the hospital is back that way." Terran jerked his thumb toward his parked truck.

"No, Earthman, she isn't here. But this path we've begun will lead you to discover truths that will not correlate with your narrow-minded understanding of the world and current scientific fact. If you choose to stand beside me, know your life will change in ways you've never imagined."

Earthman? What the hell is he talking about?

This whole scenario hit a new level of insanity. Odd did not even begin to describe Nodin's behavior. The vampire theory was actually looking reasonable at this point.

"Terran, if I were a vampire, how could I be out during the day? Maya is attempting to heal from damage done by a very dark evil. A real evil. Little time remains. Mother believes you're the only one capable of healing her. Choose."

A gentle breeze spun around Terran's body. The draft calmed his confusion and created a link with Nodin—a kinship, a core of trust. He closed his eyes, and the vision of the pool came to him. The film on the pool's surface cleared. He now saw beneath and knew what he had to do. "Take me to her."

Nodin shuffled a little and rocked back on his feet, still buried in snow. "We need to hug."

"What?" Terran lifted a hand, warding him off.

Nodin cursed, grumbling something about his Mother, but spread open his arms and gestured for Terran to step forward.

"I'm doing this for Maya." Terran wrapped his arms around Nodin in an awkward bear hug. If Nodin asked him for a kiss, he was heading back down the mountain. Alone.

"Ah, Terran, I'm hurt. I've been told I'm a very good kisser." A hearty laugh shook Nodin's chest, rumbling against Terran's body.

Strange, how does he know what I'm thinking? Terran started to draw back, a few choice words on his tongue, when a strong wind beat against their bodies. The brisk breeze stirred through his hair and whipped against his clothes then he held nothing but air. Nodin had disappeared.

What the hell?

An air funnel stirred the snow at his feet and circled around him. Once the current reached his head, only a stir brushed upon his skin before he was lifted off the ground. Disoriented, he tried to scramble back to earth, but the vortex tightened around his body. A great fog enveloped him and cool air blasted against his face. His body went horizontal, and his muscles locked tight as he jetted across the sky.

How is this possible? Did I ingest a hallucinogen at the lab?

Frozen in place, he traveled through the upper atmosphere. The earth flew by in a blur of greens and browns.

Where has Nodin gone?

Terran bit his lip to determine if he could still feel the pain. *Very real.* The smell of the ocean cleared his senses. *How far has this wind tunnel travelled if I'm near an ocean?* The air temperature went frigid, and an icy mist formed on his skin. The faint squawk of seagulls further alerted him to water's presence.

His body flipped. Vertically. Diving headfirst—a perpendicular plunge. Terran tried to lift his arms over his head in order to ease into the water. The whirlwind refused any movement as he sped through the air, like an arrow straight toward the sea.

Braced for contact, Terran held his breath as the ocean waved in welcome. He tensed and closed his eyes, but the impact was minimal. His natural instincts, however, struck with maximum force, and he scissor kicked toward the water's surface. *A futile fight.* The air cyclone swirled his body deeper and deeper.

Panic engulfed him and he struggled against invisible bonds. Gasping for air, surrounded by water, and continuing the plunge, his survival reflex hit red alert at the unnatural state of his body.

A voice reverberated in his head. Nodin's voice. *"I will not let you drown. Breathe. Relax your body, my brother."*

Lips locked against his mouth, and he was finally able to breathe. Terran had always wondered what he would do in a life-or-death situation. Apparently, kissing a man fell in the "do" category. If, in fact, he was locking lips with a man, he'd left all rational thought back on the mountaintop.

Ears popping, his body a human popsicle, he traveled farther into the sea's sapphire depths. Water pressure started compressing his body. Sure death was imminent, he relaxed and let it come. But then, his body shifted direction. No longer heading straight down, he leveled out, and then shot vertical. He surfaced like a rocket and erupted onto a rocky, moss-covered platform. Gasping for air, he filled his lungs—more a natural reaction to an unnatural submersion than out of any true loss of breath. He rolled onto his back and observed his surroundings. Above him, bright light shined down, making him blink against the glare. Somehow, his glasses had remained on his face. Somehow, he was alive.

His body trembled from the cold, and he scrunched into a fetal position, trying to get warm. He glanced around, noting this cave was similar to the one in his dreams. *Or the same cave.*

A shimmery light crossed the floor and stopped right before his eyes. The beam continued its trail over his body, heating him from the inside out. Only the tip of his nose retained its chill when he felt the hairs on the back of his neck rise in attention.

Someone stood behind him.

Heart pounding, he sat up and turned around.

A woman, with a hazy golden glow surrounding her, watched him from her stance in the rocky cave. Otherworldly. Not human. Standing over eight feet tall, her auburn hair branched out as if she were an ancient redwood hidden deep in the forest. Her amber skin glimmered when she knelt beside him. Her eyes were the color of a blade of grass in spring.

Mother Nature.

Calmness swept through him, as if he'd been hypnotized by her beauty. How he knew who and what she was, he could not say. But in that moment, he understood exactly—awareness exploded in his mind. Awed by her, he bent his head.

He felt his body warm in her presence, and his connection to his current environment became magnified by an intense degree. The bond to the earth, and an understanding of how he fit, clicked like a final puzzle piece in his mind. *And yet, is this real? Can this truly be Mother Nature?* Doubt prickled as he regained his senses.

Mother held something in her arms. Protectively, cradling the figure. She brushed her chin across the wet clumps of blonde hair—Maya's hair.

As the shot of recognition rocked him, he noted Maya's pale skin. His nightmares of the past week were now very real. Maya's body trembled in Mother's arms.

A sweet song echoed through the cave but did not ease her shudders.

Maya jerked and screamed his name. Her intense cry struck him with a vision of her bound to a stake that had been lit on fire, and the flames were devouring her body.

Terran stood, intent on soothing her pain.

Mother raised a hand, and her stick fingers beckoned him closer.

Maya's raspy breathing filled the silence.

Mother stroked her face tenderly as he stood beside them. Then the woman's golden hand reached out and she brushed a stray hair from his forehead—a mother's touch, the kind given to a child after they've fallen and scraped their knee.

A breeze ruffled Mother's red locks. Nodin appeared at her side.

The presence of someone from an existence Terran understood brought reality front and center. "I don't understand. This woman, she is… and Maya she…she needs medical attention. Take her, please. Just like you took me, however, whatever, you did, take her now. She needs a hospital."

Again, a voice reverberated in his mind. A musical lilt accompanied the words when a soft feminine accent spoke in a comforting whisper. *"Terran, you are Earth. You are the thread that binds us all. We are all connected through your unifying force. You are the great accommodator. Without the earth, the air would not flow freely. The fire would have no foundational spark. And Maya, she is the spring rain making your blossoms grow. She chips away at your shores and you yield to her, letting her sway against you."*

Mother bent and handed him the shivering bundle. Maya was weightless, like some fairy waif this golden woman had conjured from another plane of existence.

"Lie beside her." Mother spoke out loud this time, and the lyrical splendor of her voice almost brought tears to his eyes. "She must find refuge in your strength. Water does not exist without the earth. Let her anchor at your shore. She must grab the thread of your stabilizing connection, and once that ties into place, her fight to follow your link to the surface begins. Give her the will to join with the living. Call to her. You are the only one who can lead her home. Her mortality begins and ends with you—the blessed earth."

Nodin dropped to his knees next to Terran, fear obvious in his glassy blue gaze. "I know you have questions, but now is not the time. Lie beside her. Let your spirit envelop her. Please."

Terran's mind refused to accept this empty shell in his arms was really Maya. She couldn't be this close to death. This whole situation was incomprehensible. "I don't believe in spirits or souls. I believe in hospitals and doctors. Those are what she needs. I cannot heal her."

"You must believe in your connection with her, Earthman, or she will die—a final death. The perpetual rebirth she experiences will no longer occur." Nodin tugged on his pant leg. "Please, undress."

His arms tensed around the cold body in his arms. "Why do you keep referring to me as Earthman? And why in the hell would I undress? What happens then? How is that supposed to heal her? I don't believe in ancient medicine man bullshit. Spirits do not commune with each other. Look. At. Her." He knelt with Maya in his arms. "She needs a hospital. Belief in healing by nature does not work. Medicine works. Now get her out of here. Wherever here is."

Mother moved beside him, the smell of freshly tilled earth circulated through the air. She bent and pressed her hands to his cheeks. "Become one with your nature."

A series of pictures flashed through his mind—a seed sprouting, corn stalks standing tall, piglets rolling in the mud, and a field of green lily pads floating upon a lake, their yellow blossoms straining in his direction.

Mother brushed a hand over his head. Her eyes seemed to shimmer as they gazed into his. Hypnotizing him into serenity. "Do not fight your new reality. Cast aside all doubts. Free your mind to absorb the truth. Love is not a fact. It is a belief. The question now becomes, do you love her enough to believe?"

Do I love her? How could he when he had no idea who or what she was? Still, what choice did he have? He couldn't very well let her die. Terran handed Maya back to Mother and undressed to his boxer briefs. If someone didn't show up with reality show cameras soon, he'd start to question his sanity. He couldn't escape this cave alone, so he'd play along with their little theatric production. "What now?"

Mother gently nudged his shoulder. "Lie on your side."

As Terran did, he watched as Nodin stripped off his clothes as well, which took all of a second since the man didn't grasp the concept of proper outwear.

"I understand it, Terran. I just choose to live unencumbered."

Terran narrowed his eyes at Nodin, unsure how he'd picked up on his thoughts. *Again.* Actually if Nodin could read his mind right now, he'd get a very clear picture of how he felt about all this.

Feelings he would refrain from revealing in front of a lady. "I'm sorry, ma'am, but who are you?" He knew, but sanity was returning, bringing reason laced with apprehension.

"Terran, you know who I am." Her voice echoed through the cave. "The clarity before you is blurred by your rational mind. Now is not the time to focus on your internal war." Mother laid Maya beside him. "Focus instead on healing."

Nervous laughter erupted from him. *Right, empty my mind.* Perhaps next she'd give him a yellow-haired voodoo doll and tell him to pet it every day. *Where are the chickens and toadstools?*

"Terran, wrap your arms around her," Mother's lyrical voice commanded. "She is not a doll, but flesh and water."

Nodin gripped his hand. "Do it, brother. The only chicken here is you."

Apparently, reading his mind was another inexplicable item of the day. Sure that his brain was unable to handle any further discoveries, he followed their directive, spread out on his side, and drew Maya close. Her body shivered so, what the hell, he closed his eyes and envisioned the sun generating heat through nuclear fusion. Regardless of his current alternate reality, energy radiating as heat from the sun remained a fact. He clung to that one iota of normalcy.

What was not normal was what he held tight in his arms. If not for the short intermittent puffs of breath against his chest, he would believe her dead. Death, what had Nodin nattered on about a final death and perpetual rebirth? She was no doubt suffering from hypothermia from this dank cave and her soaked skin. How had she lost so much weight since he'd last seen her? Would she ever recover from this wasting disease? Maya's bones protruded from under her skin. A wilted petal was all that remained of his bright yellow lily.

Blonde tufts of her semi-dry hair stuck out all around her head. Racked with occasional shudders from the cold, she whimpered out soft cries. Her lips and skin were an unnatural hue of blue.

Nodin sank next to them and wrapped his body around her back. At his ease, he began a native tribal chant.

Mother stood behind Nodin and stared down at their entwined bodies.

A vision of Cerberus, the three-headed hellhound, rose in Terran's mind. With their three heads together, he imagined they resembled the beast.

Mother laughed. The musical sound flowed through the chamber, and her voice was like soft velvet when she spoke, "Do not worry, my son, I do not have the power to transform you into such a creature."

An understanding smile lit her ethereal face and reassured him somehow. As if he was a child and she was pleased he had learned a lesson.

Her skin gleamed with gold and green sparkles before her entire body shimmered and disappeared to whatever plane of fairyland existence she lived on—perhaps she was a magician. His mind *had* left the building. Nothing in his knowledge base explained anything that had happened.

Nodin had warned him at the top of the mountain.

Quite an inadequate preparation for this particular scenario.

If they thought he had questions before, they'd be overwhelmed by the overflow in his mind now.

Maya shivered again, immediately diverting his attention. Her appearance was like a golden raisin dried too long in the sun, and then left overnight in the rain. He ran his hands over her body, accidentally brushing Nodin's arms. The contact did not, however, distract the native from his trance-like murmur.

This moment remained surreal. Terran refused to consider how the only thing separating him from a naked man was a naked wisp of a woman.

He'd been instructed to heal her—how was that possible? Only thoughts of hospital beds, nurses, and doctors came to mind. Needles and medicine were instruments his mind understood.

A play-by-play of moments spent with her flipped through his thoughts—the first time at the stream, leather boots at the strip club, her smile across the crowded bar. All lies. A mask to cover what she really was. Which was what? What kind of game were these people playing?

He had almost lost his heart to her and she...was she even human? Anger and denial at these irrational thoughts smothered his softer sentiments, like an avalanche pouring down a mountain.

He was freezing his balls off next to a corpse and a mind-reading Indian. No doubt, they'd both had their laugh keeping secrets from him. Whether or not this situation or these people, were real—he was done. Joke over.

CHAPTER 26

Nodin finally quieted.

In the silence, Terran tried to rationalize, which brought about the return of his headache, so he started talking—rambling in a one-sided conversation. All the questions lined up in bullet points in his mind flowed out, yet remained unanswered. The sound of his voice helped maintain a modicum of sanity in this insane situation. Perhaps Nodin and Maya were some organic-living-based cult or live-action role players and had somehow used magic to create this illusion.

How much longer am I supposed to lie here?

He pulled back and studied Maya's face.

What is she doing with these people? What is wrong with her body?

A medical explanation for her condition had to exist. He turned that thought over in his mind.

Is she contagious?

The rocky bed was not meant for comfortable naps, but eventually, the heat their entwined bodies created relaxed him, and he drifted off.

At the bottom of a small wooden boat, he rocked back and forth. Waves threatened to topple him over.

A blast of air against his face had him gasping for breath.

"Terran, time to wake up." Nodin jostled his shoulder.

Terran stretched and yawned as he emerged from his dream. A filmy sheen of perspiration covered his skin. Heat remained from where his body rested next to Maya. Her skin was still pale, but he noted a subtle change. Her face appeared less wrinkled. Her bones

150

were no longer like piercing shards under her skin.

"We must take her to water now." Nodin lifted her off the ground and carried her toward the back of the cave, indicating with a jerk of his head for Terran to follow.

A familiar oval, semi-deep pool gathered between the ancient rocks, creating a tub. His strange dreams now had a place of origin. The Twilight Zone theme song played, like a scratchy record, in his mind.

Nodin extended Maya over the edge and dropped her with a slight splash.

Jarred from his sci-fi zone, Terran had only one thought—get her out of the water. "What are you doing?" What kind of mental patient dropped a dying girl into a pool of water? "Are you trying to kill her? She's unconscious. She'll drown." Terran shoved Nodin out of the way and jumped over the pool's side. He lifted her and placed his ear over her left breast.

Her heart's faint vibration answered.

"Terran, you must release her. She has a symbiotic relationship with water. It is the only sustenance she requires to live."

"We all need water to live. Don't expect me to stand here and let her drown in it." He brushed Maya's wet hair from her face. If he got any angrier his jaw would crack. Ice flowed through his veins from fear, anger, disdain, disbelief. This wild range of emotions had him gripping Maya tighter. "This has gone far enough. I don't know what kind of tricks you're up to, but I'm done. I want out of here. You all can live in this Frodo-fantasy world on your own. I don't do these role-playing games."

Nodin gripped the sleeve of Terran's soaked shirt. "Listen." Wise blue eyes stared into his, and Terran heard Nodin's voice inside his head. *"She will die if you do not let her drink from this pool. The time has come for you to accept that she is more than your understanding will allow. We need you, but I will not burden you with my concerns now. When Maya has healed, we will have much to discuss, Earthman."*

Terran kept her frail body, balanced in his arms, above the pool's surface. "First off, stay out of my head. Second, you expect me to leave her in this tub where she can't breathe and the water will magically heal her? You and Mama Tall Tree have lost your minds. I do not accept this. No matter how many voices I hear in my head, I still believe Maya belongs in a hospital with doctors and medicine.

Look at her, she's dying of some wasting disease." He glanced at the hand still tight on his shirt. "Let go of me."

Nodin tightened his grip. "Tolstoy says, 'Science is meaningless because it gives no answer to our question, the only question important for us: 'What shall we do and how shall we be?'" What shall you do and who will you be, Terran?"

"*Science* is not meaningless—every word that comes out of your mouth, however, *is* senseless. The only important question here is how can *you* let her die?" His shouted response boomed through the cave. Could he compromise his entire belief system and let her float in this icy pool?

"Terran, you must compromise." Nodin gripped the side of the pool and met his gaze. "This moment couldn't be any more real. You know what you should do and how the water will affect her. Release your disbelief. I need to regain my strength on the surface. I will return shortly with food and drink. Please, release her into the water. Do not remove her until I return. Let her heal." Nodin stepped back and stood in the dim ray shining down from the top of the cave and once again disappeared.

Neat trick.

Terran refused to believe Nodin's magical vanishing act could be anything but that, a trick.

His only companions were the faint light from a full moon, which cast a shadowy beam into the cave, and a hollow water-girl whose life seemed perched on the edge of those shadows. The cave's environment reminded him of a PBS special he'd watched on a Sacred Cenote in Chichén Itzá. What type of sacrifices had dropped from the well above? Gold? Jade? Virgins?

No matter, now he needed to make a sacrifice. Nodin wanted Maya placed in her tub to drown then that's where he'd put her. Maybe some show of compliance would have them surrendering their ridiculous roles.

His gaze scanned over her half-comatose body, still so weak and frail. The overwhelming sense of compassion remaining for her irritated him. Even half-dead, she still made him feel more alive than he ever had, but at what cost? She'd never been honest about anything. Though, she'd had plenty of opportunities to explain her lifestyle.

What is wrong with her body? Why did I dream of this pool? What am I meant to do now?

He stood with the wet bundle in his arms until a faint voice—Maya's voice—reverberated in his head. *"Release me."*

"What?" He lowered his ear to her lips, but he felt only a slight puff of her breath against his skin. He shivered, surely on the verge of hypothermia in this ice-cold water. How long could he stand here holding her above the water? If he let her go would she really heal? His sense of right and wrong clashed heavily in his mind. He readjusted her in his arms.

Her hand escaped his grasp and fell into the water. She moaned and arched away from his body. *"Please."*

Fine. Unbelievable, but apparently what she wanted.

He placed a hard goodbye kiss against Maya's head and released her into the "sacred well."

# # #

Five hours! Five hours had passed. Luckily his waterproof watch still worked, or unluckily, since he was still stuck in this deserted well able to watch the passage of time.

Terran paced back and forth in front of Maya's pool, like a guard on duty over an alien species. Every half-hour, he vaulted into the water and tested her pulse, amazed her heart still pumped in her watery grave. His body started to resemble hers, although he looked more like a hairy prune. Half-frozen, he sank to the ground and wrapped both arms around his knees in an attempt to retain body heat. The effects of no caffeine or food turned his already sour state into an acid rage.

Watching a flaming bolt shoot down from the cave opening, he worried his anger had presented in a disembodied form. A man emerged from the flames, steam billowing off his naked body. A flash of recollection crossed Terran's mind from the night he and Maya took their drive out to the lake.

What is his name? Hadn't he been naked the last time, as well? The details were vague. Immunity had set in from the constant state of undress these people seemed to have no trouble exhibiting.

Fireman produced a silver backpack from over his shoulder and pulled out a pair of jeans, which he tugged on. He dug into the pack and produced a pair of black sweatpants and a sweatshirt then tossed them at Terran's feet. "Sweats are easier than trying to guess your size. I'm Flint."

Terran raised a single brow.

Flint just shrugged and tapped his temple then handed over a Coke bottle and a paper-wrapped breakfast sandwich.

Terran placed the food on the floor and shrugged into the sweatshirt, taking a moment to appreciate the soft cotton before sliding on the pants.

Fireman walked to the pool and peered over the edge. "She's looking better."

"Where the hell is Nodin? She's been sitting in that water for hours. I want answers, or I'm taking her out." He grabbed the soda bottle off the ground. "Imagine that, it's hot." He closed his eyes and prayed for calm. "Not only that, you expect me to sit here and believe she's not dying in there, but healing. I don't appreciate having to baby-sit a corpse." Terran hurled the bottle against the cave wall.

The soda crashed and sprayed before fizzing to a stop on the rocks beneath.

"Still, such a child," Flint reflected, as the bottle rocked on the floor and poured out its carbonated contents.

"If she dies, I don't care what kind of symbiotic relationship you or Nodin have with her, or whatever the hell you flaming fucks believe. I will take you down."

"Flaming fucks?" A burst of laughter followed. "Surely, you can do better than that."

Terran dove at Flint's legs, which knocked him back but not down. A barrage of intense heat struck where he held Flint. Terran tried to push past the burn, but the heat was too intense. His arm hairs curled and the air filled with a nasty burnt hair smell.

A firewall flickered between them, so he backed off, more than pissed at these games.

"Drop the magic tricks, Flint. Let's see who'd win then." Feet braced apart, Terran stared down Flint, daring him to step forward. A flare within the flames stretched out, and stopped an inch from his nose. Unaffected, Terran remained still.

A funnel of fire swirled around him. Terran took a moment to enjoy the heat against his half-frozen body. As quickly as it had formed, the flaming vortex dropped and created a fire circle on the stone floor. Terran picked up his sandwich and pointed a finger at Flint. "You're crazy."

"Insanity runs in this family, brother." Flint laughed and plopped down within the flaming ring, making himself at home. "Actually, I did go through a few years of insanity after I first turned. I'd been working on the Hypatian Codex, at the Ipatiev Monastery in Kostroma, Russia, translating from the sixth century Greek manuscript of John Malalas. I'd become entranced with learning all I could of Svarog, the Slavic god of celestial fire and blacksmithing. Little did I know I would soon follow in his footsteps. I imagine I've had various sparks of insanity since my transformation. Something pleasant for you to look forward to, insanity can run hand-in-hand with being peri-mortal. I wonder how you'll handle it, Earthman."

This Earthman moniker started to grate. "Interesting bio. Did you come up with that all by yourself? How about using your memory recall to focus on the fact that I'm still human?" Terran rubbed his palms together over the fire. "Turn up the flames on your little campfire. I'm already at stage one hypothermia in this death dungeon I've been dropped into by your buddy and Mother Nature."

A little bonfire formed between them, while the outer circle sputtered out. Terran rubbed his nose, trying to ignite circulation into the icy tip.

Flint stood and again made his way to Maya's pool. He stuck a hand inside the water and steam wafted off the surface. "Maya's not a corpse. The water will heal her. Water is who she is, as I am fire and Nodin is air. You, my mad scientist, will be Earth. We are the Elementals. You've been allowed a glimpse into our world prior to your transformation. Count yourself blessed. Nodin and Maya were offered no warning or prior understanding."

"Elementals? Right, like some kind of superhero team?" Terran mindlessly chewed his sandwich, wishing he hadn't wasted his carbonated caffeine in a burst of rage.

"I've claimed many titles throughout my vast lifetime, so call me what you will. But accept this, the water and your presence *will* heal Maya. Mother believes your destined relationship will fill in the emptiness she needs to resurface. Quint almost destroyed her. I find I do not wish for her to die. She exudes a liveliness, a cleansing spirit I am drawn to. Mother has instructed that you remain here. I will return to sit with you, but for now, I must go and gather my strength."

The inevitability of Terran's circumstances began to clarify. "I don't really care what you wish or what Mother has instructed. I want out. And believe me when I say, Maya dying due to your mystical-powers nonsense will not go unanswered by every law enforcement agency I can convince to believe me." Terran stopped eating, concerned about the presence of mind-altering drugs in his sandwich.

"Earthman," Flint scoffed, "if I wanted to make you believe something, I'd compel your mind. I don't need to drug you."

"What do you want from me?" Terran crumpled the sandwich wrapper in his hand. "Who are you?"

"I am a part of you. Can't you feel our bond, brother?" Flint tapped Terran's stomach with a fist. "I am your core. I live in your belly. I form the fire, you now feel. It courses through your blood as anger, as denial. But the flame exists, you will see. We will work together, fight together. We're all a part of you. Maya needs your strength. Do not doubt you will deliver her from this abyss."

"Right, I forgot, my super hero name is Abyss-Deliverer." Terran pinched the bridge of his nose. This tale just got taller. "Everything's much clearer now. I'll just use my Earthman powers and cover her in dirt. Is that how it works?"

Flint laughed and slapped him on the back. "You are quite funny. Each gift works differently. I have been reduced to embers many times, only to spark again. I am a Phoenix, rising from the ashes." When Flint raised his arms at his sides, fire spread out like wings under his arms before fading to smoke. He pointed a finger at Terran. "And you will be a pig, Earthman, wallowing in mud. *That* is how it works."

Flint was still chuckling as he stood in the bright morning ray shooting down from the well. "I will return. My volcanic sustenance, Kīlauea, awaits."

CHAPTER 27

Morning passed and an afternoon sunbeam lit the cave with a single circular ray. Terran peered over the rocky tub's rim. Maya's hair was no longer in tufts. Voluminous golden waves now floated around her face and shoulders.

Her eyes opened.

Terran stumbled and grasped the rocky edge for balance.

Water bubbles floated to the surface due to her wide smile.

"Not funny." He rubbed his chest where his heartbeat kicked against his chest.

Her enticing curves were back in full glory. Her slim arms lifted out of the pool.

He hooked his hands under her arms and pulled her up.

"Move back, please." Standing in the pool, she shook the water from her hair and upper body, like a wet cocker spaniel fresh from its bath. Again, she reached for him.

He hefted her semi-dry form out of the pool then carried her to the only level spot in the rocky cave and placed her on the ground.

Maya shot him a quick glance then crossed both arms over her chest. "So you're here."

"Yeah, been here for a while now." He averted his gaze from her perfectly toned body—perfectly *healthy* body. How could she entice him when every molecule in his body warned against her allure?

"I see," Maya responded.

Her gaze remained intent on his, as if...*Damn it.* "If you are doing that mind-reading trick, I'd caution against it. You might not like the thoughts in my head. I don't want anything upsetting you and forcing me to stay longer to 'heal' you." *Heal her*—as if that whole scheme hadn't been some farce. What was the truth? He couldn't deny the proof of her restored body.

"Of course." Her hand shook as she brushed a strand of hair from her face.

He removed his sweatshirt and passed it over. "Your role-playing partners are really good at their game."

She held his shirt frozen in mid-air. "But Terran, surely you understand that you did heal me. I was—"

"No." He raised a hand, palm out. "I don't want to hear the ridiculous tale from you, too. If you choose to live this kind of lifestyle, that is fine, I don't judge. But I've never been much of an actor. I can't fake how I feel, Maya, so drop the pretense."

She pulled the sweatshirt over her head, where it settled at mid-thigh. She padded closer and with an unsteady hand reached up to touch his face.

He jerked away. "Don't."

Tears glimmered, but she kept her gaze locked with his. "Terran, please, I know there are many things I did not tell you but you said… that night, you said…that—"

"Maya, the time for you to answer questions has passed, all right?" He pinched the bridge of his nose. Maybe if he pinched hard enough, he could hold back the pain of betrayal throbbing behind his temples. Maybe he could forget that this woman had ruptured his heart. "I don't want any part of this. I'm sorry to upset you. I realize you are ill, so let's bypass this discussion and concentrate on getting out of here so we can get on with our lives."

He couldn't do this. He had to leave this cave, this woman. His imagination stirred with thoughts that didn't compute. He'd never truly known who she was. Even now with her body laid bare before him, nothing made sense. How had she regained her health so quickly? From a deflated piece of rubber to a full-blown rosy, pink balloon that had a silky string wrapped around his finger. How could that thread still exist? He refused to accept its pull. He'd break it. Cut it off.

But reality blurred—a shining braid crisscrossed with blues, browns, and greens glimmered in a strand between them. Taunting his mind with an unrealistic vision. Pushing him to the edge of sanity. The silky string tugged against his heart, to forgive her, to believe in the purity of what they'd shared.

He shook his head and closed his eyes. When, he opened them again, the thread had vanished and along with it any thought of remaining by her side. He had to escape this nonsensical prison. He was hallucinating for shit's sake.

"Maya, please, just get me out of this cave. I hope you'll continue to get better, but your recovery will be without me."

CHAPTER 28

Defiant. Distant. Lost. He'd shied away from her touch.

Maya did as he wished and stayed out of his mind. Peering inside would most likely cut deeper than any black blade Quint possessed. The dark matter deluge had mostly washed away, but the wounds Terran inflicted would ice over and never fully melt. This rejection on top of her physical pain wasn't fair. A scream stopped at the top of her throat. Her hands clenched with the need to rip out her hair, destroy everything and all. A raw desire to fling herself in Terran's arms and beg him to take her, to understand, to love her, snaked through her body, hissing, and striking against her brain. He wasn't the only one who begged for escape.

Why? Why heal her only to deliver more pain?

She forced her emotions behind a wall, slammed it shut, boarded it, and locked it down. Knowing all along this was her true fate, she had to let him go.

Drawing a deep breath, she turned to face him, her stoic mask firmly in place.

He stood in the light shining down from the hole in the well. Dust particles swirled around his body, free to float and drift before gently falling to earth. Her heart was no longer welcome to circle and spin in the comfort of Terran's sphere. Her reality had slammed into his consciousness and crashed into oblivion.

She raised a hand to touch him, but drew back, knowing he would not welcome her comfort. "When Nodin returns, you may go. I would deliver you, but I cannot leave as yet. I need to drink from this well Mother has prepared a little while longer." She turned away and stared at her reflection in the pool, before running her hand across the warbled image. "Terran, please know that I am truly sorry for the trouble I have caused you. I tried to remain in the background, but circumstances forced us together. If your wish is for our friendship to end then I understand."

Destiny was for fairytales and children's books, not Elemental girls and human boys. The night they spoke at the stream, he'd made clear what he believed, but she had maintained her presence by his side. Attempting to keep him safe, yes, but also because she refused to walk away. Now, once more, his choice was clear.

Terran spun her around. "Friendship? We were never friends. Friends have a certain level of trust between them. You are incapable of telling the truth. I don't know if you are so wrapped up in this world you can't see that, or what?" He paused for a moment, and when he continued, his words sliced across her heart. "One thing is clear, though, you are completely insane for letting them do whatever they did to your body. You should have seen yourself. You almost died."

This last was shouted out, and she, mentally and physically, eased away from his fury.

Her heart gave one last thump before it squeezed dry and wilted in her chest—dead just like her. Wasn't this what she deserved? She'd lived her life in deceit, both as a human and as an elemental. She played with people's minds and their lives freely. Actions had consequences. Mother had asked her to prepare him, and she'd kept him in the dark. Her tendency to strike her own path foiled her once again.

"You are right, Terran, living this Elemental life I did almost die. But not in the way you think. I was supposed to prepare you and I failed. So let me tell you the truth now—all of this isn't a game or magic." In her palm, she formed a pool of water, and then dripped the trickle down her fingers and onto his arm. "We are real. Our gifts are real. I did heal in the water."

"Enough!" He knocked her hand away. "I don't know why you picked me for this little farce, but I'm not falling for any of it. If anything, get help, Maya. I'll admit you had me going, and for that, I doubt I'll ever forgive you. You're a misguided mess."

His words struck like ice picks against her frozen heart. "What mess?" She pulled her hair back from her face until the pain tore at her scalp.

"Nodin, Flint, and the tall lady."

"You've met Mother and you still doubt?"

"Doubt is too small a word for how I feel, believe me."

"And you think I belong in a white jacket in some asylum. Well, welcome to the loony bin, Terran. Believe *me*, you'll fit right in." She shouldered past him. Weak from the fight, she sought solace in her pool. In here, he couldn't see her falling tears. Couldn't see that with each word, her heart iced over, layer by layer. As she plunged into her pool she wondered, why was there no cure for heartbreak when it's the mostly deadly disease of all?

CHAPTER 29

The blessed smell of coffee alerted Terran to another presence in the cave. He ignored the visitor and finished laying out his still wet work clothes.

Nodin appeared by his side with a paper cup in his hand, shaking a fast food bag. "Burger?"

Terran reached for the huge coffee cup. The warmth instantly heated his cold fingers. After removing the plastic lid, he blew against the liquid's dark surface.

"Need some help with that?" Nodin offered with a chuckle.

"No, I'm good." Terran refrained from rolling his eyes before biting into the semi-warm sandwich. Hamburger, cheese, and a sesame seed bun had never tasted so good.

When he got out of this freezing hole in the ground, he'd grill an enormous steak and savor each juicy bite. He'd follow that with a monster brownie, covered in hot fudge. For now, a second burger would have to do.

Rejuvenated with food and caffeine, Terran deliberated the best way of convincing Nodin to deliver him from this well.

Yet, there were still so many unanswered questions. And doubt, that slippery slope, had wheedled its way into his brain. Maya had seemed so genuine. Unshed tears had shimmered in her eyes before she'd escaped into her watery isolation. How was she breathing in that pool? He hadn't located any air tanks. No apparatus was attached to her nose or mouth. *So how?*

And how had her body healed from its previous deathlike state?

He'd been here the whole time, so how had they cured her? What if they were telling the truth? *Earthmen, water-girls, flaming firemen, tree ladies, and wind funnels—in this reality two plus two did not equal four.* He'd turned this puzzle over in his mind for hours. *What am I missing? Did I depict them as live-action role players to keep my sanity?* His head ached from overanalyzing his situation and caffeine-deprivation. One cup of coffee barely scratched the surface of his addiction.

Terran wiped his mouth with a napkin from the bottom of the bag and glanced at Nodin, who watched him with a quirked grin and raised brow. "All right, Nodin, let's say for a few minutes I'm willing to swallow this tale. I'd like some answers if you don't mind. That's the least I can ask after being kept here."

Nodin waved his hand before him, indicating his wish for Terran to proceed.

Terran paced in the late-afternoon sunbeam pouring down from the top of the well. "I'm unclear how I fit in all this. Why do you keep calling me Earthman? How do you know what I'm thinking? Where do you go when you leave? How does the water heal Maya?"

"The answers I can give you will never compute in your rational mind, Terran. You must look into your heart. Close your eyes and feel your connection to the earth and to each of us."

"Do you realize how insane you sound?" He stopped pacing and gripped his hair in his hands. He didn't want to look into his heart, the rawness and ache of duplicity was blocking the red pulse. Because Maya, she…hadn't she…he deleted her from his thoughts, took a deep breath, and focused on Nodin. "I don't process concepts in an irrational manner. Facts are real. I need some way to classify this information in my mind."

"What about this doesn't feel real?" Nodin raised his hand and delivered a blast of air across his face. "Your denial does nothing but waste time. We are at war."

A strong wind whipped through the cave beating against him, but not a single hair stirred on Nodin's head. "War against whom? And I'm cold enough as it is, I don't need the special effects."

"Maya did not have time to properly prepare you. But, that is irrelevant now, we must move forward. Our basic life facts have been shown to you. I was not given the same opportunity to reject or embrace this life, and yet, I have walked this earth a very long time. Think long on accepting this offered gift. As Earthman, you represent our core. Embrace your power. Acknowledge fate. You've been given a perfect mate in Maya. I would be proud to walk beside her through this life, but she is not for me."

A mate? "And if I refuse?"

"Then we will walk away from you forever."

"You'll leave?" Terran walked over to the pool and checked on Maya.

What is she doing in there?

"We will have no choice. I ask you to consider how much more you can give back to the earth. Your intelligence, added to a peri-mortal life, strength, and the ability to transform, will be an advantage. The capacity to glean the actions of others and their intentions will also be given." Nodin stood beside him at Maya's pool. "Using your mechanical mind to process the most strategic step forward will be an asset to our team. With each passing day, our environment grows worse. Take the tools offered to stem the tide of destruction. You may say no and walk away. We can make you forget. Another Earthman will be born. The cycle always repeats." He swirled a circle in the water with his finger.

Terran turned away and walked back to the warmth and link to reality found in the sun's beam. "You think you're immortal? And you can detect, or 'glean' as you say, what I am thinking right now? On top of that, you believe you can change my thought patterns?"

"Not immortal, we are peri-mortal. Do you know what a "Peri" is?"

Terran shook his head.

"The mythology has been misinterpreted. Peri's are thought to be spirits who have been denied paradise until they have done penance three times. Not completely accurate, as we were *chosen* by Mother Nature, but our mortality *is* perpetual. Our elemental sustenance is required to sustain our life force. If Maya were to go without water for a time she would die. If I were placed in a vacuum, I'd cease to exist. As for redirecting your mind, we've done so on a few occasions."

"We?" He narrowed his eyes at Nodin. "When?" He'd consider this peri-mortal notion later.

Nodin laughed and shook his head. "The night you and Maya stopped at the stream. I made you forget a few minor details. Delving into your mind and switching your gears wasn't easy. And now, your mind is full of human concerns and disbelief. Maya and fears for her health also weigh heavily."

"So my role in all of this is as this Earthman character? What happened to the last one?"

An air of sadness crossed Nodin's face, and he pursed his lips before glancing away.

A ripple and faint splash came from the pool.

"Maya stirs. I'll leave you to learn your answers."

"Wait. One last thing, why did you take me through the ocean when you first brought me here? You could have dropped me down from the well."

Nodin slapped him on the back. "After all those dreams of yours, you were expecting water, so I gave it to you." Nodin's deep chuckle vibrated off the walls as he spun into an air funnel and whipped up and out.

This Elemental thing just might be worth it for payback alone.

# # #

Maya opened her eyes and swallowed a deep gush of water. It filtered through her body, washing away pain, but sloshing right past her heart. Terran was still here. The tingle thrumming through her body in his presence had not dissipated. Her worst fear had played out, like a bad horror movie before her eyes. She was different—not welcome in his arms. And yet, she could not stop the need to soak up every moment with him before everything was erased from his memory.

Can I request the same clean slate?

Rising from the water, she glanced around the cavern, anxious to see him. Life coursed through her body, and the water droplets streaming down enhanced awareness of Terran on every level. She shook off the lingering liquid and flipped back her dry hair. Her absorption levels remained high and would until all the murky matter delivered by Quint was cleansed.

Terran stood with his face tilted toward the sky, his view transfixed by the exit above. Keeping him here so long was unfair. He had a human life outside of her world.

She stepped out of the pool and padded to his side. "Terran? Are you all right?"

His gaze took in the entire scope of her body, and then locked on her lips. "You appear much better."

A cloud of sexual awareness surrounded them. A very vivid picture projected into her mind of them entwined together. His kiss in the vision was not gentle, but punishing.

She gasped; surprised he could desire her still. Her fear he would not chose this Elemental life remained, but her greater fear was for his safety against Quint's twisted plans. She shuddered at the reminder of Quint's plan to use her as a pawn against Terran.

"Terran..." She stepped forward. Ready to answer the need in his eyes, in his mind.

But once more, he held back. "Maya, please don't." He turned to speak, but just huffed out a breath. "Right now...I'm unclear on a lot of things. And you...whatever you think you are, whatever this is, you are still the biggest...the most... I'm at a loss of how to even speak rationally at this point." He ran a hand over his stubbled chin and shook his head. "I just want away from this place."

Every bit of her wanted to turn him to ice, strike back against his rejection. But, none of this was his fault. Innocent, he was so innocent, and only a bystander in this hazy existence.

"Terran, I know I have no right to ask, but I'd appreciate if you would, for a moment, suspend disbelief and hear me out."

He crossed both arms against his chest then waved a few fingers in her direction. "I believe I'm a captive audience."

"Would you like to know how old I am?"

"Sure, if that's where you want to start."

"I was born in 1877, and I died in 1898."

CHAPTER 30

I was the only child of a couple who had me later in life, and because of this, I was spoiled. They gave me trinkets and bought me pretty dresses. My mother died when I was eleven, leaving me to care for my father. I was expected to cook and clean as she had, but I had not been raised doing those chores.

I was the important one. I was the one who needed care. I grew up as a friend to the children on neighboring farms. One boy in particular, Luke Hastings, had always been enamored of me. When I came of age, he wanted to marry me. I was only interested in what he could give me—an adventure.

He wanted to head west, and after my father died, we decided to leave together. Luke promised me the world once we got there. I read an employment ad for Harvey girls out in San Francisco. They paid for the transportation and provided room and board once you arrived. Harvey girls worked in Fred Harvey's restaurants. The company was one of the first to hire women. Some say Harvey girls are what tamed the Wild West. They'd build a train stop, Harvey would put a restaurant there, fill it with girls, and they'd have a civilizing effect on all the rowdy men that came to town.

Luke and I scraped together some money, and we took the train out of St. Louis, not traveling together, of course. Harvey girls had to remain unmarried. There were always opportunities to sneak time together, though, and we found every one. We were on a real adventure. Rules were made to be broken. However, once we settled in California, things did not turn out as we planned.

He worked as a brakeman for the Frisco line, and I worked as a Harvey girl. Hard work. I waitressed twelve hours a day, at least six days a week, and I even had to be ready in the middle of the night if a train came in off-schedule. I had to learn cup codes, how to brew coffee, and we constantly polished silverware.

The sound of a train coming no longer filled me with excitement, but with dread for the labor that would follow. Although I enjoyed my female companions, I became worn down by the long hours, and I wanted more.

In 1896, Luke joined the stampede to Canada to find riches in the Klondike Gold Rush. I stayed behind on call as a Harvey girl at the Ferry Building in San Francisco. Every time I heard the train whistle blow, I had to be prepared.

Then, His Grace, the Duke of Rutford, Edward Somerset came to town on business. The English way of life was changing, and forward-thinking men like Rutford came to America to invest in the railroads and steelworks. He set his eye on me to become his mistress. He succeeded and showed me the "more" I had been waiting for my whole life. I had my own apartment, jewels, clothes, and shoes that hadn't been worn through. As his mistress, I gave my body in return for material things. I set out to please him, and I was rewarded amply. Luckily, he didn't stay with me all the time, as he had a wife back in England, and only visited when he was in town for business.

Luke came back from the gold rush. His pockets were heavy with gold. After he learned of my relationship with Rutford, he called me a soiled dove and thrashed me good for not waiting. We were supposed to stick together and build a shop of our own. He left, but returned a month later. He begged my forgiveness, and being lonely, I acquiesced. We rekindled our love affair, but when Rutford came to town, I refused to see Luke. When Rutford left, I explained to Luke how we would continue. The Duke would provide for me, and Luke could stay as long as he skipped out when Rutford was about. The servants were loyal and wouldn't alert him.

I didn't see Luke for a few weeks, but then he visited one evening. He had a picnic basket and asked me to join him on the beach for a late-night rendezvous. At the beach, I opened the basket, which held only a bottle of wine and two glasses. He poured a glass and toasted our future together. Relieved by our reconciliation, I took a deep drink. Then, he refilled my glass.

My lips numbed and my eyelids refused to stay open. I left the sandy ground, as if floating on air. Cold water washed over me, and a salty spray rushed across my tongue. I could not move—he had drugged my wine.

I was listless as I drifted into death.

I awoke in a sea of blue, a school of fish surrounded me, and a woman floated before my eyes. Her face was too beautiful to describe. I could not encompass everything in one glance. She spoke with no voice, but an echo in my head.

"How much more do you want to be?"

I couldn't respond. I started to realize the strangeness of the situation. What was I doing in the water? I couldn't breathe. I kicked my legs, straining toward the surface, but was held in place.

"Yes, you can breathe. Free your body and mind."

Panic raced through me. Who was she? Had I died? How could I survive so deep in the ocean? Where was Luke?

Then her musical voice flowed through my mind with each waving current. "Maya Conway, you have spent the first twenty-one years of your life in selfish endeavors. That changes now. I have a plan for you, a journey, but you must put aside your petty wishes and foolish material desires. I expect more, and I will keep you here until you grasp your situation and understand you no longer live for Maya Conway alone. The world needs you. I need you. Drift, rest, and accept the elemental nature within. I will return."

# # #

"Mother's idea of 'returning' was two months later. By then, I had drifted down to a Hawaiian island. I stayed on Ni'ihau, the Forbidden Island, which had been purchased by a Scotswoman in 1864. Her descendants still owned the island, but, at the time, only natives lived there and they frequently walked the beaches to collect shells for jewelry.

I remained confused about what had happened to my body. I didn't need to eat. If I did, I'd spit the food back up. I didn't sleep and I was afraid to stray far from the water. It drew me back, over and over. Each crashing wave filled all the empty spaces inside of me, calmed me. I didn't understand what sort of witchcraft this was. I thought perhaps I should eat fish, but I couldn't digest the meat."

Maya quieted and peered over her shoulder at Terran. He had remained silent, as she'd paced through the cave, exhuming her sordid past.

"One day, when I came to shore after a long swim, the vision I'd begun to believe I'd imagined stood before me. Mother's arms opened wide. Nodin and Flint stood at her side. My first emotion was acute embarrassment, since I was stark naked. Then I felt a wash of shame for the life I had lived up until that moment. I knew my future direction had changed, and it would center on these three people."

"I could feel the energy swirling around them, so strong. And I laughed, joyous, so happy to finally be free. Unique. Important. In my human life, I'd had an inflated view of my charms, but I

170

understood I'd use them now to make a difference in the world. Why that fact crystallized for me, I don't know. Perhaps they projected those thoughts into my mind. This new path was the adventure I had sought my whole life. It confirmed why I always felt I deserved more. I sure got a lot more than I bargained for, and my life since then hasn't always been the best or the happiest. It can be very lonely. I do find a level of satisfaction, though, when I help people, especially children."

Maya leaned against the cool cave wall. Hidden in the shadows. Afraid to look into Terran's eyes, afraid she'd glean his thoughts without consciously wishing to do so. Digging into those brown depths would no doubt fell her like a blow from Quint's fist. "So that's everything—my all, every secret laid bare. Answers to those questions you've asked so many times. You've insisted I wear those tiny, glass slippers. Only my foot will not fit. My water flows straight through. Never stopping to fulfill the fantasy of who you think I am."

Terran shook his head. "You really believe all this, don't you? I wish I could as well, but I can't. Do you understand that, Maya? I'm sorry for the life you've led up until this point. Sorry you feel it necessary to create this fantasy world. I have tried to suspend my disbelief, tried to see things from your perspective. Now I ask that you see this crazy reality you've invented from mine, can you understand why your world can't be real for someone like me?" He sighed, ran his fingers through his hair, and massaged his temples.

"May I help with the pain?" Maya moved away from the wall and lifted her hand to his face.

"No." He waved her off. "I'm fine."

He'd obviously had enough, so she padded to the pool and sank against the side. Shivers brought goose bumps to her skin, though not from the cold. *Where did I put that sweatshirt?* Baring all physically, when she'd just revealed her soul, brought a rush of embarrassment. She wrapped both arms around her knees, covering herself. Nudity was a way of life, due to her transformations, but this exposure felt shameful. Did he find her body repulsive? Why, oh, why hadn't someone brought her clothes? She rested her head against her hands, linked on top of her drawn knees. As tears trailed down her cheeks, she stiffened as a scrape against the rocks indicated Terran's presence. And the heat, that vaporous haze of lust, remained between them—desire had no shame, nor pink-cheeked blush. It still raged in every shade of red.

He placed a hand on her shoulder. "Maya, this situation, it's just been...difficult. I'm more comfortable in my lab away from everyone. I'm not one for adventures like this. We should...I just...listen, we'll both be better once we're back where we belong. I'm sorry, but I can't live this life."

Maya nodded, unable to face him. His double-tap against her shoulder was more like a brotherly pat.

"*Nodin!*" She broadcasted in her mind. "*Flint. Get me out of here. Mother! I beg you to release me. Please. Please. Take me away.*"

Maya contemplated the blue-gray rock wall before her. How long had this pool existed? Would she revisit this place someday, fifty, a hundred years from now? Would it remain the same?

Even though she hadn't begun her duties with Terran, she'd finish them. She appealed to the Goddess Isis for strength, wisdom, and calm. She tugged on his sweatpants and met his gaze. "Fate has offered you a path. Choose which road to take. If you do not choose an Elemental life, you will not see me again. Nodin, Flint, and I must live in secret. As soon as this business with Quint is finished, I will go. I won't come back until you are gone." She closed her eyes, sealing tears behind her lids. Her mouth went dry, and she pinched her lips together to hold back the swelling scream. The pain inflicted by Quint was nothing compared to that final step away from Terran. She loved him and was entangled in the web of stability and humanity he'd weaved around her lonely heart.

Terran braced his arms against the rocky side of the pool. "I'm not sure who Quint is, but if you have to go, then perhaps that is for the best."

CHAPTER 31

Flint chose that moment to fire down from the top of the well. Maya rushed to his side.

"May I have this dance, Lady Conway?" Flint locked her in his arms and twirled her around the cave in an old-fashioned waltz.

The dance gave her some much-needed time to compose her shattered heart. *"Thank you for coming. Sometimes I really do love you."*

Flint dipped her before Terran. "Ms. Conway, serving you is entirely my pleasure."

Maya closed her eyes, refusing to look at Terran. He'd made his decision clear. He wanted nothing to do with her or the Elemental life. Which served as a reminder, so she halted Flint's circle around the cave. "Flint, Terran is in desperate straits. His temper rests on a very thin edge. We need to remember he is human."

Flint offered a cheeky smile and lifted her hand to his mouth for a kiss. "That's right, I forgot, human males aren't endowed with much stamina."

Maya rolled her eyes.

Flint hefted the pack off his back, unzipped it then handed her some clothes. "Sorry, Pigpen, no new clothes for you."

"No caffeine either?"

Flint shrugged. "Sorry, no. We'll get you something on the surface. Quint has switched again. His latest persona is Neb Aether, CEO of Aether Pharmaceuticals. Should have seen that one coming."

After dressing in jeans and a black sweater, Maya took Flint's hand, gathering strength through his warmth. "At the lake, Quint told me about the vaccine to fight BSE. It's a lie. His dark matter covers the prion's presence, but it's still alive and deadly. Cows who receive the vaccine may still acquire BSE, especially, if like Crowder, ranches use illegal feed. We need to stop production and destroy any delivered vaccines."

Terran wrenched her from Flint's side. "What do you know about the Mad Cow outbreak? Dr. Houser and his team from the Prion institute were unable to detect anything. You're saying this person uses dark matter to black out the prion's presence? I'm afraid I've missed something here. Who is Quint? Neb Aether is a renowned virologist. He would never be a part of false science."

Maya took a deep breath and placed her hands on his where they dug into her shoulders. "Terran, Quint *is* Neb Aether."

Flint snapped his fingers together, sparks flying with each flick. "I can see you two didn't spend much time talking. Quint is an evolved form of dark matter living inside a human host. Nodin can explain better."

Terran's brow narrowed. "Quint is a parasite?"

"Of a sort, yes." Flint agreed.

"To be clear, you believe a parasite made of dark matter is living in Neb Aether's body? And that this Quint person is what exactly?"

Maya grasped Terran's upper arm. "This Quint person is dangerous and unpredictable. He's the reason I was so ill. It's hard to explain who he is and what he's capable of, because we don't know. Nodin has some theories, and he's anxious to discuss them with you. I didn't want to burden you with worries about Quint on top of everything else, but you must prepare. Quint tried to take over my body to get closer to you."

"Take over your body in order to take over mine? That should take no time at all to process." Terran scoffed. "Why would he do this?"

Maya looked to Flint, when he just shrugged, she gave the only answer she'd been able to piece together. "Because as an Elemental, as Earth, you are the strongest. You are our grounding force, the center. Quint's essence cannot exist in a human host for any significant amount of time because their bodies deteriorate. With you, he will have a body that can renew, essentially forever."

"I am not an Elemental."

Maya released Terran's arm and took his hand, brushing her

fingers across the blue veins lining his wrist. "No, you are not, but he's aware of your potential. We worry he'll tire of waiting and push along your transformation. I won't let that happen."

Terran lifted a strand of her hair and rubbed it between his forefinger and thumb. "The way you looked when I got here, was because of something Quint did?"

"Yes." His slight touch trickled through every pore in her body.

With a tug on her hair, he said, "Then you'll stay away from him."

"Terran, you understand better than I what dark matter is and how much is theoretically in the universe. We are like fleas fighting an elephant. We can make him itch, but eventually, he'll stomp. Regardless of that, this health hazard he's created must be contained using our Elemental gifts."

"Health hazard? You mean the masking of the prion and the fake vaccine, right? I'm still unclear, how do you know all this?"

Flint stepped forward. "It's time to dispense with questions, Pigpen. Unless you can figure out how to detect dark matter, we're doing this our way. Are you ready to join the fight? This isn't some grade school science project. Plus, you haven't undergone your transformation. Might be best if you sat this one out."

"The first thing I do after I've 'undergone my transformation' will be to kick your ass." Terran poked Flint's chest.

Maya braced a hand against Terran's shoulder. "Boys, please, let's focus our animosity where it belongs."

"Still calling him a boy after being alone with him last night... hmm... how unfortunate for you, Maya." Flint laughed when she shoved him. "Are you taking Terran or am I?"

"I've got him."

Terran scoffed, "You've got me all right. Got me more confused about what's happening than I was before. We're supposed to stop Neb Aether from creating and distributing a false vaccine, but he isn't Aether, he's really Quint, a parasitic form of dark matter. Great. It all makes sense now. On top of that, I'm to become some kind of immortal Earthman, but when I do, Quint will inhabit my body. Perfectly clear."

Maya bit her bottom lip then mumbled, "Peri-mortal."

"What?" Terran said, steel lacing his tone.

"Sorry, it's just that it's not, um...immortal. Sorry, I was just..."

Maya threw up her hands. "You're always saying you want facts."

"Facts? You want to talk facts now?" Terran shook his head. "No. I'm sticking with denial. Perhaps this is all some coma like state I've entered due to caffeine-withdrawal."

Flint slapped Terran on the back. "I imagine Columbia offers a variety of caffeinated mud flavors."

Terran covered his eyes with his hand and muttered, "I really hate this rabbit hole."

#

As he watched Maya fold his clothes, Terran pondered all he had learned over these past few days. She snapped out his now-dry T-shirt before folding it into a neat square. This visible proof of her water-gift provided one more conundrum. An overwhelming urge to punch something had him cracking his knuckles. A five-mile run would be a proper way to vent the backlog of resentment and disbelief piled in his mind. The sordid story this blonde beauty before him had revealed without so much as a stutter or blush, jabbed through his thoughts. *A duke? Really?*

He remained in the light from the well. Maybe if he stood here long enough someone would spot his presence and rescue him.

What is she doing now?

"I'm ready. Can we go?"

She stilled before placing his shoes on top of the neatly folded clothes pile. "No. I need one more night."

"Are you serious? You expect me to stay here another night? Why didn't you just let me leave with Flint?"

She crossed both arms over her chest. "I'm sorry. I didn't realize."

"Didn't realize? Haven't you been listening? I've expressed my desire to leave over and over."

"Do you want me to call Flint back?" Her movements were jerky as she braided her hair and twisted the mass in a bun.

"No, just forget it." He trudged over to her pool and sank down against the outer wall. Scrubbing his hand over his face, he clapped his hands together, before steepling his fingers under his chin. Dark matter. What did he remember about that? He refused to think about Maya. Because he didn't want her to read his mind, see his true feelings. Love? Had that passed?

Step away from those thoughts.

Was Neb Aether really conducing false science? He'd need to contact Houser.

"I can't believe you're actually considering facing off with this Quint person after what he did to your body. Was it some kind of experiment?"

Maya sat along the pool's edge and ran her fingers across the water's surface. She paused and cast him a sideways glance. "I thought you were beginning to believe."

"Why would you think that?"

She shrugged and resumed her finger swirls in the water.

"Do you have any idea how I felt when you were gone. I couldn't find you. Then, after searching for days, I'm delivered here and you're a shriveled, emaciated death doll." He shot up and paced before her. Visions of her in Mother's arms pierced his thoughts. Her quivering body lying next to his. The soft hum of Nodin's chant, as she lay enfolded in their arms. Protectively cradling her even as he railed in disbelief. He stilled his pacing and was quiet for a moment, containing his emotions. Then he whispered out, "Why did you pursue me?"

Sadness gleamed in her aqua eyes before she turned away. "I never had any choice. I was told we were matched by destiny. That we belonged together."

"You understand how that sounds, right? You're willing to let others match you up with men. Use your body." Her sharp intake of breath alerted him that perhaps he'd gone too far. And perhaps he had. Perhaps he shouldn't take his distress out on her, but she was the one who had gripped his heart. Seized the thumping, lusting red mass in her watery grip until, with fingers slick from her lies, her hold had slipped and his heart had crashed against the rocks of this damp cave.

She hopped down from her perch and shoved against his chest. "Go ahead and chip away. Use your words to defile me. I'll endure."

"Endure as some sort of water-girl? That's your plan?" He could not stem the cascade of bitter words. Being here, discussing her mind-boggling existence shot his anger into vitriol's red-light district.

She scrubbed at her head until her braid broke free from the bun. "Don't do this, Terran. Please. Get some rest. Your anger is making you say things against your nature. You're not cruel." She patted his forearm.

The pale beauty of those gentle fingers served as a reminder of other moments that same hand had passed over his skin. She sought to comfort him when her own pain and uncertainty must also be prevalent. "You're right. I apologize. What should we do now?"

"You can rest. I need to return to my pool." She unzipped her jeans.

Any other time a different reaction to this might have occurred, and he did feel a slight stir, but no, right now he needed clarification. He couldn't allow lusty thoughts when he barely remembered his own name. "And tomorrow you plan to face this Quint?" His ire rose once more as disbelief and fury replaced desire.

"Yes."

He gripped her arm. "I don't think so."

"You have no say."

"I believe I do. Fate and linked destinies, remember? I have every right to stop you. Nodin brought me here to heal you. I held up my end of the bargain. Don't think I'm going through that nightmare again."

She jerked her arm free. "Terran, tomorrow you will remember none of this. We will deliver you back to your world. No memories of your time here will remain."

"Oh no, I won't be forgetting anything. I don't trust these people you're with. I'm not letting you walk into another situation that could destroy your body."

"You don't want this life. You don't want me."

"How can I know what I want? Can't you give me time to contemplate?"

"We don't have time." She roared back.

He opened his mouth, but closed it once more. Her heaving chest and the feral light in her eye was wreaking havoc on his libido. He stepped away from the temptation. As he paced under the well opening, he squinted against the glaring light. Yelling at each other would get them nowhere. A level head was necessary.

He stepped before her and titled her chin with his thumb. "Here is how this will play out. I'm going tomorrow. Based on what I find there, I'll decide whether or not I will let you work your mind meld. *I* will choose."

Maya shook her head. "I don't want you there. Did you not

listen to a word *I* said? Quint is too unpredictable. I can't make that fact clear enough. He wants to take over your body. You. With any means at his disposal." She cursed under her breath. "I know you may not believe me, but what happens to you matters. Deeply."

"If I'm staying here tonight, I'm going in the morning."

"I don't have to take you." Her chin rose and she poked a finger against his chest. "I'll make you forget everything right here, right now."

Terran grabbed both her shoulders and gazed into her sapphire blue eyes. "I wouldn't suggest leaving me behind." If she left, she would rue the day. He'd find a shaman, a voodoo master, a dark witch—whatever means necessary to find her again.

She visibly drew a deep breath and closed her eyes. When she opened them once more the fathomless aqua had returned. "Seeing Quint might not be the answer. You need to believe in this life, the inherent dangers, before we go."

"Fine, I believe."

"You are such an asshole."

"No, an asshole is an external opening of the—"

"All right, no more. You're so literal."

He heard a stifled chuckle.

"I'll take you." She shoved against him and walked to her pool. She stared into the depths for a moment then said, "It's against my better judgment. But if meeting Quint is the extra push you need, perhaps it's the right move. I never know. I'm at a loss at which path to take with you. I doubt I'll ever figure out our direction."

"Join the club, my tricky water lily. Join the club."

CHAPTER 32

Terran squinted against the sun on an atypical Seattle afternoon. Temperatures had settled in the mid-eighties, but after days in a freezing crypt, each hot ray was like a shot of heaven.

He remained at Maya's side as they approached the entrance to Aether Pharmaceuticals. Quint's façade was housed in a redbrick building in the Fremont district. Flint and Nodin followed close behind. No one stopped them, even though they were the only ones without employee badges.

Not surprising, especially after their morning shopping spree. They had entered the back of an upscale boutique and appropriated clothing while the owner stood silent and still at the register. After that, Nodin breezed through a café and grabbed a sandwich and steaming coffee cup—without paying. Terran removed a damp twenty-dollar bill from his equally damp wallet and slammed the money down on the counter. Thievery was uncalled for.

Flint rolled his eyes and commented they were just accepting rewards for their good deeds.

Terran had suggested he shut up.

Now that they were actually at Aether, Terran regretted succumbing to human needs. His stomach churned—unsettled from the odd food and timing between each meal.

Plus, this Quint person troubled him. Would he send security? Regardless of all the preposterous revelations, his protesting stomach, and his overwhelmed mind, he didn't want Maya arrested over this madness.

Security measures similar to those in place at the Conservancy seemed likely at this facility. Or was this Quint his own security measure? This dark matter turning into a human theory just about blew the top off his skull. He needed Magic Maya fingers to ease his steadily building headache.

As he entered the main lobby, he struggled with the concept that dark matter could take a human host. Especially since current theory held that dark matter didn't interact with any matter, nor was it detectable. The possibilities of this discovery were endless. Even with the potential for the greatest scientific breakthrough ever before him, his mind played one question over and over—*If Maya spends her time recuperating in water, as Earthman, where does that leave me? Wallowing in the mud?*

Flint chuckled. "That's right, Pigpen."

Mind-reading ass. Terran took a lengthy drink from his coffee, which kept him from dumping the steaming brew over Flint's head. "Stay out of my mind."

If they got to Quint's office and he was the CEO of a video game company and they were all part of some whacko gaming experiment—the ass kicking would commence.

He followed Maya up the stairs to the second floor.

At the top, Maya punched open the door and walked down a hallway lined with royal blue carpet. By her non-hesitant march, she was apparently aware of Quint's location. A receptionist guarded an office with connected glass walls and stainless steel double doors. Without taking a moment to huddle up and form a game plan, Maya pulled open the door.

Terran grabbed her arm to keep her at his side.

Neb Aether sat behind a desk, conducting a meeting with Chinese businessmen and recognizable senators from Washington and Oregon.

"Get out." Flint, dressed in the finest clothes from the boutique, addressed the men in attendance.

"Gentlemen, forgive this interruption." Aether spoke from behind his desk, his fingers steepled under his chin. "They've obviously mistaken our meeting time. I'd planned on dealing with them later. Please, excuse us for a moment."

Quint's harried receptionist now stood at the door.

"Nancy, please see to their comfort." He waved a hand in the men's direction.

As Nancy shuffled out Aether's guests, the safety sprinklers suddenly erupted. Water poured from spouts lined across the ceiling. Nancy and her finely suited crew hustled to the stairwell, no doubt planning to exit the building. Puzzle pieces began locking together in Terran's mind. He shot a sideways glance at Maya and raised a brow.

She winked.

"Terran, do you see the manipulative games I'm forced to deal with?" Aether trapped him with a pitch-black gaze.

How does this man know my name?

"You're not Neb Aether." Terran wasn't sure if he uttered a question or a statement. A conundrum he found himself facing a lot lately.

"No, I am not." Aether grinned and the whites of his eyes went full black.

Terran must have stumbled a little, because Maya took his hand, offering support. A vision of Aether's mouth locked onto his wormed into his thoughts. Terran wiped the back of his hand over his lips, while he watched Aether laugh.

A fine mist fell from Quint's office sprinklers while spouts outside the glass walls still erupted with a heavy flow. Tiny droplets covered Terran's lenses, hindering his vision. If he wiped off his glasses, what would he see? After twenty-seven years of living in one reality, would he now see another? Doubts about Quint and the Elementals' abilities could no longer fester in his mind. They had to wash away. He used his wet shirt to wipe his glasses. With them perched back on his nose, his vision remained blurred by streaks of water, which matched the hazy perception he could no longer deny.

Quint, the lecherous being who wanted to control his body, who had tried to kill Maya, stood costumed before him in Aether's skin. The vision of his future altered slightly as another seemingly impossible supposition became fact. Dark matter could take human form, Maya was a water-girl, and they were in a world of shit. He shook off those thoughts. Concentration, before this man, was key. Forced to face this reality without proper study of all the variables rankled.

Adrenaline surged and he stepped up to the plate. "If we were playing games, then consider this checkmate. We will burn down this building and destroy all your false science. What was your plan anyway, *Quint*? If everyone dies from Mad Cow disease, who is left to leach?"

Quint walked around the far side of his desk. "Terran, we both know, I only need you. These others think to stop our progress. Profitable progress. I'll ask once. Join me. I built this company for you, to do with as you please. We can unravel all the world's mysteries together, become gods among men." Quint sneered as he glanced at Maya. "I realize, Maya has some charms, but she's not the only woman you'll ever want."

Terran stepped farther into the office and countered, "We never have everything we want, because once we attain it, we no longer wish to have it. We want more, always more. I'll never join you, Quint. I will not use science as a means to deceive people."

"Maya is deceiving you." Quint locked gazes with Maya and presented a teeth-baring grin.

With measured steps, Nodin moved to stand beside her.

"Never, for a moment, believe she won't use her abilities to keep you and control you." Quint tapped his steel letter opener against his desk. "She's already altered your mind. I can see her influence raining in blue streaks through your body. You may think you're sailing along safely, but she'll suck you in like the Bermuda Triangle." A black substance drifted from his finger and he swirled it around in a circle until it formed a vortex.

Flint jumped on the coffee table, set between two chairs at the front of Quint's desk "Enough talk. Let's finish this."

Quint shook his head and exhaled a deep sigh. "This show of force is futile. I am as *I* will. I exist but do not exist. I am everywhere and nowhere. What is it you think to do, Flint? How will you stop me? You've tried for, how long is it now? Over five-hundred years?"

"Terran, I'll ask you once again to be reasonable." Quint once more met his gaze. "I would hate to start our mutually beneficial relationship on the wrong foot." He waved a hand. "The rest of you may leave. I'll deal with you later. Flint, keep your sparklers away from my building. Maya, you're looking hale. I enjoyed drinking from your cup. I suddenly find myself quite thirsty."

Quint's sly grin was the only warning before an invisible force rocketed Maya against the office walls. The glass barrier shattered and razor shards rained down. She quickly regained her footing, but scratches lined her arms and face. Jagged glass pieces remained embedded in her skin.

"Maya!" Terran shot to her side. "Are you all right?" As this moment became very real, his primal instincts to protect his woman took over. Any lingering thoughts this was a fantasy world left as he watched water ooze from Maya's wounds.

A sound, like the flick of a lighter, erupted as Flint snapped his fingers and set Quint's desk on fire. A bellow of air fed the flames, spreading them across the papers on the desk and onto the carpet.

A voice beckoned in Terran's mind, screeching, drawing him in, *"Come with me."*

With a wave of his hand, Quint smoldered the flames, leaving behind a black char. Quint studied him and crooked a finger.

Terran's legs moved in his direction. Multiple voices fought for supremacy in his mind. He flinched as the words bumped and jarred against each other.

Maya appeared before him, bracing her palms on his chest. *"Stay with me...Stay."*

As he struggled against the momentum driving him forward, he felt Nodin's arms wrap around him from behind. Water blasted from the sprinklers, stinging his skin. A strong wind drove Terran two steps back then Nodin released him.

Quint's clothes rippled and his lips and hair created a frightening mask as a strong gale blasted against his face. Flames rained down from above, yet blacked out an instant before they touched him.

Maya maintained the pressure against Terran's chest, her eyes turned deep blue and water poured from her nose. She wiped the liquid from her lips and kissed him, which reestablished their connection on a physical level.

His forward motion stopped. *What is real?* Maya was real. Since he'd discovered her in the cave, she hadn't deceived or lied. None of this could be explained. He could no longer blame Maya for not exposing the truth, he knew now he'd never have believed her without proof. Proof that might get them all killed.

A black seed dug through his mind— compelling him to push away Maya.

No!

Then everything stopped.

No one moved.

No one spoke.

Without support for his forward motion, Terran fell to his knees before Quint's desk. He glanced at Maya, but she stood still, arms frozen as if they were still locked against his chest. The only sound was water dripping from the sprinklers.

Eyes wide, Maya lowered her arms in small increments. Her body shivered and her shoulders hunched. Her attention was riveted by something behind him.

What could possibly frighten her?

He used the edge of Quint's desk to lever to his feet, and then followed Maya's gaze to the shattered interior office wall.

A lovely petite creature, most likely in her mid-twenties, with flame red hair stood in the jagged glass frame.

Did they fear this girl? If so, why?

The flat screen TV on the wall exploded. The laptop on Quint's desk whined and sparks shot out of the screen. His watch burned his wrist.

Flint glared at the girl, pulled his cell from his pocket, and threw it to the ground.

Apparently, Maya wasn't the only one rattled by her presence.

A blue light field surrounded her. Her red hair stuck out straight from her head as if she'd inserted every finger into a light socket.

"Pillar, welcome back." Quint broke the silence, speaking to a tall woman with white-blonde hair standing behind the glowing girl. "The timing of your arrival couldn't be more convenient."

The redhead focused on Quint, who had stepped in her direction. She tilted her head then opened her arms in welcome.

"No, please," Maya pleaded. "I beg you. Don't do this."

Don't do what?

"Pillar, what have you done?" Nodin's words were whispered agony.

Quint skirted around them. "She's done as I wished. Pillar, bring her to me."

Maya took Terran's hand and squeezed. *"If this is our end, please know I loved you."*

Our end?

Did she think they were going to die? How? The clarity of Maya's beauty inside and out shone like a beacon during this dark moment. No longer hidden in the pools murky depths. He cupped her face in his palm, blocking the strange scene playing out before them.

Maya stiffened under his hand.

"What is it?" Terran turned to see what had startled her.

Quint was frozen in motion. One hand suspended in the air and his feet no longer touched the ground.

The redhead smiled then clapped her hands together, drawing the blue field between her fingers. A bright violet sphere formed.

An inky black substance, once more, crept from Quint's fingertips, but drew up short against an invisible barrier surrounding him. His mouth opened and the scream echoed through Terran's mind. The others were similarly affected, cupping their hands over their ears.

The redhead's glow began to wane.

Quint fell to his knees. "You…You've m-m…made the wrong choice."

The redhead generated a violet light in her hands then shot it like a laser beam at Quint. The beam struck his torso, knocking him across the room.

The pulse sent a subtle shockwave over Terran's skin. Every hair on his body stuck up straight and yet he refused to blink.

A white circle now existed in Quint's chest.

Terran stared at the hollow core. Physics lectures stirred through his mind. Bits and fragments struck his brain. What just happened? Photons? A mental science class for another time as he watched rage darken Quint's face. Would he retaliate? Was this redhead capable of unleashing another pulse?

With eyes as black as night, his fists clenched at this sides, Quint released an unearthly bellow. "You dare to defy me? Me? I will return and I will destroy each and every one of you and everything you hold dear." And then he beamed away like he'd entered the transporter on some science fiction show.

Flint turned to the redhead. "Who are you?"

"I am Violet Levina."

"Come with me." He stepped forward and grabbed her arm then instantly released her. Very slowly, he opened his hand.

Terran glimpsed angry red blisters on Flint's palm.

"I will not be led by any man, especially you." Violet's soft lilting accent contradicted the strength latent within. She turned to Maya.

"Why do you continue to put yourself in harms way? After assisting you at the lake, I would have thought—"

"Violet, not now." The blonde woman Quint had called Pillar, placed a hand upon the redhead's shoulder.

Violet continued her perusal of Maya, and then she cast a glare at Flint. "I cannot continue to intervene. It is too dangerous for—"

"Violet, we discussed this," Pillar interrupted once more.

Violet nodded at the woman and offered a weak grin. "I'm sorry."

A pulse of violet flashed, temporarily blinding him, and after blinking, Terran noted that Pillar and Violet had disappeared. "Well, at least, gamma-girl didn't turned green and destroy the place." Levity seemed appropriate. Anything else would have him screaming for the exits.

Flint's brow furrowed as he faced Terran. "Gamma-girl?"

Terran paced alongside Quint's desk. "I'm going to go with this, so follow along. It's theorized that a high-energy magnetic field can convert dark matter into a photon within the visible spectrum. That was why the cylindrical hole in Quint's chest appeared white."

Eyes wide, Maya stared at the place where moments before the redhead had used her gifts to incapacitate Quint. "I have no idea what you just said, but she was amazing. We have to find her."

Nodin reached over and shook Terran's shoulder, jolting him out of his mental physics class. "Let's get this done. We'll discuss the she-hulk later."

Flint led the way as they fled down the stairwell.

Terran noted Maya's cuts and gashes from the broken glass had healed. The memory of all that glass breaking, reminded him of their greater purpose. "Flint, follow me. Maya and Nodin, make sure everyone is out of the building and far away."

Terran raced back up the stairs and down the second floor corridor. A lab was on this level, somewhere. The familiar smell of hexane solvents had evoked a wave of homesickness for his lab when they'd arrived on this floor earlier. Ahead, an old-time showerhead stuck out from the wall and a Plexiglass box stuffed with safety glasses hung beside a door—standard safety precautions outside every lab. Clear signs he'd found his mark.

Once inside the lab, he yanked off the rubber hose leading from the natural gas nozzle to the Bunsen burner then turned the gas valve wide open. He twisted open two more valves before turning to Flint. "Concentrate, please. Is anyone left in the building?"

Flint closed his eyes and after a moment, answered, "No."

"Give me five minutes. Then light it up."

Flint was staring at his palm again. He closed his hand in a fist. "It will be my pleasure."

Terran sprinted down the hallway and bounded down the stairs. The stairwell door opened to the lobby. He made for the front doors and ran outside. Aether's employees milled about on the sidewalk across the street. They were soaked from the sprinklers and were bundled together in clusters. A strong wind kept them at bay.

Arms waving, Terran crossed the street. "Stay back. There's a bomb."

A loud boom reverberated and all the windows on the second floor shattered in a fiery explosion. More blasts erupted as additional flammable material exploded, lit by the massive fireball shooting through the lab. Glass rained down around the building. Flint did his duty and controlled the flames before they spread. Nodin controlled wind patterns so the debris was contained.

Sirens sounded in the distance.

Terran stood next to Nodin on the sidewalk and kept an eye on the crowd. To glean what people were thinking would be interesting. Most were probably worried whether or not they would have a job tomorrow.

Nodin suddenly shifted.

Terran stiffened and turned.

The willowy blonde, Pillar stood apart from the crowd, beside her was the redhead.

The scientist in him longed to speak to Ms. Levina. He wished to understand all her capabilities. If his theory was correct and she could control the whole electromagnetic spectrum then she was more powerful than all of the Elementals and Quint combined. The most frightening thought was what she could do to Maya. *Vaporize was too kind a word.* He'd try to comprehend that nightmare later. Right now, he was fascinated by the palpable waves of emotion coursing between Nodin and the blonde.

Nodin remained still as the woman called Pillar glided toward him.

"You're on your final chance with me, Pillar." His voice was deep with muted warning. "There is only so much more I will tolerate. Do not believe our past will keep me from destroying you."

"You destroyed me a long time ago." Her gravelly voice rasped, as she halted before him.

Nodin shook his head. "Enough." He kissed her. Hard. Deep. Determined.

Terran turned away on the pretense of searching the crowd for Maya.

Nodin's soft laugh brought back his attention. "You know I prefer salty over sweet." He licked his lips as Pillar marched off.

Violet continued staring with curiosity plain in her eyes.

Sudden warmth at his back indicated Flint's presence.

Violet's eyes narrowed before she turned and followed the blonde away from the fire and the men watching their retreat.

Apparently, woman trouble exists for Elementals, as well.

CHAPTER 33

"Do you even have a license?" Terran stood in a Ford dealership's parking lot after escaping the chaos surrounding the smoldering remains of Quint's brick building. Distress remained high after hearing Flint's plan to steal a vehicle—a shiny red Ford SVT Raptor.

While Terran understood the necessity, he couldn't compute the idea of driving a bright red stolen truck down a major interstate.

Flint ran his hand over the Raptor's hood. "This beauty is a trophy truck in street clothing. She has extra long wheel travel so she can handle rough terrain, something we may need. Plus, she looks mean with the muscle to back it up."

"I don't care about any of that." Terran gritted out, and then pointed across the street "The used trucks in that lot will serve our purposes. And they aren't waving a bright red flag to police officers in search of a stolen vehicle."

"Terran, do you really believe after all you've witnessed in the past few days, the police pose a problem for us?"

"Do you or do you not have a license?" Terran stood guard by the driver's side door.

Maya ran a hand up his arm. "Terran, we need to move on."

Nodin interjected, "Flint gave up on human laws a long time ago, brother. He'll never listen to reason. Besides, this truck has over 400 horsepower with a 6-speed automatic."

"Really?" Terran cupped his hands on the truck window and perused the interior. The shiny, steel lined dash and intricate dials brought back thoughts of the vehicles expense. "Wait, no. No. I can get cash out of the ATM for a used truck. I'll leave the money in their mail slot. Why do we have to steal this one?"

"Because we can." Flint shoved him aside and sidled into the driver's seat.

"Brilliant answer."

"Just get in, Pigpen."

Terran opened the back door for Maya then hopped into the passenger seat. He planned to keep an eye on Flint's driving. Pilfering high-end trucks was out of his comfort zone. These Elemental road-trippers may no longer care about such petty matters, but adopting the same nonchalance about breaking laws would take a long time.

After a finger fight with Flint over the touch-screen navigation panel, they were set to head east.

Terran twisted in his seat to speak to Nodin and Maya. If his mind sat idle then this new reality would come crashing down. "Based on what happened today, I have no choice but to reconsider my stance. However, please understand I'll need time to analyze all the factors. I will have more questions and you *will* give me answers. I comprehend dealing with Quint is not a game. I imagine accepting this Elemental lifestyle happens in stages so consider me in stage one. I suppose I understood upon meeting Mother Nature, but I blocked the truth from my mind."

Lights from streetlamps and business signs lit up Nodin's face. "I asked you who you will be and what you will do. Tonight we unearthed answers to those questions. In the face of danger, you took charge. You completed the task we set out to accomplish. I'd say you've already blown past all the stages."

Terran didn't want to dwell too much on levels of acceptance now. He ran a hand over his chin. "I've been considering the possible range of Violet's capabilities. I believe she can control the entire electromagnetic spectrum. Radio waves, Microwaves, Infrared, Ultraviolet, X-rays, and Gamma rays." He ticked off each one with his fingers. "That petite redhead holds unimaginable power."

Nodin nodded. "What's worse is Quint's aware of what she can do and who she is. He was thrilled to see her until she blasted that hole through his chest. I've never seen anything like her. We've struggled against him for so long. If we could get her in our corner, we'd finally have a chance to win."

Maya finished fiddling with the buttons on the panel by her leg and sat back. "Quint will come after us harder now. He wasn't just spouting off when he said he'd make us pay. He'll have no trouble locating us. Scientists theorize that the universe is made up of sixty-eight percent dark energy and twenty-seven percent dark matter, so in essence, that leaves normal matter bringing up the rear at less than five percent—Normal five versus darkness ninety-five. We don't stand a chance." She combed her fingers through her hair. "When he says he's everywhere and undetectable, he's right. We've never been able to detect his presence. We merely pick up on his subtle menacing vibe. And now, he's finally been in a situation out of his control. If we thought he had no scruples before, now that he's been challenged, he'll pass sanity's edge reasserting his authority."

Flint flipped through the radio channels and settled on a classic rock station before he knocked Terran on the shoulder with the back of his hand. "Can Quint heal from this?"

Terran turned down the guitar solo blasting through the cab. "You're asking *me*? How would I know? I have no comprehension of who this Quint is, what he's derived from, or how as dark matter he interacts with matter. I'll have to dust off my physics book." Terran adjusted the seat belt lever, to keep the strip from rubbing against his neck, as he twisted in his seat.

Maya glanced at Nodin. "We've never understood how Quint came to exist or why. Maybe Pillar knows. I wonder why she and Violet were there? Nodin, do you—"

"No, Maya. I don't know her mind anymore. I begin to wonder if I ever did." Nodin's gaze settled on the view outside the window.

A tense silence settled over the sounds of Led Zepplin belting out "Kashmir." Not privy to the undercurrents circulating through the truck, Terran searched for a way to change the subject.

Do I need to? Are they having telepathic conversations right now?

He certainly was.

Talk. Talk. Don't dwell.

"So, Maya, any more surprises? Adding Pillar and Violet into the problem throws off my whole mental math equation. I had enough to compute with the three of you."

"I'm glad you're finally viewing this Elemental life as real, Terran. Let's begin by focusing on where Aether's false vaccines were sent."

Nodin scrubbed a hand over his chin. "Flint and I can determine which farms are using illegal feed then detect and incinerate livestock infected with Mad Cow."

"Good plan." Maya tapped her fingers against her knee to the beat of the music. "We'll worry about Pillar and Violet once we've finished."

Flint grunted, and then glared at his open palm.

In the faint light from the dash, Terran noticed a light pink mark still marred his skin from Violet's burn.

Flint rolled his fingers into a fist and faced him with a feral smile. "The redhead is mine."

#

Reminding Flint again that both he and the truck had needs, Terran suggested they take the next exit.

After pulling into a gas station, he jumped out, headed across the parking lot, and then hiked through a narrow strip of grass to a fast food restaurant. Upon seeing to his most basic human need, he exited the bathroom, wiping his hands on a paper towel.

Maya stood by the soda machines, a grease-stained brown bag in hand.

His first thought was to apologize for not believing her, but his heart still chafed over her incomplete honesty. The complexity of their relationship was on a level he hadn't quite grasped. Plus, the fact he hadn't showered in two, or was it three, days now pushed his mood way past acidic all the way to caustic.

Maya remained leaning against the counter with both arms folded across her chest as he approached. She passed him the bag filled with greasy goodness.

Nothing beats a Five Guys burger and fries. Nothing.

"Did you get some water?" Terran tilted her face with his free hand and peered into her blue eyes.

She blinked and turned from his touch.

Perhaps, stage two meant accepting her. Just her. He could do without the rest, but at this point, he had to play his hand or fold. And that string, that braided thread of need, of desire, thrummed a primal beat through his body. Each strike wore down his resistance, pounding only one wish over and over—take her and forget the consequences. Their connection would never break or snap in two.

The band would only stretch. Ready at any and every moment to boomerang them back together. He took a sip of ice-filled soda, which did nothing to cool the lust burning though his body.

Damn her for putting him in this position. She'd said she loved him. They had stood on the edge of death and her final thoughts had been of him. He couldn't let that pass unanswered. The time for childish tantrums was over. They wanted him to take charge of their party of four. Fine, he'd take the reins.

He dug deep into his nature and exhumed those ancient tools men had developed over thousands of years. He took a deep breath and blew it out, expelling doubt, fear, and anger.

Earthman rising.

Maya studied him, a slight tilt to her head. "You look like a statue frozen in place."

Parts of him might still be frozen from that inhospitable well, but his will broke through the clay mold and charged through stage two. "Get some water, Maya."

"I'm fine."

"Three days ago, you were a dried apricot. You are anything but fine."

Her aqua blue eyes darkened to sapphire and she fired back, "I've been taking care of myself for a long, long time. I don't need your sudden interest in my welfare." She flicked a finger at his paper bag. "Enjoy that while you can."

"Believe me, every bite will be pure bliss, but not as much bliss as this—" He pulled her closer, bent his head, and kissed her. Hard. Punishing. She struggled, but he tied her up. Not allowing her resistance to the cord between them, but winding their connection tight. In a world that no longer made sense, this was real. With each rasp of his tongue over hers, his world went from hazy gray to vibrant blue.

He locked his hand at the back of her neck.

She slid her arms up to his shoulders.

Their kiss expelled waves of emotion dammed up for days.

Catcalls from late-night customers reminded Terran of where they were. Reluctantly, he pulled back, grasped her upper arm, and led her outside.

Maya clasped his hand, halting their progress to the truck. "I thought Quint had you. I'm so frightened he'll harm you before your transformation. And even though I know I should keep these feelings to myself, I'm scared of what my future will be without you. I thought everything was over."

"I don't know what is over and what is beginning. We can only move forward. I imagine Nodin would have some perfect quote for this moment, but I'm more basic. I want a shower. I want you. Most likely at the same time. The rest, I'll take as it comes." He brushed a stray hair over her ear. "I'm so very sorry for all my harsh words." He dropped his forehead against hers. "You were amazing today. So brave. Who are you, Maya Conway? And after all this time, why me?"

In answer, she kissed him—a flagrant reminder of all that was between them. They reaffirmed life and their burgeoning love in the most basic way possible. Though they would have to wait for completion—fast-food parking lots were not conducive to life-affirming sex acts.

Maya smiled and bumped their hips together. "Are you sure? I could make everyone leave."

He paused for a moment, but then pulled her along toward the truck.

CHAPTER 34

For over a hundred years, Maya's service as an Elemental had focused on helping humans and fighting water pollution. Now, her life focused on one thing—Terran.

As his head rested on her lap, she studied his profile. *I would die for him.* She would give every last drop of her Elemental gifts to keep him safe.

But would an Elemental life be too much for Terran? She'd never tasted whisky before, but right now, the amber liquid seemed a viable way to ease this torment, to make her forget. Customers at Mo-saw's enjoyed liquor's effects, and in this moment whisky seemed an appropriate way to drown her sorrows. Unrealistic, because she couldn't walk away from this situation, she had to sail through to the journey's end. Whisky would have to wait.

Does he love me? Want me? Forgiveness for his words in the cave had already leaked from her thawing heart. His bluster had come from fear and uncertainty.

The tick, tick, tick of the turn signal brought Maya out of her contemplations.

Flint practically boosted the truck on two wheels exiting to Buzzy Bear Campground.

Mending the frayed threads of her relationship with Terran could not be realized under this state of emergency. Diving deep into a sexual well and absorbing every facet of pleasure they could create was unrealistic with Quint on the loose.

"Nodin."

He twisted in the passenger seat. *"I understand, Maya. Flint and I will deal with the consequences of Quint's vaccine while you keep Terran safe."*

"I can't leave him." She ran her fingernails through his sexy stubble. Days had passed since he'd shaved. A shiver went through him as her tickling caress registered.

Terran blinked open his eyes. "Where are we?" He stretched and sat up.

Of course, the first words out of his mouth were a question.

"As you've so often reminded us of your human needs, we too have elemental needs. Flint pulled off here because there is a river running on the outskirts of the campground. Plus they have some higher-end amenities."

"Good, I can finally take a shower." Terran rubbed his eyes and yawned.

"A shower is a wonderful idea." If he planned to enjoy water, she'd be right there with him.

At a previous stop, they'd appropriated toiletries and towels, plus extra clothes. Maya grabbed the bags off the floor and hopped down. "Showers are this way."

Nodin hopped out of the passenger side and visibly breathed deep. "Maya, Flint and I will be waiting outside the door. I'll do a quick perimeter search." He stripped then disappeared into the wind.

Flint jabbed Terran's shoulder. "Don't hog all the hot water, Pigpen."

Terran stepped toward Flint with a feral growl.

Maya jerked his hand and led him through the campgrounds to the brick building that housed the showers.

"What is the story behind Nodin and the tall blonde, Pillar?"

"She is the salt of the earth. I don't know many details of her history—how she came about or even her age. I do know, she and Nodin were together for a time, and then something tore them apart."

"He seemed interested in rekindling their affair today."

"Did he?" Maya halted before the bathroom door. "I was terrified when Violet stood outside of Quint's shattered office wall. A purple fog masked her mind. I've never felt so much power emanating from one source. I don't know Pillar's game, but she saved our lives today. Whether she planned our rescue or not, that was the result."

"Flint seemed eager to volunteer for the mission to locate Violet."

"He's baffled. Quite amusing that someone finally burned him."

"Burning, I am familiar with the sensation. I'm unsure of your expectations, Maya, and I'm not sure of our future path, but right now I don't care." He stepped toward her, pushed open the bathroom door, and backed her through.

Slackening defenses with Quint at large wasn't the smartest idea. But Terran obviously wanted her. They were alive and together. A short celebration seemed in order.

He buried his hands in her hair. "I'm tired of thinking. I just want to feel."

"My thoughts exactly."

He moved his lips lazily over hers, a slow climb from sweet to demanding that scaled past sanity straight to crazed lust. She parted her lips and he swept in, deeply evocative, seductive. He settled to play with her lips, advanced and retreated, enticing her to capture more. Her nerves were stretched tight, and she aggressively returned each hard-edged caress. Intensity grew and she outlined his body with her hands. Frustrated by the clothing barrier, she pulled back. "Get undressed. Hurry." She whipped her shirt over her head and wiggled her jeans over her hips.

Terran copied her actions with his own clothing, but stopped and helped unhook her bra. He lingered, sliding the straps off each shoulder with a brush of his finger.

That fingertip drew a hot line over her lips before pressing into her mouth. She licked and sucked, keeping her gaze on his.

Withdrawing his finger from her teasing ministrations, he trailed down her neck and delved under each lace-fringed cup. Her bra floated to the floor, and he teased each revealed tip. His tongue replaced his finger, flicking over each pink bud.

His touch elicited a torrent of need that shot straight to her core. Their future unclear. Their lives in danger. Their worlds separate. Yet, their connection endured—fluid and steady.

In this moment, the outside world evaporated. Their cog on destiny's wheel ground to a halt. They'd suspend this moment in time.

Maya grabbed his arm and tugged him to the showers. The stalls had cream-colored curtains hanging from silver hooks. The rings jangled as she ripped open the curtain and adjusted the temperature dial. "The water's not going to be overly warm. But I can fix that." She shoved his boxers down his thighs and pushed him under the spray.

"Hey, still a little chilly," Terran shivered and backed into the corner.

"I believe I said I'd fix it." Maya dropped to her knees, held his thick root in her hand, and encased the seeping tip in her mouth. Peering upward, she watched his face as she skimmed her tongue around the rim of his engorged head. "You aren't the only one who knows how to tease, Terran."

His knees buckled and he wrapped a hand in her hair, attempting to ease her away.

"No. You want to feel. Want to know what's real in this world. I am. We are." As she licked her way up and down his turgid flesh, she held his heavy sacs. "I want to discover what happens to *your* body when *you* come. Why don't you explain it to me?"

"Not now. I'm all talked out. Science is all fucked in my head, and I'd much rather fuck you." He placed his hands under her arms and twisted her so he was at her back then reached around and cupped her breasts.

Her body arched as he massaged each tip with his thumbs. With his mouth, he brushed fevered kisses over her neck and shoulders.

He slid his hand across her belly and past her wet curls. A single finger crossed over her slick folds and journeyed deep.

Maya's hands were flat against the shower wall while his teasing finger moved within her body. She reached behind and positioned him where she ached for him most. "Terran, please."

He placed her hand back against the wall. Not allowing her a modicum of control as he nudged her shoulders down, bending her, and then braced one hand on the wall linking his fingers with hers. A few teasing glides had her rising on her toes. He positioned his heavy head at her slit and slammed home in a single thrust.

She recognized his quest to regain control over this basic element in his life and let him ease his troubles within her welcoming flesh. She studied her hand, linked with his on the wall. Such a simple joining, but each slap of his body against hers, the feel of his heavy sacs striking her with each plunge, symbolized their complete link. A steamy mist surrounded their entwined bodies, enfolding them in a hazy veiled world.

Their union so complete, she easily swept past stormy seas to where he stood waiting on the shore. Her body rode out each rhythmic slide. Pressure percolated and he reached his hand around to skate magic fingers over her straining bud. A husky moan escaped Terran's lips.

The sound joined each droplet as they struck her back and trickled down her body.

Control gone, he gripped her hips in both hands and heavily ground against her, working faster, harder. Words spilled from his lips in incoherent murmurs.

Her hands remained pressed against the wall as the wick lit and fired through her body until it reached their joining point and exploded in a blazing rain of pleasure, storming over and over.

He held her still then after two quick strikes, he sparked and his hot seed erupted like a red-hot lava flow, deep inside her body. His spasms fed her own.

She quivered until the final sizzle faded, and she felt his head fall against her shoulder. His heart pounded against her back.

After a moment, he spun her around and kissed her, a wet dip of his lips against her own. Toying, with a quick, teasing tongue. "Maya, you want to know what happens when I come?" His thick voice whispered against her mouth. "My body asks, how can I ever leave you?"

She held tight and wished he never had to.

Now clean in every nook and cranny, Maya watched Terran's reflection in the mirror as he shaved. He'd let her rub the shaving cream all over his cheeks—a real couple's moment. Times like this would be locked away in her memories forever, which for her was a very long time.

She grabbed a dry washcloth out of the shopping bag. Seeing him perform such a simple human act was like a slap of ice-cold water. "Quint flew over the cuckoo's nest years ago, but his reaction to this defeat will make a psychopath look like a fairy princess. Not to mention the fact, we destroyed his pharmaceutical company. Vengeance. Death. Destruction. Pain. All on his to-do list. He terrifies me, even more so now that you and I are...that we are...not the same." Not what she wanted to say, but she wouldn't be a burden. The thought of losing Terran was unbearable.

Terran wiped the dry cloth over his freshly shaven face. "Perhaps we were a bit precipitous in our actions, but Quint needed to be stopped. I didn't believe he was Aether until I stood before him and watched his eyes turn pitch black, and I know this sounds crazy, but in that moment I glimpsed pure evil. The thoughts he projected in my mind…" Terran shook his head. "The science behind all this— you, Nodin, Flint, purple hulk-girls, and dark matter able to mesh with matter—it can't be explained." He sat on the bench, holding one sock in his hand, staring off into space.

Maya took a quick peek into his mind and saw Quint's black eyes staring into his. Terran's fear and helplessness at his inability to break free broadcasted quite clearly. *A chalkboard filled with an electromagnetic spectrum chart. Equations. A physics book. Her body bent before him. Quint's voice screaming, "Come with me."*

At that thought, Terran shot a glance her way, unable to mask the confusion in his eyes. Sad brown pools like a basset hound sitting on a front porch waiting for someone to come along, pat his head, and lead him down the right path. How could she make this elemental life easier for him to comprehend?

He furrowed his brow and he finally worked his sock over his toes. "Maya, I know you are used to digging through people's thoughts, but you don't need to comb through mine. If there is something you want to know, just ask. If you want to know how I feel, I am more than willing to tell you. It isn't fair you can see everything, and I am still stuck in the dark."

"You're right. I'm sorry. Gleaning is a habit and you looked so lost. You're not in the dark. I'll guide you through this. My love for you would light up any path. I know you are unsure of everything, including me. I will make it right. I promise."

She ran a hand over his damp hair and considered using her elemental powers to erase his fear and soothe his worries, but as he said, that wouldn't be fair. Instead, she sat on his lap and ran a hand over his smooth cheek. He had not spoken of his love for her, but as he kissed her, she could feel it as his lips moved languidly over hers. A subtle, evocative melding as if he had all the time in the world to get drunk on the cocktail mix of their mint-flavored breath.

He angled his head and enticed her with a playful advance and retreat.

She squirmed in his lap, and she crept her hand under his waistband.

A loud bang sounded on the bathroom door. Hinges rusted over time creaked open.

Flint shouted, "We're coming in."

"All of a sudden you care about privacy?" Terran quipped.

"Not really." A fact Flint demonstrated by stripping down in the center of the room. He flopped over and held out his hand to Maya. "Soap?"

She slapped the squeeze bottle into his hand.

Flint winked. "Nodin, I'm sure there's plenty of hot water left. Terran's human stamina being what it is."

Nodin laughed. "I know today was a lot to take in, Terran. But you handled yourself well."

"Ass kisser," came a mumble from behind the shower curtain. "Nodin, go whip us up a couple of willing lasses."

"I'm not your air-tran delivery service. Find your own."

Terran and Maya slipped out the door as the argument continued.

The water called to her, so she led Terran to the river's edge. Tension held her in a tight grip as she gauged the approximate forty-foot distance between the truck and the stream. "I'm not sure about this, Terran. I can wait."

"You are not completely healed and after today's attack, you need water. Go. I'll be here." Terran kissed her forehead and the tip of her nose. He held her tight in a prolonged embrace before he reassured her once more and strolled back to the truck.

How many times would she watch him walk away? The dangers of life as an Elemental had presented themselves quite drastically today. Terran remained strong through all the confusion, anger, and feelings of betrayal. Not overly frightened, but stepping up and taking charge. They were a mish-mashed group without a strategy, but today, he'd emerged as a levelheaded leader. With Terran at the wheel, they would finally have a sensible driver. He'd know when to stop, when to go, but would he choose to sit in that custom-made seat?

CHAPTER 35

Throughout the night and into the next morning, Maya kept her head above the water's surface. A constant state of awareness was necessary, because they couldn't detect Quint through their gleaning. His dark essence existed outside of their elemental realm, which left them vulnerable. Once the golden streaks of dawn lit the horizon, she made her way to the river's bank and shook dry. Nodin and Flint had not yet returned from their own recuperative wanderings.

Throwing on her clothes, she chuckled, because she intended to take them right off again. She jogged over to the truck, planning to wake Terran with a proper good morning.

As an icy chill shot down her spine, she skidded to a stop. A shroud of darkness dropped, painting her mind with grays and blacks, pitched against a canvas of unstable red rage.

Quint, still clothed in Neb Aether's skin, stood by the truck, staring in at Terran. The skin on Quint's face drooped and revealed bloody eye sockets. His fingers against the truck window were shriveled and black. Only a few hair tufts remained on his head.

Nodin!

Flint!

An early morning breeze blew the ragged pieces of Quint's shirt open and revealed the white void in his chest. He registered Maya's existence by snarling—a crazed look in his raven eyes. Impatience and something never registered from him before—fear, printed in black type across her mind.

"Shocked to see me so soon." His voice rasped out. "I believe I said I would return. Terran is mine, Maya. I will do with him as I please. I will keep him as my dog and break him. Chained. Bound. Obedient. He will beg to lick my hand. And then, I may decide to bring him back to you and your Mother for his transformation. You will see what it means to fuck with me as he rips out your throat. I will own him, body and soul."

"Quint, in case you aren't aware, you've got a little something on your shirt." Maya smiled, and then shot a ray of water, like a full squadron of fire hoses gone mad. The burst knocked him back, but not down.

Quint roared and pitched toward the truck. He wrenched open the back door and yanked on Terran's legs.

Terran fought off Quint by kicking his face and arms.

A gust of wind knocked Quint down. Nodin landed in the truck bed, followed by Flint.

Quint regained his footing and pulled Terran out of the truck. A slithering black sludge began crawling over Terran's clothes.

"No." Maya charged forward and wrapped her arms around Terran. She held tight as Quint tried to wrench him from her hold. She released a flush of water into Terran's mouth, beating back the murky substance continuing to spread. Blue waves clashed with the black tar coloring his skin. As one vein of darkness stopped, another started.

Wind howled around them, beating against Quint. He released Terran and turned his obsidian gaze toward Nodin.

The morning sky faded to black.

They were trapped in a dark world envisioned by the soulless monster trying to snuff out their existence. Maya wrapped an arm around Terran's waist and yanked him away from Quint.

Fireballs lit the obscured expanse around them. The intense heat bubbled her skin so she stepped away from the battle's epicenter, tugging along an incoherent Terran.

Trees were uprooted and flung through the air. One after another, they burst into flames before striking Quint.

Maya steadied her grip around Terran's back and led them toward the stream. "Are you all right? Can you breathe?"

"S-s-s…Stop….let…h-h-him…t-take me." Terran scratched his arms, forming deep, bloody grooves in his skin.

Lightning crackled and struck the earth. A loud boom resonated across the campground, shaking the ground. The universe shifted and shimmered before her eyes in a colorless blur. One focus, one goal had her straining toward the stream, passing everything trying to block her mission. Black rays shot down from the sky, striking the path before her. Maya hefted Terran in her arms and weaved around each bolt.

Don't look back. Move. Move.

Maya converted into a waterspout, enveloping Terran in the center. A strong surge from Nodin pushed her forward. An invisible field blocked her, boxing her in at all sides. She spun against the barrier, again and again, unable to break free. A searing swell broke against her mind as Flint's voice ordered, *"Use your will, Maya."*

Their combined Elemental resolve broke through her confinement.

She tumbled to the ground with Terran in her arms. "Keep Quint back."

A sticky black sap poured down her face, seeping into her eyes and mouth. She blinked, trying to see through the muck. "Terran, hold on. We're almost there." She tightened her grip and allowed her elemental nature to lead her toward the water.

Quint's voice ripped through her mind. *"There is no escape. Terran will pay for your defiance. He will beg for death. Perhaps, I'll make you watch as I strip him down and invade every facet of his body."*

"No," Maya screamed. "You won't take him."

"He's already mine."

Terran gasped for breath. His heartbeat slowed as Quint's dark matter coursed through his body.

Quint is winning.

Wind whipped against her. Heat flared at her back. Water, she needed water.

How many more steps?

Rock edges poked her feet and water seeped over her toes.

Just one more step—

No!

Terran was ripped from her arms.

Maya dropped to her knees and splashed water on her face, washing away Quint's tar. Eyes still blurred, she saw Terran suspended above her. His body arched and writhing in pain.

His human body couldn't withstand much more of Quint's

barrage. She had to get him to water. She misted and shot upward, *"Nodin, help me push him down."*

A giant rumble groaned across the forest floor, like a mighty dragon in the throes of painful death. The ground trembled and shook, and then split into a deep chasm exactly where she planned to land. Earth welcomed Terran's arrival, shaking in anticipation, fighting her for control over his destiny.

"What can I do?"

"Push him into the earth." Flint compelled.

"No, not like this. He must have a choice."

"It's too late." Nodin's voice was full of sorrow. *"His transformation is inevitable. Let him go."*

Nodin and Flint combined forces and propelled Terran into the wide crevasse.

Knowing he spoke the truth, Maya switched back to her human form and hooked onto Terran's legs. If he were falling through the earth, he'd receive her shelter.

Quint's malevolent voice scraped against her mind. *"I'll be back."* A chilling laugh trailed his declaration and followed her into earth's abyss.

They tumbled over and over as the ground split open before them and filled in behind.

No escape. Their fates were sealed.

Tree roots and boulders stuck out of the ground, gouging her skin. She adjusted her body around Terran's, absorbing the brunt of nature's gauntlet. They jerked to a stop as a huge root hooked onto his jeans.

"Let him go," Maya screamed.

With a final rumble, earth rushed in from all sides.

CHAPTER 36

Maya shot out her hands, halting her landing above Terran's body. The impact fired a rod of pain from her wrist to her shoulder. A dirt cave, no bigger than a coffin, surrounded them. She couldn't breathe. Every suppressed human fear surfaced, and an unearthly scream ripped from her throat.

They were buried alive. *Buried alive. Buried alive!*

Vibrations from her cry caused a trickle of dirt to fall on her face and brought back her focus. She didn't need to breathe, yet her mind screamed a different story.

Focus. Concentrate.

Terran was the one who needed to breathe and he was…barely. After gleaning all his injuries, Maya was grateful he remained unconscious. She pried open his mouth, clamped hers over his, and released her medicinal brew down his throat. Her elemental current flushed the darkness from under his skin, eradicating the remnants of Quint's black stain.

His heart still beat. She hadn't failed him. Not yet. "Terran, don't go. Please. I can't do this without you." Sobs racked her body, and she shook against him.

She sent a mental message to Mother to come—to save him. Prayed the Goddess Isis would hear her call. She would sacrifice anything. Give all she had if they saved him.

Her life meant nothing. She was nothing.

"Terran, I'm so sorry. I wish I'd never brought you into this. I should have walked away. If that's what it takes, then I'll do it. Please,

Mother, haven't I given you enough? Don't let him die now. Take him. Transform him. I don't know how the conversion is done, but he can't survive much longer."

Maya lifted her shirt's neckline, wiped the tears from her face, and listened. Silence. Only silence reigned. No one called. No one comforted or soothed her worried soul. No team of Elementals communicated plans for rescue. Alone, trapped in a cave with the only man she'd ever love. No matter how long her peri-mortal life lasted, Maya was certain her heart would remain sealed in this dirt casket.

She dug through Terran's pockets, found his phone, and flipped on the power. A faint light source, but the glow allowed her to see his face. "Do you know that? Do you understand how much you mean to me? How much I need you? I've waited so long." She buried her head against his shoulder and breathed in his scent of balsam and cedar. His heartbeat brought a slither of relief. "I need you to wake up. Tell me how to get out of this pit. I can't think straight. I need your rational mind. Please, Terran." Between her desperate pleas, Maya delivered small sips of water into his mouth.

Dizziness waved and she blinked again and again to regain focus. She licked her dry lips. Needing more liquid, she placed a hand against the floor of the dirt cave and drew water from the earth.

Her tank only half full, Maya ran a hand through Terran's hair, brushing out dirt clumps. "Damn it, why aren't you waking? I don't know how much more water I can give you and still journey to the surface to get help."

His left arm lay broken at his side, the bone in his forearm sliced through his skin. A deep gash on his temple was matted with blood, likely due to striking a tree root during his fall. The warm, red gush of blood had spread down his shirt, leaving a copper stain. Her healing blue flowed with his red pulse and meshed in a swirl of violet through his battered body.

Terran did not speak. His mind remained locked in a quiet place, empty of all thought, of all pain. *How long can humans remain unconscious?*

Over and over, she drew water from the earth, giving him every drop she could muster. Her arms started to look like the dried apricots he'd once compared her to. Her tongue shriveled and her eyes were too dry to blink.

The dried earth began to crumble around them. A cave-in seemed likely.

No more tears fell down her face. They'd been wasted earlier when she could have given the liquid to Terran. Only one option remained.

His breath rasped out as she placed her dry, crackling lips upon his, and gave him a final pour of her healing elixir until her needle hovered above empty. Her efforts had kept him alive thus far, but drawing moisture from the ground around them was no longer safe.

She croaked a whisper against his ear, "Terran, I have to go. I'll come back. Love you." She kissed his lips and forced herself to leave. Taking one last look at his handsome face, she tattooed the memory in blue ink across her heart.

A trickle was all she had left. She transformed then wiggled up a tiny fissure, traveling back and forth in an underground maze, like a slinking worm inching toward the surface.

Fear she wouldn't return in time to save him increased her pace.

Finally at the surface, she let her senses stretch, keeping alert for danger. Water lay ahead. She coalesced into her human form and stumbled forward. Her knees buckled, and she fell against the rocky bank. Only a short distance remained so she crawled forward on her hands and knees. *For him. Make it for him.*

Water lapped against her fingers and she released her human form into the river and let gravity have its way.

The cool water cleansed her mind and body, re-hydrating every pore. *"Goddess Isis, grant me your guidance and strength."* Would Terran survive in that cave alone? A thought struck. *Where did I surface?*

Half healed, she rushed out and marked the spot by stabbing sticks into the crack where she'd emerged.

Back in the water, she floated on the bottom, not allowing the current to carry her away. Her body re-hydrated, her vision cleared, and the sediment of Quint's debris and Terran's injuries flushed out of her system. She surfaced as the sun set across the eastern sky. Too much time had passed. Water was closing in from all sides and for the first time a drowning sensation overwhelmed her. Her reliance on water was a prison that kept her from Terran.

What is he doing down there? Is he conscious? Oh please, don't let him wake until I return.

Alarmed at his reaction to being buried alive, she gulped down water over and over.

The wind picked up and the river's calm flow suddenly became a raging rapid. She shot out of the water and shook dry.

Nodin stood on the shore. "What happened? How did you—"

"There isn't time. I have to get back." She scurried over to her stick marker and trickled down, faster, stronger, but when she arrived at the dirt coffin—Terran was gone.

The only evidence was their filthy clothing left like a rag pile in a corner.

She swished around and around, searching, seeking, backtracking as a ripple of water, gliding, sliding through the earth.

No. No. He is here somewhere.

She spread out in an ever-widening circle around the cave's perimeter, but he was nowhere to be found. She slithered back to the top.

Flint stood with Nodin. "Maya—"

"No. Help me look." She weaved through evergreens, splashed into the river all the while calling for Terran. *No answer.* She dropped to her knees and dug at the small crack in the earth where her solitary stick still stood.

"I know it was here." She sat back on her ankles and glanced around the area. "Or maybe... maybe I surfaced over there, you'll see, I was just looking in the wrong place." She scrambled over a few feet and dug a new spot.

Flint wrapped his arms around her from behind. "Maya, calm down."

Nodin crouched at her front and pried the stick from her fingers. Her nails were covered in dirt. She wiped at her cheeks, welcoming the smear of earth. No need to cry. She would find him. She had to.

"Maya, look at me."

The concern in Nodin's eyes pushed her over the edge. "No. Don't look at me like that." She beat against his chest in agony over the futility of fighting destiny.

Flint pulled her from Nodin and rocked her against his chest. He crooned soft words until her sobs quieted. "Maya, stay with us. We'll find him."

Maya steadied her breathing and clenched her jaw against the wrenching vice locked around her heart. "We can't leave him in that dirt grave. What happens when he comes out? He won't understand. He'll need our help, our guidance."

Nodin covered her hands with his and squeezed, transferring his strength. "Maya, the earth shifts. He may not come back to this spot."

"Of course, he'll come back. It can't end this way." She pushed Nodin away and untangled from Flint's arms. "He'll come back and when he does, I'll be waiting." With those words, she grabbed another stick, and stabbed it into the dirt.

The wood splintered.

Nodin knelt beside her and brushed the remaining wood slivers from her hand. "Mother had no choice but to begin his transformation. She will guide him during the dawn of his new life as an Elemental. You must be patient. The earth will take its time to heal him."

Maya stared at her empty hand and whispered, "If he doesn't come back, who will heal me?"

CHAPTER 37

While waiting inside an ancient relic on the outskirts of town, Quint propped his feet on the kitchen table and contemplated his next move. He folded both hands across his stomach and felt heat emanating from the hole. A hole put there by a backstabbing female. Guess those classic country songs were right. He'd underestimated Pillar. She'd slipped right under his radar. He'd enjoy making her pay, but not all at once. He would go slowly and enjoy each ear-piercing scream.

Was no one loyal anymore? Would he have to bring everyone to heel? Pillar had turned his beautiful Violet against him. But no matter, everyone had a breaking point and he'd find Violet's. She was the most amazing human he'd ever seen. Of course, he could appreciate her gifts, after the fact. All her raw power would be his, but he'd have to contain her in a roundabout way since she was capable of destroying him. As evidenced by the glaring hole *IN HIS CHEST!*

Quint had no intention of returning to the vacuum of darkness, the never-ending abyss. He would stay here—on earth. At this very moment, Terran was undergoing his transformation into Earthman. Quint had laughed with glee as Terran tumbled into the dirt pit. What a fortunate string of events. Sometimes these creatures needed just the slightest nudge. Once he rooted into Earthman's body, he'd glory in his newfound Elemental gifts and rule over Violet for as long as her heart beat.

Speaking of pounding hearts, his partner was finally home. The key clicked in the lock then another lock slid open. Quint heard four beeps from the security pad. *Silly fool.* It wasn't the people who could set off the alarm he needed to worry about—it was those who didn't.

"Good evening, Schwarz."

"Waaah. Goodness. Mr. Aether? You frightened me." Quint noticed Schwarz's German accent went thick during excitable moments. "How did you get inside?"

"Don't be coy, Schwarzy. It doesn't suit you."

"Where have you been? We've been trying to reestablish Aether Pharmaceuticals." Schwarz turned on the light and gasped as he took in Quint's appearance. "What happened to you?"

"Are you referring to my general state or this enormous hole in my chest?" Quint sank back in the chair; aware he looked a mess and didn't care. He wanted to see this vision each time he looked in a mirror so he wouldn't forget. The daily reminder of deceit fueled his rage. "This is what happens when you grant a sweet violet access to your heart. She shoots a bullet through your chest. And you, of all people, know the theory that a high-energy magnetic field can convert dark matter into a photon within the visible spectrum. Well guess what, Schwarzy, the theory is correct."

"Dark matter?"

"Had you ever truly believed anything about me was human?" Quint kicked a kitchen chair across the room. It slammed and splintered against the wall. "Stop acting like an incoherent idiot. I'm not in the mood for your mousy snivel."

"But wh-what can I d-do?" Schwarz stammered.

Quint stood and grabbed him by the throat. *"What can I do?"* He mocked. "Are you nothing without me? Can you not find your own path? Must I do it all?" The man under his hand gasped, and his face turned blue. Interesting how they all opened their mouths and stuck out their tongues. Quint dropped his hand as he got a whiff of Schwarz's breath.

Schwarz crumbled to the floor.

"Get some water." He kicked Schwarz's heaving side. "Quit hacking all over. Who knows what vile germs you've exposed yourself to during your experiments, you sick fuck."

"What are you doing here?" Schwarz stood with his back against the kitchen cabinets. He held one hand at his throat and the other dug through his pocket. "What do you want?"

"Oh no, my little rodent, what is in your hand? A utility knife?" These ridiculous humans, would they never learn? "Go ahead. Stab me."

Schwarz lunged and stabbed him in the heart. And once again, he removed the knife and plunged. His eyes went wide, and he backed away when nothing happened. No wound appeared. No blood poured.

"My turn." Quint took the knife, pushed Schwarz into a kitchen chair, and then slammed the blade into his thigh.

"Aaaarrghhh…Verpiss dich, du hurensohn!"

"Shut up, you German fool, or I'll remove the knife and stab your other leg."

The fool whimpered and breathed heavily.

"What did you eat? Your breath smells like someone took a rotten coffee shit in your mouth. No wonder you never get laid. Even I use a toothbrush." Quint leaned against the kitchen counter as far away from the foul-smelling man as he could get. "Now, have we established the hierarchy? Or would you like to test me again?" Quint paused a beat until Schwarz shook his head. "Good. You work solely for me, regardless of what sick practices you have going on in the basement of this house. All your twisted fun becomes a side project. I have a time-sensitive makeover I'm entangled in at the moment. So you, my sneaky little rodent, will do reconnaissance."

As he held a hand over his bleeding leg, Schwarz chuffed out, "What are you?"

"I'm undetectable darkness. I'm the monster that hides in dark corners. Your worst nightmare." Quint pulled a long knife from the butcher's block on the counter and ran his finger along the blade. "Are you through with your irrelevant questions? You should be asking what do you need, my master? How can I serve you? Those questions are more to my liking."

Schwarz stared at the blood drying on his hand before meeting his gaze. "What's in it for me?"

"Now that's the Schwarz I know and love. My plan is simple. Find Violet Levina and in the process, discover all you can about her family, her life, her job, then report back."

"Again, what's in it for me?" Now the mouse began to squeak. *Very good.* He didn't need weak players on his team.

"Once we have Violet, we'll be able to fund your science

experiments *ad infinitum*." Quint tapped the blade's tip against his lower lip.

"What are you, really?"

"I see that little nose twitching. Keep your vials and needles for your basement creatures."

Schwarz hobbled to the sink and poured a glass of water. "Where should I start?"

Quint buttoned his white dress shirt, and then tucked the shirt into his pants. Sulk time was over. Retaliation was the new order of the day.

"You're the one who enlightened me, my dear Schwarzy. Remember? Go back to where Violet's history began. Where the first witch was burned alive at the stake—Kilkenny, Ireland."

CHAPTER 38

Maya leaned against an old barn's faded red planks. Anticipation raced through her body, because an outlet for her misery was on the horizon. Her mission to find and destroy all Quint's vaccine vials would end very soon. Unfortunate, as this assignment had kept her miserable mind occupied.

Flint and Nodin burned diseased cattle in an empty field, miles from where she stood. The white-gray smoke billowed in the distance—must be one hell of a barbeque. No doubt, they waited for her to join them, but completing her duty without a bit of a brawl wasn't as much fun.

The ranch vet headed to his office in the newly constructed pole barn, funded with a bribe from Aether Pharmaceuticals.

Apparently, research subjects didn't come cheap.

Maya left her spy post and headed across the pasture. Her feet crunched in the tall grass and curious cows snuffed out their greetings. At the open barn door, she passed cardboard boxes stamped with the familiar logo of Quint's now-defunct drug company.

She stood at the vet's office door, her lips curving as he gave her a very blatant once-over. *Oh, he'll be a fun one.* "How's it hanging, cowboy? I noticed you have a few boxes of Aether's unapproved vaccine. I'm afraid I don't take too kindly to your conduct."

The vet propped his feet on his desk. "We've heard about other ranches being hit by vandals who come in and destroy the vaccine. Glad to see you took the bait. I imagine the boys and I *will* take kindly to *you*. Did you think we wouldn't be prepared?"

Maya gleaned the energy patterns of three men making their way to the barn. Their minds pumped for a fight, rifles loaded in their hands. "Three men, is that what you call prepared? All that firepower won't work against me, cowboy, but please feel free to try."

A shot of water against the vet's chest knocked him out of his chair. Maya slammed shut the office door to block out his sputtering and cursing.

As a cloud of vapor, she circled above the ranch hands as they rushed to the vet's office after hearing his shouts.

Eeny, meeny, miney, moe. After peering through their minds, she picked the blond with a penchant for mistreating horses and women.

Maya rained a heavy stream over his head, which knocked the shotgun from his hands. She drifted around them as a dense fog.

His partners scrambled to his side with their guns lifted at the ready. The youngest of the crew shouted and wildly swung his shotgun. He fired a single shot that struck the box of vaccines. The buckshot ripped through the cardboard and the sound of shattering crystal vials filled the air.

The soaking wet blond cupped his hands over his ears that were no doubt ringing from the percussion of the youngster's ill-advised shot. Her foggy fingers wrapped around his neck, and she lifted him while the others stood frozen in fear.

The blond choked and gasped for breath, clawing at his neck

"What is it you thought to do? I am fog, mist. A clear, unending stream. You cannot stop me with your human weapons. I will rain down upon you until you beg for mercy at my feet."

A massive wave from her body flowed out and knocked down the stunned ranch hands.

The vet opened his office door, but after surveying the scene, he shut it again.

The boy in her hand turned an interesting shade of blue.

Violent winds pummeled her and knocked loose her grip on the ranch hand's neck.

Nodin stood in front of the boy, who had fallen to his knees and was clutching his throat, gasping for air. "Enough, Maya. Go. I'll take care of this."

She morphed into her human form and stood her ground before him.

Flint appeared at the barn door, and a blast of heat struck her balled fists. "You want to play with all that power, little girl?"

Her need to evict all this emotional turmoil erased all rational thought. Eagerness for a true fight rippled through her body.

Flint stepped closer, his lips curved in a half-smile. He blew her a heated kiss.

The blast of heat struck her face and dried her throat. "I'm through with these fools. Do with them what you will. I'm done." She blasted out of the barn like a feral waterspout.

Away from Flint. Away from Nodin. Away from everything tying her to earth.

For weeks, they had worked tirelessly discovering which animals were infected. Flint burned them once she and Nodin gathered them. The science world now knew the BSE vaccine was false. Nodin used his mental influence to lead Dr. Houser, head of the Prion Institute, to the truth.

How much longer must she serve the earth and its people? How many days of suffering would she endure in a fog without Terran?

Nodin held no sympathy, telling her to stop pouting and believe in Mother's plan. She tossed back that following that path had worked out just peachy for him. Her sarcasm had gone unappreciated.

Snowflakes lit the skies in Wyoming. The water no longer freely flowed, and the temperatures were tipping toward frigid.

After her outburst today, she needed isolation and warmth.

She drifted south, traveling as a storm cloud through the sky. Coasting along, until she reached the warm waters of the Kaulakahi Channel, the watery passage between Hawaiian Islands, Kaua'i and Ni'ihau.

Ni'ihau, the Forbidden Island, where she'd first learned and adapted to her new life as an Elemental. Her solitude. Her escape. She'd drink salt-water cocktails and soak up the sun—until Terran returned. She could only hope that as he began his journey through his new life as Earthman, he would start by finding her.

CHAPTER 39

"At least Maya will be around to hose me off." Mumbling to himself, Terran swiped at the dirt clumps clinging to his arms and legs

At a farm in the Ukraine, each day he'd grown stronger by lying in a pit of rich, black soil. He emerged frequently, like a real life version of dawn of the dead, to eat plants, and discuss his new existence with Mother Nature.

As he gazed across an empty field where farmers would soon be planting wheat or barley, he acknowledged the passage of time. It was time to leave. Head home to the people that loved him.

Fear for their safety overwhelmed at times, but the first step in his new journey was hindered by inner turmoil and physical weakness. Terran shuddered as he remembered Quint's dominating power that fateful morning at the campground.

A depraved malice had violated his mind and body, traveled along his veins, and threatened his humanity. But Maya, his Maya, remained strong. She alone kept him sane.

What did healing him cost her? Where is she now?

His gleaning powers were not yet under his control. There hadn't been anyone with which to practice in this remote corner of the world.

The flat field before him was covered with remnants of winter's snow. Three months ago, he'd been surrounded by white and not only in his environment but also in his mind. A blank slate in a new consciousness he hadn't asked for, nor desired to achieve.

Adjustments to his Elemental life tossed him through a gamut of emotions. Denial. Rage. Helplessness. Fear. Anger.

His welcome into this new world had started with a mouthful of dirt. His eyes blinked open and were instantly speckled with black. His scream was muffled as he shot up from his shallow grave. He gasped for breath and shivered in fear. The effort involved in rising so quickly tired him and he collapsed. He frantically searched back and forth as he'd tried to understand where he was and how he came to be there.

A soft hum sounded through his body, calming him, and the earth folded against him, like a soft fleece blanket. Its energy began warming his skin, giving him strength, which flowed through him and cleared his mind.

He drifted in and out of consciousness those first days until finally, he was overwhelmed with a strong need for the sun and sprouted from the earth. Glancing around, he felt connected to every blade of grass, every chunk of bark, every leaf on every tree. A link forged to them all. The water, the sky, the earth's hot core settled in perfect harmony and alerted him to his change in circumstances.

He was an Elemental—Earth.

Did he want this? He couldn't change back, could he? Where was he? How much time had passed since the fight at the river?

He lifted his hand in front of his face, looking for obvious changes, but saw none. At his core, a strong energy flow pulsed just under the skin. Unseen but felt.

Aware of the powers Maya said he would receive; he'd done a little test. He listened with his mind and heard the flap of a bird in flight, the soft chirping of a cricket, the scurrying of a mouse. How far could his mind travel? He'd reached out further and further until he'd heard voices that spoke of their farm and found minds full of pleasant visions of children playing by a hearth.

The only shelter was a weather-beaten barn, decades old, in an empty field. A rustling sound came from under the faded planks.

How can I see without my glasses? Wait, am I wearing glasses? No, he wasn't wearing anything. At all. *Of course.* He rolled his eyes and laughed hysterically. Nudity was par for the course as an Elemental

He headed for the sanctuary of the barn, curious as to what was inside.

Mother Nature stood just as he remembered her—tall, majestic, glittering with a fantastic mixture of golds, greens, and browns. She waved a hand before her, indicating a cornucopia of vegetables laid out on a makeshift table of old wood.

She had asked him to sit and eat, gather his strength and feed on the bounty of the earth.

That awakening had taken place over three months ago.

After his mental walk down memory lane, once again, Terran entered the barn and found Mother Nature standing by the table. "What's for dinner? Steak? Pork Chops? Ribs? How about an ice cold beer?"

Mother laughed, a musical chime, and pointed to a carrot pile on the table.

He walked over and picked up a carrot. "I've never eaten so many carrots in my life. No wonder I no longer need glasses. The next time I look in the mirror, I expect to see Bugs Bunny staring back."

She placed a hand on his arm. "How are you faring?"

A twinge of guilt rumbled through him, because she was always so patient and kind. Those two words did not in any way describe his behavior the first time he'd walked into this shelter. A colorful speech had flowed freely from his mouth. *His human mother would not be proud.* Petulant and pissed were light indicators of his attitude during that time. He'd made clear his displeasure at having this Earthman life and all its responsibilities foisted upon him.

But they were past that now.

He twirled a carrot by its leafy, green root. "I'm well. I no longer feel weak, nor that constant tug toward earth to restore my strength. I'm ready." He sat and ate in silence.

They had already argued and debated his questions: *What are my gifts? What do you expect from me? Can I visit my parents? Where are Nodin and Flint? Are they taking care of Maya? How is she? Where is Quint? How do my powers work?*

Can I die?

Laughter and tears had filled the barn as she'd calmed his fears and entertained with her version of earth's history.

Though Mother had patiently explained everything, once he left this barn, he would be on his own. Reality would come crashing down and he'd make many mistakes.

Whispers constantly resonated in his mind. They remained too remote to glean. Could he handle all the clambering voices? How would he muddle through enough to determine who truly needed his help?

"Mother, how is Maya?" Terran rubbed two fingers against his chest bone where a dry ache had sprung. The only cure was a drink from Maya's spring. He had almost died and hadn't revealed his feelings. At the time, he'd had less than a week to reconcile who and what she was. He understood so much more about her now. Forever may lie before him, but he swelled with impatience to see her again.

"You ask after Maya, but your true question is when will you see her again? I agree it is time for you to leave. I have given you all the guidance I can. You must walk the path to truly understand this Elemental life. However, I have one more revelation to disclose. As you are aware, Maya received the extra gift of healing."

Mother circled the table and came to stand beside him. She placed a finger under his chin and added a push of pressure so his gaze met hers.

Her eyes flashed bright green before settling to moss. At times, she was like a mood ring from a grocery store candy dispenser—interchangeable and spooky.

Her eyes turned brown, and she quirked a grin. "Terran, listen, please."

"Sorry."

She nodded and continued, "You are the circle of life. You are solidity and stability. You are tactile and real. Within your circle, air, fire, and water meet. Without your grounding force, they would fall into chaos. Your extra gift is the ability to control them all—wind, fire, and water. All four Elemental gifts are yours."

"But, I haven't felt anything. I don't know how to—" One gift carried enough complexity for a lifetime or even a peri-mortal lifetime. How would he control all four?

Mother placed a single finger against his lips. "The Elementals will teach you. Guide you. Your connection to the earth will remain the strongest, while the others will serve as needed. Use these gifts wisely, my son."

"I know I need to leave, but I'll confess to you what I'd never admit to another. I'm afraid I won't adjust. I'm afraid of Quint. What is normal now? Earthman is fighting against an army of science soldiers in my mind. It's a war of the worlds in there." Terran pulled on his hair, creating tufts.

"You may scoff at Nodin's quotes, but let me offer one now. D. H. Lawrence wrote in *Phoenix II*, 'Man is a thought-adventurer. Which isn't the same as saying that man has intellect.... Real thought is an experience. It begins as a change in the blood, a slow convulsion and revolution in the body itself. It ends as a new piece of awareness, a new reality in mental consciousness. On this account, thought is an adventure, and not a practice. In order to think, man must risk himself. He must risk himself doubly. First, he must go forth and meet life in the body. Then he must face the result in his mind.'"

Mother gently brushed a hand through his hair. Warmth and comfort flowed from her touch. "I cannot answer all your questions, Terran. So many things you must discover on your own. It is time for your adventure to begin. Take risks. Go forth."

He paced in front of the table, tapping a carrot in his hand.

Thought-adventurer?

At this point he was still too flabbergasted to delve too deeply into his thoughts. "Where am I to go? To Maya?"

"Yes. She is lost in worry. Soak in your reunion. You may be peri-mortal now, but savor time. Many dangers exist. Do not become complacent. Your existence is not guaranteed. Love your brothers and care for Maya. Although she is an Elemental, her heart beats the same as any girl. Quint still wishes to control you. You must prepare yourself for battle. His defeat will come at your hand."

"How will I defeat him? What about Violet Levina? Her powers far surpass mine."

"Violet's time will come. Yours is at hand."

CHAPTER 40

Maya refrained from rolling her eyes as Randall Neville ran his fingers down her arm. His immaculate business suit and the gray-lined temples of his perfectly layered hair highlighted his metrosexual lifestyle. The ring on his manicured left finger had disappeared into his travel bag pocket. A tanning bed smell remained on his skin. Always a pungent odor—Eau du baked sweat.

Neville droned on, "...and so I'm down here leading the conference on bio-engineering. This is the third year I've made this business trip. I'm set up in the platinum suite at the Hawaiian Bay Resort. The views get more beautiful each year." With that comment, he ran a finger across her jaw.

Neville had approached moments after she arrived at the resort's beachfront bar. As the sweetener to his arrival, he had the bartender deliver a fruity concoction decorated with a neon pink umbrella and speared with pineapple wedges. Bored with her island isolation, she came here to vent frustrations on troublesome bar patrons. Tonight, she struck gold at the end of her rainbow-flavored drink.

Neville flashed his gold card, so sure she'd be lured in by his high-dollar symbols. His plan entailed adding her to the string of women who'd spent a horrific night on his 1500 thread count sheets. When away from home, Neville discarded the rules of decency and his wedding vows. Unfortunate ladies had left his hotel room victims of a sexual dominant. Safe words went unheeded. His dark nature was revealed in angry shades of scarlet left on his victims' pale skin.

Maya played a submissive role, shyly peering from under her lashes every time she spoke. "Oh, I've never seen a platinum suite. I bet they're luxurious."

I'd love to stab him in the eye with my straw.

Maya twiddled with her drink's paper umbrella and wrapped her arms around her middle. She smiled when he drew closer and rested his arm on the back of her chair.

That's right, strutting peacock, come get your feathers wet.

"Thanks for my drink. It's so pretty. Where did you say you're staying again?" She sipped her drink and twisted on her bar stool so her knee brushed against his thigh.

A rush of heat shot through her body that hadn't initiated from alcohol burn or interest in Neville. She choked, eyes watering as she coughed. Her nostrils burned as the drink spilled out her nose. Grabbing a napkin, she blotted her nose.

What is Flint doing here? Asshole.

"Excuse me. Must have gone down the wrong pipe." Maya coughed and sputtered.

Neville patted her back. "Let's head back to my suite. I'll get you a glass of water."

Her internal temperature flared, flushed through her system, and sparked into lust. She stepped off her seat and wrapped both hands along the bar's edge to maintain her equilibrium.

Something was off. This feeling was unfamiliar, yet amazing. A light draft swirled around her tied hula skirt, and a heated breeze danced down her back. *What is happening?* An invisible hand caressed her body. Only one person evoked this response.

Neville reached out to steady her—

A hand batted him away.

A hand that led to a broad chest covered in a white T-shirt with neon pink letters asking, *Where's the Beach?* Her gaze travelled down to a red-and-white hula skirt, tied around a tapered waist.

Then *he* spoke, "Maya, sorry to keep you waiting."

Her knees wobbled and she leaned against his body. Balsam and cedar flared in the air, filling her empty heart with their warm, welcome scent. Colors appeared before her eyes once more, and her link to the earth returned.

Terran held her close—an umbrella after months of pouring rain.

"Who are you?" Neville slammed his Scotch on the bar.

With a grin, Terran extended his hand. "I haven't quite figured that out yet. And you are?"

"He is leaving," Maya interjected.

Terran's hold on her waist tightened. "Yes, he is."

Neville raised his hands, palms out, toward Terran. "She approached me."

Terran laid a hand on Neville's shoulder. "You will remember you are married and act according to your vows. You will no longer hunt these tropical shores for women to sate your fetish. Finish this trip, but do not ever return."

Maya detected immense power emanating from Terran as it flowed over into Neville. The mental stream gleaned strong, powerful, overwhelming. How could he appear so calm after everything that had happened? Why was he here?

Giddy laughter threatened to escape.

Neville shook his head and knocked Terran's hand from his shoulder. He peered down his nose. "Nice skirt."

"I know, brown is more my color, but we could try black and blue. You decide." With a gentle nudge, Terran shifted her behind him.

Neville raised his glass in a mock toast and retreated.

Terran turned and cupped both sides of her face in his hands. He trailed his thumb across her lower lip.

She clutched his arms in case she fell from shock.

Using his thumbs, he wiped at the tears pouring down her cheeks.

Is he angry? Does he think I am interested in that man? Why isn't he speaking?

She prodded into his mind.

"Don't delve." He pinched her chin. "We're on an even keel now, but will only remain so if you allow that one privacy. May we leave here? I'd like to speak privately." He pulled her away from the bar toward the ocean.

Every gentle touch, every husky word, brought hope. "I'm not sure. I don't know where to go."

"Take me to your island."

"My island? How?"

His lips lifted in a cocky grin as he answered, "Through the water, of course."

Her thoughts remained in a fog as he led her to the ocean's edge. The water's familiar feel lapped against her feet and ankles, bringing back reality.

All her fears and worries melted into the surf. She jumped him—arms, legs, and mouth locked tight. She kissed him and ran her hands over every reachable inch of skin.

Alive. He's alive.

She refused to care if he didn't want her this way. She'd take this heated moment to make up for months of despair. Her emotional dam had burst, and this beach side reunion wouldn't be complete without a kiss in the moonlight.

Terran matched her ardor. He slipped his hand beneath the navy blue triangle covering her breast.

Their kiss wasn't enough. They were still too far apart. Where to begin? Where to touch? A multiple-choice test lay in black and white before her, but the only answer was a long drawn-out essay and he held the pen. What would he write?

Maya pulled back, but kissed his lips between each word. "Take...you...island."

He tucked her head against his shoulder and led her into the ocean, away from the sandy shore. "My beautiful yellow lily, you've traveled very far from home."

"I hope I am home. Now. With you."

"Take me to your island, and I'll show you my welcome mat."

"I can't believe you just said that, but I'm so happy, I'll laugh anyway." Happiness bubbled down her spine. She wrapped her hands around his face, peered into his eyes, seeing past the deep brown. "Are you all right? Have you been with Mother? That man, at the bar, I was going—"

He silenced her with a quick kiss. "Maya, I know what you were doing. As for the rest, I'm adjusting. I don't want to talk about this here. I'd rather go for a swim. I want to experience this moment together. The feel of the water as it rushes over our skin. The clarity, the silence found deep beneath the surface. And then I want to lie down in the sand and complete this vicious circle I've been spinning in for months. The circle of my life ends with you. It always will."

Maya kissed the side of his neck and licked his thrumming pulse. "If this is a dream, don't wake me. Your words give me hope. I've been cross with everyone and everything. Without you, I'm lost. I don't know which direction to turn."

"Follow me. We'll figure it out together." He took her hand and drew her further into the ocean.

"Terran, wait." She grabbed his arm and towed him toward shore. "You can't—"

"Watch me." He dove and pulled her along.

She fumbled for his arm and scissor kicked toward the surface, but only went deeper as he towed her into the sea. Oh, this was amazing, sharing the water with him. How was this possible? He'd returned and hadn't rejected her. Promising signs—beautifully wondrous signs. She'd take them, even if her bliss only lasted until they reached her island.

He squeezed her hand and together, they swam past schools of fish and coral reefs. Leaving a trail of happiness in the bubbles dancing to the surface behind them.

# # #

The first rays of sunlight glistened against the water droplets pearled on the curves of her nude body. Her wet hair lay tangled in the sand.

"Enjoying the view?" Flat on her back, Maya rested on the beach, her gaze on the sky.

"Most beautiful view I've ever seen." He'd never be able to trick this girl. Never catch her unaware. Out of all the gifts he'd been given, he believed she was the most glorious one. Without her, he'd feel like Sisyphus, carrying the weight of this new life uphill only to have it roll down, flattening his efforts. But he'd made it here, to her island, and now, their Elemental link clamored for immediate attention.

"I see your compass is working."

He glanced down at his hard shaft straining in her direction. His gaze locked with hers and he shrugged.

She levered up, rested on her elbows, but shifted her gaze to the vast ocean. "I've been lost without you."

Terran kissed her shoulder. "The choice to leave was not mine. I remember falling, and then I woke up covered in a pit of black dirt. I'm sorry I took so long to return." He paused for a moment then admitted, "I've had some difficulty adjusting."

"I understand. I'm so sorry. So, very sorry you didn't get to choose. It's unfair and maddening. I never wished this life for you. I tried to—"

"Maya, please, I don't blame you." He turned on his side and ran a finger along her arm. "I see now there was never any other path. My parents, my job, my dreams all pointed in this direction."

Her ocean blue eyes shimmered with tears, before calming and turning deep indigo. Turning on her side, Maya reached over and traced his body with her fingers.

The shackle binding them began to rattle and shake. The pull to reestablish their connection made him grasp her hand and link their fingers. He kissed her hand, sealing their union.

Her hand twitched in his and she blinked. As startled as he by the jolt of lust his kiss had caused, that simple caress had almost brought him to completion. And by the heated look in her eye, she experienced the same.

"Terran, please. I need to know. Are you truly all right? I do not wish you to feel obligated in any way."

"No, Maya, I chose to be here." He gave her hand a squeeze, "When astronaut, Russell Schweickart, returned from an Apollo mission he said, 'You become startlingly aware how artificial are the thousands of boundaries we've created to separate and define. And for the first time in your life you feel in your gut the precious unity of the earth and of all living things it supports. The dissonance in this unity you see and the separateness of human groupings that you know exist is starkly apparent.' I finally understand what he meant."

"Good lord, you've turned into Nodin."

He laughed. "Only partially."

"Mother helped you?"

"Yes. She helped me embrace the unity of earth and all living things. I've always felt a connection to the earth, but now I feel so much more. And the artificial boundary I erected between us was placed there out of fear and anger. I want to live a life that properly defines Earthman's purpose."

"I'm grateful Mother helped you grasp your role. I was so worried." Head bent, Maya swirled small circles in his chest hair with her finger. "What will you do now?"

Terran leaned closer, tipped up her chin, and kissed her. "I'm doing it."

"I searched for you after the cave-in and when I couldn't find you, your disappearance became too much to bear. I've isolated myself here, waiting for your return. I'm sorry I didn't protect you, and that I returned to the surface. It's more dangerous now than before. Quint will come. He can find us." Her clasp on his shoulder became a death-grip. "We must get you to—"

Terran interrupted her by placing a finger against her lips. "Those worries will wait. Right now is what matters. Mother said you contained the BSE and destroyed the vaccine. I think you deserve a gold star for that. Shall I give it to you?"

He claimed her mouth in a possessive kiss and desire flared bright. He stroked his tongue both rough and gentle against hers. The kiss became more fervent, out of control, soothing an ache that had erupted months ago.

Terran pulled back, dropping kiss after kiss on her nose, each brow, her cheeks. Mindlessly, he covered her neck and shoulders with licks and bites. "I need you. I've missed this skin that smells of spring rain and mists at my touch." He closed his hand in a fist, created a pool of water, and poured the liquid down her chest.

She gasped and stared with wide eyes. "How did you do that?"

"I'm gifted. How else could I swim with you? I'm not sure how each Elemental gift works." He paused for a moment unsure how to explain. "I thought about what I wanted to do and water formed in my hand."

She took his hand and ran her finger through the water pooled in his palm.

Though he understood he was just showing off, he blew a soft breeze through her hair.

"That's not fair." She pushed both hands against his chest. "You got all the gifts?"

He chuckled and distracted her by pouring more water over her chest. Her head fell back and she arched against him as he licked the water from her sun-kissed skin.

He returned to her lips, tangled in her web and reveling in each silky, clinging caress. "Maya, look at me. After being alone for so many years, you deserve to hear the words. I love you. I should have said them before, but three words can't encompass all this." He swept a hand over his heart. "Mother said I'm a circle. That may be so, but know this—I begin and end with you. Over and over, I will mark you as mine. Establish our bond in every way. I want to drape gold on each of your fingers as a symbol you belong to me."

"You truly mean to stay?" Her gaze was direct and seemed to shimmer with hope.

"Maya, how can you doubt? I know you've felt alone through the years, but that is no longer the case. I want you at my side as I begin my adventure. I need your guidance and your love."

Excited delight erupted in her eyes, and her hand worked up and down his arm. "What shall we do? Where do you want to go? Did Mother say we could work together?"

"Look at who has all the questions now. After months of ice and snow, I want to bask in the sunshine. Make love for hours. Everything else can wait."

The crashing current that had raged through his mind for months stilled. Her presence drenched his heart and rooted deep. He glanced at his chest half-worried flowers would sprout.

She chuckled and placed a kiss right above his blooming heart.

They played and teased for long moments, savoring their rediscovery of each other—mindless to all else.

When they finally joined, they experienced a blessed healing. A glorious rhythm followed the tide crashing against their entwined bodies. The sun's heat was no match for the erupting volcano overtaking them as together they plunged into the pool of fire. Bursts in vibrant reds, yellow flares, and a golden glow of orange flames flowed like hot lava under their skin. Release pooled and then burst like magma in wave after wave down the fiery fount.

Once again whole. Once again joined. Once again at peace.

Their hearts melded by heat refined into a sharp blade and pierced them both. Two Elementals bound by nature and touched by destiny's hand, allowed primal lust complete control. Skin against skin, they forged an unbreakable bond.

CHAPTER 41

Terran stood at the foot of an old mine. Late spring in Colorado brought about the snowmelt, which trickled through abandoned mines and created a brew laced with the dissolved metals: arsenic, cadmium, copper, and zinc. Keeping this toxic discharge from contaminating water sources occupied his spare time.

As the Elemental—Earth, he focused on healing the earth and helping humans in danger—an overwhelming, never-ending responsibility.

Today's mine survey hadn't resolved any issues. He kicked the loose rock outside the entrance. How much could he ingest, and how long would it take to heal? Lying naked in a dirt pit when Quint came calling wasn't an option.

Terran stepped inside the mine, transformed to dust, and traveled home. He and Maya lived in a cabin on the outskirts of Monte Vista near the Rio Grande National Forest. Three bliss-filled months had passed since their retreat on Maya's Forbidden Island.

He'd landed a job as a consultant for the Environmental Protection Agency. *Easiest job interview ever.* Guilt remained over that mind meld, but a nine-to-five job was no longer viable with his Elemental duties.

Closer to home, he became aware of another's presence—an invader of his sanctuary.

This particular creature, he didn't mind, not that he'd admit it. During his stay in Colorado, he'd learned a lot about his Elemental group and himself. As an only child, he'd never known the intricacies of having brothers. Complete pests one day and someone he'd willingly die for the next. Nodin and Flint served in his quest to become a better Elemental, although in completely different ways.

Terran breezed through his laboratory's front door, re-formed, and grabbed a pair of sweatpants hanging on a hook by the door. Spare clothes were stashed everywhere—in his house, in town, and in the surrounding forest. Nudity remained out of his comfort zone.

Flint sat at his desk, clicking through YouTube videos on the laptop.

Terran wadded up a sock and threw it at Flint's head. "Make yourself at home."

"I thought I was." Flint propped his feet on the desk.

"Where have you been?"

Flint shrugged.

Terran headed for the mini-fridge and pulled out two organic Hoppy Head beers. "Find what you're looking for?"

"It's your turn to stay out of my head, Pigpen."

Terran grunted in answer and skirted the table filled with beakers, graduated cylinders, and an optical microscope.

Flint took the offered beverage and twisted off the cap. "How was Mommy?"

"Very well, as was my father. Thanks for asking."

"Domestics," Flint scoffed and shook his head. "Did you tell them?"

"No, but I think my Mom knew something was different. Mother's intuition and all that." His parents had been furious he'd been out of touch for so long and had even contacted the local authorities.

He and Maya had returned yesterday from a three-day reassure-the-parents trip. Maya had driven him crazy with worries his parents wouldn't like her. She'd packed, repacked, and overanalyzed her entire wardrobe. His parents' warm welcome had laid her fears to rest, and they'd already planned a return trip.

Flint stood and stretched. "I'm heading out. Been in this backwater burg too long."

"Redheads are known for their tempers. Sure you want to stir up Ms. Levina?" Terran leaned against his table and took a long draw from the only beer he could still drink. Overly hoppy, and not his first choice, but beer was beer.

"She started it."

"How old are you again?"

"Just focus on keeping me old by defeating Quint, and let me worry about my hot-house violet."

Terran eyed the samples in the Total Organic Content machine. "Nodin checks in every other day. The problem is we don't know much about dark matter, and after I read any physics book, I have to stick my head in the mud for hours to recuperate. Physics theories are mind-blowing. Your Violet is our best bet, unless you know where I could get a super-cooled magnet."

"Just stick a magnet in the freezer." Flint joked. "Between your science talk and Nodin's constant philosophical quotes, I should get paid with barrels of silver wire Dengas for speaking to either one of you."

Flint headed for the door, but stopped and leaned against the frame. "I know you didn't ask for this life, but you're adjusting well." He bumped his fist against the door pane. "I've been through it all. Everything. More than once. I know most of the time I'm blowing smoke, but the four of us, we're all each other's got."

Compassion? From Flint? Terran nodded, unsure of the conversation's direction.

Flint lifted his beer in salute before setting the bottle on a chair by the door. "Take care of Maya. I still don't understand what she sees in you, when all along she could have had this." He waved a hand down the front of his body.

"Maya prefers fresh meat, not an ancient hunk, left at the bottom of the freezer then served charred on all sides. Speaking of burnt meat, stay on Violet's good side, Flint. You have no idea the power that girl harnesses. I'd hate to see her turn on you."

"No worries, Pigpen. I find most women burn in my presence."

"You've lost your mind if you think Violet is 'most women.'"

"Levina is Latin for lightning bolt. I'd let her strike my body anytime." Flint waggled his brows.

"Leave it to you to turn a pleasant discussion into crude perversion."

"Either that or we'd be drinking lemon tea and breaking out the crumpets."

Terran tipped his beer bottle toward Flint "You're the one who just gave the whole emotional spiel. I was about to hand you a tissue."

"You can take that tissue and shove it—"

"I thought you were leaving?"

Flint raised his middle finger in salute. "Keep it hot, Pigpen."

Terran shook his head as Flint fired away and left a smoke trail through the afternoon sky. Although it went against "bro code," he hoped Ms. Levina taught Flint a few things about women and humility. Flint covered loneliness with a cocky demeanor, but there were occasional flares of kindness. If Violet "lightning bolt" Levina decided to shine the spotlight on Flint, she might burn him to ash.

And yet, Violet had not returned to shine her light on anyone. She'd disappeared, leaving them floundering in the dark. Mother's warning rumbled daily through his mind. He pounded a fist against his lab table. Glass clanked then settled.

His defeat will come at your hand.

Preparation was crucial. Quint was coming.

CHAPTER 42

"I've been considering a trip to South Dakota," Terran announced from his perch on their kitchen barstool.

Maya grabbed a glass from the cabinet and filled it at the sink. "Why do we need to go there? Have you sensed something? We could stop at Mt. Rushmore."

After arriving home from her library job, Maya always drank a full glass of water. Amusement struck at how happy he was to see her each day, like a puppy greeting his master at the door. His "tail" between his legs had even twitched when he'd kissed her hello.

Terran grabbed her arm, kissed her again then answered her questions. "No dead presidents. Though we might strike gold in the Black Hills. The LUX detector is located in an old gold mine at the Samson Research Facility. LUX stands for Large Underground Xenon experiment. Maybe if they ran Quint through their tests, there would be proof dark matter exists." He took her glass and finished off her water. "Quint's a WIMP."

"No, he's anything but that." Maya shot him a glance that suggested he was crazy.

Terran chuckled and tweaked her nose with his finger. "You misunderstand. Dark matter is theorized to take the form of particles called Weakly Interacting Massive Particles—WIMP."

"If those scientists ever met Quint, they'd change that name in a heartbeat. I imagine Quint steers clear of South Dakota and dark matter detectors."

"I'd still like to tour their facility. After that, we could go to

Italy."

"Oooo, how romantic. We could go to Saint Mark's Basilica, Pompeii, The Colosseum, and then we could tour the wine—"

"No, no wine…What would happen if you drank wine?" He studied her for a moment then continued, "Never mind, we'd be visiting the Gran Sasso National Laboratory. It's the world's largest underground laboratory. They do—"

"You want to vacation in Italy and spend the entire time in a lab." Maya sighed deeply. "What am I going to do with you? You want to do research, study what happens when particles collide? How about you start a collision with me?" She ran her hand over his semi-hard flesh covered by sweatpants. "Mmm, almost ready, but this time you'll have to catch me."

As she misted, her clothes fell to the floor. Her misty form swirled around his body. Reforming by the fireplace, she smiled and crooked a finger.

"No cheating by switching forms." His luscious lily never failed to entice. Light shined through from the patio door's tilted blinds and highlighted her silky, blonde strands. He entered the game by making the first advance.

She stepped to the side.

He vaulted over the couch.

Shrieking with laughter, she ran down the hall toward their bedroom.

He followed and found her standing on their king size bed. His feral nature now provoked, like a savage lion stalking a golden gazelle. He slammed shut the door and leaned against it. "Come here."

"No. Catch me."

"There's nowhere for you to run." Voice calm, he waved a hand before him. "I'd say you're caught."

His tricky siren misted again and disappeared through the crack under the door.

As he whipped open the door, it bounced against the wall. He trekked back down the hall, rearranging his very swollen cock in his sweatpants. "Cheaters never prosper. Haven't you ever heard that, Ms. Conway."

When he came around the corner, he spotted her standing behind his recliner. She wouldn't get away this time.

He rushed her.

A crazed squeal erupted before she burst into an almost hysteric laughter.

They raced around the couch then circled the kitchen block, like two cars around an oval track.

He reached out and grabbed her elbow. "Don't you dare mist again." He drew her closer, hefted her in his arms, and carried her to the bedroom.

They both were breathing heavily when he lowered her to her feet by the bed. She kept her arms wrapped around his neck and kissed him, a lingering, tender caress warming his mouth. He returned every brush of her lips then took over, gripping the back of her head to hold her steady for his show of conquest. "I caught you. What have I won?"

She pulled back, her mass of hair swaying gently around her face and shoulders. Her full breasts peaked, a clear sign of her arousal. Her eyes turned sapphire blue as she ran her hands over her body and up through her hair. Lifting the golden tendrils away from her shoulders cascaded a heady sea scent through the air.

Impatience to claim every inch of her coursed through him, gaze still locked with hers, he started to shove down his pants. Her lips formed a playful pout.

"Stop." She knocked his grip from his pants. "You, sir, have won a trip to my laboratory. We do extensive research here. Our test subjects are subjected to many, many trials."

Another playful tease of her hands over her breasts had him reaching for her, ready to take over that caress, ready to repay her teasing with some play of his own.

But she re-directed his hands to his sides. "No, the subject must remain still." Maya relieved his straining erection from the elastic band of his sweatpants. She molded her hands around his heated flesh. A teasing play of her fingers mixed with hard strokes.

He allowed her control over the experiment, enjoying her thorough study.

She squeezed his tight sacs. "I have you in my hands. What tests shall I run? Checks for weight and length are above average." She laughed and tightened her grip, stroking harder and faster.

The effort required to remain still as she ministered to him was medal worthy.

"The feel of you in my hand and knowing it's my touch creating such a hard and heavy reaction results in my stimulation as well." She ran her thumb over his erect head.

He jerked in response and hitched out a breath. Body primed to claim his captured prey. But he'd let her experiment or whatever game she wanted to play, because he knew satisfaction was the only result of this study.

Maya dropped to her knees and licked the beaded tip on his erect head before drawing him deep in her mouth, over and over.

He tightened his hand in her hair as he edged toward release. No longer able to wait, he gripped her under her arms and lifted her. "My turn to experiment. Let's see how you taste." He seized a rosy tipped breast between his lips then laved each peak with his tongue until her whispered pleas brought them back on even ground.

She tugged on his hair. "Terran, kiss me."

He obliged and locked his mouth over hers. Her tongue grappled with his for supremacy, one test he met her at with full measure. He slid his hands around her back and down over her hips. He boosted her, locked her legs around his hips, and set his aching head at her honeyed core.

She gripped his shoulders, lifted, and then sank down, taking him deep into her body. Her eyes opened and she directed, "Sit on the bed."

They remained joined as he sat on the edge of the bed. She rose up and glided down then repeated the tortuous motion.

Terran met her second thrust with a hard nudge of his hips, "I thought you wanted to test me. See how many times we could collide before we both exploded into fragments. You'll have to pick up the pace."

"You want a hard ride, Earthman? I'll give you one."

All tenderness was lost as she pushed him back on the bed, readjusted, and rocked against him. Out of control, her wild gallop increased in stride, and his hips rose with hers to jump over each hurdle. Sweat beaded on her body as they leapt through a wall of flame.

The red-hot glow of her brand seared his body again and again. He bucked out his surrender and left his mark deep in her body. Each strong pulse led her to the edge and pushed her over. Her body went rigid, but he held her tight in the saddle, rolling his hips against her as she called out her triumph and finished the ride. Her throaty cry of his name thundered through his system and kept the onslaught of his release sprinting through his body. Tremors and twitches slowly abated, and he relished the glorious vision mounted between his thighs. He bent his knees and corralled her sweat-slicked body, lowering her against his chest.

A satisfied sigh passed her lips

"Well, Ms. Conway, what were the results of the experiment?"

"I think further study is needed."

A chuckle rumbled from his chest as he traced his fingers up and down her spine. "I was very satisfied with the results. You can be my lab partner anytime. Although, sometimes I worry I get carried away. I strive for gentleness, but end up losing all control."

She remained quiet for a moment then kissed his shoulder. "The intensity comes from our fear it will end." Her whispered words touched on a fear he equally shared.

His defeat will come at your hand.

No, those fears were not welcome here, in this moment. "Nodin is the wise one, he must be rubbing off on you." With his forefinger under Maya's chin, he nudged to study her face.

They rarely mentioned their fears, choosing instead to focus on actions with immediate solutions. Quint's next foray into their lives could mean the end of their existence. During these private moments, when they were sealed together, they regained a semblance of control in the barest way possible.

Maya kept her worries hidden. But as connected as they were, their concerns and fears eddied around them.

He refused to delve into her mind. Although he wasn't sure she could say the same—old habits died hard.

She leaned down and softly kissed him, lingering, playing with his lips.

At times, this expression of her softer side did more to excite him than anything else.

She nipped his bottom lip. "You're right, sometimes I do peek into your mind, and I'm sorry for that. The world gets hazy and unfocused, but when I glean your thoughts, I find reassurance. I still struggle to believe this is all real."

Terran caressed her face and whispered against her lips, "I love you, Maya. What more do you need?"

"I need and want it all. I was only half alive before, but with you, I see life so much clearer and brighter. I am complete now that I've followed destiny's path to you." She shifted and lined up their bodies by lying more fully atop him.

"You are like that yellow flower left on my pillow, back in full bloom. Bright and open after a full dose of Forrester Fertilizer."

Her body vibrated against his as they both laughed at his ridiculous reference.

"Is that what that was?" She placed her elbows on his chest and swirled a finger around the dent in his chin. "I'm not sure. Did you spread it over my entire field, Earthman? Or did that big red tractor miss a few spots?"

He cocked a brow. "No, I'm sure I hit all the areas needing application, but if you want a double dose, I've got a ready supply."

"Been storing it up for me, have you?" *Apparently, agricultural references turned her on.*

She brushed his damp hair off his forehead and kissed him. His effect was the same and the hunger in their kiss increased. He could still lose her, but she was hale and whole now, meeting his desire equally. A repeat experiment seemed in order. She lifted and set him at her core, plunging down, erasing all thought, but sprouting heat between them.

Maya's eyes remained open, gazing into his, her hands were braced on his shoulders, and she panted out, "That's right, once more. I'll never get enough." She ran her hands over his chest and up to cup his face.

Their kiss turned flagrant as he met each grind of her hips. A moan erupted from her throat as the tension steadily rose. A slow build, now that their initial heat was satisfied. This ride would be a leisurely climb, leading them to the heights of a firestorm until they thundered through the rain. He set a measured pace until a filmy sheen covered their bodies. Her mouth released his and she breathed heavily against his lips. He allowed no solace in the storm. Once again, he locked his mouth to hers, and his tongue matched the motion of his body's rise into her dewy heat.

The torrent continued pouring down and she rose above him. Eyes closed, she bit her lower lip as her body started to shake with the ripples of her release. The hazy heat created between their bodies fogged his mind, and he joined her with a final gust against her flooded core. Every muscle relaxed and his arm flopped over his head as she fell upon his chest.

Total devotion to this water-girl filled every corner of his heart. "I will never leave you."

Her head made a slight nodding motion and a trickle of tears wet his side.

"Don't cry. This won't end. I promise."

"You've captured me. I can't lose you now."

He trailed his fingers up and down her back. "We're bound by an Elemental spell. Nothing will break it. Trust me."

This Elemental life was something neither had asked for, but they were connected now and tied together forever. Every triumph, every joy, every sorrow shared for an eternity.

Destiny had dealt them a hand. He dreaded the day he'd play his ace.

CHAPTER 43

Maya finished downing her third supersized glass of water, more thirsty today than usual. Her Earthman had left, sated for a time, and ready to tackle the world's problems in his makeshift lab in the backyard pole barn. After watching Terran walk away, she headed to the master bath to shower.

Terran's phone on the bedside table rang with a warbled ringtone. She checked the caller ID, but the screen was blank. His cell rang and rang, never going to voice mail. A sickening sense of foreboding churned her waterlogged stomach.

"Hello."

"Oh no, dear, this will never do. Playing the part of jealous lover already, are we?" The voice seemed to come from a young girl, but the words were all Quint.

"How did you get this number?"

"Who says I'm using a phone? In all this time have you learned nothing of my abilities? I am everywhere. All."

No. Not now. She needed more time. She couldn't lose Terran now. "I won't let you take him."

"As if you have any say."

And wasn't that the ultimate truth. She'd never had any say. Never. How could she respond when she knew he was right? Silence reigned on the line. Silence that defined the moment and highlighted what she'd known all along. The sacrifice she would have to make—was willing to make—for love. For Terran. "Take me instead."

"Take you?" A purr came from the girl's throat and vibrated

across the line. "Interesting. I'm listening."

"I've never understood why you didn't want me anyway. Or Flint or even Nodin. I'm peri-mortal. I can give you the longevity you crave."

"Just give?"

"No, I'll play along. Put up a fight. Who knows, maybe I'll even defeat you. Knock you back until we can re-group. Get Violet on our side."

"Them's fighting words, Water Witch."

"Frightened of a mere slip of a girl, Quint?"

"Why don't you come out and play? I may even take you up on your offer, although I did have my heart set on Terran. He is the strongest, you know. And the smartest."

Maya refused to back down. "Take me."

"Just like that? Never as much fun without any suffering. And there will be suffering."

"Where?"

"In the woods, dear. Come join me by the river. I'd like to deliver your demise at the water's edge. And I'd hurry, or I might get antsy and visit his lab. Oh, what fun explosions we could create." The call ended with a girlish giggle.

Should she do this?

She hadn't chosen her death so many years ago. Hadn't chosen this Elemental life. But she held no regrets. She'd found love, been loved, and in the end, that's all that mattered.

Her life for Terrans.

Choice made.

Under the shower stream, rejuvenation and resignation spilled over Maya's body. The life-giving liquid didn't ease the drip of finality pounding through her mind.

The water turned cold, yet she remained under the flow, frigid and afraid of what would happen when she left its secure presence.

Quint circled the woods like a wolf roaming closer and closer to their door. The time to face the snarling beast had come.

Always inevitable—her journey would end.

The joy she gleaned flowing through Terran every time he helped someone was a feeling she'd forgotten, but he'd helped her remember. Being around him, re-opened her heart to the pleasures found in her duties as an Elemental. Integrity. Growth. Sharing. And love, that four-letter word she'd feared so long, would now lead to another four-letter word—dead.

Determined in her course, she turned off the cold spray, shook dry, and stepped into the bedroom. She refused to look at the rumpled bed.

This walk to death's shadow could only be completed with an emotional shutdown. Yet, she paused at the threshold between the bedroom and hallway—aware of the risks upon stepping past. Defeat lay on the other side. She would fight and she would lose.

Her death. Her choice.

She stomped on the golden carpet strip, over and over, until the flimsy metal divider dented. Her hands squeezed into fists and water dripped to the floor. Tears poured down her cheeks. Her heart gurgled as she crossed the threshold and headed down the hall, not surprised at finding Mother standing by the patio door. The glass doors behind her framed the old barn where Terran toiled away with chemicals and glass beakers.

Mother opened her arms in greeting.

Maya turned away and gripped the back of a chair set alongside the kitchen island. "I can't, Mother. I'm sorry. If I lean on you now, I'll break. I must be strong. I can't cry or hold on too tight, because if I come to you, I'll drop to my knees and beg you to take it all back." She faced Mother once more. "Please. Take Terran to a place he'll be safe. I'll do anything. Tell me what I need to do."

Mother clasped her fingers together before her. "That is not my purpose here."

"Not your purpose, right." Maya scoffed. "I've been fumbling around without any sort of direction. Until Terran, Mother, he gave me purpose. I love him and that serves in everything I do." She pounded a fist against her chest, where her heart overflowed with love. "He's my reason in this crazy existence. Without him, I am only a vessel filled with water."

"My daughter, the fight with Quint is for Terran alone."

"We don't live alone, Mother. There are four of us and we fight together." She kicked the bottom of the kitchen chair, knocking it over. "Why would you have him face Quint alone? What kind of game are you playing?"

"I see with a view beyond your understanding." As Mother waved her arms out to her sides, amber and emerald streaks shimmered under her arms.

"Then make me understand, tell me what it is you know. Why make us suffer? If you encompass so much then tell me the answers." Maya blinked back unwelcome tears.

"You've chosen to take his place then?"

"Without question. I won't allow you to take *this* choice from me."

"Quint is close. Impatient. Panting with greed and anticipation. Do not face him alone, Maya. Take Terran with you."

"So I can watch the man I love get devoured and turned into a disgusting dark smear on the earth. *Never.*"

"Don't be foolish, girl."

"At one time that was true, I was a foolish girl, but then *you* chose to change me. You forced me to live this Elemental life. Now I will choose when it ends. I get to decide." She jabbed her finger against the countertop, emphasizing each point. "I choose to exchange my life. I choose to face Quint alone. I choose when I die."

"Maya, you have grown from a selfish, vapid human into a compassionate Elemental. Yet, the adventurer in you remains. Come." Mother spread her arms open.

"No." Maya shook her head. Done with this conversation. Ready to move forth with her plan. Mother's soft embrace would weaken her resolve. "I won't take your comfort."

"Not comfort, strength. Come."

"It won't be enough."

"Daughter, my beating heart, let me give you this last gift."

With each step, Maya attempted to solidify her purpose in her mind and heart.

Golden arms that shimmered from the light through the window enveloped her body. Maya closed her eyes and let Mother's warmth seep in. A vision appeared behind her closed lids.

An arid seabed. At the center, a solitary tree rises from the dust. Defiant, unwilling to fall. White bark faded from the sun. An intricate puzzle created by cracks crisscrossing the dry earth. Wind stirs and fish bones appear at her feet.

A single tear's wet glide dripped and broke through the mirage.

Maya opened her eyes. Mother had disappeared and left her holding empty space. Empty arms.

Maya snapped open the lock on the patio door, and then glanced down at track on the floor—stupid thresholds.

Sliding open the door, she stepped outside and headed for the forest. Never once looking back.

CHAPTER 44

The solution in the Erlenmeyer flask turned green. *Odd.* Terran lifted the flask and swirled it around. *Why did it change color? Is residue left on the glass?*

When the liquid in the graduated cylinder turned brown, he felt the hairs on the back of his neck stand up straight.

Someone was behind him.

He turned.

Mother stood in the open doorway with a bushel of carrots in her arms.

He shook his head. "Very funny."

She placed them on a chair by the door. "I thought to lighten the mood since I've come to tell you the time has come, Terran. Quint is here."

"Now? Maya, she—"

"She is heading for the river."

Acid fear churned in his gut. "What?"

"It was her choice."

"We get to make choices now?" Why was Mother in his lab and not protecting Maya? *Where are my truck keys?* He unplugged the heating mantle. *What else?* He glanced around the lab. He wasn't ready.

"Terran, you are ready. Power lies within. Use the Earth. Harness its energy. Gather the force of your gifts and unleash them."

"Right, gather, unleash. Thanks. Excuse me." He tore off his lab coat, threw down his safety glasses, and stepped outside. Mind open, he allowed his senses free rein across the forest floor. Maya tried blocking him, but he jumped her hurdles. Mental roadblocks wouldn't work. Not today.

Hopping into his Raptor, he followed their connection through the trees. Their thread remained strong and guided him to her location. He slipped the truck into 4-wheel drive and bounced along until leveling off on a dirt path heading toward the river.

Here. The search ended here. Braking hard, he slammed the truck in Park and jumped out.

Screened behind a copse of evergreens, Maya stood by the river. *"Maya, What are you doing?"*

"Go back." Visible now as she'd moved to the gap between two bushy branches.

Her eyes went wide and she waved wildly. Her terror vibrated along their connection. She rushed forward, but plastered against an invisible wall and fell back. Her mouth formed words, but he couldn't hear.

A void crashed between them. Pain burst in his head, hammering like a thousand nails into his brain.

Quint had arrived.

The fight for control of his body was no longer a question of when, but of surviving the day. Terran kneeled on the ground and he clawed his fingers deep into the earth, drawing strength, using his elemental connection to maintain control over his mind.

Quint strove for dominion, like a farcical circus trainer with a whip, lashing for control again and again.

But Terran was king of this forest and refused Quint even a portion of his mind.

Do not acknowledge. Refuse his will.

With a roar, Terran stood and released a strong wind gust against the barrier erected between him and Maya. The wall shattered to black dust.

Maya misted and her voice ripped through his mind, *"Run!"*

CHAPTER 45

Applause sounded from behind a thicket of bushes. Quint appeared, cleverly masked in the form of a teenage girl, wearing skinny jeans and pink and white striped top.

Maya's mist turned to flakes and snowed to the ground. She reformed, but remained frozen in place.

Quint-girl had similarities to Maya—tall, blonde hair—such an unfortunate waste of young life. Evidence her teen body was incapable of containing Quint's evil essence was obvious as deterioration had begun. Her skin hung on her bones like an oversized cloak. Full black eyes raged as she snarled with rotted teeth.

Maya's faint power tried to break through Quint's barrier to seam with his.

"It's over. I win." The poor teen's voice sounded as if she'd been chewing glass. "As if there was any other choice. I alone evolved into this existence. I deserve the prize of immortality. What will you do with forever, but waste it on ridiculous endeavors. You fight to rebuild this planet, but your efforts are futile. Destruction and mayhem rule, because greed always wins."

Terran planted his feet in a wide stance. "Then why do you desire to become human? You hate them, yet you are desperate to live among them. You have not won. I remain standing. I will not allow you to use me."

Quint stepped closer to Maya, but kept his gaze on Terran. "I wish there were time to use you over and over until I've filled your every cavity with my black seed. I'm a bit impatient and will have to set aside that fantasy, although, my fantasy of destroying your Elemental friends will soon come to fruition. Once they're erased, I will rule, as is my right."

"Fantasy is the only part of that speech you got right. You won't survive the day."

"Terran, I had thought you so clever, but you carry a fatal flaw, compassion. You would never have survived as an Elemental. I see mad scientist in your future—an entertaining direction. Perhaps I'll continue down that path, and get my dear friend, Schwarz to join in the fun."

"I'm done listening to you drone on about how superior you are. Back it up, Blondie." Terran calmed his fury, breathed deep of the surrounding air, and soaked up the purity of the forest. Fire burned deep in his belly. Earth beckoned, rumbling at his feet, ready to bend to his will. Everything coalesced to the surface of a pin. In this moment, he and Quint sat perched atop.

"Ah, yes, let's do discuss your penchant for blondes. I'd hoped you would appreciate my costume. I picked her out of the schoolyard just for you." The sneering and jeering from the young girl was, no doubt, incongruent with the beauty she'd once been. "To be honest, she's starting to chafe, perhaps I'd fit better in a Maya suit."

At the threat, Terran's Elemental nature went primeval. The air around him heated and swirled in a fury.

Quint laughed and clapped his hands. "All four gifts, what fun I shall have." Then the giddy schoolgirl mask slipped, and a cloying evil pulsed in the confined space.

Recess over.

"You've made the oldest mistake in the book, Terran. Did you think I wasn't watching, waiting for the perfect moment? You've shown your single ace. But I carry the Dead Man's hand and the fifth card is the Queen of hearts."

Maya's body shot up and floated in the air. Her back was bent in an unnatural manner.

Terran formed a fireball in his hand and shot the flaming mass at Quint.

The force knocked him down, and his clothes went up in flames.

A rank stench of burnt human flesh filled the air as the teen's skin melted. Quint's voice screeched inside Terran's head, *"How dare you strike a girl.*"The flames blanked out and left a charred mess.

Maya broke through Quint's grip and plunged to the ground. She quickly rose to her knees and, with a strong water gush, blasted Quint into the river. She maintained her narrow stream and followed.

As the earth rumbled and cracked at his feet, Terran stumbled to the ground.

Focus.

Control.

Wind whipped through the air, and the river churned and flooded the bank.

As he rose from the ground, a horror-filled scene froze his heart in his chest.

Quint had beat back the river's current and wrapped his arms around Maya from behind, squeezing, seeping his darkness under her skin.

Terran transformed into a flaming vortex and spun to save her.

Muddy water poured from Maya's nose and mouth. Her eyes full black as she raised one hand and smiled with tears shining in her eyes "This is my choice."

What choice?

She transformed and wrapped Quint in a foggy embrace. They passed through his fiery funnel in a flash of black and blue.

What is she doing?

She couldn't defeat Quint on her own. Terran's smoky form flowed with them, following their path to the river.

As Maya pulled Quint deeper into the water, Terran could only watch in horror when Quint lifted his head and winked.

Quint was letting her win.

"Maya, let him go. We must do this together." Terran reformed to his human state. As he entered the river, water splashed and churned around him.

Maya's eyes were hollow shells, black streaks coursed under her skin. *"I cannot remain."* She dived with Quint in her arms.

"Maya, No—" Terran plunged beneath the surface but only one blonde appeared. The other had dispersed, fading into the cold blue surrounding them.

Their elemental link faded—their connection like the frayed edges of a whittled-down string. Fiber after fiber snapped in two, leaving only a single thread, thin and swaying with the current.

"Goodbye, Terran."

"Maya. Wait!" He circled through the water, but an empty vacuum flooded his heart. She'd disappeared from his radar.

Where did she go? Is this her choice? To leave him? To die?

The river rose in swells, tossing his tormented soul through each crashing wave. Rage burned. Firing his need for vengeance. For punishment. For power to erase Quint from the earth.

Terran shot out of the water—desperate to destroy the creature that had harmed his mate.

A black blanket covered the river and sank down, covering and eradicating the water's existence from the earth.

Barren, dry, dust.

Quint growled, "Your siren sings no more."

Terran stepped on black sand where the water once ran freely. Not a drop remained. Not a drop. His Maya. Gone.

Gather. Unleash.

Terran sank to his knees, he fisted his hands, and he pounded into the dirt over and over. Then he heard it—water rushing to fill the emptiness.

The river still flowed.

Quint's power was not all encompassing or far-reaching.

Gather. Unleash.

His defeat will come at your hand.

He stood before Quint. "You are temporary. An aberration. The earth will continue without you, and I will not fall to your will."

Quint-girl circled him, bones visible through flapping, charred flesh hanging off her bones. Ebony claws grabbed Terran's hair and yanked him to his knees. Her black eyes blinked and her wilted tongue wet dead, gray lips.

Gather. Unleash. For Earth. For Maya. For love erased.

"Let's end this." Terran grabbed Quint's head and locked their mouths together. Eyes closed, Terran released the reins, freeing his Elemental nature.

Earth, fire, water, and air streamed around and through his body. Swirling past his heart and up his throat. Four elements fused into a golden orb and blocked Quint's dark matter from diluting his soul.

Terran envisioned the earth spinning through space as a blue-and-white circle. He wrapped his arms around the sphere and joined its rotation around the sun. Encompassing, nurturing, containing life. Glowing bright with power waiting to be contained and used against darkness.

Terran opened his eyes and blinked against the sun's glare and heat. He spread his arms wide, conducting the magnetic field surrounding the earth. Raking his hands through that warbled field, he gathered the earth's harvest in his hands. A current sizzled from his fingers through his veins and power swirled in his hand. A glowing indigo-and-white sphere coalesced into a violet seed. He swallowed the gift and it germinated in his body.

Awareness returned to the earthly struggle raging on the dry riverbed. The seed bloomed and violet branches sprouted and twined around his body and arms.

Quint's scream was muffled as he tried to break free from Terran's vine-like grip.

Earth's power rose.

One shot.

His aim must be true. A deep breath pulled the purple branches to his core—his heart. Intense heat created a pulsing violet bullet in his chest.

Focus, pinpoint.

Terran opened his mouth wider over Quint's and pulled the trigger. The bullet fired out of his mouth and shot straight through Quint's face.

Terran blinked but white dots danced before his eyes. He no longer held Quint.

Energy waning, Terran tumbled face first onto the ground. He dug his hands into the dirt at his sides, and he rubbed the earth over his eyes.

Then, *damn it*, he ate it. After he swallowed, his vision cleared.

Quint stumbled along the shore, like a blind hunchback, and when he turned, the empty hole in his face matched the one in his chest. His neck led to ears and a thin hairline, but no face in-between.

Time to finish him off. Sparks of static electricity built as Terran ran his hands over the earth's surface. Dust swirled and carried him to where Quint had collapsed near a tree.

With his foot, Terran kicked Quint's body over. "Roots, bind him." The ground around the tree groaned and trembled as roots surfaced and wrapped around Quint's form.

"Wind, deliver him." Air swirled, spinning Quint higher and higher through the air. "Fire, rocket him," flames shot through the air and carried Quint up past Earth's atmosphere into space. "Don't come back."

Terran wiped at the mud pouring from his eyes and nose. "Asshole made me eat dirt." Power fading. Limbs heavy, eyes gritty, mouth lined with gravel, he crumbled to the ground

Maya. Where is Maya?

Spent. Empty. A vision of her face before she'd dispersed into the water appeared before his eyes. Her voice once more echoed through in his mind, *"This is my choice."* He had to find her. He struggled to his knees only to fall again. Elbow after elbow, he crawled his way to a tree and used its coarse bark to pull up.

"Maya!" His scream startled the birds from the trees.

His head fell back as tears poured from his eyes. Hot rage and a heavy sense of emptiness filled his heart. "It's you that did this to me." With his fist, he jabbed the tree. "I didn't ask for this. I didn't want this Elemental life." He kicked and punched until the tree fell. He started on another, yelling, crying, and screaming out in anger and pain.

The skin on his hands was ragged and brown muck oozed from the wounds.

How can I be earth without water?

As he collapsed, his head bounced against a tree. As he fell into the welcome arms of oblivion a single thought surfaced—he'd fought off Quint's darkness and yet, his world had still turned black.

CHAPTER 46

"She's not dead."

Each word dropped like a boulder against Terran's aching head. Was he hearing voices or speaking a futile wish? "What?"

The familiar voice repeated, "She's not dead."

Terran rose on an elbow and looked at the familiar surroundings of his barn. His dirt pit was new, deeper.

Nodin sat Indian-style at his side. The fingers of one hand held his place in a volume of *Being and Nothingness* by Sartre.

Terran scrubbed a hand over his face. "How long have I been out?"

"Three days."

Three days, three years, three minutes, what did time matter at this point? He sank back down in his dirt coffin and closed his eyes.

"What happened?" Nodin nudged him with his book.

"Wait. *She's not dead*, you said that, right?" Terran shot back up and shook Nodin's knee. "Maya's not gone?" Air finally reached his lungs, and he breathed in the barn's subtle nuances—wet hay and fresh tilled earth.

"Mother delivered Maya to a safe place before Quint could destroy her spirit."

"Spirit?"

"Soul, psyche, life force—whatever you chose to call it. Terran, your yellow lily lives."

Terran peered into Nodin's eyes searching for the truth. As the words sunk in, he rested his forehead against the dirt. *My yellow lily lives*. His heart thumped, kick-starting the stalled beat. He clenched his jaw, refusing to cry in front of Nodin.

Nodin flicked his ear. "Osho's *Discourses* says, 'Life is always moving into the unknown, and you are afraid. You want life to go according to your mind, according to the known, but life cannot follow you. It always moves into the unknown. That is why we are afraid of life, and whenever we get any chance we try to fix it because with the fixed, prediction is possible.'"

He raised a palm. "Don't, Nodin, please, not now." With each breath, dust particles filtered through his nose. He brushed his cheek against the cool earth, giving himself a moment to focus on the reality of his environment.

Maya was alive. He was alive. That was enough to decipher.

Nodin shuffled beside him. "How did you do it?"

"Do you know where she is?"

"Recuperating on her island."

Terran grunted, "Sure, she gets to lay on a warm sandy beach while I'm stuck in the dirt, literally."

Nodin tapped his book against his knee.

Terran returned his focus to Nodin's question. "Sorry, I'm a bit distracted. I'm not sure how it all came together. I'll have to write it all out, each facet. I should take my blood pressure then perhaps test my blood—"

"Terran," Nodin interrupted with a shake of his head.

"Sorry. Give me a moment…" He crushed a dirt clod between his forefinger and thumb, concentrating on the coarse feel as the clump crumbled in his hand. The earth, his gifts, he'd used them all to defeat Quint. "Mother said to gather and unleash, so that's where I focused my energy. I gathered the earth's magnetic field within my core, where it meshed with my elemental powers. Everything coalesced and fired from my body, leaving a void in Quint's face."

Terran sat up and wrapped his arms around his knees. "He'd taken a young girl's life. He'd taken Maya from me. I hit him with everything I had then shot him into space."

Nodin nodded. His face serious. "The final frontier."

Terran gaped at Nodin, because he'd uttered the words so seriously. Words from a modern movie coming out of the ancient Indian's mouth brought a rush of hysteria. He laughed until his eyes watered and tears poured down his cheeks. He shot out of his pit and wrestled Nodin to the ground. "The final frontier. Ah, that's funny." He smacked a kiss on Nodin's lips, and then stood. "I did it. I destroyed Quint and sent him packing. We're safe now. He can't touch us."

Anticipation of a time without Quint's dark cloud over their lives had him breathing easy for the first time in months. Focus could return on serving the Earth. And Maya, once he found her, he'd serve her a helping of anger at her sacrifice then he'd make love to her until she was tied to him, like a ship at dock.

Nodin remained on the barn floor. "And here I thought we'd never kiss again."

"I don't care. I don't. I'm relieved, ecstatic that it's done."

Nodin stood and dusted off his pants. "Well, I wouldn't say—"

"Stop. It's done and I need to see my girl."

# # #

Maya opened her eyes then blinked—underwater. Her heart rate kicked up as a blurry form appeared above her.

Where am I? In a tub?

She blinked again and the blur became a woman's face. Maya shot out of the tub and blasted a water stream from her hand.

Pillar collapsed to the floor.

As she stood knee deep in a tub above Pillar, she felt the water sluice off her skin. "What are you doing? Why am I in this tub?"

Pillar glared and sputtered. "You bi—"

"Pillar." In a tailored black suit and white silk blouse, Violet Levina stood in the doorway. Her gaze remained on Maya as she spoke to Pillar. "Leave us."

Pillar glared for a long moment, and then squeezed water from her shirt and left.

Salty dogs can learn new tricks. Perhaps Violet could offer training tips.

"Welcome back, Maya."

"Violet. May I have a towel, please?"

Violet nodded, "One moment."

Maya studied the area outside the bathroom door, searching for exits.

Violet returned with a fluffy sea-green towel with the store tags still attached.

After accepting the cotton towel and ripping off the plastic tags, Maya said, "Where am I?"

Violet kept her face averted as she answered, "An apartment in Switzerland. My grandfather brought you here as a favor to Mother."

"Mother?"

"Yes. I'm afraid now that you're awake, I must leave. I'm being tracked, and I find you are a very large beacon. You've been in this tub for three days. If you're well enough, you should go." Violet twisted her hands together and picked at her thumbnail. "I wish things could be different. I've heard so much about you and your friends from Pillar."

"Pillar? I'm sorry. I am not sure where...I thought—"

"Your Earthman survived."

Maya dropped to her knees, splashing water onto the floor. "Terran survived?"

"I'm sure he'd prefer telling the tale himself. Men like to brag about their victories."

"Victory?"

Violet giggled. "I'm sorry. I realize you're confused, but you've been repeating everything I say, only in question."

"Repeating...right, sorry. Switzerland, that's what you said, right? Flint is here. I'll contact him." *And get to Terran like yesterday.*

"No!" Violet's hand shot up and covered Maya's mouth then she glanced around the room as if monsters would burst from the walls. "You mustn't even think his name."

Maya spoke between Violet's fingers. "Why?"

"It's too late. I must leave." Violet scurried out the door.

Maya tried to glean Violet's thoughts, but crackling static blocked her attempt. She focused on Pillar, but a purple field road-blocked her efforts. *No admittance into the girl's club.*

Maya rose from the tub and quickly absorbed the water from the soaked towel. "Violet, please wait. I just want to talk—"a door slammed shut—"to you."

Had Pillar left as well? Maya didn't sense her salty presence. Why had Pillar hovered over the tub? *Pervert.* And why was Violet protecting her?

"Just great." She wouldn't get answers by standing in this tub. She stepped out and tiptoed down the hall. Phone, phone, where was the phone? No phone. Glancing around there was nothing—no couch, no tables, no chairs. Only a department store bag on the floor lying next to a crumpled fast food bag and drink.

No one lived here so how—

The apartment door banged open and a gray-haired man appeared in the entrance. He wore a long black coat, almost like a cape.

Maya wrapped the towel tighter around her body. Power exuded from this man. Not Elemental, but something else rested behind those bushy brows.

"Greetings to you, Ms. Conway. Glad you're awake." He carried the same lilting accent as Violet.

Interesting. "I'm sorry. Who are you?"

"I am Mother's helpmate and friend. I see to her needs when she is unwell."

"Unwell?"

Could Mother get sick?

"But of course, how else do you think you stand here today? You always underestimate her power and willingness to guide you along the proper path. Still such a child and yet, you are older than I. It seems those who live peri-mortal lives miss out on the wisdom old age brings. But that's a discussion for another day. Mother suggests a return to your island to fully recuperate and your Earthman will join you."

"But how did Terran win?"

"Do we ever really win? Or do we just live to fight another day? That is what your Earthman has done. It is for another to finish. For now, the four Elementals will work together and grow stronger. Your leader has proven his merit. The battles ahead will require your bond remain strong. Unbreakable."

She circled closer to the bag. Were there spare clothes inside? "I didn't catch your name?"

"I didn't give it."

"You are related to Violet. The accent."

"Be careful, my dear, your curiosity steers you into trouble."

"We need her to join us. I'd like to speak with her." Maya snapped her fingers. "Wait, she said something about her grandfather."

"Ms. Conway, shall I make you forget everything about today? Violet is operating under a bit of a misconception at the moment, but she must continue on her own path. Move forth without my interference." He shook his head and mumbled, "Or much interference."

He paused a moment before continuing, "Now, I must leave. I sense your fiery friend drawing close, and it is not yet time for our paths to cross. Ms. Conway, a pleasure." He waved his cloak before him and disappeared with a poof.

A poof.

She'd even heard the poof. Her brain must be waterlogged.

Pounding followed the poof. Someone bounded up the stairs outside the apartment door.

She stepped into the hallway and stood at the top of the steps. A sudden warmth flooded her system. "Flint, is that you?"

"Maya?" Flint appeared at the landing, and he stomped up the final five steps. "Where is she?" He fired past her into the apartment.

Maya leaned against the door pane. "She left."

"What did you do?"

Maya straightened and shoved her hands on her hips. "Excuse me. I just woke up from death five minutes ago. I've had two unintelligible conversations and have no idea what the hell is going on. Don't you start in on me."

Flint's jaw clenched and he stared at the floor for a moment before casting her a side-ways glance. "Did you speak to Violet?" He growled out each word.

"Yes."

"Well, what did she say?"

"She said hello then goodbye. Basically."

Flint threw up his hands and went to stand by the open window. "I can't pin her down, but when I do…"

"Flint, let her go for a time. Her grandfather says, I don't know what he said, but anyway, Mother says I need to recoup at the island. Come with me, hit a couple volcanoes then come back. You look like you could use a refresher."

"What are you doing here?" He glanced around the apartment.

"I'm not quite clear on that and I don't care, because the sooner I leave, the sooner I'll see Terran. Let's go."

CHAPTER 47

Maya soaked in the sea, desperate to regain her strength. Only green and brown strands of seaweed floated by to hear her thoughts on life's trials and tribulations.

Waves surged around her and a soft breeze brought goose bumps to her skin.

A voice floated through her mind, *"I never did taken you shoe shopping, did I?"*

She laughed. *"No, I don't believe you have."* How could he make her laugh when all she wanted to do was cry with joy? Focusing on the beach, she watched as Terran stepped toward the shoreline.

"No, I'll come in." Maya waved him back, and then dove under the surface, swimming until she was close enough to stand. Waves broke against her knees then her feet as she met him where the water eddied against the shore. Her gaze rose and met deep, comforting brown eyes. "Your shoes are getting wet, so we'll have to get you a new pair, as well."

His only response was a single raised brow.

As she tiptoed into the shadows of his memories, she flipped on the switch and shined a light across everything. Tears slid down her cheeks as she gleaned the pain he'd endured and the anguish her disappearance had caused. "I'm still here. Water to your Earth."

"How could you? I can't believe you'd…" He clutched her shoulders and gave her a bit of a shake. "Do not ever *choose* to leave me again. We fight together, not apart."

Maya glanced down at their feet—hers in the water, his in the sand. "It will always be so for us. We'll always meet here. At the shore."

Terran cupped the back of her neck and kissed the tip of her nose. "That is partially correct. I believe the more accurate term is we'll always *join* at the shore. Shall I show you?" He wrapped his leg around the back of her calve, tripped her, but twisted so she landed on top.

Her heart beat freely once more as he proved his assertion.

They would always join at the shore.

EPILOGUE

In a field alongside a stream on a rural farm, Maya leaned against the tailgate of a faded green pick-up. "Dumping acid whey into the ground could create an environmental nightmare. If the product flows into a water source, it could potentially exhaust all the oxygen. Fish need dissolved oxygen to survive. Do you understand now?"

"Sure do, sorry miss. We just had all this extra, and well, it was taking up too much space in the barn. And we didn't want the grandkids climbing on the barrels."

The farmer shuffling his feet before her had used Greek yogurt's byproduct, acid whey, as a land-applied fertilizer and as a protein supplement in their livestock feed, but after overstocking had decided to dump the remaining barrel contents into a stream.

Fortunately, she and Terran arrived before the pouring began.

She kept her mental grip on the farmer and explained she would properly dispose of the product. As he hopped back in his truck, the only thing he would remember was the environmental repercussions.

She glanced out over the rows of corn. Terran and Nodin stood in the middle of the field, the green leaves brushing against their knees. As Terran spoke to Nodin, he rubbed his hand over the wide shoots, maintaining his link to the earth.

Winter had passed and with spring turning to summer, they had celebrated life in a myriad of greens, blues, and browns. Surrounding their lives with nature's bounty. Searching for answers to keep nature clean and humans safe.

In their Colorado cabin, they lived alongside the forest's edge. Working as an Elemental team.

Maya approached the two handsome beasts, marveling at just how gorgeous two naked men could be as the first rays of dawn struck their bodies. She fanned her face, knowing she should only be eyeing one figure, but peeking at the other. Although, due to their frequent transformations, she was very familiar with both forms, one more so than the other. *Lucky me.*

Terran swiveled and smiled—a grin that lit up her world. A world with exciting possibilities and an optimistic future. Dirt crumbled under her feet as she ran across the field and jumped into his arms.

"Maya...what?" With an "Oomph," he stepped back for leverage.

She kissed him.

The sun warmed their skin as it rose over the horizon. Welcoming a new day. Offering life to the plants surrounding her.

What was meant to be a quick kiss of pure bliss took an interesting turn to pure lust. He ran his tongue along the seam of her mouth. She welcomed the plunge. Terran did everything methodically. A point made clear by this kiss. When they came up for air, they grinned at each other like a couple of loons.

"Well, that's my cue to leave." Nodin's voice startled her and brought her back to the present. Though she and Terran had made use of fields before, they had company now. *Shame.*

"I've got a field you can explore." Terran whispered through her mind.

She pinched his arm then flashed Nodin a sheepish grin. "Sorry, I'd kiss you too, but Terran might get growly."

"Growly?" The man in question tweaked her hair.

"Grrr."

Terran shook his head at her bared teeth. With one arm supporting her bottom, he reached out with the other and shook Nodin's hand. "Brother, good to see you. It's been too long."

Maya stuck out her tongue at Nodin. "He's a wanderer, Terran. Always flying solo."

Nodin raised a single brow. "Actually, I had altruistic motives. Figured I'd leave you lovebirds alone. Let you settle in your nest."

Terran shuffled her in his arms. "Where are you headed now?"

"Not sure."

Maya unwrapped from Terran. "Come stay with us." She poked Nodin's rock-hard stomach.

"No. I have my own battles to fight." Nodin kissed her cheek. "Take care of each other." Dust stirred at his feet before he rose with the wind and disappeared.

Terran wrapped his arms around her and brushed a falling tear from her cheek. "He'll be back."

"I know. It's more that he's lonely and sad. Pillar confuses him."

"Love is complicated enough, but when you add in all the factors of an Elemental life, relationships become more problematic."

"I sure hope you are not saying I'm complicated, because I—

He stopped her rant with a kiss that was not complicated at all.

When he pulled back, he flashed a cocky grin, very aware he'd averted trouble. "Race you back home?"

"What do I win?"

"Catch me and see." Terran vanished before her eyes. At one with the atmosphere, he flew across the earth—exulting in his Elemental nature.

Alone for a moment in the field, Maya breathed in the sticky sweet scent of corn, peered up at character-shaped clouds, and reveled in a warm summer breeze crossing her skin. Earth's purity amazed her. True beauty could be found by standing in a field that for decades continually produced a gift from the earth. She should do this more. Take a moment. Breathe in her surroundings. Appreciate the peace.

Revel in a love that was at this moment flying across a deep blue sky.

No longer did her link to humanity drip away. No longer did she question her purpose in this peri-mortal existence.

No longer would she wash away. Love linked her.

She misted and shot through the air, eager to win the race.

#

Flint walked the cobbled streets of Zurich or Turicum, as the Swiss city was known in Roman times. He walked passed Fraumünster, an old church. Stopping at the popular tourist destination was the last thing on his agenda. Flaming red hair, plump pink lips, oval face, petite frame—that picture remained seared across his mind.

Heat flared through his body, alerting him to danger. He stilled and checked his surroundings.

Finally.

Pillar sat at an outside café, watching him. She lifted her cup in toast. *"I will help you."*

"What's in it for you?"

"Redemption."

Thank you for reading *Water's Threshold*. I hope you enjoyed Maya and Terran's story. If you did, please leave a review at your purchase site. Reviews are very appreciated by the author. I'm "moose"-assuredly grateful.

Visit www.jillianjacobs.com
for all new release information.

Please enjoy the following excerpt from *Ember's Center*, Book #1 in The O-Line Series. Jillian's Contemporary with Suspenseful Elements.

Owen smiled when she finally met his melted-chocolate eyes.

Seemingly aware she'd given him an once-over—a very blatant once-over. *Awkward.* She clasped together her trembling hands. "Was there something you needed?"

"Yes, actually."

His voice matched his body: deep and heavy, and she bit back a sigh.

"I have a small problem you might help me with."

"Absolutely. What is it?" Ember folded both arms across her chest. *Where are my shoes? Can he see the tea stain on my shirt?*

"I'm glad you agree. You see, I hate when women cry."

What? That was quite the non-sequitur. Laugh lines appeared beside his eyes. Unsure what her answer should be, she replied, "I hate when women cry, too."

Not comfortable around men, especially huge, handsome ones with square jaws sharp enough to cut ice, Ember calmed her breathing and tried stilling her pounding heart. The Marauders' center stood in her cube entry.

Her entry. *Oh no! Where has my mind strayed?*

Did he live up to the rumors? The "O" in Offensive-line raised many a woman's curiosity across social and traditional media platforms since all the players were extraordinarily gorgeous. Not hard to imagine Owen's reputation for bedroom proclivity was very accurate since his shoes were so big, which meant he was big everywhere. *Ridiculous.* She would not stare *there.*

Maintain eye contact. Keep it!

About the Author

In the spring of 2013, Jillian Jacobs changed her career path and became a romance writer. After reading for years, she figured writing a romance would be quick and easy. Nope! With the guidance of the Indiana Romance Writers of America chapter, she's learned there are many "rules" to writing a proper romance. Being re-schooled has been an interesting journey, and she hopes the best trails are yet to be traveled.

Water's Threshold, the first in Jillian's Elementals series, was a finalist in Chicago-North's 2014 Fire and Ice contest in the Women's Fiction category.

Jillian is a: Tea Guzzler, Polish Pottery Hoarder, and lover of all things Moose.

The genres she writes under are: Paranormal and Contemporary romance with suspenseful elements.

Connect with Jillian Jacobs online

Website: www.jillianjacobs.com

For more information on Harvey Girls, Jillian recommends reading: *Appetite for America: Fred Harvey and the Business of Civilizing the Wild West- One Meal at a Time* by Stephen Fried

For Fresh-water Conservation information: The Nature Conservancy: www.nature.org

www.ingramcontent.com/pod-product-compliance
Lightning Source LLC
Chambersburg PA
CBHW071453170626
46811CB00007B/2565